First published 2020

First printed edition published 2023 by Drollery Ltd.

Copyright © Alice Coldbreath, 2020

ISBN 978-1-916736-03-0

More books available by Alice Coldbreath:

The Vawdrey Brothers Series:

Book 1: Her Baseborn Bridegroom

Book 2: His Forsaken Bride

Book 3: An Ill-Made Match

The Brides of Karadok Series:

Book 1: Wed by Proxy

Book 2: The Unlovely Bride

Book 3: The Consolation Prize

Book 4: Her Bridegroom, Bought and Paid For

Book 5: An Inconvenient Vow

Book 6: The Favourite

The Victorian Prizefighter Series:

Book 1: A Bride for the Prizefighter

Book 2: A Substitute Wife for the Prizefighter

Book 3: A Contracted Spouse for the Prizefighter

This book is dedicated to my good friend Diane in NYC who is an angel.

Hill Boarding School for Young Ladies, Bath, England, 1843

Mina glanced down at the untouched bowl of soup sitting on the tray. "How about some beef tea, Papa? Would that go down any easier?" she murmured, looking at his dry, cracked lips. He had not taken any sustenance in days now.

His dull eyes, once so bright with intelligence, flickered. "Mina," he wheezed; his hand on the counterpane twitched.

She reached out and covered it with her own. "Papa, you *must* eat, dearest," she urged gently.

He gave a wan smile. "You must listen…" His words trailed off painfully. "I want you to go with him. He will take care of you."

Mina frowned. "Please, Father, you must not fret yourself. We need to concentrate on rebuilding your strength now the fever has left you."

His eyes fixed on her urgently. "Promise me!" he burst forth at last. The effort of his entreaty left him weak and trembling.

Mina paused, looking at him intently. What was all this about now? While feverish, her father had railed and babbled a good deal, but she had thought that stage had now passed. "With whom, Papa?" she asked carefully, patting his hand.

"Lord Faris," he said, confounding her completely.

"Lord Faris?" she echoed blankly. She did not know the name. It was not one of the patrons of their school. She had never heard of him.

"You must go with him, Mina," he said, carefully forming his words as though it took great effort. "For he'll take care of you when I am gone."

At this, Mina's resolve to stay calm fled her. "Go with a stranger, Papa? Who is he to me?"

"Family," her father managed to gasp out. She noticed how his gaze kept drifting to the door as if he was waiting for someone. She glanced that way herself in confusion.

"Family?" If anything, she felt even more bewildered, for she knew herself to have no other kin in the world apart from her father.

"Your…your brother, Jeremy."

Jeremy? Mina felt a sudden shock, as the world as she knew it lurched violently off its axis. The only brother Jeremy she knew about was the brother her mother had told her had died in infancy. Mama had been buried with his lace cap and booties in her coffin. It had been her explicit wish. "But surely, Papa—?"

He cut her off with a quick movement of his hands. "Forgive me, child," he said, closing red-rimmed eyes. "Forgive."

"Forgive you? Dear Papa, you've done nothing wrong and have always been the very best of men," she assured him. He gave a small sigh, and Mina bit her lip, wondering if she should send again for Dr. Carruthers, but how could she, knowing both the meagre contents of her purse and the fact the good doctor had assured her there was precious little else he could do for him now. Dr. Carruthers had assured her the ravings had passed, yet

2

here was Father talking so strangely that she scarcely knew what to think.

A tap on the door let her know Hannah, their maid of all work, stood on the threshold. "Yes, Hannah?"

"I wanted to tell the master I done it," Hannah said with a nod, folding her hands over the front of her apron.

"Done what?"

"Posted his letter off."

"What letter?"

"The one to that address in Cornwall. To that Lord whatsit."

Mina pressed a hand to her brow. Was she dreaming this entire exchange? she wondered, her head swimming. She had scarcely slept a wink these past three days, and the whole thing was starting to take on the strange properties of a dream.

"Miss?" said Hannah, starting forward from the doorway. "Oh, miss!"

Seeing the fixed direction of Hannah's gaze, Mina turned back to her father. "He's just sleeping, Hannah," she said, leaning forward to catch the labored breathing, but found she could hear nothing. "Papa!" She stood so fast she caught the edge of the bowl of soup on the side table and overturned it. "Papa!" Heedless of the soup stains all down her navy crepe skirts, Mina pressed forward. "Please, Papa!"

It was Hannah who had to pry her fingers from her dead father's shoulders some minutes later. "He's not dead, Hannah!" she said wildly. "He's not dead, he's just sleeping!" When Hannah's capable hands clamped over hers and turned her from the bed toward her solid form, Mina clung to her stout waist like it was the only thing that kept her afloat in an uncertain sea. She wept wildly and unrestrainedly as she never had allowed herself when Mama had passed five years before.

"There now," Hannah murmured. "There, child." *Child*. No one had called her child in years. Now here was Papa and Hannah both addressing her as such, in the same day. She had been Miss Walters to all their pupils as soon as she had turned seventeen. "You let those tears flow freely now, miss," Hannah encouraged. "He was a good gentleman and an honest master. None can say fairer than that."

Mina sobbed until her throat was raw and her face sore from tears. She scarcely heard the words which flowed from Hannah's lips in a steady stream. She caught the odd sentiment. "We'll soon have him laid out and then buried like a good Christian," and "A real gent to the end he was—even his manner of passing was mild as a lamb." But the words held no meaning to her at the time. It was Hannah's steady, solid manner she derived comfort from.

Over the next three days, she found herself grateful all over again for the dependable Hannah. The servant had stood stalwart beside her in her best black bombazine during the funeral service, then again when it came to facing their landlords, Messrs. Roberts and Simpkin Esquire, who called at the school the very next day to collect the outstanding balance.

"She's just put her father in the ground, God rest his soul," Hannah had said fiercely when Mr. Simpkin seemed to take issue with the amount of outstanding rent Mina made over to him.

Mr. Roberts hastily intervened. "Quite, quite," he said, stroking his large handlebar mustache. "I am sure we most heartily lament the loss of your dear father. Of course, my colleague is quite correct, usually we would require three months' notice before one of our properties is vacated…" He caught Hannah's

4

eye and coughed. "However, under such regrettable circumstances, we will, of course, make an exception."

"You are very kind," Mina said flatly. After paying the sum owed for the burial and interment, she had a matter of mere pennies left in her purse. As it was, she knew not how she was to pay the rest of Hannah's wages.

"So, you will be leaving Bath imminently, my dear Miss Walters," Mr. Roberts continued as Mr. Simpkin continued to brood heavily beside him.

"Yes," Mina said briefly. "I await my new direction any day now, by return of post." Her lips felt numb, as the private living quarters they occupied were very cold that morning, for they had not yet dared light a fire. She could not feel her fingertips, despite the black lace mittens which Hannah had dyed along with the rest of her raiment. They had closed the schoolrooms and the dormitories weeks ago, but they still could not keep the few rooms they used warm. Not on the small amount of coal they had been rationing. The scuttle was practically empty.

The last paying pupil had left well over a month ago, long before Papa's illness had really taken grip. In truth, their admissions had been sadly dwindling over the past couple of years. Their little school had never been fashionable, but it had been solidly respectable. It was almost frightening, Mina reflected, how quickly a steady paying business could go down the drain and one could be out on the street. Their patrons had distanced themselves, and none had replied to the last few letters she had written.

"To relatives?" Mr. Roberts pressed. Mina stared at the broken blood vessels on his bulbous nose and wondered if he was a secret drinker.

"I am hoping to secure a position as a governess," Mina corrected him.

"Now, if you gentlemen would excuse us," Hannah said loudly, pursing her lips. "My young lady has several matters she needs to wind up before she can pack her bags."

This was another lie, Mina thought, but she was grateful for Hannah's intercession. She had neatly packed up her things the day before. All packed up and nowhere to go. Nosy Mr. Roberts and sour Mr. Simpkin were ushered out of the front door, and Mina sat at her father's walnut writing desk and laboriously wrote out a set of glowing references for Hannah.

As she laid down her pen, she felt the beginnings of a dizzy terror at what was to become of her. Her future yawned before her like a frightening chasm which would swallow her up into nothingness. She had no one. Even Hannah had prospective employment lined up with a young widow in town, though she professed herself quite willing to stay on until Mina was ready to leave.

To leave for where though? She had given up hoping for employment from the several schools in the area. She had applied to them for any teaching positions when their own pupils had trickled away, before Father had even grown sick. Since Father's illness, she had sent dozens of letters asking after private governess posts but had yet to receive a single reply. The trouble was, she was still relatively inexperienced at four-and-twenty, and the only school she had ever worked in was her own father's.

Governess positions usually took a while to secure, and realistically you needed a sponsor to work on your behalf who had the necessary connections. She had hoped that Lady Ralph, who had been a sponsor of the school, might help her, but the lady had been sadly uncommunicative of late. Mina's family had kept very much to themselves. Although regular attendees at church, they had not mixed much with the congregation, for her parents had really only cared for one another's company. They neither moved in society nor kept up any acquaintances in Bath. They also lacked family connection for, as Mina understood it, both her parents had been orphaned at a young age.

A rap at the front door startled her out of her bleak reverie. She hoped to goodness it was no tradesman expecting payment, for the coffers were now well and truly empty. She craned her ears and to her surprise heard a tread on the stair. Surely Hannah was not bringing any caller upstairs to her? She half turned in her seat and widened her eyes when she heard a short knock on the door. Quickly touching her hands to her head, she felt her nut-brown hair was still smooth and glossy in its arrangement of side braids which looped below her ears and then swept up into a neat bun at the back.

"Presenting Lord Faris, miss," Hannah said, bobbing a curtsey and withdrawing promptly.

Mina stared at the beautiful young man who sauntered into the room. He wore a most elegant outfit of evening wear complete with black opera cape, top hat, and a walking cane topped with a silver pommel. His hair was a bright, burnished gold and stood around his face like a halo, and it was only after staring at him a moment that Mina realized he had a rather cynical mouth, and his eyes looked slightly glazed.

"Good evening, Lord Faris," she said, rising from her chair and giving a graceful curtsey. It was easy to fall back on deeply ingrained manners when all else failed.

He was looking at her rather hard. "Dear me, you are not *at all* what I expected," he drawled. "Are you indeed she?" He extracted a letter from his pocket. "Miss Mina Walters?" He

7

read the words as though they were slightly distasteful to him, and Mina felt herself bristling. "You do not look," he added thoughtfully, "like I imagine a Mina." He twirled a hand about indicating her appearance. "You look more like…" He pouted a moment in thought. "A Prudence," he pronounced with displeasure.

"My parents always called me Mina," she answered repressively. "Though my true name is Minerva, after the goddess of wisdom and strategy."

"Minerva?" he repeated with a faint wince. "Ah yes."

At that moment, Mina caught sight of the handwriting on the page he held between his elegant fingers. Surely that was her father's writing? She felt her heart leap. It must be the infamous letter Hannah had posted. "I'm afraid you have the advantage of me. Are we acquainted?" she asked with a calm she did not feel.

He threw himself down onto a chair and then winced. "This chair," he pronounced carefully, "is damnably uncomfortable."

"Perhaps you ought not to have hurled yourself down into it in such a fashion," Mina could not help suggesting. "It is hardly designed for such ill treatment."

He ignored her, his eyes roaming over the room with a fascinated and leisurely sort of contempt. "Dear me, so this is what a young ladies' boarding school looks like. How very disagreeable. I can scarcely credit she would have left my father for *this*."

Mina looked back at him steadily. "I'm afraid you will have to be a good deal less cryptic," she said frankly, "if you expect me to respond at all meaningfully."

He frowned. "Do sit down. I can't concentrate when you're hovering above me like some kind of carrion." He eyed her full mourning with disfavor. "That gown makes you look like a crow."

"Yes, so I gather. A crow called Prudence," she agreed tartly. "I am in mourning," she said, taking a seat opposite him and drawing her black fringed shawl tighter about her.

"Oh? Did he actually die then?" His gaze flickered back to the letter. "He *said* he was dying, but I did not know if that was merely artistic license."

"My father died three days ago," she corrected him quietly.

"A man of his word," he replied with a humorous quirk of his lips.

"Always," Mina agreed and saw by his quick frown that he would like to always have the last word. Immediately, she determined she would never let him have it. She folded her hands in her lap and waited as he crossed his legs, encased in cream silk breeches, and stared at her in moody abstraction.

"Shall I go and order tea?" she asked when the silence started to stretch.

"Filthy stuff," he answered swiftly. "I never touch it. I will take a glass of brandy."

"I'm afraid my father kept no liquor in the house."

"Good God. Was he some kind of puritan?"

Mina did not trouble to answer this for she saw he was not really interested in her father at all. "Am I to take it there is some kind of familial connection between us, my lord?" she asked coolly, though she still could not credit what her father had told her in his last few moments.

9

"Oh yes," he said, nodding slowly. "We are brother and sister, my dear, though only half blood. Through our sainted mother." Mina felt her color rise, and seeing her expression, he laughed softly. "She divorced my father and married yours," he said. "Did she never speak of it even once?"

Mina clutched the arms of her chair. "Not of divorce, no."

"Of me?" he asked, looking intrigued. "She spoke of her own darling boy?" His lips twisted.

"Of you, yes," she admitted, feeling as though the words were dragged out of her. "She spoke of her first-born child, but I never dreamed…" She had never said he was by a different father. Mina took a deep breath. "It was her expressed wish that she was buried with your baby bonnet."

That caught his attention, for his eyes widened. "And was she?"

"Of course."

"And with nothing of yours?" he asked with a trace of malice.

"With nothing of mine, no," she confirmed, feeling like she was soothing a jealous child. He smiled, and she realized with a sinking heart that he did indeed look very like their mother. Only her image was distorted in him, for he did not have Mama's gentleness to temper her beauty.

"Then pack up your things, sister dear!" he cried extravagantly. "For I am come to provide for you, as your late lamented sire wrote and entreated me." He flung a negligent arm across the chair back. "Far be it from me to refuse an obligation or a matter of honor." He spoke the words mockingly, and she wondered if he was directly quoting her father's words. Taking her by surprise, he leaped suddenly from the chair. "There are debts, I presume, for me to take care of?"

10

Mina rose stiffly from her own chair. "Our debts are paid," she said, her color rising. "I discharged the last of them not an hour ago."

"All of them?" He sounded incredulous. "From your father's letter, I imagined you quite sunk in penury."

Was he suggesting her father penned a begging letter? Mina took a moment to get her temper under control before she replied very carefully. "Due to the doctor's fees and funeral costs, I was not able to set aside a sufficient sum to pay our servant, Hannah, for this past month's wages in full…"

"Say no more," Lord Faris said, drawing a pocketbook from his waistcoat. "The good Hannah shall be handsomely tipped. How long, do you suppose, before you could be ready to leave this place?"

Mina stared back at him. "My bags are practically packed," she admitted. "I was hoping to hear word of some position—"

He cut her off peremptorily. "Good. I believe I have sampled all the delights Bath has to offer and am now ready to wend my weary footsteps homeward."

"But how long would it take to travel to your home?"

"A week," he answered with a shrug. "Depending on weather and traveling conditions."

A week? "Are we to take the stagecoach?"

"I have my own conveyance," he answered with a yawn. "And we will change horses at Exeter."

The next hour was a blur. Hannah, very excited, helped to round up the last of Mina's meagre possessions into a battered trunk and a large, rather ugly carpetbag. Methodically, Mina walked through every single room in the small school and ensured she had not overlooked any treasured possession including the matching Staffordshire china dogs or her mother's engraved silver teapot. As a last act, she slipped into her father's empty room, and taking up his watch and chain, she secured it in the hidden pocket at her waist and pinned the chain to her bodice. Then she and Hannah threw dust sheets over the piano, the tables, the mirrors, and the desks.

Lord Faris came looking for her long before they had finished, and Hannah assured her she was more than capable of completing the task before she secured the property and returned the key. Mina embraced Hannah, and the servant slipped a weighted piece of paper into her palm as they drew apart. She shot a warning look at Mina as she bobbed a curtsey to Lord Faris.

"Thank you for everything, Hannah. I have left your references on the desk. I do hope you will be happy with Mrs. Fortescue."

"Yes, miss, I'm sure. And you take care of yourself."

Touching a hand to the locket at her throat, Mina turned and followed her half brother out of the door and out of Hill School for Young Ladies forever.

One Week Later

The carriage lurched again, and Mina's hand shot out to brace herself against the padded sides. Lord Faris's coach was luxurious and flaunted his crest on every available surface, yet even wealth, it seemed, could not shield you from all discomfort on the open road.

A succession of inns and the merest glimpse of bustling Exeter had been all Mina had experienced en route, for Lord Faris had not wanted to tarry and had pressed his coachman hard. The four white horses had been exchanged at Exeter for four gray horses, and they had pressed on. Now, on the seventh day, they had set out bright and early for the final leg of the journey.

She wished she could take the opportunity to enjoy the Cornish scenery, for what she could see from the window was astonishingly varied. Rocky outcrops one minute and lush green barley fields the next. As for the glimpses she caught of the coastline, they were tantalizingly lovely even when the sea mist obscured the detail.

Mina had now spent six and a half days in the company of her half brother and was no longer surprised by his mercurial changes in mood. Her heart sank when she saw his silver hip flask appear midmorning, and at every inn they passed, he demanded it refilled. Usually, he waited until their evening meal before he began imbibing, and it seemed an ill omen for his homecoming that he would make it blind drunk.

As the day wore on, he became steadily more wild-eyed and disheveled in appearance, his necktie hanging untied, his collar open. Mina watched him with pursed lips. Now she could recognize the signs, she thought he must have been drinking heavily on the first occasion she had met him.

"You look nothing like her," he said, suddenly rousing her from her ruminations. "You must take after the schoolmaster. A great pity."

"Apparently, my lord," she corrected him in a low but firm voice, "I take after my paternal grandmother, who was a woman of great resolve."

He gave a soft laugh at that. "I just bet you do."

"How do you know I look nothing like her?" she asked, her curiosity getting the better of her. "Do you tell me you remember her? Despite the fact she left when you were so young?"

His eyebrows rose. "There is a full-size portrait of my—our— dearly departed mother hanging in the gold sitting room at Vance Park."

A portrait? "I have her miniature," she admitted. "My father commissioned a matching pair for their first wedding anniversary."

"Indeed?" His eyes flew to her locket. "May I see it?"

She had half a mind to refuse him, but her mother's memory forestalled her. Instead she reached wordlessly for the clasp on her bronze locket and unfastened it. The catch was stiff and fiddly; she opened the oval locket before passing it to him.

He took it from her and sat studying it a moment. "Undoubtedly the same sitter though my father's artist was infinitely more skilled."

"Doubtlessly infinitely more expensive also," she replied dryly.

14

The smile on his lips grew. "You get your coloring from your father, I suppose," he said, transferring his gaze to the opposite side of the locket. "That middling brown shade of your hair. I had hoped you would resemble her more."

Jeremy Vance, Viscount Faris, was starting to grate on her nerves. "She was also a very sweet-tempered person with excellent manners. It seems we neither of us resemble her in temperament, brother." It was the first time she had addressed him as such, and certainly the first time she had shown him outright the sharpness of her tongue. To his credit, he threw back his head and laughed. She had a suspicion he was more than half-cut at this point. A vulgar expression she had learned from Hannah, but she remembered it now and applied it in her thoughts.

She did not know this man, and she did not believe him to be the protector her father had hoped he would be. A dull sense of panic had been rising in her for the past few days like a nasty wellspring that might eventually bubble up and overwhelm her. Now she had left Bath, any meagre acquaintances she might have were over a hundred and fifty miles behind her.

Hannah would have already taken up her new position, and she had precious other friends. Lady Ralph no longer responded to her letters, and Canon Whitehaven seemed to have disappeared off the face of the earth. Of their ex-pupils, several had written her pretty letters when they had first left Hill School, but those had naturally tailed off with time when they had entered society or married.

It was a bleak thought, that this was the only family left to her. This blond, laughing drunkard with eyes full of spite and malice for all he was so pretty.

"Sadly, I already have one viper-tongued shrew in residence at Vance Park," he said with mock regret. "My viscountess, the

Lady Amanda. I had hoped…but there. Things rarely turn out as we anticipate." He passed her locket back to her.

He had hoped she would be some simpering miss who would cast herself on his chest and beg for his clemency, she thought with shrewdness. Perhaps he had thought to find a gentle confidante in his half sister. A sort of saintly shadow of his long-forgotten mother. Willing to flatter and cajole him and hang on his every word. Their mother certainly would have, she realized bitterly.

"In short, madam, you are not what I expected." He drew out a cigarillo case and, without asking her permission, lit up a thin dark cheroot. Her nose wrinkled, for it smelled vile. He noticed her reaction and smiled again. "I cannot see that we would suit."

A strange way of putting it, she thought. Almost as if he were jilting her.

"I agree," she answered shortly. If he thought she was going to beg for his mercy, he was sadly mistaken. "Perhaps you should set me down at the next inn and I can make my own way back to Bath at the next opportunity." It was a bold statement, full of stiff-necked pride, for she knew both how little remained in her purse and how little was left for her back in Bath. In truth, nothing.

His eyes flared, and for one horrible moment, she thought he would take her up on it. "No, no, there can be no question of anything of that sort," he said vaguely, his mind clearly miles away. "You are my own flesh and blood and gently reared. I cannot see you cast out on the streets."

Her back stiffened, but it was no more than the truth. After paying the costs of Papa's funeral she was practically destitute.

Still, courtesy would have dictated he did not draw this to her own attention.

"No, I must see you provided for…" He trailed off, sunk in sudden thought. He tugged on his lower lip in contemplation.

"Perhaps you have a small cottage on your estate," she suggested with sudden desperation, for she did not like the unholy gleam now shining in his blue eyes. "I could give lessons from there—art or music lessons? Or perhaps your wife will know of some acquaintance who has need of a governess?"

"Teaching? There's precious little demand for ladies' lessons around Penarth," he said dismissively. "As for Amanda, any acquaintance of hers would have no respectable use for you. No, I have a much better notion."

"And that is?" she asked with a sinking sensation in the pit of her stomach.

"Why marriage, of course," he said slowly. "That is the traditional manner ladies are provided for, is it not? And as your fond brother, am I not required to provide a match and a suitable dowry?"

Mina felt her color rise. "You are insolent, my lord. My father asked for no such favor!"

"Now don't go back to being all formal," he sighed. "Did you not address me as brother earlier?"

"I will never do so again," she said angrily. "You do not deserve the title."

He smirked. "Well, then let us get around this obstacle by calling one another by our given names, at least whilst we are the two of us alone. I will be Jeremy and you will be Mina."

17

She glared at him across the carriage as he took another liberal swig from his flask.

"And just how do you propose to serve up this husband for me?" she asked caustically.

"I have someone in mind, Mina," he admitted. "Someone who…shall we say, wants something from me?"

"You are indebted to him?"

"Not exactly." He shrugged.

"What should compel him to offer for a relative stranger then?" she asked with mounting ire.

"Oh, he will make no such offer," he chortled.

"If he does not offer then the whole thing is impossible!" she pronounced with some feeling of relief.

"We shall turn up at his doorstep, then send for a parson and a veil, dear sister. He will speak the vows, though I will need some private conversation with him beforehand."

She stared at him open-mouthed. "You are joking, my lord."

"Jeremy," he corrected her.

"Jeremy, I think you have run quite mad!"

"I have never been more serious in my life, my dear Mina, I assure you."

She had to break off her words as the carriage, which had been climbing a slope, came to an abrupt halt.

Lord Faris twitched the curtain and gazed bleary-eyed out of the window. Mina peered past him but could make out precious little for it had grown dark and blustery outside. In the distance loomed a solitary and lonely-looking inn. Mina bit back an exclamation of annoyance, for she had thought they were to reach their destination before nightfall, not put up at yet another roadside tavern.

Jeremy reached up with his silver-topped cane and hit the roof three raps. "Make for The Harlot," he called.

The Harlot? Surely she had misheard him. "Do we make for that inn?" Mina asked in dismay.

"We do," he said thickly and turned his empty flask upside down.

"Are we staying the night there or are you simply stopping to refill your flask?" she asked coldly.

"You'd best learn to curb that tongue, young lady," he said, wagging a finger at her. "Or I very much doubt married life will be easy for you."

Mina glared at him, but his eyes had drifted shut and did not open again until the carriage came to a halt. For a moment he gazed about him, blinking as though unsure of his surroundings. "Do my ears deceive me, or can I hear fisticuffs?" he asked before darting with a bound from the carriage.

Mina leaned forward to peer out of the open carriage door. There was certainly a raucous crowd in the vicinity. Whoops and yells and jeers could be heard from what sounded like a very rough and ready bunch. They did not sound at all like the sort of people you would wish to meet on a dark night. She craned her neck out until she could see the coachman.

"Where are we?" she asked.

He did not answer, but simply pointed wordlessly with his whip. Mina glanced up and saw a swinging inn sign of a busty woman with plunging neckline and the name The Merry Harlot proclaimed over her tumbled, blowsy curls. Drawing her cloak closer about her, Mina hastily retreated inside the carriage.

The public inns they had frequented along their journey had been respectable hostelries that kept good tables and comfortable beds. She had thought Lord Faris liked his comfort far too well to stay anywhere disreputable. This place, however, was of an altogether different caliber. She could only suppose he had gone in search of more alcohol to fortify his plunging spirits.

Ten minutes later, she was dismayed to see Lord Faris striding across the courtyard toward her, holding a pewter tankard in one hand and a shapely blond in the other.

"Here she is, Ivy my love," he proclaimed, wrenching the door back open. "Come, Mina, show yourself. I have one here who would fain take a look at you." He turned back to the blond. "I assure you Mina is no shrinking violet."

Ivy threw back her head and laughed heartily, though Mina failed to see the joke. Given little other choice, she was forced to clamber down from the carriage unaided as Lord Faris did not have a free hand to offer her. She landed in a puddle that splashed up her skirts and made her mood even worse. She gazed back coldly at her half brother. "Am I to understand we are to put up here for the night?"

This dissolved both Lord Faris and Ivy into fresh mirth. "See?" he gasped, squeezing the blond's waist. "Did I not say she was a regular gorgon? I vow, she can turn a man to stone with one look from those eyes."

"I wish that were so, my lord," Mina answered, cutting across Ivy's giggles. "For I would have found a statue a far pleasanter traveling companion, I assure you."

"Oho! Would you indeed?" he cried, releasing Ivy and grabbing Mina's upper arm in a surprisingly strong grip. "Well, I fancy I have a new companion for you. Though whether you will find him pleasant is another matter altogether. Is that not so, Ivy my sweet?"

"If she does, she'll be the first," Ivy replied doubtfully.

Mina found herself propelled in the direction of the inn. Surely he could not mean that the man he intended her to marry was putting up at this den of iniquity.

"Wait!" she cried, struggling to turn back. "My things!"

"Juggins will bring your bags." Lord Faris tightened his hold on her arm.

"You're hurting me, my lord!"

"Then stop struggling, my dear." To his credit, he did loosen his grip on her arm to seize her wrist instead. Once they reached the courtyard, Mina was surprised by the number of lanterns and torches illuminating the place. Straggling groups of villainous-looking people were strewn around, smoking and drinking and speaking in low voices. Their murmurs fell off to silent stares as Lord Faris marched her across the cobbles and—horror of horrors—into a common taproom.

If Papa could see her now, she thought, her cheeks flaming as her eyes adjusted to the murky light within. Someone was playing a fiddle, and there was a good deal of laughter and jocularity. She could even see other women, she noticed as an old toothless crone cackled loudly, slapping her thigh.

Hanging above the bar was the most indecent wooden carved figurehead she had ever seen. It was in the semblance of a voluptuous woman flaunting her bared breasts for all to see. It

21

must once have graced a ship's prow, she supposed, but was now suspended from the beams in this gruesome establishment.

Lord Faris towed her in the direction of the bar, and all at once the noise seemed to stop and an eerie hush fell over the room. A horrible prickling sensation traveled up Mina's spine as she realized all eyes were now turned on her.

"Take off your bonnet," Lord Faris said softly as he held up a coin between two of his fingers for the barmaid to take.

"I will not!" Mina hissed back at him furiously, and he chuckled, shaking his head. The barmaid, by contrast to the wooden effigy hanging above her, was plain and angular. She cast a look of undisguised curiosity at Mina before taking Lord Faris's coin.

"What'll she have, your lordship?" she asked, nodding at Mina.

"Alas, my companion is teetotal," he answered with a sorrowful click of his tongue. Mina could have sworn she *heard* the disapproval in the room around her.

"I'll take a large gin," she said loudly over his shoulder.

"Good for you, gal!" cackled the wicked-looking old woman she had spotted earlier. Lord Faris cast a startled look her way.

"And I thought you were temperance folk," he muttered reproachfully.

"Did you?" Mina asked him pointedly. The barmaid plunked a glass down before her, and Mina tugged at the wrist he still held. With a lift of his eyebrows, he let her go, and Mina reached boldly for the glass. "Assumptions are dangerous things to make, Lord Faris," she said, looking him dead in the eye. Then she lifted the glass and knocked back the noxious fluid.

A cheer went up in the barroom, and Mina gulped it down, swallowing down the instinctive cough and blinking rapidly to dispel her watery eyes. *Well, gin is disgusting*, she thought as she slammed the glass back down and dragged a black lace mitten across her mouth.

Lord Faris smiled at her a moment, before pushing away from the bar and turning slowly in a full circle, meeting all eyes which turned his way with a challenging gleam in his own. "William Nye!" he shouted challengingly. "I have something for you!"

Once again, an uncanny hush fell over the room.

A whiskered gentleman sat up to the bar and removed the pipe from his mouth. "He be out back, milord," he said in a slow, drawling voice. "Cleaning up after the fight, I'll warrant." His manner was pleasant and ponderous, and for an instant, Mina could have sworn he winked at her. Mind you, her head was swimming from the gin, so she could not be sure.

As if on cue, a door from behind the bar swung open and a large, dark, bare-chested man with a towel slung over his head and shoulders prowled through. "Who's calling my name?" he demanded in a nasty, confrontational tone, gazing around the bar with narrowed eyes. Mina felt a trill of alarm when his gaze flickered over her and seemed to dwell a moment before settling with an expression of extreme loathing on Faris.

"I did!" Lord Faris answered in what Mina felt to be a needlessly theatrical manner. "I've come to settle a matter of unfinished business between us, Nye."

William Nye's lip curled. "Have you?" he asked contemptuously and, reaching for a bottle of liquor, poured himself a liberal slug and knocked it back, before shaking his wet hair out of his eyes like a dog. With a start, Mina noticed his knuckles were raw and bleeding. She watched as he caught the edge of the towel and dragged it back over his head, rubbing at his dark hair as if for all the world he was in the privacy of his own room, instead of a public house. Slowly, as though taking its cue from him, conversation started back up around them, and the fiddler retrieved his bow and started picking out a tune.

Glancing at Lord Faris, Mina thought he looked rather deflated for a moment before he recovered himself and swaggered back toward the bar. "Perhaps we should take it into a private parlor, Nye," he suggested.

Without even a word, Nye turned on his heel and marched across the taproom, heading for a side door. Lord Faris turned toward her and showily offered his arm. Ignoring it, Mina stalked past him, trying not to stare at the almost indecently masculine display in front of her. William Nye possessed the broadest shoulders she had ever seen, and a muscular tanned back she found almost shocking to behold.

Certainly, her papa had possessed no such body, the heavy muscle mass speaking of the almost animalistic strength of an ox or a bullock, she thought. He seemed more like a beast than a man. His fawn trousers were damp and clinging to muscular thighs and buttocks in a fashion that made her blush. She could only assume that he had stood under a pump or partially submerged himself in a water trough to get so thoroughly soaked through.

Her cheeks burned with indignation as the door swung shut behind him and she had to make a grab for the latch to drag it open for herself. He was no gentleman! Showing a rudeness that her mother would likely have swooned at, she in turn let it close in Lord Faris's face as she hurried down a dark passage after William Nye's heavy tread.

One solitary oil lamp burned in the corridor, casting its sickly yellow light over the garish wallpaper. For a moment, Mina paused, unsure which of the paneled wooden doors Nye had passed through. Hearing a step behind her, she plunged into the first on her right and almost barreled into Nye's massive bare chest.

"Oh!" She took a hurried step back but was prevented from retreating by Lord Faris's coming in behind her. The private parlor was wood paneled and sparsely furnished with a large covered screen, a scarred table, and two benches. Mina glanced disparagingly at the dusty benches and fancied the table surface would be sticky.

"Take a seat, Mina," Lord Faris requested, sidling past her to sit at the bench. "Nye." To Mina's disapproval, she saw he had caught up a dusty bottle from the bar and held three glasses which he set down before him with great ceremony before filling them a third full with a dark purplish-red drink. "To our bargain," he said, raising one of the glasses and draining it. Neither Mina nor Nye reached for the other glasses.

Covertly she watched as William Nye folded his massive arms across his chest in an attitude of utter intractability. "Bargain?" he bit out. "What bargain?"

Lord Faris smacked his lips. "Excellent claret, my dear Nye," he murmured with a sly smile. "Almost as good as your French brandy."

"If you have a point, I suggest you get to it." Nye's cold eyes flickered to her again, then slid away.

Lord Faris reached for the second glass and paused with it a moment. "It's about that small matter of Vance House," he said thoughtfully. "We both know my father intended it for you, but alas made no such reparation in his will." Mina watched Will

Nye stiffen perceptively. Whatever he had been expecting, it had not been that. "I am prepared, shall we say, to make over the necessary documentation to you, the deeds etcetera to make good on my father's wishes." Lord Faris paused, clearly expecting an answer, but Nye gave him none. "There is, however, one small condition."

Mina tensed as she watched Nye's green eyes narrow to mere slits. He looked like a venomous snake at this point who might strike at any moment. "Which is?" he said through gritted teeth when he realized the other did not intend to speak without a response.

Jeremy Vance, Viscount Faris, smiled. "I wish to simplify my arrangements and gather my loved ones closer about me. It is not convenient to have them scattered so far and wide. As such, I have had my son and heir recalled from school, and shall require you to marry Mina here and bring her into the fold."

Mortified, Mina shut her eyes tight a moment, her fingers gripping the table edge hard. When she opened them, she found Will Nye staring at her. Then slowly and deliberately he spat on the ground and then raised his eyes to her in cold contempt. "You'd have me marry *her*?" he said, turning back to Viscount Faris.

"Indeed. A real lady and a fine wife she'll make you, Nye," Jeremy replied heartily.

Mina could feel her expression was stony and unresponsive as Nye's eyes roamed over her with an insolence that made her palm itch to slap him. It seemed almost like her vision blurred as she flared hot as a furnace before the next instant turning as cold as the grave. Her feet felt so heavy on the floor she almost feared she might splinter the boards and sink through it. She felt short of breath and yet, if her lungs didn't feel so empty, she would have screamed with impotent rage.

26

"Lose the cloak," Nye said, jerking his chin at her.

"I will not," she answered through gritted teeth. Did he really expect her to display herself like cattle?

"Is she with child?" he asked abruptly, turning back to Lord Faris.

Mina gasped at this, but Jeremy merely gave a choked laugh. "Nye, you wound me," he said, pressing his hand to his chest. "You think I would foist some bastard brat on you?" Nye went very still at his words, and then Jeremy added with silky malice, "I am not my father."

They stared at each other, and Mina noticed it was her brother whose eyes lowered first. He had a hectic flush on his cheeks now. He was at the reckless stage of intoxication that Hannah had described to her before. It was at this point that men could be their most dangerous. To others and to themselves.

"I am not with child," she said in a clear, carrying voice. When Nye did not tear his angry gaze from Jeremy's face, she started unfastening her cloak with clumsy fingers until it fell at her feet and her slim figure, in its starkly black buttoned-up gown, could plainly be seen.

Nye's gaze turned to her. His eyes were hard and glittered with fury. He barely seemed to register her words.

"I am not with child," she repeated. Finally, he seemed to focus, and his gaze raked over her again, coldly assessing this time. With a short nod, he acknowledged the truth of what she said.

"Shall we proceed?" asked Jeremy, clapping his hands together unsteadily. "Send for the parson!"

"I do not think that is how it works, my lord," Mina said urgently. "There are banns which must be put up for three weeks beforehand and—"

"Mina, Mina." Jeremy Vance chuckled. "I am Viscount Faris and half these lands hereabouts belong to me." He extended one hand before him, palm up. "You seem to forget the local rector's living is mine to bestow, like so many others. Is that not so, Nye?" Nye looked contemptuous. "If I have Reverend Ryland summoned now, he'll perform the ceremony at my say-so. Then we simply apply for a pardon afterward to make up for the lack of a special license. If you two are shacked up together like a regular pair of lovebirds, there's none who would stand in the way of making it legally binding."

"It's hard to forget something I did not know in the first place," Mina commented caustically but was ignored.

"I want the deeds to Vance House in my hand before I'll take her," Nye growled.

"Not the most trusting soul, are you, Nye?" Jeremy commented with a wry twist of his lips. He drained the second glass of claret. "I will give it to you as a wedding present. I am a gentleman and as such my word should be—"

"In my hand!" Nye roared.

"Oh, very well!" Lord Faris sighed with a roll of his eyes. "Lord, was there ever such an untrusting fellow!"

"And I want to be married from a church," Mina said, bracing herself for argument. There was a short, heavy silence.

"Have Ryland unlock the church," Nye said at last with a shrug, not looking at her, but straight at Jeremy. "You pay his living, so you call the shots."

28

"People seem to be forgetting just whose show this is," her half brother complained and was ignored. "Oh, very well," he said, clambering to his feet. "Let us first go and make the announcement in the bar, drink a few rounds, and then I shall get Juggins to take me home to Vance Park to fetch the deeds and then on to the village."

"No," said Nye heavily. "*First* you go and fetch the deeds and *then* we'll all make our way down to the church."

"All?" Mina echoed incredulously.

The faintest ghost of a smile touched Nye's lips. It was not pleasant. "Aye, all," he said. "Weddings need witnesses after all."

Remembering the motley assortment of patrons in his barroom, Mina shuddered.

3

If Reverend Ryland blinked at the strange congregation who awaited him at the church door some three hours later, Mina could not blame him. The clock struck midnight as he fumbled with the huge key in the lock, and when two burly men stepped forward to help him drag the creaking door open, Mina saw blood splatter on their breeches and deduced they were likely prizefighters who had recently been brawling in The Merry Harlot's courtyard.

"'Ere, darlin'," said a redhead in a scarlet silk dress which clashed violently with the profusion of sausage ringlets framing her face. "Put this on instead of your bonnet. This is a wedding, not a funeral." She laughed and drew a shabby cream silk shawl from around her neck. Mina opened her mouth to protest it really wasn't necessary, but the redhead was already tugging on the black ribbons of her bonnet. "It can be your somefink borrowed too, can't it? My name's Effie by the way. Jeb's my man." She nodded toward one of the hulking brutes who had helped with the church door.

"Is he a fighter too?" Mina asked, watching as Effie cast her second-best bonnet onto a pew. She must remember to pick that up on the way out.

"That's right, but we ain't from round these parts. We only roll up in this hole in the corner every few months." Effie draped the scarf over Mina's bared head. It was still warm from being tucked about her bosom. "There, now you look the part," she said with a nod of approval. Her scarf smelled strongly of perfume and some other musky scent Mina could not identify.

She peered through it with difficulty for the heavy pattern was elaborate.

"Much better. Shame you ain't got no flowers though," Effie lamented.

"Excuse me, ladies, did someone say flowers?" asked a voice on her right, and Mina made out a short figure sketching a bow. "I gathered these from the roadside as we made our way down to the village." Mina thought it was the older gent with the fluffy whiskers who had winked at her back at the inn but could not be sure. Everyone presently looked like mere shadowy outlines to her now. "Hold your hands out, my dear."

"Ooh, them delphiniums are your somefink blue too, my dear!" Effie said approvingly.

Mina stuck her hands out blindly in front of her and felt a bunch of wet stems placed into them. "Thank you." She grasped the bouquet and took a few steps forward.

"'Ere, don't you try escapin' now, my lass," some wag wheezed close by, and Mina deduced she was heading in the wrong direction. She stood stock-still, then spun around in confusion, until someone caught her elbow.

"This way," a gruff voice said, and strangely enough, Mina felt herself relax, for she recognized who this was. It was quite unmistakable. Nye marched her up to the front of the church, not relinquishing his firm hold of her elbow for an instant.

"'Old up, Will Nye," Mina heard Effie cry out. "She ain't got nuffink new!"

"Give her a shiny sixpence for her shoe!" someone else suggested. Mina heard the chinking of people checking their pockets. "I'd better get it back," she heard someone grumble. "Here!"

"Take off your shoe," Nye rumbled impatiently close to her ear.

Mina stood up straighter. "I can't—"

He swore and the next thing she knew, his large hand had seized her ankle and was forcibly removing her shoe. Mina let out a small yelp as he then shoved her foot, none too gently back into it. She could now feel the intrusive sixpence against the ball of her foot. Indignation swelled in her breast and, rather imprudently, she drew in a large breath, only to be overwhelmed by the scent from the scarf.

Lifting the edge of the veil, she had the presence of mind to bring the fresh wildflower posy under her nose and take a large gulp of that to dispel the fug.

Someone in front of them cleared their throat. "I will require your full names, please, and the place of your birth," requested a ponderous voice Mina guessed must be that of the clergyman.

"William James Nye of this parish."

He squeezed her elbow and Mina lowered the flowers to speak. "Minerva Walters of Castle Combe in Wiltshire," she choked out, then sneezed.

Mina heard a pen scratch over paper as their dates of birth were duly recorded and the names of their parents.

"Do you solemnly swear there exists no just impediment to your marriage?"

They both swore and then the vicar's voice rose querulously. "Whoso giveth away this woman in holy matrimony?"

"I do," her half brother's voice rang out with self-importance, and Mina heard his hasty step approach. "Let the record show Jeremy Vance, fifth Viscount Faris," he proclaimed.

The ceremony proceeded, and Mina concentrated on surreptitiously lifting her veil to get a gasp of fresh air when she could. The church was lit only by a few candles and added to the overall impression of murky gloom. Afterward, she could not have described the interior of the little church, not for a hundred pounds. She could see though that it was a far more rural affair than the austere limestone one she was used to attending in Bath. St. Stephens had painted ceilings, a wide chancel, and an extensive vestry whereas this poky church seemed more like a cave. With a start, she realized their vows had ended.

"Give 'er a kiss then, Nye!" called out a raucous voice.

"Fuck off, Jeb" came her new husband's surly reply as he turned away and stalked back down the aisle, leaving her open-mouthed and deeply shocked at his profanity in a sacred place. The congregation, such as it was, erupted into hilarity, as though for all the world he had uttered some grand jest. Mina turned back toward the vicar with flaming cheeks, but Reverend Ryland was feigning a deaf ear as he fussily moved his bookmark and closed his Bible.

"Good luck to you, madam," he said with pursed lips, casting his eyes heavenward.

"She'll need more than luck," Jeremy predicted with a short laugh. The place was rapidly emptying now as people jostled and bustled out of the pews, almost falling over each other in their haste to follow the bridegroom back out of the church.

Mina whirled around, glared at her half brother, and then started hastily back up the aisle. What was she supposed to do? Where was she supposed to go? She only knew one certainty and that was that she was being left behind. She had only managed a few steps when she stumbled over her own unfastened shoe as her stockinged foot came out of it. She had to grab at the back of a nearby wooden pew to stop herself from tumbling into a heap on the floor.

Suppressing a sob, Mina cast down her posy of flowers and tore the shabby veil from her head. She would not cry, not in front of this ill-bred rabble. Sinking down onto the floor, she made a grab for her shoe and pulled it on as the silver sixpence fell out.

"Come now" came Lord Faris's mocking voice. "Don't tell me the erstwhile schoolmistress is so summarily defeated by a few sundry whores and villains. And you named after the goddess of wisdom and strategy."

Mina yanked her shoelaces tight as she did her best to gather the scraps of her lost dignity about her. "Go away, Jeremy," she said in a voice that shook with anger.

He gave a low laugh. "And just how do you propose to return to The Harlot without me?"

"If I must return to that loathsome place, then I shall walk," she told him through gritted teeth.

"If you must?" he echoed, sounding vastly amused. "My dear sister, is it possible it escaped your notice that you are now the landlady and proprietress of that establishment?"

Between her nerveless fingers, Mina's shoelace snapped.

4

Mina hobbled around the last bend in the road and leaned heavily against part of a fallen-down stone wall. She had a blister on one heel and was out of breath from the steady uphill climb. She fanned her hot face with her bonnet, which she had finally found lying under a wooden bench, sadly crushed and dented. No doubt it had been trampled underfoot in the hasty exodus from the church. Her hair was coming down around her ears in straggling rattails, and even in this light she could discern streaks of mud at the hem of her skirts. She had long since discarded the delphiniums by pitching them over a stone wall, though Effie's makeshift scarf was still draped around her neck as likely the redhead would want it back. The silver sixpence she had tucked into her hidden pocket, resisting the impulse to fling it after her bouquet. She could not afford such gestures, she told herself sensibly, even though it did seem an unlucky charm to have about her.

Looking on the bright side, she could at least see the faint lamplight ahead of her from the inn and hear the squeak of its sign swinging to and fro. At the beginning of her climb, she had caught snatches of faint laughter and voices on the path ahead of her, but they had fallen off after a while, leaving her alone to plod on in pitch-black darkness, prey to her own fears. In the distance, she thought she could hear the crash and boom of the sea over the cliffs, but she had not yet caught a glimpse of it.

Who even knew what horrors could lie in wait for her on such a lonely stretch of road? She shivered, thinking of highwaymen and goodness only knew what. *Foolish Mina*, she upbraided herself, drawing her cloak tighter around her. *Afraid of goblins, pixies, and ghosts when you're a grown woman and should*

know it is beasts of flesh and blood that pose the biggest risk.
One in particular sprung to mind, and she dashed a forearm
across her eyes.

They were tears of thwarted anger, she told herself hastily, that
kept filling her eyes. Nothing else and certainly not self-pity.
She had wanted to rail and scream at the aggravating Lord
Faris, but of course she had not. Sometimes being raised a
perfect lady felt like a real burden. Try as she might, it did not
seem to come to her as naturally as it had to dearest Mama.

She tried to imagine now, what Mama would have done if she
had been left to tramp miles on foot, alone in the dark, scorned
by her own wedding party, and failed. Papa would never have
treated her mother in such a fashion. Indeed, he had always
shown the most tender-hearted solicitude and consideration
toward his spouse. But Nye was as different a man from her
own father as chalk and cheese. In truth, she had no one else to
compare him to, she thought, having never met such manner of
man before.

She wondered what flaming redhead Effie would have done if
her "man" had left her like that at the altar, humiliating her in
front of all gathered there. Probably screamed and cursed like a
fishwife, Mina thought with envy. She would likely have flown
at him and clawed his eyes out, spitting and hissing like an
angry cat. How she would have liked to have done that! To
have picked up her fallen shoe and flung it at his head as hard
as she could throw it!

Mina's bottom lip trembled, and she bit on it until she could
taste blood. She hated him. Not Jeremy Vance, but William
Nye. The sudden realization brought her up short and she stood
a moment shivering in the dark. Why did she blame Nye so
much for the debacle? After all, he had been as coerced into
their farcical marriage as she.

36

Maybe that was *why* she was so angry, she thought, comprehension dawning. She thought there should exist some fellow feeling between them, some kind of sympathy for a fellow sufferer. They had been in the leaky boat of their marriage together, until he had pitched her over the side to the sharks! Yes, that was it, she thought with a decisive nod. *That* was why she blamed William Nye. Squaring her shoulders, she strode onward, ignoring her sore heel and the dull ache in her chest. She needed to forget all notions of allies or friends. For these days she was quite alone and had none.

By the time she reached The Merry Harlot most of the lamps were extinguished, though she could still hear occasional bursts of merriment from the public barroom. Avoiding that entrance altogether, she skirted the edge of the courtyard and surreptitiously tried another door. For the first time that day, luck was in her favor and the handle turned. Stepping inside with a thankful sigh, she pulled it closed behind her, leaning heavily against it while her eyes accustomed themselves to her surroundings. She seemed to be in another bar, this one a more genteel version with rugs on the floor, upholstered sitting chairs, and round tables. Were parlor bars a thing? she wondered with a frown. If so, then The Merry Harlot had one, although, she realized with a sneeze, it was rather dusty and seemed little used. She moved slowly across the room, bumping into little tables as she went.

The only reason she was tiptoeing, she told herself, holding her breath as creaking footsteps crossed the floor above her, was to keep things simple. All she wanted to do was find her bags and an empty room for the night. She could reopen hostilities on the morn, but for now, she simply wasn't equal to them. She had risen at six and it was now long past midnight. It had been a long day; she was cold and weary and wanted her bed. When her questing fingers found the door latch on the opposite wall, she slowly levered it open and gazed out into the dim hallway.

There they were! Her trunk and carpetbag had been dumped unceremoniously in the corridor. The trunk was far too heavy and would have to wait until the morrow, but she pounced on her carpetbag and brought the large, ugly piece of luggage to her chest and hugged it as though it were an old friend. She nearly wept with relief at being reunited with it, and that was when she realized she was overwrought and needed the seclusion of a quiet room to collect herself. She didn't even care about food or washing her face. Just sleep.

Lifting the ribbons of her ruined bonnet, she plunked it on her head and caught sight of her reflection in a large etched mirror on the opposite wall. *My God!* She looked like she had been dragged through a hedge backward! Telling herself there was nothing she could do right now to repair the damage, she headed for the staircase instead.

Three brass candleholders with snuffers were laid out on a side table next to a silver candelabra. Transferring one of the lighted candles into a holder, she held it up before her and with a muttered prayer that her luck would hold, started to limp up the stairs, wincing at every step. On the first floor, she found two locked doors and one that opened onto a room strewn with personal belongings and an unmade bed. The fourth room was a bathroom with discolored porcelain tiles and a matching roll top bath with clawed feet. Next to it was a smaller hip bath which would not take so long to fill and a handsome washstand. Opening the last room on that floor, she heard two sets of loud snores and beat a hasty retreat.

There was nothing for it, she would have to go up another flight of stairs. Her heart in her mouth, Mina mounted the steps until she found herself on another landing. This floor seemed a good deal livelier than the first. The first room she did not try, for she could hear a fully-fledged row erupting between its occupants.

"Just you wait!" a woman screeched. "I'll see you hanged first, Clem Dabney, you see if I don't!"

"Woman! Hold your tongue!" came the deep and furious response. There was the sound of something thudding against the wall and the shattering of glass. *Seven years' bad luck*, thought Mina, hurrying past that one as fast as her blistered foot could take her. Unless it was a window, of course.

The second room, disappointingly, was locked. The third she could distinctly hear giggling from. If she wasn't mistaken, it was that blond barmaid named Ivy.

"Oh, you rogue!" she cooed. "You know that costs extra."

Mina pursed her lips and passed on to the fourth room which she prized open gingerly. At first, she thought it was a sitting room, for there were several chairs dotted around it, then she noticed a mattress in the middle of the floor and on it a half-dressed man sprawled out swigging beer from a stoneware jar. He looked up in surprise and she saw his head was bandaged.

"That you, Ivy love? Frank didn't take long then!"

With a hasty apology, Mina withdrew her head and shut the door. She thought he called something after her but didn't stick around to find out what. There was only one door remaining untried, and it was right at the end of the passageway. Mina approached it with some trepidation. Even as she set her hand to the latch, she heard an earthy moan from within and recognized the cockney accents of the redhead from the church.

"Ah Jeb, that's it," Effie groaned. "Do not spare me, my love. Oh, do not spare me!"

Do not spare her from what? Mina wondered as she hastily retreated from the door. From Effie's loud moans, she guessed Jeb was heeding her entreaties well. If her hands were not full of luggage and candlesticks she would have covered her ears. She took three hurried steps backward and felt herself collide with a wall where there should not have been one. Swinging around in alarm, she found a large figure looming out of the shadows before her and realized with horror that it was none other than her new husband.

"Excuse me!" Mina burst out in mortified embarrassment. Something was thudding now against the wall in the room behind her, punctuated by animalistic grunts that made Mina's ears burn. "I need to find an empty room," she added shrilly, trying to dodge to one side of the bulk that was William Nye. "That one is taken."

"Are you sure?" he asked dryly and seemed to block her path entirely whichever way she tried to barge past him. He shot one brawny arm out and braced it against the wall, leaning down so his mouth was close to her ear. "There are no free rooms," he said slowly, possibly so she could hear as Effie was now starting to wail with increasing volume. Mina dropped her carpetbag and clapped a hand to her neck to shield it from his hot, tickling breath. His eyebrows rose. "We're full," he added bluntly. That took the wind out of her sails, and she gazed up at him in dismay.

"Full?" she yelled as Effie approached a pitch only dogs could hear. "But where am I supposed to sleep?"

Nye frowned at her. Behind them, Jeb bellowed like a bull. The thudding stopped abruptly with the sound of a masculine groan and collapsed mattress springs.

Mina drew a deep breath and picked up her carpetbag. "If you could be so kind as to direct me to the staff quarters," she said, striving to sound composed, but even to her own ears sounding slightly hysterical. To her shame, she could feel herself beginning to tremble all over with strung-out nerves. Hot candlewax spilled onto her fingers and her bag nearly slipped once more from her grasp.

He did not speak for a moment, just looked at her hard. Then he uttered one word. "Attic."

Mina sagged with relief. She couldn't help it. She felt exhausted and perilously close to tears. "Thank you," she muttered, a slave to politeness even in the face of the worst manners she had ever been subjected to. He made no response, just turned his back to her and walked back down the way he'd come. Mina's eyes burned. Pray God he never knew how close she had come to humiliating herself and blubbering like a child.

With a suppressed sob, she started up the last flight of stairs. The ceilings were much lower and sloping up here, and she could well believe it was where the maids slept. The first room had two narrow beds in it, both unmade and strewn with clothes, and a dresser covered over with a good deal of ribbons and combs, perfume bottles, and spilled powder. The room reeked of a floral pungent scent, and guessing that one was likely Ivy's, she opened the second which was scrupulously tidy but had a quantity of hand sewing laid piled up on the one bed and a handmade patchwork quilt on the other. As this, too, was clearly occupied, she made wearily for the third and final room, which was on the opposite side and much bigger than the other two. Indeed, it was quite as big as both the other rooms combined.

This room had a bare dresser and a large bed in the center with a brass bedstead. The fire was unmade, and the bed stripped back to its mattress. Mina almost cried out with thankfulness to see it was not in use. She whisked inside and shut the door behind her, setting her candle down on the dresser. Unfortunately, there was no lock on the door, so after dropping her bag, she seized a rickety wooden chair instead and shoved it under the handle.

Her safety seen to, she cast about for blankets and sheets to dress the bed. A trunk under the window looked promising so she made for that, and by another stroke of luck, found it contained a quantity of much darned and mended linen. She dragged out sheets enough for her needs and made up the bed.

Sadly, there was no water to wash, and anyway, she was too tired to comb her hair or do anything other than strip down to her chemise and drawers, blow out the candle, and crawl under the covers. She lay awake for a few minutes, telling herself that though she despised her half brother, it was pointless saving her wrath for a morally weak character and a drunkard such as himself. She had sent him away with a flea in his ear and expected he was probably passed out in a drunken stupor by now in his four-poster bed. A four-poster likely emblazoned with the Faris coat of arms, she thought with faint scorn.

As for William Nye… She set her jaw. She would make that man sorry he'd ever met her, if it were the last thing she ever did! A small smile curved her lips even as a tear trickled from the corner of one eye. Comforted by her vow of vengeance, Mina fell into a deep sleep.

5

Mina rose early the next morning and established the routine that she would stick to for the next week. She rose, dressed in her serviceable black gown, and descended to the kitchens in search of hot water and something to eat. Her first glimpse of the large kitchen almost made her recoil, it was in such a squalid state. Every surface was covered in a thick coating of grease and dirt. The fire was lit in the coal fire range, though there was not a soul in sight. Someone was up and about though, for on the table was the remains of a round loaf and a dish of butter which still had a knife set in it.

Peeking her head in the room next door, she discovered a large scullery which had a copper set in the corner for heating water and a bread oven, both of which shared the same chimney. Peering under the lid of the copper, she found the large pot was only half-full of tepid water. First she lit it with a spill from the kitchen range and then, casting about, found a large pail in the corner and, remembering she had seen a pump in the courtyard the previous night, carried it outside to fill it with water.

As she waited for the copper to heat, she helped herself to a piece of bread and butter, reflecting she had not eaten since dinner the previous day and was ravenous. A cupboard next to the sink revealed a jar of blackcurrant conserve which, after sniffing, she thought looked edible, so she added a scraping of that and had just perched on a wooden settle to eat it, when the sharp-faced barmaid bustled in, tying her apron strings. She did a double take when she saw Mina and her face grew tight.

"Oh," she said. "You did make me start. I didn't expect to see you again." She sniffed and strode through to the scullery before returning rapidly. "Who lit the copper?" she asked in surprised accents.

"I did," Mina said, swallowing her mouthful of bread and jam. "I'm heating water to wash. Good morning," she added briskly. "My name is Mina Nye. What, may I ask, is yours?"

The maid flushed to the roots of her hair. "It's Edna," she said after a moment's heavy pause. "Edna Lumm." She ran her hands down her apron distractedly. "No offence, Mrs. Nye," she said stiffly, "but I got things to be getting on with. I can't stand around here passing the time of day like a lady o' leisure."

"That's quite understandable, Edna," Mina said pleasantly. "I feel the same way. May I ask if the kitchen is considered your province?"

Edna bristled. "Hah! If only," she snorted. "My duties extend far and wide in this godforsaken hole!" Her cheeks were two spots of bright scarlet now. She was practically vibrating with indignation.

"Yes, I think I saw you serving in the taproom last night," Mina agreed calmly, finishing off her meal and brushing the crumbs from her lap.

"My poor mother would turn in her grave if she knew I had to serve at the bar!" Edna burst out. "Ivy's supposed to man the bar of an evening, but on fight nights…she's got other duties," she finished bitterly. "I don't like it, but needs must, and a girl's got to earn an honest crust."

"Yes indeed, it sounds like you must be spread very thinly," Mina said with sympathy.

Edna's mouth worked a moment before she could speak. "I got pasties to make before lunchtime and then I got to make a start on the laundry. It's no good expecting that slattern, Ivy, to wake before noon!"

"I see." Mina nodded. "Well, if you've no objection, I can see there's plenty of things I could be helping out with down here." She glanced around the filthy kitchen. "I can't cook, so the easiest thing for me to do would be a spot of cleaning."

Edna stared at her. "*You're* going to clean?" Mina nodded. An expression of heavy skepticism passed over Edna's face. "I see," she said, plainly thinking this some whim of the moment. "Well, help yourself. I'm not about to stand in your way, I assure you!"

"Thank you," Mina said mildly, standing up. "Will you share the first lot of warm water with me? Where do you usually wash? In the scullery?"

This spirit of camaraderie had Edna blinking, but she fetched a china basin and the two of them went companionably into the scullery where they stepped into the alcove, unbuttoned their necks and cuffs, and rolled back their sleeves. Edna shared a block of carbolic soap with her and some faded but clean washcloths. They were performing their ablutions side by side when Mina heard the kitchen door slam and the heavy tread of boots across the floor.

Feeling Edna's gaze on her, Mina forced herself not to react as she heard someone slamming cupboard doors and a filthy curse word muttered before the rattle of knives in the drawer. It had to be him.

"He'll be getting himself bacon and eggs from the larder," Edna muttered. "And splashing hot fat all over the back of the range, no doubt," she added bitterly.

Mina nodded, realizing the household seemed to shift for itself when it came to meals. "I don't suppose there's any tea to be had about the place, is there?" she asked wistfully, for she knew the drinking of tea to still be considered a luxury in many places.

"Tea, why to be sure," said Edna. "We've a cupboard full of the stuff. We'll brew some, when he's cleared out with his foul temper," she added in a low voice.

A cupboard full? Mina's spirits rapidly rose. "Wonderful," she breathed, setting down her washcloth and picking up a towel. Halting footsteps in the passageway outside had her turning her head to see Will Nye staring straight at her. For a moment, she held his gaze, and then with a slight shake of his head, he was gone.

Mina breathed out again with relief. She rebuttoned herself carefully and checked the pins in the neat knot at her nape, giving him time to finish frying his bacon. "Do you have any headcloths or scarves I could use to cover my hair? And perhaps a spare apron? I have one," she added quickly at Edna's expression. "But I have not yet unpacked my trunk."

"I've one I can loan you," Edna acceded grudgingly. "But it's nothing fancy."

Mina held her tongue rather than pointing out a fancy housemaid's apron would be of little use to her when scrubbing down greasy surfaces. The slam of the kitchen door let them know Nye had departed. "He can't possibly have eaten already," Mina commented with a frown.

"The likes of him don't sit at a table," said Edna told her dryly. "He slaps it between two pieces o' bread and takes it with him."

"I see." Mina climbed to her feet and picked up the empty pail. "I'll go and fetch more water for heating while you make the tea," she said.

Edna acquiesced and Mina traipsed back out to the pump. Feeling eyes on her, she grabbed the handle and started vigorously working it. By the time she felt able to take a surreptitious glance about the courtyard, all she caught was a glimpse of Nye's back disappearing into an outhouse.

Edna made their tea strong and hot, and she added sugar but no lemon. Mina drank her cup with a sigh of pleasure, for the blend was a surprisingly aromatic and unusual one. "What kind of tea is this?" she asked, lowering her cup. "It's got a lovely flavor."

Edna shrugged, opening the cupboard to show paper packets tied with string. "I just picks one off the shelf," she said. "There's plenty to choose from."

Mina gaped at the extensive choice of tea leaves. She had never seen so much in one place outside of a tea merchant's establishment. "Someone must enjoy tea a good deal, I think," she commented.

Edna's gaze swerved away evasively. "There's plenty of tobacco and brandy about the place too," she said dryly. "But I don't poke my nose in what don't concern me."

Mina frowned, but Edna did not elaborate, so she set about tying a scarf around her head as the water heated. "Do you have any white vinegar or lemon?" she asked, thinking of Hannah's tried and true methods when it came to domestic cleaning.

"No lemon," Edna said succinctly. "But we got white vinegar." She indicated a cupboard, and Mina set about making her diluted solution.

She spent an industrious morning scrubbing down every surface in the kitchen. When she'd done all the obvious ones, she opened all the cupboards, turned them out, and set about scouring the shelves. At various points, she heard people come in and out of the room, but steadfastly ignored all comers, her upper body usually wedged in a confined space in any case.

Edna made a good quantity of flat pastry pies with mince and onion and baked them in the scullery oven, before she set about boiling up a load of linen and bedclothes which looked none too savory. "Prizefighters bleeding all over the sheets," Edna complained crossly. "And worse!" She took a half a raw potato to the worst of the stains and rubbed it to the discolored spots while muttering to herself. She made them another pot of tea at midday and wordlessly slid one of her pasty pies toward Mina for her luncheon.

In the afternoon, Mina replaced all the contents in the cupboards and attacked the scullery with the same zeal. By four o'clock, she was exhausted and realized she had somewhat overdone it. She had to work hard to pick her feet up and not drag them when she once more trailed out to the pump to refill the copper for washing. She was far too tired to lug a load of buckets of warm water up to the porcelain hip bath on the first floor, she thought wryly. Instead, she would have to settle for a strip wash in the scullery.

It was a shame as she felt simply filthy, and despite the scarf wrapped around her head, her hair would now need washing, as she had worked up such a sweat. Then she noticed a small tin bath hanging from a peg in the scullery. That would be just the ticket. She filled it and fetched out the abrasive carbolic soap once more, thinking longingly of the scented cake in her trunk. In reality, the carbolic would serve her much better in her current dirt-covered state, though she did not know in what condition it would leave her long brown hair.

There was a tatty folding screen in one corner which someone had once covered laboriously with cut-out scraps of what looked like programs and flyers for various music hall and circus performances. It was coming apart now, but Mina saw with interest that it had once been edged with velvet ribbon and studs and had clearly been a labor of love. She dusted it with a damp cloth and arranged it around the tin tub to give her some modesty as she bathed.

Edna had not reappeared since midafternoon, and Mina could only assume she had duties elsewhere. Other than Nye, she had not seen any other men about the place since the previous evening, so she thought she would simply get on with it. Kneeling beside the tub with a jug, she first washed her hair and soaped it up with the red carbolic soap. Then she swiftly undressed and lowered herself into the water, lathering up her limbs and dragging a washcloth over her skin until she began to feel much refreshed. Reclining in the tub a moment, she covered the tops of her breasts with the washcloth and with a sigh, fell back to lazily contemplate the colored illustrations on the screen.

She was just examining a flyer for The Amazing Ormerod Sisters, whose act seemed to comprise of juggling in their frilly drawers, when she heard banging on the kitchen door which she knew she had secured by turning the key into lock. Sitting up with a muffled exclamation, she reached for her towel and wrapped it about herself before peering around the doorway into the kitchen. It was Nye, stood at the door with a face like thunder. Hurrying across the kitchen, she turned the key and swung the door open.

"We don't lock this door—" he started furiously before catching sight of her barefoot and dripping on the flagstones.

"I was taking a bath in the scullery," she explained with as much dignity as she could muster, considering she had wet hair

49

straggling down to her waist. To her annoyance, she could feel hot color rushing to her face.

He paused a moment. "There's a bathroom on the next floor," he said through gritted teeth.

Mina inclined her head. "I am aware, but I simply did not have enough energy left to carry cans of water up and down the stairs."

"Next time," he said shortly, "tell someone."

Mina's chin came up. "Such as who? I've only seen Edna all day, and she already has enough duties without waiting on me."

He gave an irritable shake of his head. "Such as me," he answered gruffly.

Oh. She eyed him apprehensively. "I need my trunk carried up to the attic," she said after clearing her throat.

His eyes ceased roaming over her bedraggled figure, and he nodded, stepping past her. Mina turned her head to watch him stride out of the room. He had his shirtsleeves rolled up to his elbows, and instead of a collar, he wore a twisted neck scarf like a laborer.

Until the past month, she had never seen her father arrayed in anything but full correct attire for a gentleman. It crossed her mind that her schoolmaster father would have been very shocked indeed to learn she had been married off to a publican. Ironically, in allowing herself to be led by Lord Faris, she had been carrying out her father's own last wishes.

"Any reason you're still stood here, dripping all over the floor?" Will Nye asked her harshly from the doorway. She gave a start. He had her trunk on his shoulder, as though it weighed no more than a few pounds. "Which room are you in?"

"The only free one," Mina answered tartly. She supposed he meant she should follow him up the stairs. Gathering her neatly folded clothes from the scullery, she hurried after him. He was already halfway up the first flight of stairs, and she made sure to keep the span of a few steps between them.

At the top of the stairs, he paused, raised his eyebrows quizzically, and angled his thumb in the direction of the largest room. Mina nodded. She hovered outside the room, waiting for him to deposit her trunk, and sure enough, he emerged mere moments later and strode right past her, heading for the stairs.

"Thank you!" she called after him pointedly. He gave no acknowledgment, and Mina, balling her fists, marched into the room, once more wedging the door shut with a chair. He had no manners whatsoever, she told herself grimly as she unbuckled the straps of her trunk in search of her nightgown and robe. She would not descend below stairs again today. She had had quite enough of The Merry Harlot and Will Nye for one day. Besides, she felt fit to drop and she needed to apply some lotion to her poor hands which were red-raw.

Once she had dragged her high-necked white cotton nightgown over her head and rubbed the last of her lavender-scented hand lotion into her sore fingers, she felt sufficiently revived to set about making the room her own. Unpacking her familiar things in these unfamiliar surroundings was a bittersweet experience. She hesitated before placing her silver-backed brushes on the dresser.

It seemed strange to see them there after all the years they had sat on the same dressing table in her small bedroom at Hill School. She laid her glass-topped hairpins next to them along with her lavender soap and glass-stoppered bottle of rose water, but the dresser still looked empty. Its large proportions proclaimed it for a gentleman's dresser in truth, along with the

51

large rectangular swivel mirror that topped it and the two-drawer locked hatbox that stood above the drawers.

Nothing about it looked dainty or feminine, despite her scattered things. She thought fleetingly of Ivy's cosmetics and perfume bottles strewn across her chest of drawers in the room opposite, but she had nothing like that. Only once, Mina had dared to spend her saved pennies on a thrilling box of pearl powder done up in pink tissue paper which promised miraculous transformative powers for a rosy glow. Some of the girls at Hill School had sworn by it, and in truth, Mina had not been so very much older than many of their pupils. Her mother, however, had been so horrified and disappointed that Mina had been forced to throw it out before she'd even had a chance to try it.

Painting your face is the height of vulgarity, her mother had denounced in shocked, hushed tones. *Only fallen women would indulge in such depravity.* When Mina had wept penitently, her mother had patted her shoulder and promised she would not tell her father of her fall from grace. *Not all girls are intended to be beauties*, her mother had explained gently. *We must accept our lot in life with good grace. Your father and I are simply glad you have been spared the snares and temptations that a beautiful face brings with it.* No doubt, she had meant it as a heartening pep talk, but Mina had been left feeling plainer than ever.

It was only when Mama had died and Mina had been clearing out her toiletry case that she had come across the secret compartment which held Mama's own stash of rice powder for the complexion, a handful of burnt sticks for darkening her lashes, and a tin of pink balm for her lips or cheeks, Mina wasn't sure which. *Dear, hypocritical Mama.* Mina had thrown the contents out without ever telling anyone. The fancy walnut lacquered box with its velvet lining and silver-topped bottles had been sold along with Mama's French bronze vanity set with the pretty blue guilloche pattern. The proceeds had been used to buy a new morning coat for Papa to meet with their esteemed governors.

Now, picking up her hairbrush and running it through her damp locks, she almost wished she had kept the contraband beautifying products. She was a pale, drab thing, she thought, looking herself full in the face. The mirror showed her depressing reflection. Like one of those gloomy paintings of Ophelia floating down a stream, singing to herself with her hair full of weeds. It was no wonder her groom had left her in the church. Setting down her hairbrush, she caught herself up short. She hardly wanted William Nye's attentions, she told herself sternly. What on earth was she thinking of?

Then she remembered she did have some jewelry to her name after all and went to fetch her stocking. Upending it, she retrieved her mother's silver locket and her father's gold watch and chain which she had stashed in the toe for safekeeping while she bathed. Jewelry would add a finishing touch to the dresser. She set them down in a few different places before she was satisfied, and then ran to her trunk to find the small china dog that one of her ex-pupils had given her as a farewell gift. Her father had laughingly said it looked like a long-haired ferret stood on its back legs, but Mina knew it was supposed to be a pampered little lap dog such as society ladies owned. She set him carefully down and then returned to her trunk.

Mama's engraved silver teapot, spoons, and sugar bowl she set on an empty shelf next to the window. She'd love a cup of tea now, she thought longingly, but could not face running the gauntlet downstairs even though there was a cupboard full of the stuff. Perhaps she could keep a packet upstairs for her own use. It really ought to be stored in tins to keep it fresh.

Of her mother's bone china tea service, she had kept two settings and the milk jug only. It had not been such a wrench as she'd feared, for in truth, it had been far from complete, gaining a few chips and cracks over the last thirty years. She placed these pieces of pretty yellow floral carefully on the shelf next to the silver teapot and surveyed the results with a critical eye, moving one cup and saucer closer to the edge and nudging a silver spoon closer to the others for the purposes of symmetry. She hoped Hannah had found somewhere to display the rest of the set to advantage, for she had gifted the remaining pieces to their old maid, who had professed herself most pleased with the oddments.

It was only then that she recalled the folded, weighted paper that Hannah had pressed into her palm at their hurried farewell. Mina frowned, remembering she had stuffed it in the concealed pocket in her skirts at the time. Returning to her trunk, she lifted out her dresses in turn, searching for the one she wanted. It wasn't so easy now they had all been dyed a uniform black, and she smothered a sigh for the loss of her best green silk which now looked sadly streaky. Still, it couldn't be helped, and quite honestly the green silk had been on the tired side for a while now, however many times she had replaced the trim and then cuffs. Besides, she would be in mourning for twelve months at least, so what difference did it make?

Sifting past her stiffened horsehair petticoats, she delved into the discreet pocket and found the folded paper. Sitting back on her heels, Mina unwrapped it and found it to contain one of the two shiny gold half sovereign coins Lord Faris had given Hannah for her tip. Tears sprang to Mina's eyes at Hannah's unexpected generosity. The dour servant had shared half of all her wealth in the world with her. Wiping the back of her hand across her eyes, she read the smudgy message their old maid had painstakingly printed on the cheap yellowing paper.

Be sober-minded; be watchful. Your adversary, the devil, prowls around like a roaring lion, seeking someone to devour.

Mina blinked, then reminded herself that Hannah had never met William Nye. If anything, it was likely to be a warning against her half brother, Jeremy, who Hannah must have taken against despite his munificence. Scrambling to her feet, she crossed to the dresser once again, and put her half sovereign into the top drawer along with the handwritten warning.

Returning to her dreary black dresses, she carried them over to the wardrobe, but on opening the second door, was surprised to find some of the hangers already occupied. Drawing them out, she found several gleaming white shirts with elaborately pleated fronts, a necktie of flaming red silk and a waistcoat of striped scarlet and black, the like which quite took her breath away with its garishness.

Her father had always said black and white were the only two permissible colors for a gentleman's evening attire, and everyone knew that neckties should be as small and soberly colored as possible. The final hanger displayed a walking suit of a loud and vulgar plaid, which she was sure no gentleman would ever deign to wear. Touching the fabric and feeling the silk lining there could be no doubt the clothes were expensive though they were wholly lacking in any kind of taste.

Remembering Will Nye's spartan dress of plain black wool waistcoat and breeches and collarless shirt, she could not imagine who these garments could belong to. With a shrug, she shoved them to the one side of the wardrobe and hung up her own lackluster gowns and stiffened petticoats at the other end. There could be no greater contrast, she thought, between the two sets of clothes at opposite ends of the rail. If one side belonged to a fine cock pheasant, then the other side was that of

55

the corresponding female bird with its dull feathers of mottled brown and black.

With a shiver, Mina returned to her trunk and slung a warm blue woolen shawl over her shoulders as she unpacked the last of her things. After all, it wouldn't matter if she wore colors in the privacy of her own room, and the black-fringed shawl was thin and provided no warmth whatsoever. At the bottom of the trunk lay her white cotton chemises, drawers and handkerchiefs, her spare corset, and black stockings. These she dropped into the second drawer down, and considering herself unpacked, she climbed into bed to open one of the few periodicals she had managed to slip down the side of her packed trunk.

It was an old favorite, despite her father's disapproval of such literature. Their pupils had brought swathes of them over the school terms, and instead of throwing them out, Mina had built up quite a collection over the years, which she had kept in neat piles under her bed. Papa thought the serialized fiction and poetry within their pages to be of low quality and betraying poor moral fiber, though he did not object to her reading the domestic household pieces or the cooking recipes. Mina read them from cover to cover and consumed them like guilty treats. She knew the stories to be mere fluff, but the thrill of a female protagonist triumphing over the odds stacked against her was a lure she could not resist.

There was something entirely comforting about rereading familiar articles, and she had only just begun a fashion article on how to revive a "tired-looking bonnet" when the volume slipped through her fingers and she nodded off to sleep.

*

Mina woke suddenly in the night, uncertain of the hour but with the conviction some noise had awoken her in the sleeping inn. She lay a moment, breathing in and out, but after a moment, she knew it had not been from inside her own room, but rather somewhere outside. Craning her ears, she caught it again—a sort of rumbling and dragging sound out in the courtyard. When she had steeled her nerves enough to slip out of bed, she crept to the window and peered out of it onto the courtyard below. Sure enough, the hanging lanterns had all been extinguished, and she could see no lights in the window of the taproom or any other downstairs. The hour must be extremely late, she thought. Indeed, it was highly likely the early hours of the morning.

She stood a few moments in the pitch blackness, but the only sound that now assailed her ears was the familiar swinging of the inn sign with its distinctive squeak. Mina shivered and was just debating returning to her bed when she heard it again. Something dragging over the cobbles and then a sort of scraping sound. Mina held her breath. What was it? For just a second, she thought she caught sight of a flickering flame, but just as her eyes darted to track it, it was extinguished. She had no matches or even a tinderbox in her room to light her candle, and so left with little other choice, she made her way back to her bed and pulled the covers up to her chin. Tomorrow she would ask for matches. Tomorrow…

*

The previous day set the pattern for the rest of the week. Nye studiously ignored her while Mina set about making herself useful around the inn. After the kitchen and scullery, she set about the pantry and larder, which, though well stocked with grain, wheels of cheese, and hanging meat, were in dire need of cleaning and organization. While it was true Hannah had done this sort of work in her previous home, Mina was no stranger to lending a hand below stairs, especially in the days when they had all ten beds in their girls' school filled, and it was frankly too much for the one maid they had employed.

Mama had not been good for many tasks beyond fine needlework, but circumstances had not dictated that her own daughter should be such a stranger to the practical workings of a household. Which was just as well, Mina thought as she shook up a pungent mixture of eggshells and vinegar for deep cleaning and getting rid of unpleasant smells. As the wife of a tavern owner, she had more need of the skills their maid had taught her than anything she had learned from her parents.

The day after turning out and scouring the laundry and pantry rooms, she turned her attention to the private sitting rooms and disused parlor bar. First, she stripped them of all their rugs which she hung outside on the washing line. Next, she saw to the cobwebs and washing down the paintwork with diluted water and soap. While she was doing this, Edna appeared with a cup of tea for her and hovered in the doorway.

"Shall I help you in here, Mrs. Nye, or will I continue stripping the bedrooms from last weekend?"

It was the first time Edna had come to her for any direction, and Mina thought a moment before answering. "No, you carry on with the bedrooms, Edna. I'm sure you know what you're about."

Edna nodded and then withdrew something from her apron which turned out to be a tin of beeswax polish for the furniture. "Thought you might be wanting this for the furniture," she said shortly and placed it on a table.

"Thank you," said Mina, coming forward to take her cup and saucer. "Polish will be most useful."

"Brought you this, too," said Edna, withdrawing a bottle of gin. Mina opened her mouth to explain she did not care for it, but Edna forestalled her. "It's for polishing the mirrors," she explained.

"Gin?"

"Gives it a lovely sparkle, it do," said Edna wistfully. "My auntie swears by it."

This was a new one to Mina, but, looking at the profusion of etched mirrors on the wall, one she gratefully accepted. The room was so ingrained with dirt that she did not get around to polishing anything until the next day, after leaving the rugs out to air overnight.

She had just started polishing the wooden modesty screens when a knock on the door startled her. Looking up, she found it was her half brother, dressed impeccably in red-coated riding attire complete with a crop which he swished against his gleaming top boots. He gave her a quizzical look and sauntered into the room.

"Mina," he said with a nod. "Dear me, we are industrious this morning."

She straightened up, ignoring the twinge at her lower back. "Good morning, Lord Faris."

He looked slightly pained at her formality, taking a seat and crossing his legs. Mina ignored him, reaching for the tin of polish and dabbing the corner of her cloth in it. "What is that on your head?" he asked when it was clear she was not going to volunteer any conversation.

"A headscarf," she responded, applying her cloth to the scuffed boarding and buffing it ruthlessly.

"Well, it is singularly unbecoming," he responded critically.

"It is not intended for embellishment. Besides," she added dryly, "I would have thought my wearing a head covering could only be a good thing. To hide my headful of snakes?" she suggested when he looked blank. After a moment she realized he probably did not even remember calling her a gorgon. He had definitely been drunk by that point.

"Am I to take it that in my cups, I so far forgot my manners as to address you as Medusa?" he asked a little sheepishly when she turned her attentions back to her polishing.

"Take it however you like." Mina shrugged, and he fell to silent contemplation of the handle of his whip. Mina dragged a couple of chairs out so she could get better access to the carved wooden divider which separated the seating areas. It probably needed restaining, she thought, examining the scuffed panels along the bottom.

"I wish you would sit awhile," he said plaintively. "You're hardly making things easy for me."

"Oh, am I not?" Mina turned to look at him impassively. "I expect you have a whole household of people whose job it is to make things easy for you, my lord. But you see, I am not one of them." Deciding to give the abused wood the benefit of the doubt, she knelt down and slathered some polish onto its dull surfaces.

"I suppose I deserved that," he mused. "So, Nye has turned you into his scullery maid, I see. Vengeful devil, isn't he? By the by, what did he say when you told him of our connection?" He gave her a look of amused, idle curiosity. "I'm simply dying to know."

"Why on earth would I tell him?" Mina retorted, not bothering to correct him on the duties of a scullery maid. "He has reason enough to resent me, without that added insult to injury."

Now she had shocked him. He stared at her. "You didn't tell him?" he said incredulously, setting down his whip and leaning forward in his seat.

"Why should I?" she asked in clipped tones, turning her back resolutely to him. "What difference does it make?"

"Tell me what?" rumbled a deep, ominous voice from the doorway, making them both jump.

Mina looked back over her shoulder and saw Nye looming in the entrance with a nasty gleam in his eye. He took a step into the room. "Tell me what?" he repeated with gathering menace.

Jeremy cleared his throat. "Why, the small matter of our shared parentage, that's all," he answered lightly.

Nye cast him a look of utter contempt. "And why would she know anything about that?" he said scornfully.

"Not *our* shared parentage," Jeremy stressed, gesturing between himself and Nye. "Hers and mine."

Mina's startled glance flew to clash with Nye's, and she was almost comforted to see him look as startled as she felt.

"What?" he barked, advancing further into the room. "Explain."

"Oh dear, what a tangled web I have woven," Jeremy sighed. "And to think, I actually thought this would make matters simpler."

"You and Nye share a parent?" Mina persisted. "But…" Her eyes wide, she stared from Jeremy to Nye. "But—"

"Not the same parent," Jeremy interrupted succinctly.

"You m-mean…?" Mina stammered.

61

"Nye was my father's bastard," Jeremy explained, making her flinch.

"And she?" Nye pointed at Mina with a complete lack of manners. "Who's she to you?" he asked bluntly.

"Oh, my half sister," Jeremy answered with a bland smile. "On the maternal side. Do you not see the resemblance?"

"None," Nye answered grimly.

"Hmm," Jeremy mused. "I wonder what you *thought* she was to me, Nye?" he commented with a soft laugh. Nye stiffened, but Mina was far too absorbed trying to unravel their various bonds to notice.

"So, you, Jeremy, are brother then to both of us?" She looked from Lord Faris to Nye before returning quickly to the former. She could see no likeness between the two half brothers either. "But surely…surely there would then exist some bar to *our* marrying?"

"Why? There is no blood connection between the both of you," Jeremy said with a shrug. "And you have never lived under the same roof, so I fail to see why there should be any impediment whatsoever."

Mina opened her mouth and closed it again. After all, if William Nye was illegitimate, then his relationship to Lord Faris would not be legally acknowledged. They did not even share a name. She cast an uncertain glance at Nye, only to find him staring back at her. This time, he was the one to glance hurriedly away. "I see," she said weakly. "And why did you imagine this would make things neater for you?"

Jeremy shrugged. "Oh, I don't know. Having all my siblings under one roof," he said airily.

62

Mina's jaw dropped at this.

Nye uttered a sound of disgust and turned abruptly on his heel and left the room.

"Taciturn chap, isn't he?" Jeremy commented.

"If you'll excuse me," Mina said, turning her back to him and picking up her cloth again. "I'm very busy this morning."

"Birds of a feather," Jeremy sighed. "But why am I always the odd one out?"

When she did not respond, instead applying herself wholeheartedly to her task, he finally took the unspoken hint and left.

Mina's shoulders slumped the minute he exited the room, and she stared down at her work-roughened hands, lost in thought. Then just as swiftly, she sat up, squaring her shoulders again. It was no good dwelling on spilled milk, she scolded herself. What's done was done. All afternoon she threw herself into her work, and by the time she dragged her tired body up to bed, the wood in the parlor bar was gleaming, including the floorboards.

6

The next morning Mina woke and remembered the rugs had been on the line for two whole nights now. Hopefully that should have dispelled any lingering fusty smells. She would have to bring them in today, but first, they would need a good stiff brush in the yard. She had entreated Edna to save their tea leaves for the purpose and should have quite a collection now after three days. As she dressed and coiled her hair into a bun, she reflected she had heard no noises during the night and made her way thoughtfully downstairs.

As had become the routine, she and Edna shared the hot water in the scullery to wash, and Mina made the tea this time in a brown earthenware pot as Edna toasted tea cakes for their breakfast. Mina refilled the copper with water from the pump, ate her breakfast, and then carried her bowl of dried tea leaves and a bristle brush out to the yard where the rugs were swaying to and fro on the washing line.

She had been lucky it had not rained for two days, she thought, glancing up at the blue sky. It was a crisp day in early March. The sun was nowhere to be seen, but at least there were no rainclouds. Unpegging the six rugs, she laid them out side by side and sprinkled them liberally with the tea leaves. She was just picking up her brush when a voice at her elbow startled her.

"Putting the place to rights, aren't you, missus?" Turning, Mina saw it was the old man who had winked at her in the bar and given her the bunch of flowers at the church.

"Good morning," she said politely. "Just giving the place a sprucing up."

"Arrr," he commented, clamping his pipe between his teeth and rocking back on his heels.

Mina cleared her throat. "I'm afraid I didn't catch your name the other night."

"That's alright, don't you fret none," he said comfortably. "Reckon you had enough to occupy you that night. The name's Gus. Gus Hopkirk."

"Well, it's very nice to meet you, Mr. Hopkirk. I'm Minerva Nye."

"Minerva?" he repeated with a frown, taking his pipe out of his mouth. "That's not a name from round these parts."

"No indeed," she agreed. "I believe it's Latin in origin."

"A Roman name?" He gave her an appraising look.

"Yes."

"Bit of a mouthful for me," he said frankly. "Reckon I'll just call you Minnie." Mina was so taken aback by this piece of familiarity that she couldn't think how to respond. "Saw one of your birds last night, out at Gull Point," he continued.

"One of my birds?"

"Aye," he agreed and touched a finger to his nose. "An owl." His eyes twinkled and he turned away, ambling across the yard.

Mina's mouth fell open. There was certainly more to Gus Hopkirk than his rough outward appearance let on. Otherwise, how would he know that owls were sacred to the Roman goddess Minerva? She stared after him a moment, wondering if Gull's Point would be on the cliffs and remembering she had not yet caught even a glimpse of the sea.

65

Why should she not take the afternoon off and go for a walk until she found the beach? The idea appealed to her. Even as a schoolteacher at her father's school she had taken every Wednesday afternoon as a half-day holiday. It was nice to have something to look forward to. Her mind made up, she sat back on her haunches and started briskly to brush down the rugs.

A good deal of dirt came away with the tea leaves, and floral patterns and borders emerged as she worked. By the time she had finished, her own cuffs, hands, and apron were decidedly worse for wear. There was no point changing her apron now, for she had decided to tackle the grimy windows that afternoon, so after hauling the rugs indoors, she simply went and washed her hands and face in the scullery and then went in search of newspapers to clean the windows with. Edna's tip regarding the gin had worked wonders on the etched mirrors, but when it came to windows, Mina knew that nothing was as good as newspapers and vinegar.

Remembering she had seen a pile tied up with string in a cupboard, she retrieved a stash of them and carried them through to the parlor room along with a pail to make up the cleaning solution of half vinegar and half water. Mina untied the bundle and started separating the pages out. It wasn't long before she started noticing that the headlines were a lot more sensational than the ones that had graced her father's favored broadsheet.

Half-Naked Somnambulist Finds Herself in Deadly Peril, she noticed, had a rather salacious drawing of a scantily clad female dangling from a rooftop, her underwear having fortuitously caught on a chimney pot and spared her from plummeting to her death below. She scrunched that page up for use with her lips pursed. She was of course glad that Miss Fanny Jones had been spared a nasty fall but failed to see why she needed to be depicted in a state of undress for all to see.

The next page contained the highlights of a case against a wicked poisoner who preyed on rich widows, a scandalous divorce case with accusations of infidelity on both sides, and an improbable haunting. Mina's eye had just fallen on an article about a twenty-four-year-old female thief who had masqueraded as a fifteen-year-old errand boy for four years when a footfall startled her and she looked up to find Will Nye frowning down at her.

"What are you doing with those?" he growled accusingly, snatching the pages out of her hand.

Mina bridled, both affronted by his rudeness and uncomfortably aware that she had been caught out reading scandal rags. "I was about to clean the windows with them," she answered, flushing hotly.

This seemed to take the wind out of his sails. "Oh," he said, swallowing back whatever he had been about to say next. "With newspaper?" He gave her a hard stare, and Mina wished she weren't so smudgy with dirt. "Won't the print smear the glass?"

"You'd think so, wouldn't you," she admitted, touching her headscarf to make sure it was still firmly in place. "But no, it actually has the opposite effect." *What was he staring at?* She glanced down to check she wasn't disarrayed in some way, but everything seemed to be in place, if a little worse for wear.

He breathed out heavily. "These are set aside," he said shortly. "For clippings."

"Oh, I didn't realize—"

"Why should you?" he interrupted her rudely.

Mina's eyes stung. To distract herself, she reached for the pages she had detached. "I'll just parcel these back up," she said stiffly, but again, he rejected her help.

67

"Don't touch them," he said, reaching past her and scooping them up. Mina drew back her hand as if he had slapped it. She stood mutely by as he gathered all the newspapers up into a bundle and walked them to the door. He halted in the doorway and turned back. "It's not me putting you to skivvy," he said ungraciously. "I neither asked for a wife nor needed one."

Mina felt her color drain away. She stood entirely still as he exited the room and continued to stand there for a good few minutes after. Reaching for her apron strings, she untied them with trembling fingers, cast the apron down on a chair, and then reached for the headscarf which she also tore off her head. Then she was out of the parlor bar, striding down the passageway and out in the yard. She was halfway across it before she broke into a run. When she reached the road, she did not turn right, down toward the village, but instead swung to the left, her legs flying despite her long skirts and the uphill climb.

Her arms worked, her legs pumped, and she flew just like the carrion crow Jeremy Vance had said she resembled. She felt good, she felt *free*. Her blood, which had felt so sluggish since Papa died, coursed through her body in a wild, fizzing rush. The brisk air whipped against her cheeks, but she did not feel cold despite the fact she lacked both cloak and hat. Her hair streamed out behind her as she burst through a hole in the hedge and made for the sound of the sea like an arrow from a bow.

She could see it. The ocean. She had never seen it before, except in books. She felt a sort of frenzied joy fill her at the sight, and her face was suddenly wet. It was tears, she realized with surprise. Then she heard shouting behind her. They would not stop her, she vowed. She was going to feel the sea spray on her face, the sensation of sand between her toes. Suddenly she was desperate to stand on that beach. If she could only get on that beach, everything would be alright. Nothing else would matter.

Coming upon the edge of the cliff was a shock. For one horribly thrilling moment, she thought her momentum would carry her right over the edge. Instead, she swerved and came up short, a shower of small stones falling instead onto the rocks below. Again, she heard voices carried on the wind behind her but refused to look back. Almost she felt as though she were pursued by furies or her own overwhelming misery which she had managed for an instant to outrun. But she would not let it catch her. They would not prevent her from her aim.

Instead she crouched a moment, panting to catch her breath and steady her wildly beating heart before lurching unsteadily to her feet in search of a path down the cliffs toward the beach. The fates for once were with her, as almost straightaway she hit on a rough-hewn path. Slipping and stumbling, she made the steep descent, her heels dislodging clods of earth, her hands clutching at tufts of grass to stop herself from losing her footing and sliding the whole way down on her backside.

By the time she reached the bottom of the cliff she was out of breath and aching all over from where she'd scraped and bumped herself on the way down. She didn't care. Clambering over the rocks, she headed for the patches of golden sand. When she reached the wet sand, she collapsed onto it, whimpering and tearing at her ankle boots, throwing them one after the other over her shoulder. She didn't bother stripping off her ripped and torn stockings. She could already feel the sand through them in any case. She had reached the sea and was wading out into its cold waves when she felt hands close onto her upper arms, whirling her round.

Will Nye's face was livid. "What the hell do you think you're doing, you crazy woman?" he bellowed. "I thought you went over the edge! I thought—"

Mina's balled fists rose up and struck against his chest as she struggled wildly against him. "I don't want you either!" she screamed in his face. "I don't want you! I hate you! Do you hear me? *I hate you!*" He didn't react, just stood there solid and stoic as she pummeled and yelled, she knew not what, until her lungs burned and her voice broke. Then her legs went from underneath her, and the next thing she knew, her cheek was pressed to his chest, he was holding her up, and she was being carried back up the beach, sobbing as if her heart would break.

*

Mina kept her eyes tightly shut during their ascent. She was humiliated beyond belief. Her face felt sore from all the tears. Straggles of her hair kept blowing across her face. The gulls screeched and the waves crashed as they broke on the rocks below. She was sure that any minute now, he would set her down and either tell her to climb the cliff path for herself or simply dump her there and leave her. After all, it wouldn't be the first time.

Yet, for some reason, he did neither of those things. At one point, he did set her down on a rocky ledge, and Mina was just struggling to sit up when she felt herself seized once again and slung over his shoulder, like a sack of potatoes. She had no fight left in her by this point and just hung there limply as he started, sure-footed as a goat, up the steep track.

When she heard voices hailing them from above, she did not raise her head to see who bore witness to her shame. She told herself she didn't care, but her hot cheeks and sweaty discomfiture spoke otherwise. She had made an embarrassing spectacle of herself. She hoped Gus Hopkirk was not aware that Minerva was supposed to be a goddess of wisdom, but even as the thought fervently crossed her mind, she realized he most probably did.

70

She was the wretchedest creature alive. Without friends, without family, reduced to helping herself to a bowl of whatever stew Edna cooked for the bar patrons for her evening meal alone. She had no one even to break bread with. Fresh tears sprang to her eyes, welling up and spilling over. Because she was upside down, they dripped the wrong way up her face and ran into her hair which felt sweaty at the roots. Beating the rugs that morning felt like days ago. She had been a different person then. One who was not broken.

Someone cleared their throat. "She alright, is she, Nye?" she heard a man's uncertain voice ask nearby. She felt Nye's body twist at his waist as he turned to look at this person, but he didn't utter a word. From the pregnant silence, Mina could only suppose he had directed a scathing look in his direction She could hear several pairs of boots thudding against the ground, trotting alongside Nye's long-legged stride, but none of them dared address him again, even when the flattened earth gave way to the cobbles of the inn's courtyard.

The door banged shut behind them, and she heard another pair of feet running up the corridor. "Get water heated," she heard Nye order tersely. "Fill the bath." Then they were climbing the stairs. Mina kept her eyes shut, telling herself she didn't care, but the moment they reached the second floor and he dipped his shoulder to put her down, she tensed and braced herself. He set her down on her dirty stockinged feet carefully enough. Seeing spots of blood on her shins she guessed she must have scraped them on the cliffs on the way down. Mina kept her eyes averted as Nye straightened up. She was in the tiled bathroom.

"You're shivering," he said flatly. "You need to take those wet things off."

71

There was a knock on the door. Edna's head peered around it. "The water was already on," she said matter-of-factly. "For the next lot o' washing."

Nye grunted, and she carried a pail of hot water in, sloshing it into the hip bath. To Mina's surprise, Ivy entered the bathroom behind her with another bucket which she also emptied into the bath. She stopped next to Mina and tossed her head. "Here," she said and held out her upturned hand to her. Mina looked down and saw a round cake of pink soap in it in the shape of a rose. "Take it, then."

"Leave it on the side," Nye said curtly. "Can't you see she's not in a state to take anything right now?" Ivy shot him a curious look and set it down on the basin.

"Thank you," Mina murmured through numb lips. Ivy made no reply and exited the room. Edna entered again with a third bucket of steaming water, a towel slung over one arm. Nye took these from her and ushered her out the door, shutting it firmly behind her.

"Can you take your clothes off, or do you need me to send Edna in to help you?" he said over his shoulder as he emptied the bucket into the bathtub.

"I can manage," Mina muttered.

"Don't lock the door. I'll stand outside."

Her eyes widened. "Why?"

"You look fit to drop."

He thought she would pass out in the bath? Surprised by his solicitude, Mina nodded her head, and he let himself out, shutting the door firmly behind him. She reached up to start unbuttoning her bodice. Her skirts and petticoats were harder to

72

wriggle out of as the bottom half were sodden and clinging to her legs. She felt limp as a rag and slumped against the wall a couple of times to muster the energy to carry on unfastening the hooks and eyes. Her eyes felt gritty. Everything ached. By the time she lowered herself into the bath, she was exhausted and the water lukewarm. She clutched Ivy's rose soap to her. Vaguely she recognized it smelled like sandalwood and rose petals.

A sharp rap on the door roused her. "Are you in that tub yet?" Nye's voice penetrated the fog of her thoughts.

"Yes," she croaked.

The door squeaked open just a crack. "Answer me, Mina."

"Yes!" she repeated louder, twisting her head round to look at the door. Had he just called her Mina? She thought it was the first time he had done so. Apparently satisfied, he shut the door. Swallowing, Mina shuffled down the tub to wet her hair and soap it up. By the time she had rinsed it through twice and run the sweet-smelling soap over her body, he was knocking on the door again.

"I—I'm nearly done," she called weakly. Why was her throat so raw? Then she recalled yelling herself hoarse on the beach. Oh, that was why. She had just about gotten the towel wrapped about her when the door opened again. She started hobbling in the direction of the door and found herself once more caught up in those strong arms.

They were halfway up the stairs to the attics when she lifted her head from his shoulder, with effort. "I left my boots on the beach," she murmured, but Nye made no reply to that, just shouldered the bedroom door open and carried her inside, twitching back the blankets.

"Get under the covers," he ordered, laying her down.

Mina blinked up at him and reached for her cotton nightgown which she had hooked over the rail that morning. It seemed to be caught there, and she dropped her arm in defeat. It ached too much from the earlier exertion to persist tugging at it.

"You want this?" Nye reached past her and caught up the white garment. He eyed it a moment doubtfully.

"My nightgown," she said feebly.

"It looks about ten sizes too big for you."

Her towel still firmly about her, Mina determinedly pulled the voluminous white garment over her head but the ribbons at her throat defeated her. She was too drained to fasten them.

"Take off that damp towel or you'll catch a chill."

Mina lay limply on her back. "I will in a minute." Her sore eyelids drooped shut.

She heard Nye click his tongue, and the next minute two strong hands had reached beneath her tent of a nightgown to drag the fluffy towel down her legs. Mina gave an outraged squawk but could not muster the energy even to bat his hands away. The next thing she knew, she was jerked into a sitting position; the towel enveloped her head and he was vigorously rubbing her wet hair with it. Mina gasped, feeling her back against his warm front. Was she sat between his thighs? Oh God, why did it feel so good?

In general, she had never been much of a one for physical closeness. *Such a prickly little thing*, her mother had always objected when Mina wriggled off her lap as a child. *Mama's little hedgehog.* Now, though, she felt weak as a kitten and certainly in no fit state to object to his familiarity. In any case, it gave her an excuse to just sit there with her eyes closed and feel his strength surrounding her. She wished she could tuck her knees up and just lie back against him, but of course, she could never allow such a thing.

A knock on the door startled her eyes open. It was Edna carrying a tray with the brown teapot and a cup on it. "She'll get an inflammation of the lungs, if you're not careful," she warned direly as she set it down on the small bedside table. Mina tried to sit forward, but Nye's firm hold on her did not permit it.

"Make her some soup," he ordered. "And pass me that brush."

"There's oxtail on the stove," Edna replied, picking up the hairbrush and handing it to him. "But it needs another two hours."

He didn't reply, but it was still the most words Mina had ever heard them exchange. Edna nodded to her and left. Nye set the towel aside on a chair and started running the brush through the ends of her hair at her waist.

"You don't have to do that," Mina said wearily as her head drooped forward.

"If I don't, you'll sleep on it wet," he said dryly. "And we both know it."

Mina's eyes drifted shut as she submitted to the strokes of the hairbrush down her back.

"Put your feet under the bedspread," he recommended at one point. "Your toes will get cold." But Mina was already fast asleep.

When next she woke, she was tucked in bed, extra pillows behind her head and her nightgown ribbons neatly tied.

75

Someone was bustling through the door with a tray. It was Edna, and this time it bore a bowl of soup.

"You didn't drink your tea, Mrs. Nye," she scolded.

"Sorry," Mina muttered guiltily, sitting up. "That smells good."

Edna set the tray down across her knees and thumped the pillows until they gave enough support to Mina's back. She stood a moment, watching Mina take her first mouthful, then her eyes roamed over the room. "That's a fine silver teapot," she said with grudging admiration.

"It was my mother's."

"You ought to have a fine parlor to set it off." Mina had no reply for that. "Shall I make you another then?" Edna asked, nodding to the cold pot of tea.

"I would love a cup of tea," Mina admitted. "Thank you, Edna."

Edna picked up the tray with the earthenware teapot and hesitated. "Will I use your things?" she asked casually. Mina looked up in surprise to see Edna's gaze fixed longingly on the yellow floral cups and saucers.

"If you would not mind, that would be very nice." She hesitated. "Will you join me for a cup? If you're not serving this evening."

"Ivy always serves evening bar," Edna replied, visibly brightening. "I'll be glad to join you, Mrs. Nye."

She reappeared twenty minutes later without her apron, carrying a tea cloth and a pot of hot water. She laid the small table in Mina's room with exquisite care, setting out the silver spoons, cups and saucers, and the little jug and sugar tongs.

Mina, finishing off her soup, watched as Edna warmed the silver pot and added the tea leaves, setting it aside to brew as she polished the delicate cups with a tea towel, admiring their gilded and fluted edges.

"As pretty a tea set as I ever did see," Edna commented.

"Thank you. It used to be a lot bigger, but alas I could not bring much with me."

"Fancy having to leave your things behind," Edna said with a shocked gasp. "Would've broken my 'eart, that would!"

"A lot of it had to be sold," Mina admitted. "To pay my father's doctor's bills."

Edna's sharp gaze darted to meet Mina's as she daintily added the sugar into the cups. "That who you're mourning?" she asked.

"Yes."

"Recent?"

"Papa died ten days ago today."

Edna breathed out noisily. Mina could see a question trembling on her lips that she could not quite bring herself to ask. She looked up suddenly. "I don't care what they say," she said defiantly. "It's like I told my aunt. I know a respectable woman when I sees one."

Mina felt a little choked at Edna's vehemence. She set the empty bowl of soup onto the bedside table. "Thank you," she said quietly.

Edna gave a sharp nod and lifted the lid to peer into the pot. "I know my own mind," she said grimly. "And nobody makes it up but me." She leveled a look at Mina. "Will you be coming to church tomorrow?"

Mina could see it was a loaded question. "Of course," she replied, though the prospect of seeing that place again was far from enticing.

Edna looked gratified. "Service starts at nine sharp, so I always leaves at half eight to make it in plenty of time."

"I will be ready to join you," Mina assured her. Edna poured their tea and they drank it in companionable quiet. Then Edna withdrew and washed the things before restoring them carefully to Mina's shelf.

"Good night, Mrs. Nye."

"Edna, won't you call me Mina?"

"It wouldn't be fitting," the maid replied, looking scandalized.

"Just in private then?" Mina suggested. Edna looked torn. "Just consider it." She gave a nod and closed the door softly behind her.

Surprisingly, Edna wasn't the last of her visitors that night. Mina had dozed off into a deep sleep, only emerging from it when the clock struck midnight in the passage below. Then she heard heeled boots coming up to the attic, and guessed it must be Ivy, for Edna, she knew, had retired already for her early morning start. The click of the heels stopped outside her room and hesitated a moment, before they crossed to the other side and returned a few moments later.

Mina frowned, only hearing the tap on the door because she was listening for it. "Come in," she called, and Ivy's blond head full of curls peered round it. She seemed surprised to see Mina wide awake. "Evening," she said, coming into the room with a candle in one hand and in her other a stoppered glass bottle with a floral label on it, straight out of the pages of one of Mina's periodicals.

"Thought you might like a drop of lotion for your poor hands and shins," Ivy said. "They looked scratched to high heaven when I saw you earlier."

Mina was taken aback. "That's very kind of you, Ivy," she said, sitting up.

Ivy shrugged, dragging a chair to the bedside. "Know how it feels, don't I? Having a man promise you the world then passing you off like you were nothing." She pursed her full lips as she pulled the stopper out of the bottle. "He may be a pretty spoken gentleman," she said bitterly, "but that don't make him any better than all the rest of them."

Pretty spoken? Mina couldn't think of anyone less pretty spoken than William Nye. When Ivy held her hand out, Mina placed hers in it with an air of bewilderment. Ivy tipped a blob of white creamy fluid into Mina's palm and then started working it into her hands with her fingers.

"I'm sorry I laughed now, when he was acting ugly toward you on that first night." Ivy directed a frank look at her. "Only he's a good tipper and I didn't think about how you'd be feeling at the time." Mina's confusion grew. "Looking back on it now, I can't blame you for thinking I was a spiteful cow. I'm not proud of myself."

"I don't think I quite—"

"I don't expect you to confide in me," Ivy interrupted firmly, reaching for Mina's other hand. "Or to want to be friends." She applied more lotion liberally to Mina's other hand. "I just want you to know that—"

Mina's frown cleared. "Do you mean Lord Faris?"

Ivy finely plucked eyebrows rose. "'Course. Who else?"

"Well, he didn't make me any promises," Mina assured her. "I think he brought me here out of a misguided notion of familial duty."

Ivy's brow puckered over this. "Out of what?" she puzzled.

"Because we shared a mother," Mina explained without thinking. Ivy gasped and fell back in her chair.

"You never!" she squeaked. Mina nodded. After all, Jeremy had never enjoined her not to speak of it. "You mean, your mother was Viscountess Faris?"

"Yes," Mina agreed slowly. "I suppose she was at one point. Not when I knew her, of course, but before she was married to my father."

Ivy shook her head. "Well!" she said, staring at Mina. "They always says as he took after his mother," she mused. "But I can't say as I can see a resemblance." She hesitated. "Except maybe... In a certain delicacy in the cast of your features." She returned to massaging the lotion into Mina's fingers as Mina reflected this was probably the nicest thing anyone had ever said about her face. "And to think," she marveled, "that Lord Faris thought to provide for you—a proper lady—by marrying you off to a nasty rough brute like Nye!" She looked scandalized. "He's got a wild side and no mistake."

"Lord Faris?" Mina clarified, trying to keep track of the conversation.

"Yes him," Ivy agreed darkly, before hesitating. "The apple don't fall from the tree and no mistake. You do know that—"

She lowered her voice. "Nye's father, old Jacob Nye, ran this place before him. But he weren't the one what sired him."

"I have heard that the old viscount was his true father," Mina admitted, coloring delicately. "Making them half brothers."

"That's right. The old lord what was married to your mother. Ellen Nye were his fancy piece for years. He bought this place for her when he was done. It's named after her. Before that, it was called The Quiet Woman." Mina absorbed this startling piece of news in silence. The Merry Harlot on the sign was Nye's mother? "Jacob Nye married her, getting his hands on the inn and giving both mother and child his name."

"I see."

Ivy released her hand and moved down to the foot of the bed. She flipped back the coverlet and inspected the scratches up Mina's shin. "Nasty," she tutted, reaching for her bottle.

"You shouldn't waste all your lotion on me, Ivy," Mina said hurriedly. "It looks expensive."

"Nonsense," Ivy said, waving a hand. "You'll ruin your skin with that nasty abrasive carbolic and wind up as dried up as Edna."

"You and Edna have both been very kind," Mina murmured as the soothing, cool lotion washed over her skin.

Ivy shrugged. "You must have told her," she said with a snort. "About your connection to Lord Faris."

"No," Mina answered. "Not a word of it. You're the first person I've told."

Ivy's mouth dropped. "And she's been hobnobbing with you? Thinking you're a cast-off bird of paradise?" Mina gazed back at her blankly. "A soiled dove. Lord Faris's ex-mistress," Ivy explained patiently.

"I'm sure she doesn't think that," Mina said, stirring uneasily as she remembered Edna's words earlier. *I don't care what they say. I know a respectable woman when I sees one.*

"Bless you, sweetheart," said Ivy, plunking her hands on her hips and giving her a pitying look. "That's what everyone thinks. The whole damn village."

7

Mina woke the next morning and remembered it was Sunday. Her muscles felt stiff and sore as she donned a gown that had once been blue plaid but was now a rather dingy black. She would have to go in search of yesterday's clothes at some point. She could not afford to lose half of her petticoats, even if the gown were torn and in need of repair. Outside her room she found her black ankle boots, polished and cleaned after their mishap at the beach the previous day.

Edna was already downstairs and together they washed, ate toasted muffins, and drank tea before donning their bonnets and cloaks and setting off for church. They were halfway across the courtyard when Nye's voice hailed them. Mina whipped around and saw him emerging from the stables.

"Where are you off to?" he asked with a heavy frown. "I thought you'd sleep in this morn."

"Church," Mina answered him simply.

His gaze flickered over her and he cleared his throat. "You're none the worse then," he said, gazing at some fixed point to the left of her shoulder.

"Just a bit sore," Mina admitted. "Which is my own fault." She took a deep breath. "Next time I get an urge to visit the beach, I'll look for a more sedate path."

His eyes met hers briefly before he looked away. "You do that," he said dryly.

Edna opened and shut her prayer book restlessly. "We'll have to leave now, Mrs. Nye," she interrupted them. "Or we'll be late and Reverend Ryland doesn't appreciate latecomers."

Mina nodded, noticing that Edna did not address Nye or even look at him and his eyes were trained on her.

"No housework when you get back," he said gruffly. "It's Sunday, so you can take your rest." He swung about on his heel and plunged back into the stables before Mina could react.

"Is The Harlot open on a Sunday?" Mina asked as she and Edna hurried across the courtyard. She felt slightly discomforted speaking of harlots on the Lord's day.

Edna pressed her lips together and nodded. "I've put a shoulder of mutton in the oven this morning to roast. There's plenty of sinners spend their Sundays at this godforsaken hole," she said sourly. "And expecting meat along with their liquor."

Mina glanced up at the inn sign as they passed it and the pretty, round dimpled face of the harlot. For the first time she noticed she was winking one eye and clasping a tray of bottles to her ample bosom. She wondered if Ellen Nye had really been as pretty and as merry as the sign proclaimed. If so, her son had inherited neither of these traits.

For the first time, it occurred to her that if Ellen Nye had been the old Viscount Faris's mistress "for years," as Ivy had said, then very likely it had been during the time her own mother was married to him. Her footsteps faltered as she considered the likelihood that her mother and Nye's had been love rivals. *What a strange notion.*

She was twenty-four this year; she would have put Jeremy at twenty-seven or thereabouts and Nye not much older. Had Nye been the old lord's firstborn, despite his illegitimate status? Was it that which had cemented Ellen's place in the old viscount's affections and led to him purchasing her the inn? They turned down to the right and started down the steep hill to the village as Mina pondered these things.

It was at the first glimpse of the fishermen's cottages lining the main street through the village that Mina felt the first stirrings of unease at the reception she might receive from the congregation. Ivy's words came back to haunt her from the previous evening. Did everyone really think she was Jeremy's cast-off mistress?

A few stragglers were stood milling about outside the church exchanging gossip, but it did not seem Edna was the sociable type, for she headed straight for the church door. Her head held high, Mina followed her example. She heard a few sharply indrawn breaths as she and Edna proceeded down the aisle of the church, but Mina made sure to keep her gaze straight ahead. Edna made for a pew halfway down, and Mina slipped into it after her, sitting next to her on the wooden bench.

Despite her impressions on her wedding day, St. Werburgh's church was not in fact a cave, but rather a small gray stone church with few pretensions. Its porch was probably the most decorative part of it, either that or the colorful stained-glass windows. During the service Mina found herself wondering several times at the significance of the images on the windows which were festooned all about with geese. She recognized Reverend Ryland's ponderous tones and wondered what he had made of the impromptu wedding service he had been impelled to perform.

Looking back on it now, that whole evening had all the qualities of a bad dream and she couldn't quite believe she was even married. Glancing down, she found she was rubbing the bare third finger of her left hand where a wedding band would traditionally be worn. She didn't even have a brass one, let alone a gold. She still had Mama's of course, as Papa had not had the heart to sell it. Should she take to wearing that in the cause of respectability?

On the walk back to the inn she quizzed Edna about the geese and was told vaguely that they were sacred to St. Werburgh.

"She had a whole flock at her convent. Then some fool up and ate her favorite goose and most put out about it, St. Werburgh was," said Edna. "For they was under her protection and he had no right. So, she gathered up the bones and resurrected the goose from the dead. Grayking, his name was. He's the one with the black ring around his throat on the main window. You may have observed him?"

"I did not, but I shall make sure to next Sunday. Most interesting," Mina murmured as they turned into the inn. "The stained glass looked very fine."

"Lord Faris paid for it," Edna sniffed. "You may have observed the Vance family box pew up the front? Decorated with the family coat of arms?" Edna prompted.

Mina admitted she had noticed it. She recognized the crest from Jeremy's carriage.

"Precious little they ever sits in it!" Edna said darkly. "His lady wife"—she spoke the words with vicious disdain—"has visited The Harlot more times than she has St. Werburgh's!"

"Viscountess Faris has been to the inn?" Mina was frankly shocked to hear this. Her impression of The Merry Harlot was that the place was rough and ready and entirely unfit for polite company. "In search of her husband, I suppose, for I cannot imagine any other reason."

"Least said about it the better," Edna enounced with disgust.

86

Mina frowned. Though her husband might be related to Lord Faris, it was on the wrong side of the blanket and would not be acknowledged by polite society. "Is Lady Faris from a local family?" she asked, feeling some curiosity toward her half brother's wife. She remembered Jeremy had made some disparaging comment about her during their journey but could not what recall for the moment what it had been.

"Met her in London he did and brought her back here a bride." Edna's expression was disapproving. "Nasty fast bit of goods she is too! For all the fact her father was an earl!"

"They have a child, I think?"

"Young Master Vance has been sent away to school, poor mite. Probably for the best. Precious little moral guidance he'd receive at home and that's a fact!"

Mina felt a flicker of interest. She supposed young Master Vance was a nephew of hers of sorts. Not that the connection was likely to be recognized now she was a publican's wife. "I see," she murmured placatingly. They had reached the kitchen door by now, and reaching for it, Mina was surprised to find it wrenched open for her.

Nye stood looming in the doorway. "About time," he said with a frown, taking her arm and leading her through to the passage beyond. "What kept you?"

"It was only a short sermon," she pointed out mildly. "Where are we going?"

"You'll see." To her surprise, he led her straight to the parlor bar. A good deal of the wooden chairs had been cleared out of the room along with most of the small circular tables. Instead, two plush armchairs and a sofa had been set next to the fireplace, upholstered in a matching peach-colored brocade. To her astonishment, she saw her own silver teapot sat on one of the tables that remained along with a very pretty tea set of cobalt and gold. A rosewood workbox was sat next to the sofa on which a beautiful Chinese shawl was spread out, and against the opposite wall, an elegant lady's writing desk stood complete with little drawers, a penholder, and a matching chair.

"I—I don't know what to say," Mina blurted after staring in astonishment at the room's transformation. "Really, I don't."

"You don't have to say anything." Nye shrugged. "It's for you to use."

"Me?" She turned to him blankly. "But whose are these things?" she said, pointing to the workbox and shawl and giving a sweeping gesture to incorporate the china service.

"Yours now," he replied shortly.

"Mine? But—"

"I'll send Edna to fetch your tea."

"Wait—"

The door shut behind him. Mina wondered why every word he spoke to her seemed to take monumental effort. Was it all women he did not like, or just her? She remembered how Edna also seemed to avoid him. Maybe she shouldn't take it personally. Maybe he just loathed all women. For some reason, she thought suddenly of Ivy and wondered if he was also averse to the blond barmaid.

Mina turned in a circle, taking in the mostly empty expanse of the parlor bar now. Her new seating area only took up about a third of the space. She walked over to the large handsome mantelpiece over the fire. It had been quite bare the other day when she had polished its every carved nook and cranny, but now it had two very pretty candelabra set on it which were dripping with crystal droplets designed to catch the light.

A decorative box of gold enamel sat between them which had a coral cameo in the center of the lid, bearing the profile of a classical maiden. When Mina lifted the lid, it started to play a tinkling tune, so she quickly slammed it shut and moved away. How could they be her things? she wondered blankly. Clearly, they were expensive items and no doubt someone's treasured possessions. Moving over to the sofa, she admired the delicate peach upholstery and then lifted the Chinese shawl to examine the exquisite patterning of pink blossom adorning the teal-colored silk. She had never seen one so pretty.

Absently, she draped it over her shoulders and walked back to the mirrored overmantel. Was it merely her imagination or did the shawl immediately brighten her appearance? Not just the unalleviated black of her mourning, but also endowing her skin with an illusion of blooming. She shrugged it off quickly. It was a beautiful thing, but to imagine it could beautify her was just nonsense. She set it down carefully onto the sofa and sat down beside it.

Edna brought her hot water for her tea and seemed to cautiously approve of the new setup. "Silver teapot looks right at home," she said, nodding with satisfaction. "It's my half day tomorrow, Mrs. Nye," she said, catching Mina off guard. "I mean to hitch a ride to St. Ives to meet my aunt on the pier."

For a moment, Mina had thought Edna was going to invite her to join her. She felt a stab of disappointment. "Oh, how nice. Is St. Ives a big town?"

Edna nodded. "It's a fishing port," she explained.

Mina nodded. "Does your aunt live there?"

Edna shook her head. "It's halfway between us, so a good point to meet."

"Well, I hope you have a lovely visit, Edna."

"Would there be anything you wanted me to fetch you back, Mrs. Nye? From the shops, I mean."

"Oh." Mina thought a moment. "That's very kind of you, Edna. Let me consider and I will let you know."

Edna nodded. "I'll make a seed cake this afternoon. If I have the time," she added briskly before leaving the room.

Mina thought of her half sovereign as she measured tea leaves into the pot and added the hot water. Would it be a good idea to break into it when it constituted her only wealth in the world? It might be a nice gesture to replace Ivy's bottle of lotion and to buy Edna some scented soap after their kindness toward her.

She was still debating this when the small brass key in the latch of the workbox at her feet caught her attention. Deciding she would look inside while the tea brewed, she lifted the box onto her knees. Inside was a jumble of embroidery tools, sewing needles, silk threads, and fancy buttons. It was lined with blue silk and had lots of dividers for organizing things, so Mina could only imagine that someone had turned it upside down at some point for it have got into such a mess.

Impulsively, she upended it now on the sofa and determined to sort the contents that very minute. She spent an enjoyable twenty minutes reordering the box to her satisfaction and drinking two cups of tea during the process. Then she nipped upstairs to collect her own meagre sewing kit to add to the box. She had a silver thimble and a small pair of sewing scissors in a decorative sheath to add along with a quantity of cheap black darning wool she used for her stockings.

90

It was only after she had sat back down again that she recalled the matching pair of Staffordshire china dogs which she had not even unpacked from her trunk. They would look very well on the mantelpiece, she thought, at either side. She would go and fetch them also. She was returning from this journey, with the dogs in her hands, when she came across Nye in the passageway.

"I was just fetching these for the mantel," she said hurriedly, forestalling any demands as to why she was not reclining by the fire. He glanced down at the red and white china dogs complete with collars. To her surprise, he followed her into the parlor room where she set them above the fire. "What do you think?" she asked rather self-consciously as she stepped back to study the effect.

For a moment, she did not think he would answer. He seemed to be regarding her more than the ornaments. Then he seemed to stir himself. "What kind of dogs are they supposed to be?"

"Cavalier King Charles spaniels," she answered promptly. "They were my mother's."

Again, his gaze, which had been wandering over the rearranged room, snapped back to meet hers. He nodded which she supposed meant he approved. Suddenly, it occurred to Mina that the feminine possessions, now dotted about the room, likely belonged to his mother and had been brought out of storage. She blushed, thinking how inappropriate it was that his mother's things should now be mingled with her own as Ellen Nye had been the mistress of her mother's first husband.

"I'm having a dining table brought in before supper," he said curtly. "You can take your meals in here in future."

Mina's eyes widened. "Will you take them with me?" she asked, emboldened by the longest conversation she thought they'd ever probably had.

His eyelids flickered. "Probably not."

Oh. Well, that was certainly plain speaking. It seemed their lives were to run parallel to one another but not cross over. "I would appreciate it very much," she said, deciding to take a leaf out of his book, "if you could explain the rules to me." She walked over to one of the peach brocade armchairs and perched herself on it, hands folded in her lap. She would be civilized and calm, completely in control. The opposite of what she had been the day before.

"Rules?" he asked, looking as though goaded into speech.

"Of how we are going to conduct ourselves within this marriage," she elaborated carefully. "You have kindly made me a space in your inn. Am I to take it that my activities are to be confined to this area?"

He jutted out his chin. "You are."

"I see." She hesitated, reluctant to break their truce. Embarrassingly, she chose that moment to remember how she had screamed in his face like a banshee. "Yes, I quite see," she added awkwardly.

He breathed out noisily. "I married you to get my hands on some property that was mine by right," he said starkly. "It was promised to me and Faris did not honor that promise. I thought—" He broke off frustratedly. "What I can't figure out is why you did it."

"Me?" She paused, trying to think of a delicate way to say she was destitute and had little choice in the matter. Words failed her, so she decided to go with the unvarnished truth. "My father died last week," she said bluntly. "I was left alone in the world with a lot of debts to settle." She took a deep breath. "He ran a small school in Bath, but it had been struggling these past few years. My father's health was such…" She sighed. "He left just enough to cover our bills but no further expenses." She glanced at Nye, but his expression gave nothing away. "I taught at the school too, but I could not secure another teaching post, though I've been trying for months," she confessed in a rush.

"You're a schoolteacher?" he bit out at last with a disbelieving look.

Mina nodded. "I had hoped perhaps to find work as a governess, but as the school failed, all our sponsors fell away. None of them replied to my letters." She swallowed. "I was desperate," she admitted.

"You must have been," he replied with faint bitterness.

It occurred to her belatedly that she had perhaps been rather tactless. Ah well, in for a penny, in for a pound. "Have you been married before?" she blurted and then colored hotly.

"No," he said grimly.

"So…all these lovely things…" She swallowed. "Must have belonged to your mother then?"

He regarded her in silence a moment. "Is that a problem for you?" he asked, and something in the tone of his voice made the hairs on the back of her neck rise.

"Of course not!" His expression still closed off, he made no reply, just straightened up as though to take his leave.

"Nye!" she said quickly and watched him stiffen. "I very much appreciate what you have done here," she said painstakingly. "Making room for me, I mean."

His eyes held hers for an instant, then abruptly he swung around and made for the door. Mina collapsed back into her chair, closing her eyes. My God, why was it so difficult to speak to that man? Hearing the door close firmly behind him, she opened her eyes again and stared into space. And how was she supposed to get through the rest of her married life with him?

True to his word, Nye reappeared an hour later with a bearded man who looked vaguely familiar, carrying a large mahogany dining table with fluted legs. The ginger-bearded man tugged his cap at her and stared as though astonished to see the transformation that had taken place in the room. Mina, who was sat repairing the rips and tears in her petticoats from her misadventure on the cliffs the day before, hurriedly dropped them out of view down the side of the sofa.

They trooped out, only to reenter carrying a set of eight matching chairs with decorative backs and seats of muted gold-colored fabric which put the previous chairs to shame. They tucked these under the table and left again without any more ado. Mina, drifting over to examine the table, saw it had a winding mechanism underneath to expand it even further if necessary. It was lucky the parlor bar was such a large room and could easily accommodate so large a piece of furniture. Stealthily, she made her way to the kitchen to see if she could find the tin of furniture polish to buff it up to a shine.

Edna was just closing the door to the oven. "Oh, Mrs. Nye," she said. "I meant to bring you another pot of tea, but time has quite slipped away from me."

Mina, glancing around the room, saw the profusion of pots and pans and the way Edna surreptitiously swiped at her beaded forehead with the apron. "I'm not surprised, Edna, you could clearly do with more hands in here. What time do you serve your roast mutton?"

Edna, who had visibly bristled, slumped against the table where she had a huge pile of peeled carrots and three large cabbages. "It gets served when it's done," she said grimly. "I can't be held accountable to time, not when I'm on me own."

"Is Ivy serving behind the bar?" Mina asked absently as she picked up an apron and started to tie it over her dress.

"Mrs. Nye, whatever are you doing? You heard what Master Nye said—"

"That's just nonsense, Edna," Mina said briskly. "I can't be sat daintily in the parlor while you slave away here by yourself." She reached for a knife and began chopping up the carrots. "Is that water boiling for these?"

"Yes, but—"

"I'm sure you have the meat in hand. Allow me to prepare the vegetables."

Edna hesitated. "I put the meat and potatoes on to roast in the bread oven before church, so they're almost done."

"Excellent, then I think you should probably make the batter from the hot fat and the gravy from the juices. Is that not so?"

Edna's harried expression relaxed a little. "Well, but—if you're sure?"

"Certainly, I'm sure." Mina sent her a calm look of assurance and Edna scurried into the scullery to check the oven.

The next two hours flew. She chopped, boiled, simmered, wrestled with the kitchen range and, together with Edna, plated and bowled up at least thirty roast dinners to be served. Edna ran back and forth from the kitchen while Mina remained where she was intently focused on the task in hand. The kitchen door swung open and closed a few times, but Mina could not have said who came in and out. Edna left her stirring the gravy or carving the joints of roasted meat onto the plates. By the time all the food was served, Mina was piling up the pots and pans and carrying them through to the large sink in the scullery.

Edna returned, looking red-faced and weary. "Those two's ours," she said, gesturing to the last two plates of food remaining on the cleared table.

"Shall we eat now or after washing up?" Mina asked, thinking of the overflowing piles of tins and trays.

"Eat now," Edna said grimly. "I'll have to go and collect all the emptied plates for washing in a bit." She moved toward one of the cupboards and drew out a tablecloth. "If you'll just give me a moment to lay your table, Mrs. Nye—"

"I shall take my dinner at the kitchen table with you, Edna."

"Mrs. Nye—"

"I do not care to sit alone on a Sunday, Edna," she said quietly. "I assure you, I will sit in the parlor by myself for the rest of the week."

That gave Edna pause, and after a moment, she inclined her head and went to fetch them cutlery. "I must admit, after cooking it, I seldom have an appetite," Edna said as they took their seats.

"Small wonder. You're probably exhausted," Mina commented. "I don't understand how they take their meals here in the taproom. Surely at some point, people would have sat at the tables in the parlor bar?"

Edna nodded. "Before my time, they did. Back in the days of Jacob Nye this place was crawling with folk. Two, three times as many as are here today. There used to be four barmaids and four kitchen maids in those days."

"Good grief, really? So extensive a staff?"

"Six stable hands too," Edna said, nodding. "You see, the stagecoaches used to stop here to change their horses on the way to Exeter."

Mina paused with her fork halfway to her mouth. "I noticed the stables were large," she admitted. "So, they used to house teams of horses here?"

Edna nodded. "Sometimes as many as twenty-four horses at a time."

"Why do they not stop here now? The stagecoaches, I mean?"

Edna's gaze dropped. "Couldn't say, I'm sure."

Mina frowned. "The patrons here," she said hesitantly, remembering the motley assortment gathered the night she was wed. "Are they village folk?"

Again, Edna looked evasive. "A few maybe," she said blandly. "But there's a tavern set in the heart of the village. The Ship, it's called. The villagers prefer that one. It's not so far for them to walk and—er the reputation is more...*wholesome*."

"I see," Mina said thoughtfully. So, The Harlot was frequented by unsavory types. It was no more than she had suspected. "The—er—night I arrived," she added. "There appeared to be some form of bare-knuckle boxing match taking place in the courtyard."

Edna pressed her lips together. "Master Nye is a champion from round these parts," she said with a fleeting look at Mina's startled face. Edna sighed and shook her head. "He's fought bouts in Exeter and London too. Prizefighting, they calls it. A nasty, rough business it is and brings a nasty, rough crowd with it."

Recalling the assortment of people gathered in The Harlot that night, Mina could not help but secretly agree. "If he's a champion," Mina said slowly, "maybe that is why he does not devote more energy into making this place a successful coaching inn?"

"Mebbe." Edna did not look convinced.

Mina chewed the last of her mutton and swallowed. "A very tasty gravy, that," she said. "Do you always serve the battered pudding on the same plate? We always used to have it with gravy as an entrée."

Edna snorted. "It's all served on one plate here. Plate, bowl, whatever comes to hand."

Mina nodded. "Do you have any diners in the small private parlor rooms on a Sunday?"

"Oh yes," Edna replied. "All three of 'em usually. They just has the same as what's served in the public bar though." She shrugged. "I try to make sure they all gets matching plates, but that's as far as it goes."

"Well, that's certainly understandable, all things considered." Mina rose to go and fetch the pail from the scullery.

"What you doing of now, Mrs. Nye?" Edna asked in alarm. "You should let your food digest a while by lying on your sofa."

"I'm going to fill the copper, so we have hot water for the pots and pans."

Edna jumped out of her chair. "If Master Nye sees you out there working the pump, it's my head he'll scalp for it."

Mina turned in the doorway. "Very well," she conceded. "Though you've still got to go and collect all the plates," she pointed out.

"I'm used to it," Edna said dourly. "I'll fetch the water." She paused. "If you're truly not ready to retire to your parlor, then you could grate some soap shavings for doing the dishes."

"Yes of course," Mina said and crossed the room to search the cupboards for a grater.

It took two of them an hour, stood side by side at the huge scullery sink to wash the pots and plates. They had to replace the dishwater several times and boil the copper again before they were done. By the time Mina took herself off to bed, she was sure she would sleep like a baby.

Alas, it was not to be. Again, she woke in the early hours to strange noises outside the inn. She lay a moment listening to the rumble and drag across the cobbles. Then she threw back her blankets and crossed to the window. For a moment, she could have sworn she saw two flickering lights amid the darkness outside, but even as she craned her eyes to focus on them, they went out and all went quiet. She stood there a moment, silent and still, waiting and watching, but nothing happened. Frowning, Mina returned to bed, and when rain started pelting against her window an hour later, she finally fell asleep.

8

Mina was brushing crumbs from her skirts after her toast the next morning, when Nye appeared in the doorway of the kitchen and gave her a meaningful look.

"Good morning," she said brightly.

"Parlor," he replied abruptly. "Why aren't you in it?" Edna hastily retreated into the scullery.

Mina eyed him warily. "It seems foolish to lay that large table for just one person to eat a slice of toast," she answered, drawing herself up to her full height. He looked unimpressed. Admittedly, she did not reach further than his shoulder.

"I've got something to occupy you today," he replied darkly. "You sew?"

"Yes," Mina admitted. "As a matter of fact, I was going to start repairing my dress today."

"I've got another project in mind," he said, taking her elbow and steering her out of the kitchen into the passageway.

Mina stole a sideways look at him. "What is it?"

"You'll see." He opened the parlor door and guided her inside.

Mina saw at once there was a quantity of blue velvet fabric piled up on the dining table. She looked at it and then back at Nye questioningly.

"It's curtains," he said. "You need to alter them."

"For in here?" She glanced over at the windows.

"No," he said. "For the bedroom."

"For *my* bedroom?" she asked in surprise, glancing critically at the heavy blue fabric. "They don't really look like bedroom curtains. I would have thought a floral print—"

"For the bedroom," he said flatly. "I'll have a brass curtain rod put up in there this morning."

"Oh." On the whole, Mina felt markedly unenthusiastic about the task. She had always liked creating new things from scratch, alteration projects not so much. "Are they lined?" she asked, flipping over the blue velvet and finding the yellow silk lining. "They look expensive." She glanced at him quizzically. "Were they hanging in another room?"

He didn't deign to answer this, just walked back to the door. Before opening it, he looked back over his shoulder at her. "I want no more standing at windows in the early hours, Mina," he said with a strange tension running through his words.

Mina almost gasped. "But how did you—?"

"I don't sleep," he said succinctly. "So I see everything. Remember that."

"You don't sleep?" Mina repeated doubtfully, but he had already wrenched the door open and was striding off. She frowned as she took up the workbox to extract a tape measure and tailor's chalk. These curtains were long and luxurious. It seemed frankly a crime to cut them down sufficiently for the attic room window. She would be practically hacking them in half! She bit her lip, wishing she could hang them in this room where they would be much better suited.

How tiresome of Nye to insist she have them in the attic bedroom! He must have spotted her stood there, staring out in her white nightgown. But why did he have to make it an issue?

she wondered. If he had problems sleeping, surely he should sympathize! She mounted the steps up to the attic, deep in thought. She had finished with the tape measure when the two men from earlier came sheepishly into the room with tools to put up the curtain rail.

"Mrs. Nye," they murmured in unison, looking anywhere but at her.

It was on the tip of her tongue to tell them to have a care in her room, but glancing around the bare attic bedroom, she suddenly realized how foolish that would be. There was truly little here to show it was even her room. Instead she nodded to them briskly and left them to it.

She spent the next few hours ill-temperedly altering curtains, one of her least favorite tasks. In truth, she had only ever done it once before, but this fabric was a good deal more difficult to work with. Edna gave her the use of a flat iron and trivet from the scullery to press the material, but she had to be very careful indeed for she was not used to dealing with quantities of velvet and silk which required more gentle care than the cottons or linens she was used to working with.

A knock on the door before lunch turned out to be Gus Hopkirk, who ambled in with another bunch of wildflowers for her. This brightened her mood somewhat, though she had no vase to put them in. In the kitchen, she discovered a pretty blue jug for this purpose and then returned to place them in the center of the mahogany table. To her surprise, Gus was still waiting for her in the parlor. She offered him a cup of tea and he took the pipe out of his mouth with an expression of pleasant surprise.

"That would be very nice of you, Mrs. Nye," he said affably. "Very nice indeed." She gestured to him to take an armchair, though after gazing at its upholstery and then down at his dark brown breeches he shook his head. "I'll take a wooden chair,

Mrs. Nye," he said firmly and retrieved one of the few that had remained from a dark corner.

"Do you mind if I return to my curtains?" Mina asked after pouring the tea. "Only Nye insists they are to be finished today and—"

"To be sure, Mrs. Nye," he said comfortably, forestalling her. "I'll not hold you back from your woman's work." Mina sat back at the dining table and once more started pinning up hems. So unpalatable was the idea of wasting any of the fabric that she had determined to make two sets of curtains from the original pair. The second pair she would give to Edna, whose window also faced the courtyard, though she had never mentioned being troubled by strange sounds in the night.

"How be you finding life at The Harlot, Mrs. Nye?" Gus asked before taking a noisy slurp of his tea.

"Oh, I'm finding my way," Mina answered lightly.

"Heard you found your way down to the beach the other day," he commented, and Mina cast him a sharp look. His round blue eyes met hers with a twinkle in their depths.

"Yes," she agreed after a pause that was a little too long. "I'm afraid the route I took was somewhat precipitous. Nye was forced to come to my rescue. But I'm sure I will find a more sedate path at some point."

"You're fond of the sea, then?"

"That was the first time I've ever seen it," Mina admitted.

Gus looked shocked. "Well fancy that!" he exclaimed roundly, setting down his cup in its saucer with a clatter. "Never seen the sea before! I can scarcely credit it."

"You were born and bred here, I take it?"

"That I was not," he admitted. "I hail from Norfolk parts by rights, but I been here some ten years or so."

"Oh, I see."

"I've always been a seafaring man, me and my father before me."

"You are a fisherman, Mr. Hopkirk?"

"I am now," he agreed. "But when I were in my prime, I was in the merchant navy."

"Indeed? You must have seen a good deal of the world?" Mina spoke around her mouthful of pins in a way she knew would make her mother quite shocked. Somehow, she did not think Gus Hopkirk would care at her lack of etiquette. Her fingers flew as she pinned and tacked the curtains into their new incarnation.

"That I have." He beamed. "That I have, though if it's sights and wonders you're after, then this part of the world is the right one to come to." He lowered his voice. "There's sights and sounds along this coastline would curdle the blood in your veins," he said. "More to petrify any man who'd traveled the breadth and depth of the world! This coastline," he said ominously, "has more mysteries and terrors to rival any other in the civilized world, or the uncivilized, if you takes my meaning." When she looked up, she found him tapping his rather broad nose.

"Well," Mina said cautiously. "It rather sounds as though you are speaking of ghost stories, Mr. Hopkirk."

"Ghost stories! I should think I am!" he agreed with a chuckle. "Are you partial to a yarn or two, Mrs. Nye, on a cold, rainy day in spring?"

Mina thought of the thrilling short stories in her periodicals that her father had frowned at. "I confess, I do enjoy them," she admitted. "Though I tend to associate them more with Christmastime."

"Then, perhaps…?" He withdrew a flask from his waistcoat and tipped the contents into his tea, holding up the bottle quizzically.

Mina shook her head. "No, thank you, not if I want these curtains to be fit for purpose."

Gus chuckled and settled back in his chair. He told her tales of spectral hounds and restless gray ladies, of hand-wringing wraiths and ghostly hunts who pursued lost souls along the cliffs on a stormy night. He told her of the malevolent monks who had once lived in a medieval monastery on this very spot who had been disbanded and punished by the bishop for their wickedness and sin. If you saw them, you were surely cursed to an unhappy fate. Some travelers, he added ominously, had been known to drop dead at the sight of their sinister habits, their empty cowls creeping up to them on a dark, stormy night.

"They must surely have had weak hearts," Mina said with a shudder. "Or some other such predisposition?"

"Aye, mebbe," Gus agreed, closing his teeth on his pipe stem.

Mina hesitated, dying to know what wickedness and sin the monks had indulged in during their lives, but maidenly decorum held her back. Gus's eyes twinkled.

"The monastery had a relic," he explained. "And so, became a popular route for pilgrims in those days. They flocked there, to touch the holy bones of St. Grayking."

"St. Grayking?" Mina frowned. Surely she had heard that name before.

"Aye." He nodded. "The monks built an annex for the pilgrims to take their overnight rest in," he continued comfortably. "There, for a handsome fee mind, they served them with roasted goose and plum pudding and all sorts of fine wines."

"I see." Mina picked up her tacking thread. "It does not sound like typical monastic fare."

"No indeed," Gus agreed heartily. "They was supposed to subsist on weak gruel and pottage, but they had grown used to rich foods and vice. But that's not the worst of it."

Mina threaded her needle and looked up enquiringly. "It wasn't?"

He shook his head. "No indeed! Once these pilgrims was soused to the gills, they would lure the richest of them out to the headland on some pretext and fling them off the nearest cliff and help themselves to all his worldly goods."

"How terrible! But surely some of these murdered pilgrims must have washed up on the shore?"

"Aye, that they did," Gus agreed. "But their party would usually have moved on by then, so no one knew whence they came. If anyone stayed on, the monks would say their victim must have gone out for a walk and been set on by thieves or else sleep-walked to his death."

Mina considered this. "Yet you said the bishop punished them, so their secret must have been discovered eventually?"

"Aye, that it was," Gus agreed, removing his pipe. "Too many dead bodies washed up and someone wrote to the bishop about all the unsavory rumors of wine, loose women, and song. One time, they had the misfortune to pick out a wealthy merchant with powerful connections who wouldn't let his disappearance lie. They found his gold ring on the beach and two witnesses

106

who'd seen him take to his bed the night before, despite the monks denying they'd ever laid eyes on him. Kicked up a fuss they did, then one of the monks confessed. Some say under torture, and the rest was all hung on a gibbet on the harbor wall.

"The bishop had their monastery torn down and the annex burned to the ground." Gus nodded with satisfaction. "So may all sinners be punished. It don't stop 'em walking though. Not on a moonless night. They're doomed to tread their old path up to the cliffs and then back home again. Dragging their feet and rolling their cart with them."

Mina looked up with a quick breath. "Rolling their cart?"

"Aye, for sometimes their victims was so dead drunk they had to be dragged from their beds and rolled up to the cliffs."

Mina felt herself turn pale. That couldn't possibly have been what she heard in the early hours, could it? She lowered her sewing and stared at Gus. "How horrible." He nodded in solemn agreement. "I don't suppose—? I mean, that you've ever—?" She couldn't quite bring herself to ask it.

"No, Mrs. Nye. I ain't never seen hide nor hair of any ghostly monks. But you can bet if I did, I'd take to my heels so fast you wouldn't see me for dust." He chuckled, tapping his nose with his pipe. "Now, are you sure you won't take a nip of this?" he said, picking his tin flask back up with a flourish.

"No indeed, thank you."

"How's them curtains a-lookin' of?"

Mina broke her thread and shook out the folds of the one she was working on. "They're all pinned and tacked now, ready to be sewn up. I shall finish them this afternoon."

"That's good, Mrs. Nye. You've an industrious nature and no mistake. Think Nye said as you was a schoolmistress in your past life?"

Mina was surprised. "Nye told you that?" For some reason, she had not thought Nye was the garrulous type.

"Oh aye. You needn't look so shocked," he chortled. "I knowed him since he were a boy, so I have."

Mina frowned. "But I thought you said you only moved here ten years ago?"

She thought he blinked a moment, but then his ready smile returned. "Ah well, he were only a lad of eighteen or so then. To an old fellow such as myself, that's nowt but a boy!"

She nodded, returning his smile. "You do not take your boat out today, Mr. Hopkirk?"

He shook his head. "Too windy," he said. "My bones is too old to fight against the waves. I only takes her out now when it's calm and balmy. I shall be mendin' my nets this afternoon," he said, glancing at the window. "My word, how the time has flown. I hope I've not bored you with my yarns, Mrs. Nye."

"No indeed! I very much enjoyed them, thank you."

"No, don't stand up," he said, getting to his feet. "I'll not distract you any further." He wandered over to the door and paused there a moment, looking back at her. For an instant, Mina thought he would speak again, but he merely nodded and let himself out.

Edna appeared not long after with a fresh pasty for her lunch and more hot water for tea. She inspected the curtains and was most pleased to be told a pair was for her own bedroom window. "I can sew up the second pair, Mrs. Nye," she protested. "Now you've put them all ready."

"You're very busy, Edna," Mina reminded her. "And have plenty to be going on with already. I can sew yours up tomorrow. Besides, it never occurred to me, but do you have a curtain rod in your room already?" Edna shook her head, looking suddenly crestfallen. "It is of no matter," Mina assured her. "I shall tell Nye to have one put up."

Edna's expression wavered. "I don't know as—"

"I shall go and tell him directly," Mina cut her off firmly. "Besides, I need to stretch my legs. I've been sat here unmoving all morning."

"If I hadn't made plans already, I could have spent my afternoon off sewing them up," Edna said with regret.

"I quite forgot it's your half day," Mina said. "I did want you to pick me up a few things from St. Ives after all. That is, if you are still agreeable?"

"Of course!"

Mina stepped to the writing desk and hastily scrawled a list. *Two bottles of scented lotion, two bars of scented soap, two stamps.* The lotion and soaps were for Edna and Ivy so it was a shame she could not pick them up herself, but it was the thought that counted. The stamps were for herself. One to put on the letter she was writing Hannah and one for a spare.

"I shall run upstairs directly," Mina said. "To fetch my money."

"There's no hurry," Edna called after her. "There's another hour till I meet the cart."

Mina was already halfway up the stairs and she did not slow her step as she flew up the attic stairs to collect her half sovereign. She burst into her bedroom without ceremony.

"Oh!" Nye stood on the threshold, though the other two men were nowhere in sight. Gazing past him she saw the new brass curtain rail fixed firmly into place. "Finished already?" she asked foolishly, but she felt rather discomforted finding him in her bedchamber like that.

"I am," he said, fixing her with an intent look. "You?" He looked pointedly at her empty hands.

"They are taking shape. I have only to sew them up now which I will sit and do this afternoon."

"I see."

"In fact," she said, "there was enough fabric to make two pairs of curtains. So, I have made a second pair for Edna. Her window faces the courtyard too," she added and saw his eyes narrow. "So, I will need you to fix up a second curtain rod in her room also."

"Is that so?"

She raised her chin. "It is, yes."

"That what you ran up here to tell me?"

"Actually," she said, walking past him and around the bed to reach the chest of drawers. "I have come to fetch my money. Edna is going into St. Ives this afternoon and has kindly agreed to fetch me a few things." She reached into the top drawer and withdrew a single navy stocking from the back of it. With little other choice, she shook it out under his eyes and pulled out the bundled-up handkerchief from the toe. This she unwrapped to reveal her gleaming half sovereign.

"You'll not be sending Edna to St. Ives with that much, surely?" he asked with a frown in his voice.

"I don't have anything else," she admitted without thinking. "Can you change it for me?"

"Maybe." He hesitated. "What did you need her to fetch?"

Mina bridled. "Personal items," she said, drawing herself up. To her consternation, he walked toward her. Mina's heartbeat picked up disturbingly when he came to a halt before her and plucked the list from her hand that she hadn't realized she was still holding. She gasped indignantly as his eyes traveled unhurriedly over the list.

"Is that it?" he asked. "I'd have thought from your attitude it was a pair of drawers at the very least."

"How dare you! No gentleman would ever mention—"

He scoffed. "I'm no gentleman, Mina. I would have thought a smart woman like yourself would have realized that by now." He let his gaze rake over her. "I had no idea that fine ladies got through soap as fast as you do." His eyes dwelt on her. "Nor lotion, but I guess that's how you keep your skin so soft."

To her embarrassment, Mina could feel the color creeping into her cheeks. How did he know how soft her skin was? She remembered how he had carried her in his arms the day before. Had he touched her skin? "As a matter of fact, it's not for me," she admitted. "But to repay Edna's and Ivy's kindnesses toward me." His eyebrows rose at that. "Ivy used her own lotion on my cuts."

His eyes flickered. "You don't have any of your own?"

Mina shook her head. "I used the last of it the other night," she admitted, and even she could hear the note of sadness in her

111

voice. Why was she talking so much? She suspected it was Nye's fault as he did not talk enough and made her nervous. His proximity was extremely disquieting.

Nye frowned. "So, tell Edna to buy three lotions and three soaps."

"I need to employ thrift if my money is to last," she pointed out. "Besides, I have two bars of soap already. I brought a lavender with me and Ivy gave me a rose."

"Keep your half sovereign," he said brusquely. "I'll speak to Edna."

Mina was flustered. "What do you mean?"

"I have a few things to add to her list," he said, turning away. Impulsively, Mina reached out and caught his sleeve; he halted at once.

"But I want to buy them as a token of my thanks," she insisted.

"They'll still be from you," he said harshly. "Do you think I'm in the habit of buying gifts for the maids here?"

She hurriedly withdrew her hand. Was he offended? "No, of course not, but—"

"Fine," he said, holding out his hand. "Give the half sovereign to me. I'll deduct any costs from it you incur."

Mina handed over the sum of her wealth with some reluctance. "And you'll put up that curtain rail for Edna?" she added boldly. He scowled. Mina wasn't sure what imp of mischief prompted her, but before she knew it, she had added pertly, "After all, you can deduct any expense from my half sovereign!"

He took a step closer, and Mina took an involuntary step back. Their gazes clashed, and Mina realized they were both breathing hard now.

"Careful, Mina," he told her in a low voice. "It wouldn't do to give me an excuse, not right now."

"An excuse for what?" Mina asked, wishing her voice didn't sound so breathless. Had she fastened her self-lacing corset too tightly that morning? He took another step forward and Mina took another back. Her skirts were up against the dressing table now and she had nowhere to left to retreat. She stared up at him, transfixed.

"Nye!" The shout from the stairs startled them both.

Nye turned his head. "What is it?" he bellowed.

"Delivery!"

He growled something under his breath and turned away, heading down the stairs with a heavy tread. Mina stayed frozen where she was. Oddly enough, at that moment, she couldn't decide if her overwhelming emotion was relief or disappointment. *Strange.* She waited five whole minutes before she, too, went downstairs.

She finished the first pair of curtains that afternoon. Setting them down, she rose from her chair and stretched. She felt stiff and irritable. If she hadn't been under such pressure to finish these wretched curtains by nightfall, she could have had a nice walk at lunchtime. She walked over to the window and peered out at the rapidly darkening sky. She hoped Edna would be back before nightfall, that was all.

The curtains in the parlor bar were dingy and dark and could likely do with a good wash, she thought, fingering the heavy fabric as she loosened the cord to pull them across the window.

She would have to light the lamps if she was to dine alone in here as everyone seemed to expect her to. Crossing to the mantelpiece, she picked up one of the rolled spills Edna had placed there that morning for her convenience. Holding it to the flames a moment to catch, she walked across the room to light the two oil lamps on pewter bases that stood on two of the remaining small circular tables. They cast a soft golden glow over the room, and Mina had just turned around to survey the results when a knock at the door was followed by Edna spilling into the room laden down from her shopping trip.

"Oh, Mrs. Nye!" she panted. "I'll just set these things down in here and then get some water boiling for tea."

"Let me see to the tea, Edna," Mia said, crossing the room. "You look done in!"

"That Sam Coulter's wagon does jolt a body." Edna shuddered. "And the wind and rain didn't help!"

Mina slipped out of the room with the silver teapot into the kitchen where she set water to boil on the range. By the time she returned with a fresh pot of tea, Edna had removed her bonnet and tidied her hair and was looking a lot less harried.

"How was your aunt?" Mina asked as she set out the cups and saucers.

"Very well," Edna shared. "She's a good soul and not one to make a fuss about her troubles. We couldn't even get halfway down the pier, what with the weather, but we had a nice cream tea in our favorite tea room. Auntie helped me pick out the items from your shopping list too," she added with satisfaction. "We went into quite half the shops on the high street."

"I'm not surprised that you're worn out," Mina commented, pouring tea into two cups. "It sounds like you've been very busy indeed."

"And how has your sewing progressed?" Edna asked, glancing over at the blue velvet at the other end of the table.

Mina passed a cup and saucer to Edna. "The first pair are completed," she admitted. "And I shall sew up yours tomorrow morning."

Edna's eyes gleamed. "I told Auntie you were making me some curtains and she brought you this," said Edna, delving into a shopping bag before sliding a somewhat crushed-looking cardboard box across the table.

"What is it?" asked Mina in surprise.

"It's a cream cake," said Edna. "I only hope it's not too squashed."

"Oh, how kind of her!" Mina peered inside at the cream slice. "It looks delicious."

Edna nodded, looking gratified. She piled two more boxes onto the table and a large pink-striped tin. "I hope this was what you had in mind," she said. "Only Master Nye wasn't terribly specific."

"I'm sure you've done extremely well," Mina said, eyeing the fancy packages done up with ribbons. She dreaded to think what this little lot must have cost.

Edna beamed and took a large drink of tea. "You're not going to look at 'em now?" she asked with faint disappointment.

"Of course," Mina said, picking up the first box which was pale blue and contained a sheaf of notepaper and envelopes decorated tastefully with forget-me-nots, a pot of lavender ink, and a box of new nibs for her pen. "Oh, how lovely!" she exclaimed. Papa had been of the opinion that black ink was the only acceptable color for letter writing. "Such tasteful decoration," she said, running a finger over the borders of the small blue and yellow flowers on the writing paper.

"I picked that out," Edna said, clearly gratified. "Auntie thought violets, but I said no. If the mistress is writing to old friends and acquaintances, then forget-me-nots are more appropriate."

It crossed Mina's mind what plain, sensible Hannah might make of the flowery notepaper when she received her letter and had to suppress a wince. "How well it will look on my writing desk!" she commented instead and stood up to carry the things over to the handsome little desk. The only thing she had been able to add to it so far was the mother-of-pearl dip pen which had been her father's. She set the pot of lavender ink next to the pen and placed the envelopes, paper, and nibs into the empty drawers. "There!" she said, turning back around to look at Edna. "Now my desk is fully furnished!"

Edna nodded, setting her cup back on its saucer. "Oh, there's something else too," she said, reaching into her bag and drawing out a handful of penny stamps. "These for your letters."

Mina took them gratefully and added them to another drawer. "And now I have no excuse not to finish that letter to Hannah very soon," she murmured. Though goodness only knew what she was going to say about being married!

The next box was a pale yellow and filled with matching tissue paper. Inside it contained three little glass bottles of eau de cologne decorated with floral labels. "Oh, how pretty," Mina exclaimed.

"They're all different," Edna said proudly. "I picked out the spring flowers and Auntie picked lily of the valley. The third one's jasmine, I think the girl said."

Mina immediately passed Edna the spring flowers bottle. "Then this one is for you."

Edna looked shocked. "Oh no, Mrs. Nye! I couldn't!"

"Nonsense, Edna. A perfectly modest woman may sprinkle scent on her handkerchief and gloves. Even my mother thought so. I'm sure spring flowers is a lovely fresh scent."

Edna bit her lip. "It is," she conceded. "But—"

"But nothing! Which do you think Ivy would like?"

"Ivy?" Edna snorted. "Whichever is the strongest!"

Mina sniffed the remaining two bottles. "Then I think the jasmine," she muttered, setting it to one side. She reached the last item, which was the most intriguing. The pink tin was done up with a rosetted ribbon on the top, so it looked almost like a hatbox.

"The gentleman in the apothecaries had to help us pick out the other things," Edna admitted. "As Auntie had no more knowledge than I about balms and lotions and such like."

Mina levered off the lid and looked down at the three fancy pots within. *Bloom of Roses,* she read on one pot. *Restores youthful freshness.* Its fluffy, whipped contents smelled good enough to eat. *Emulsion of Almonds*, she read on another. *Reduces wrinkles and blemishes. Magnolia Cold Cream* was the third which apparently *reinstates natural smoothness of complexion.* "Which would you rather?" she asked Edna. "Restore freshness, reduce blemishes, or reinstate smoothness?" Edna merely looked bewildered. "What do you think of the scent of this one?" Mina said, passing her the Emulsion of Almonds.

"I couldn't accept another gift, Mrs. Nye," Edna began dubiously.

"Nonsense. I only bought three so I could share them with you and Ivy."

Edna hesitated at this, clearly loath to miss out if Ivy would receive a share. "I've never held with artifices," she muttered, looking flustered.

Mina reached across and pointed at the label on the bottle. "It says that one is a tonic and made from nature's ingredients."

Edna removed the stopper and sniffed the milky-looking contents. "It doesn't smell," she said with surprise.

"You see," Mina encouraged her. "Try a drop on the back of your hand." She poured a second cup of tea for them both as Edna sampled the lotion. "It's not as though it is rouge or powder, Edna. It's a treatment for your skin."

"My skin does get very dry," Edna admitted, accepting the second cup.

"Then it's settled."

They smiled at each other over the rims of their teacups.

As it was Edna's afternoon off, Mina threw her own supper together. An impromptu meal of cold mutton, pickles, cheese, and bread and butter was partaken of, followed by her cream slice. After weighing the likelihood of being discovered by Nye eating in the kitchen, she resisted the temptation and instead took her plate through to the parlor. She still felt unsettled after their confrontation earlier and did not want to risk escalating matters. She dined in silence, washed hurriedly in the scullery alcove, and then extinguished the lamps and mounted the stairs with her candle in one hand, the bag of shopping in the other, and her new curtains under her arm.

On reaching her room, she dragged a chair over to the window and set about fixing the curtains to the hooks. Once they hung in place, she stepped back to survey the results and thought they would look a lot better if they had a lighter pair underneath for decorative purposes, such as Nottingham lace. Pulling them to, she had to admit the heavy fabric provided a barrier against the cold blast which emanated from the attic window. It also served to muffle the intermittent bursts of rain which drummed against the panes.

Slipping across to Ivy's room opposite, she left the bottle of jasmine perfume and the magnolia cold cream on the barmaid's dresser before returning to her own room. She was not sure that she liked the lily of the valley scent that remained, but she set it on the dresser anyway as the bottle was pretty, telling herself she did not feel guilty about keeping the Bloom of Roses, for she thought it was by far the nicest of the three lotions.

It was still early, but she simply did not feel like taxing her eyes further over letter writing or reading. Stripping down, she set her clothes neatly over her chair, donned her nightgown, and spread some of the scented cream sparingly on her elbows, knees, and décolletage. Then she did her neck, face, and hands and braided her hair in one long plait and climbed into bed.

Perhaps because she had spent the whole day sat in a chair, she did not feel tired once her head hit the pillow. Instead she lay there, her mind wandering again and again in the same direction. William Nye. Doggedly, she steered her thoughts away from the width of his shoulders, the strong column of his tanned throat, and the way his dark hair fell across his forehead and toward his general objectionableness.

119

He had made it entirely clear, she thought, that he intended for them to lead separate lives. The parlor bar had been converted for her exclusive use and she was to be confined to it, leading an unconnected existence to the rest of the inhabitants of The Merry Harlot. It scarcely seemed practical, she thought, but he seemed determined to promote the scheme.

Fleetingly, she allowed herself to remember how he had come after her when she had fled to the cliffs, then hastily pushed such recollections away, before she had to examine her own behavior that day. It was too bad that he seemed determined to deprive her of any company, even if it was only Edna's. If ever she tarried too long in the kitchen or scullery he seemed to pop up and send her away. She had almost expected him to show up that morning and chase Gus Hopkirk out of the parlor. It seemed funny now that he hadn't, she pondered. Almost as funny as Nye sharing with Gus that she was a schoolteacher.

She simply couldn't imagine Nye indulging in idle conversation let alone with her as the topic. And yet, he must have, for how else could Gus have known? She shifted over onto her back and stared up at the ceiling beams. It was most odd. Irritably, she twitched at her bedsheets and remembered something that had been niggling away at the back of her mind since that morning. Namely, where she had heard the name Grayking before. Finally, she remembered. Edna had told her it was the name of Werburgh's favorite goose! Mina sat up in bed.

Gus had said that the monastery was a place of pilgrimage because they housed the holy bones of St. Grayking. *St. Grayking?* Mina frowned. Surely the early church had not sainted a goose, even if he had been miraculously raised from the dead by his mistress? Who would travel miles and weather untold hardships to pray at the resting place of a bunch of old goose bones? Mina lay slowly back down, clutching her blanket. Had Gus been spinning her a yarn? The words had certainly tripped off his tongue easily enough.

But why would he? What would be his motivation in telling her a bunch of untruths like that? Ghost stories were meant both to entertain and to frighten the listener. Slowly, she turned his words over in her mind. She *had* found Gus's tales entertaining and when it came to the sounds the hauntings were supposed to evoke—the dragging and the rolling of the monk's cart—she had been scared. For those were the sounds she had heard now several times from her window in the early hours of the morning. Involuntarily, her eyes darted to the closed curtains.

Had he known that? And if so, how could he? He would only know if the sounds were of an earthlier nature, she thought. If they were made by men, intent on some dishonest purpose, then it was not beyond the realms of reason that they might try to mask their actions by spreading tales of ghosts and apparitions. It would not be the first time such a device had been employed. Mina was sure she had read of such things in her women's periodicals. Cutthroats and thieves who had sought to ensure their hideouts were shunned by law-abiding folk, by the spreading of false rumors of specters and ghouls.

The only serious falling out she had with her own father had been on the occasion he had found out about her own juvenile scribblings. She had been reading a tale about the haunting of a highwayman by his murdered accomplice to their pupils during their Thursday afternoon sewing hour. Those stories had turned the outright pity in those girls' eyes into admiration.

Oh miss, you're an author, miss.

It's as good as anything in Milady's Fancy, *miss.*

You ought to send it in, miss, really you ought.

Her father had warned her that the female brain was more delicate in its balance and should not be overset with unhealthy stimulus which could depress or send it feverish. Mina had pointed out that more than half the stories in the ladies' periodicals were written by women, and her father had seemed to think that proved his point. Periodicals were a vastly inferior reading material and she should be cultivating her mind by devoting her studies to that of worthy books written by men.

Mina, secure in her own excellent health, had privately disagreed. She knew that her own papa was far more prone to stomach upset and colds than she. If her physical form was so robust, then why not her mind also? While it was true that she had often lay shivering in her bed as a tree branch tapped her window, imagining untold horrors, it was also true that the same frisson of fear held a lot of enjoyment for a girl whose life otherwise was rather colorless. She enjoyed reading thrilling tales, and she did not believe they were bad for her.

More importantly, Papa turned a blind eye to the fact his pupils purchased such materials, so why should he not allow his daughter a vicarious thrill or two also? Mama did not read at all, and yet Papa did not lecture her to self-improvement. He thought it charming that Mama fussed about with lace and needlepoint and took no interest in current affairs or politics. She, however, had been forced to abandon her tale of spectral highwaymen forthwith.

Turning over again, Mina acknowledged that fact still stung and forced herself once again, to contemplate Gus's tale. Had he invented his on the spot to entertain her? It seemed unlikely he would go to so much trouble on her behalf. With a sigh, Mina clambered out of bed in search of her knitted bed socks. Her feet were simply too cold tonight.

She rifled through her stockings in search of them and frowned when her questing fingers came up against something hard and round. Lifting out the object, Mina found it was her half sovereign. She stared at it a moment in astonishment before thoughtfully replacing it. Then she found her rather lumpy blue bed socks and pulled them on over her bare feet. Straightening up, she found herself staring once more at the velvet curtains.

Snatching up her shawl, she threw it over her shoulders and inched toward the window. What o'clock was it? She thought she had heard the clock chime eleven. Opening the curtains by the tiniest amount, she gazed down at the yard below and was startled to see a tall shadowy figure below seemingly staring right back up at her window. With a gasp, Mina stepped back and then whirled around to jump straight into bed, her heart still thudding.

Her only comfort was that he had not been wearing a monk's habit.

9

The next morning, she woke full of renewed vigor. The first
thing she did was check that she had not dreamed the coin in
her stocking drawer. No, there it was, shiny as ever. He had not
wrapped it back in her handkerchief but had simply tossed it
back into her drawer. Her chest swelled indignantly. The man
was a law unto himself! She would most certainly tackle him
about it, she thought grimly as she made her way downstairs.
When the moment was right.

She ate breakfast with Edna, with her hip propped against the
kitchen table. She was not poised for flight, she told herself.
Indeed, she half wanted Nye to walk in on her this morning, but
disappointingly, he did not appear even though she lingered
long after her second cup of tea. Finally, she took herself off to
the parlor room and settled to sew up the curtains for Edna's
room. She finished them at midday and took them up to place
them folded on the bottom of Edna's bed. While she was in
there, she was gratified to see that another rail had been put up
ready for them over the window.

She was halfway down the stairs again when she saw Nye
passing through the hallway below. "Nye!" she called, and
slowly he turned to look at her, a ferocious glare on his face.

"Well, what is it?" he growled before she had reached the
bottom of the stairs.

"I've finished the curtains and now I intend to clean those
parlor windows," she said breathlessly. "They're filthy. I'll
need newspaper for it. Do you have any that you're not saving
for clippings?" He shook his head and her face fell. "Oh." Then

inspiration struck. "Tell you what," she said affably. "You can direct me as to what sections you want saving and I can cut them out for you and even paste them in a scrapbook, if it will help." Nye scowled. "After all, those papers must have been collecting dust for years. They're taking up valuable cupboard space," she pointed out reasonably.

"No," he said tersely.

She crossed her arms. "No?" she repeated. "Pray then, what am I to use?" He muttered something under his breath. "I'm afraid I didn't catch that."

"I said, you're not going to let this lie, are you?" She shook her head obstinately. He wheeled about and headed back for the scullery. After a moment's hesitation, Mina followed him. He was retrieving the first bundle of newspapers, she noticed with interest. "Follow me," he said grimly and made for the kitchen where he cut the string binding them.

Mina watched as he rifled through the first newspaper, extracting one page which he set aside. "You can have the rest of it," he said. Then he opened the next paper and repeated the process. Again, he removed one page and set it with the other and then handed her the remains of the paper. "Is that enough?"

Mina shook her head. He repeated the process with another two newspapers, and Mina surreptitiously strained her eyes to scan the pages he removed. She could just about make out a headline of the top page: Nye Wins by Knockout in Third Round. Oh, they were press clippings from boxing matches. "If you separate the rest of the pile," she said, "then I could do all the windows in the inn. Edna doesn't really have the time," she added quickly, anticipating his refusal. "Not with the day-to-day duties she already covers."

He shot her a level look. "Not in the public bar," he said tersely. Mina shrugged, perfectly willing to concede that point. Not another word passed between them as he swiftly separated the rest of the pile and stuffed his pages into his waistcoat. "You can have those," he said, nodding to the discarded pile.

"Thank you." She spent the afternoon cleaning windows. Her arms ached after she had completed the parlor bar, the kitchen, and the scullery. She stopped at six o'clock to take her solitary meal that Edna brought her which was a rich beef stew. After that, she contemplated turning in for another early night, but the idea frankly did not appeal to her.

She needed a bath, for though the newspaper left the windows sparkling, her own palms were stained with black newsprint. Before this though, she wanted to tackle the windows in the three private parlors. After all, Nye had banned her from the taproom, but he had made no mention of the private parlors.

Feeling vaguely defiant, she mixed up another batch of water and white vinegar and carried her bowl to the first of the parlor bars. The solution soon cut through the film of dirt, the smell of vinegar making her eyes water. She had just taken up the newspaper and was swiping it across the glass when she saw a sporting-looking carriage career into the yard, taking the bend in the road far too fast. Mina let out an involuntary cry, for the carriage was leaning over so far that for an instant she thought it would overbalance.

Then, just as quickly, it righted itself. The gentleman sat atop it pulled viciously on the reins and the four horses came to a stop. He threw down his whip, righted his top hat and swiftly climbed down, calling to a passing ginger-bearded man who Mina vaguely recognized as the man who fixed up the curtain rail for her the day before. He took the head of one of the horses and started leading it toward the stable before the gentleman shouted again, and then wrenched open the door to his carriage, dragging out a dainty-looking female from its recesses. His rough treatment practically set the poor child on her backside, Mina noticed with disapproval. Surely the girl looked familiar, she thought, her nose practically pressed to the glass at this point.

Then she had it. It was Cecily Carswell, the ward of one of their old patrons at Hill School, Sir Matthew Carswell. Cecily had attended their school for two years before her guardian had deemed she had received sufficient education and withdrawn her. Unfortunately, he had withdrawn his patronage at much the same time. Her father had been most upset about it. Mina picked up her supplies as she saw the objectionable young man tow Cecily in the direction of the inn. Closing the door discreetly behind her, she retreated into the shadowy corridor, pulling her headscarf down to obscure her features.

"You there!" the arrogant young man hailed her. "Do you have such a thing as a private parlor for hire?" He cast his eyes around the dimly lit hallway with disdain.

"We have three," Mina answered him calmly, gesturing their direction with her arm.

"Curtsey when you speak to me, slattern!" he fired up. "Impudence!" He turned back to the shrinking young girl, not waiting for Mina's response. "There, now you can stop your sniveling, for did I not say I would find somewhere we could take some refreshment?"

He flung open the first of the three doors and instantly recoiled. "Faugh! It reeks of vinegar in there! I vow, someone has broken a bottle of it!" He flung open the second and practically flung poor Cecily into it. "If you move before I return, I promise you will regret it, my girl," he snarled and then was gone in a whirl of his caped riding coat.

Mina paused only for a moment with indecision. She did not like the way Cecily had flinched from her escort. What was the child doing in the company of this flashy-looking youth? It looked like nothing so much as an elopement gone sour. She knew from experience that Cecily's guardian, Sir Matthew Carswell, was a stern, autocratic man. Had his ward run away with the first young buck who had made up to her? Mina did not like the look of Cecily's companion's face which the lamplight had illuminated briefly. He had a cruel mouth.

Stepping into the first private parlor, Mina set down her bucket and newspapers and removed her apron and headscarf. Smoothing her hair, she approached the second door and softly opened it.

"Cecily?" she said quietly and watched the young girl wheel around, tears streaked down her cheeks.

"Oh! Miss Walters," Cecily exclaimed in a choked voice. "Is that really you?" She took a stumbling step toward Mina before pulling herself up.

"It really is," Mina responded gravely. "You seem to be in something of a predicament."

Cecily's lip trembled and fresh tears spilled over. "I've been so wicked, Miss Walters," she whispered. "This is a judgment on me."

"Nonsense," Mina replied bracingly. "But you would certainly be ill advised to continue on your current course. Are you yet married to this gentleman?"

Cecily paled and shook her head. "No! Oh no!" she said, shivering.

"When did you leave your guardian's protection?" From what Mina could recall, Sir Matthew's residence was somewhere in Cornwall.

"Not two hours ago," Cecily sobbed, and Mina deduced it was likely the longest two hours of Cecily's life. "Though in truth I left his house for a party and then I left the party for—oh, it's complicated!"

Mina held out her hand. "Come quickly now, child," she said. "With me." The girl did not even hesitate. With a faint cry, she teetered toward Mina and allowed herself to be propelled out of the private parlor and along the narrow passageway leading to the stairs.

"Quickly now!" Mina took her hand and led her up the two flights of stairs to her attic bedroom. When Cecily made to speak on reaching the first landing, Mina raised a finger to her lips to caution quiet. Cecily nodded and clung to Mina's hand as if her life depended on it. "In here," she murmured and shepherded the girl into her attic bedroom. "If you sit tight, I will endeavor to extricate you from this mess." Cecily squeezed her fingers and then obediently sank down onto the bed. "Not a peep, mind," Mina repeated. Cecily nodded, wide-eyed. "You must be as silent as the grave. As if your life depended on it," she stressed. "Until I return for you." Cecily nodded again, and Mina turned and made her way sedately downstairs until she reached the foot of them.

"You! Wench!" Cecily's companion hailed her insolently.

Mina stood very straight and proper in her respectable black gown and fixed a cold eye on him. He was flinging open the doors to all the private parlor rooms. Gus stood next to him, looking perplexed. "The lady I arrived with, where is she?"

Mina regarded him steadily. He looked flushed from drink and ill temper. She let her lip curl with disapproval, and Gus stepped in hastily.

"This young gentleman's lost his traveling companion, Mrs. Nye," he said loudly. "Have you seen any young ladies hereabouts?"

Mina lifted her eyebrows. "I've seen no one," she responded coolly.

"What?" the young man exclaimed furiously. "You saw us arrive! I saw you in the corridor—" He broke off his words now, plainly noticing the lack of apron and headscarf. "At least, I thought it was you," he added sulkily. "Perhaps I was mistaken."

Mina looked at Gus. "He's been drinking," she said coldly. "Mayhap you should ask the bar to stay the liquor where he's concerned."

"You bitch!" snarled the newcomer, making a wild grab for her, but Gus came solidly between them, preventing contact.

"Now then, young master!" he bellowed. "Less of that! Less of that! This be a respectable woman and mistress here! She's no replacement for the one you've lost!"

"What's this?" asked a rough voice ominously, and Mina watched Nye appear from the shadows, looking irritable and dangerous, in short, his usual self.

"This young fellow," started Gus affably, "seems to have misplaced—"

"I've misplaced nothing!" snapped the haughty young man, wheeling around to face Nye. "This *woman*—" Suddenly, he made a choking noise and Mina noticed Nye's large hand was

130

fastened around his throat. The young man's face turned purple as he started clawing ineffectually at Nye's wrist.

"*My* woman, do you mean?" Nye asked with quiet menace, bringing his face closer. A gurgling sound was all the other could manage by this point.

"Steady, Will," Gus cautioned, but Nye ignored him, turning to Mina.

"What is he after?"

"From what I can make out, he's drunk and looking for a doxy," Mina answered coolly. She shot a malicious look at the young man, but his eyes were now bulging, and his sole focus was Nye. Mina thought of frightened, harmless Cecily cowering in the attic bedroom and found she had little sympathy to spare him.

As suddenly as he had seized him, Nye thrust him from him and the other man fell to his knees, gasping for breath and tugging at his cravat.

Nye's lips twisted with contempt. "Get out," he enunciated and strode past him, catching Mina's elbow and towing her across the passageway with him.

"You're not welcome, my lad," Mina heard Gus telling the stranger sternly. "Best take yourself and that fancy gig o' yours and leave."

"What were you about? Skulking there in the dark?" Nye growled, propelling her toward the staircase.

Mina raised her chin. "You never told me not to go near the private parlors," she said pertly. "You said the taproom and the cellars were out of bounds, nowhere else. I had just finished cleaning the window in the first of them, that was all."

131

Nye's gaze was piercing, and Mina felt herself color. "Then I credited you with more sense than you deserve," he retorted gruffly, and Mina bristled all over. Though why it should bother her if William Nye thought her a fool was beyond her. She found herself opening her mouth to make a smart retort before thinking better of it. "If you don't want to be taken for a doxy again, you'd best keep to the parlor or above stairs of an evening," he spat, then pushed her in the direction of the staircase, and Mina watched him slam through the door into the public bar.

She stood rigid a moment, before turning to look out of the window onto the courtyard. The objectionable stranger was climbing back into his high-perched carriage. Mina watched as he scanned the lanes and hedgerows as he wheeled back out of the yard and onto the road. He was certainly taking a much slower pace on his way out than he had on his way in. Doubtless imagining Cecily fleeing him into the night like a poor, frightened little rabbit. After a few moments of waiting to make sure he had truly gone, Mina turned and made her way quickly to the kitchen to boil some water for tea. While it boiled, she retrieved her things from the first private parlor and stowed them away in the scullery and then cut a few slices of currant loaf which she buttered, not knowing when Cecily would last have eaten. Last of all, she took some milk, remembering that was how most of the girls at school had taken their tea. Then she stole away upstairs to join Cecily.

*

"I have fresh bread and butter for you, Cecily, and I'll make you a nice cup of tea," Mina told her, setting the plate down on a bedside table and filling the silver teapot with tea leaves and hot water.

132

"I declare I couldn't eat a thing!" Cecily's bottom lip wobbled as Mina helped her undo her pretty bonnet and took her cloak. "I still can't believe I'm truly out of his clutches." Her hand clasped Mina's. "Oh miss, he must have been ever so angry," she said, tearing up again. "His temper was the most wicked I have ever seen. I had thought my guardian Sir Matthew's temper was terrifying," she confided artlessly. "For he grows cold as an icicle. But Mr. Brinson's was in a *wholly* different league."

"And how is it that you are acquainted with Mr. Brinson?" Mina asked, hanging Cecily's bonnet on a peg.

"Oh!" Cecily's eyes fell. "He—he is an acquaintance of my cousin's friend. I met him through Vanessa at a party and afterward again, we bumped into him in the park. He—he seemed so very obliging and kind then that I always looked out for him." Her eyes fixed on Mina appealingly. "My cousin also thought him a most affable and charming person."

"Your cousin Vanessa?"

Cecily nodded her head dolefully. "So, you see, it was not only me that was quite deceived."

"I take it Vanessa is very young," Mina said dryly.

"Oh no, she is nineteen, quite the same age as me," said Cecily naively, and Mina reflected that Hill School had not prepared her for the snares of fortune hunters at all.

"I take it that Sir Matthew was not aware of this connection?"

Cecily quailed and shook her head. "N-no," she admitted. "You see, Mr. Brinson said that his reputation had been sadly soiled by some unfair rumors which meant my guardian would quite take against him, if he knew of our friendship. Vanessa agreed that it seemed most unjust."

133

"So now it turns out those rumors are likely well-founded," Mina pointed out.

Cecily's bottom lip wobbled. "Y-yes," she agreed, ducking her head. "Oh Miss Walters," she gulped. "Whatever am I going to do? Sir Matthew is going to be so very angry with me!"

After some gentle but firm questioning as she poured the tea, Mina ascertained that the most Mr. Brinson had subjected Cecily to had been some rough words and a little manhandling. Cecily had most imprudently allowed herself to be persuaded to sneak out of a tea party to meet with him in the garden of her unsuspecting host. She had then been bundled quite roughly into a waiting carriage and threatened with all manner of eventualities if she "played Mr. Brinson false."

Mina was not sure if the scoundrel had meant to actually marry Cecily or to blackmail her guardian for her quiet return, she only knew that she had to do her best to try to minimize any damage Cecily might have wrought upon her reputation. Speed was really going to be of the essence, she thought as she watched Cecily force down a piece of bread and butter and drink a cup of milky tea. It occurred to Mina that her old pupil had not evinced any curiosity whatsoever as to how Mina had wound up at The Merry Harlot. Such was youth, caught up only in its own toils and troubles, she thought wryly.

"I'm going to have to go back downstairs now," Mina said firmly. "To see if I can find some conveyance to take you home."

"Oh!" Cecily's eyes widened. "But couldn't I stay with you, Miss Walters?" she pleaded, looking much younger than her nineteen years.

Mina reached across and patted her hand. "Cecily, you must see that your return is imperative. If you were to remain away from

134

home overnight without your guardian's permission, I'm afraid your reputation would be quite ruined."

Cecily's lower lip wobbled. "But I would be with you," she said. "No one could be more respectable!"

Mina sighed. "You sit here and finish your supper. I will be back shortly." She wasn't looking forward to this interview with Nye. Indeed, she suspected he would be most angry when he knew how she had willfully misled everyone earlier. For an instant, she remembered how he had referred to her as *his woman*, and the color in her cheeks deepened. She couldn't focus on that right now. She needed to sort out this situation with Cecily.

A quick scout around downstairs for Nye was fruitless, and Mina deduced he must be in the public bar. She would have to use strategy, she thought with determination, as he had expressly forbidden her from entering the taproom. Thoughtfully, she took up the hurricane lamp from the hall and carried it out of the front door and into the yard outside.

Pausing there a moment, she lifted it above her head and then slowly made her way across the courtyard in the direction of the stables, giving everyone plenty of time to spot her out of the window. Sure enough, she had only just reached the stable entrance when she heard the door of the inn wrenched open and a hurried step on the cobbles.

Concealing her smile of triumph, she dodged into the stable and then turned to calmly face her pursuer. Sure enough, it was Nye, a thunderous frown on his face.

"What the hell are you doing out here?" he demanded as soon as he'd swung inside.

"Ah good, there you are," she greeted him briskly. "I need your help with a matter concerning an ex-pupil of mine."

He stared at her. "What?"

"I need to get her back to a place called Upton-Gadsby that's at least forty minutes from here if I can take Cecily's word," she explained. "It's a matter of the utmost urgency."

"Back to?" he repeated blankly.

"Yes. She's here and she needs to be there."

"Well, what the hell is she doing here?" he demanded, his voice rising with ire.

"I'm afraid there was something of a misunderstanding," Mina said evasively.

His gaze narrowed. "Such as?"

"Can we not focus on that right now? I really do need to get her home posthaste, or she will face some rather dire repercussions."

He huffed out a frustrated breath. "You always talk like that?" he asked.

"Like what?"

He shrugged. "I've not got much book-learning," he said cryptically.

"Oh." Mina paused. "You seem to follow my meaning just fine," she said a trifle awkwardly. After all, would it not be a far worse thing if she talked down to him?

He shot her another straight look. "Upton-Gadsby?"

"Yes," she agreed. "Do you know it?" He gave a short nod. "Do you have a conveyance, or could you get hold of one?" She hesitated. "I could pay." He lifted a brow at that. "It seems I still have a half sovereign at my disposal," she added boldly.

He gave no response to that, just stared into space a moment. "So, this solves the mystery of why you were accosted," he commented dryly.

"Well, it never really made sense that I would be mistaken for a doxy," Mina pointed out.

He narrowed his eyes at her before coming to a swift decision. "Bring her here in ten minutes."

Mina breathed a sigh of relief. "I will need to go with her for a chaperone," she said apologetically. "Her guardian would not be pleased if she turned up alone."

"Her guardian?"

"Sir Matthew Carswell. He used to be a patron of my father's school."

Nye looked up quickly. "Carswell?"

"Yes. You have heard of him?"

Nye's gaze fell. "I believe he's a Justice of the Peace," he said with faint scorn. "And keen on sending people to the Assizes. You know him, then?"

"Not well," Mina responded quickly, seeing the tension in his frame for all he tried to hide it. "As soon as our school hit some difficulties, he withdrew his sponsorship."

"So then, you owe him nothing."

Mina's chin rose. "I'm not doing it for him, but for Cecily."

Nye seemed to ponder on this for a moment as he looked at her with open speculation. "Very well," he said at last.

"Thank you," she said with feeling. "I really am grateful, Nye—"

"Don't be," he interrupted her. "I want something from you in return."

"So long as it's not more curtains," she answered lightly. "Then I will most happily reciprocate. I mean," she added hastily, "I will repay in kind."

A grim smile flickered over his face. "I knew what you meant," he said, then slowly held out his hand.

Mina glanced down at it a moment. Did he mean to shake? She extended her own and found it enveloped in a strong grip. She promptly tightened her own, remembering what her father had taught her about firm handshakes. His eyes gleamed, and she wondered if it was with amusement or some other emotion. He held on to her hand for a beat longer than she thought was correct form, then released it, leaving her with an impression of callouses.

Feeling strangely winded by the experience, Mina turned back hurriedly for the inn. She rubbed her own palm as she mounted the stairs, remembering his knuckles had been bloody the first night she had met him.

"It's all going to be fine," she told Cecily.

"You still have it!" Cecily exclaimed, turning from the dresser excitedly. "The little china dog I bought you for a keepsake!"

"Of course," Mina replied, remembering how mercurial Cecily's temperament could be.

"Do you remember what we called it?"

"I'm afraid not," she admitted, reaching for Cecily's bonnet and cloak.

"Lulu," Cecily supplied happily. She kept up a happy and constant prattle for the next ten minutes without once asking Mina what she had been doing in the three years since last they met. Mina led her down the stairs to the stables, Cecily talking nineteen to the dozen about her fellow ex-pupils and questioning if Mina had kept up with any of them. "Did you hear?" she asked as Mina helped her up into the unassuming black coach that waited for them. "That Polly married a curate. *A curate?*" she repeated, looking around, her eyes very wide. "Can you imagine?"

"I did hear," Mina admitted. "Lucy Williams wrote to me a couple of times and she was a bridesmaid, if I remember correctly."

"Lucy was?" Cecily cried in surprise. "How extraordinary! They were never terribly close in school. Did she tell you any particulars? Polly always used to say she would only marry if she were permitted to wear satin, orange blossom, and pearls. Do you remember? I doubt a clergyman would allow such extravagance in his spouse."

Mina glanced up at Nye, who was sat impassively in the driver's seat. He cocked an eye at her. "You sure you wouldn't rather sit up here?" he asked dryly.

Mina sent him a quelling look as she followed Cecily into the carriage. It was true, Cecily was rather voluble, but she had a good heart, nonetheless.

The journey passed quickly, and Cecily's loquaciousness was unabating until they arrived in the vicinity of her guardian's property, then she began to fidget nervously. "You will come in with me, Miss Walters, won't you?" she asked, turning her eyes on Mina in mute appeal.

"Of course."

"Oh dear," Cecily faltered. "Whatever shall I say to Sir Matthew? He's sure to be much put out."

"I'm afraid he will," Mina agreed gravely. "Anyone would be, Cecily, but I'm sure his utmost concern will be your welfare and reputation."

Cecily bit her lip and nodded but was inclined to be tearful once again. "I wish I'd never met him!" she wept into her handkerchief. "Mr. Brinson," she added, looking up. "Not Sir Matthew. How shocking," she reflected. "That such a fair face could disguise so vicious a nature." She shuddered. "Why, it's just like your tale about that wicked young gambler who haunted that highwayman," she observed, surprising Mina a good deal. "Do you remember how his well-molded lips concealed his snarling predatory sneer?"

Mina blushed at the recollection of her florid prose. "He looked to me," she said aloud, "like he would run to corpulency in his middle age and likely suffer from the gout."

Cecily's mouth fell open. "No, really?" she breathed in horror. "Do you think so?"

"That type so often does," Mina observed impassively, rightly judging this assessment would cause the last of Mr. Brinson's glamor to fade forever.

"How hideous," Cecily gasped. "Apparently, that curate Polly married is so unworldly that he often forgets to take his meals, unless he is prompted. Fancy that!"

"He must be the scholastic type," Mina agreed. "My own father was rather like that." She turned to look at Cecily to see if that prompted even a question as to her old headmaster's whereabouts, but Cecily just smiled vaguely.

"I still could not marry a clergyman though," she responded, her mind clearly elsewhere. "Not even if he was practically a saint!"

10

Sir Matthew was a lean man in his late thirties with a hawklike face and shrewd pale eyes. He was stiff with outrage by the incoherent and tearful tale his charge laid before him. Mina was obliged to both remind Sir Matthew of their previous acquaintance and at times to make sense of Cecily's tale which was interspersed with bursts of violent weeping and self-recriminations.

He was inclined to be accusatory rather than forgiving and practically demanded that Cecily admit herself complicit to the elopement plot instead of being forced into the carriage.

"You are not at the bench now, my dear sir!" Mina had been forced to interrupt at one point when his railings had reduced Cecily to a gibbering wreck. "If I might suggest you would be better employed elsewhere than in these pointless recriminations."

He had drawn himself up very tall at this, his nostrils quivering. "Am I to understand, Miss Walters—" he started cuttingly.

"It's Mrs. Nye now," she corrected him in a steely tone. "And I'm afraid I must insist on the immediate sending of a card to Cecily's hostess, otherwise my efforts will all have been for naught. You must have your footman deliver it without delay."

"A card?" he snapped, his gaze darting from Mina to Cecily and back again.

"A card," she confirmed. "Explaining Cecily felt unwell and went out to the garden in the hope the fresh air would revive her but was sadly unfit for company and obliged to return home.

Perhaps Cecily could add a postscript note, apologizing for not saying her goodbyes before she left?"

Sir Matthew's lips pursed a moment as he considered this and directed a piercing look at her. "You think of everything," he said with a curl of his lips. "And seem to possess what is to be hoped is a rare talent for forging excuses, Mrs. Nye," he said dryly. "One which I am not altogether sure I approve of."

Mina inclined her head. "You may not approve, but might I suggest that Cecily's reputation would greatly benefit from it at this present time?"

He stood very still for a moment and then strode around his desk, whipping out both silver pen and card. "Compose yourself!" he shot at Cecily, who was propped against the wall, her face streaked with tears. "You will come and add a postscript when I am done with these few lines."

"I couldn't!" moaned Cecily. "My hand is trembling like a leaf!"

"You will come and write it, you little fool!" he flared up. "To prove you are indeed safe and sound at home and not elsewhere! That was the point, was it not?" he directed at Mina. She nodded slightly. "How is your father, by the way?" he asked, stepping back from the desk and gesturing to Cecily to approach. Cecily complied, though she dragged her feet over it and took the pen from him with a large sniff.

"He is dead, Sir Matthew. Some twelve days now," Mina said quietly.

Cecily's hand flew to her mouth and she almost dropped the pen. "Oh, but you never said!"

Mina managed to stop herself from pointing out she had never asked. "The school was closed up two days later and I left Bath

143

to get married," she added with dignity. "Now, if you will excuse me. I cannot leave my husband waiting any longer."

She left the room quickly, and though she heard someone call out to her, she did not tarry but hurried out into the hall. The footman hovering in the hallway sprang to open the door for her and luckily Sir Matthew had not given her the chance to divest herself of cloak and bonnet. "Thank you," she called over her shoulder as she ran lightly down the steps and across the gravel. To her relief, she found Nye had brought the carriage around. Making for it, she was surprised when he leaned down from his perch and extended a hand to her. Clambering up the steps, she seized it and was swung up onto the seat at the front beside him.

*

They did not speak until they had swept down the drive and were back on the open road once more. Mina had a horrible suspicion the front door to Sir Matthew's house had opened as they had bowled down the drive, but she kept her head held high and had stared ahead of her the whole time, so she could not be quite sure above the sound of the horse's hooves.

Once they were out of sight of the house, she breathed a sigh of relief, and Nye relaxed the pace of the horses. "That bad, was it?" he asked wryly.

"Not really," she answered conscientiously. "Although, Sir Matthew was naturally most displeased."

"He would be."

She darted a hasty glance at Nye's profile. "I did not really explain, but—"

"You don't have to," he forestalled her. "It's none of my business and I'd rather keep it that way."

"You don't want to be involved," Mina said uncomfortably. "And I'm sure I don't blame you. But you see, I simply could not abandon Cecily to such a fate."

"Married to some ne'er do well, you mean?"

"He was a thoroughly unpleasant bully," she said roundly.

He shook his head. "It'll be him or someone just as bad, more than likely."

"Honestly, I don't see how it could be."

He was quiet a moment. "Not all girls have a Miss Walters to sweep in and save the day," he pointed out. "You didn't."

"It wasn't quite the same!" she retorted when she could draw breath.

"Wasn't it?"

"Of course not! You didn't abduct me for one thing."

"No? What about Faris?"

"He didn't abduct me either." She took a deep breath. "In fact, I wasn't far from being thrown out on the street."

An uncomfortable silence reigned for a moment, and Mina drew her cloak closer about her. She remembered how highly her father had thought of Sir Matthew as an upstanding member of society. He had been so proud to have his endorsement of Hill School. She thought of the genteel suppers they had used to throw for their entertainment. Lady Ralph, Sir Matthew, and Canon Carter-Hayes had all attended regularly in those days to be entertained by select recitals and entertainments on the pianoforte.

Lady Ralph had even awarded a prize every summer term to the "Most Improved Girl." She even recalled Cecily had won it one year. How long ago it all seemed now. The memories felt slightly embittered these days, as she recalled how dismayed Father had been by Sir Matthew's curt letter announcing his withdrawal as a governor and sponsor of the school. Lady Ralph had not even bothered to formally cut her ties; she had simply stopped answering any communications.

As for Canon Carter-Hayes, he had his own problems with some inconsistencies with church funds and had been summoned to the bishop's palace to explain. Subsequently, he had been ordered to vastly cut down any positions of authority that he held, so they had not been so surprised by his withdrawal from the board. Mama had begged them not to speak of it as it was "not nice," and she was sure the poor dear Canon had been the victim of some gross deception rather than guilty of any incompetence or dereliction of duty.

"Did he offer you a post?" Will Nye interrupted her thoughts harshly. "Looking after his half-witted niece?"

"She's not half-witted, only a little naïve," Mina corrected him. "Nor is she his niece." When he directed a cutting look her way, she added quickly, "And no, he did not offer me a post."

He snorted. "More fool he. I expect you could have kept her out of trouble until she was of age."

Mina looked at him in surprise. "She's a little old for a governess," she said mildly. "And more in need of a well-connected chaperone who could introduce her about town. I am not well-connected," she pointed out. "And would not be able to throw her in the path of eligible beaux."

"If she has money and he's not her uncle, he probably wouldn't want that in any case."

146

"What do you mean?"

He cast her an ironic look. "He probably means to marry her himself."

Mina gave a startled laugh. "I hardly think so!"

"Why not?" Nye asked coolly.

"If you'd seen the way he speaks to her," Mina spluttered. "Like an authoritarian rather than a suitor."

"Cecily's not the only naïve one, I see," Nye rumbled, and she cast him an irritable look.

"He's at least thirty-five if he's a day," she objected. "And Cecily only nineteen!"

His gaze remained steady. "And?"

Mina rallied. "I can imagine nothing less likely!"

"You think men like that speak to their wives gently?"

Mina looked at him shrewdly. "I thought you said you did not know him?"

"I don't know him," he retorted. "But I know his reputation."

"Which is?" She frowned, striving to remember what he had said before. Something about referring people to the Assizes in his capacity as Justice of the Peace.

Nye shrugged. "It's none of my business," he said evasively.

Fleetingly, Mina wondered if he knew of anyone who had suffered under Sir Matthew's ideas of justice. She could always ask Gus if Nye was determined to be unforthcoming. On impulse, she asked, "Why did you tell Gus Hopkirk I was a schoolteacher?"

Nye blinked, clearly taken aback. He did not answer for a moment. "Must have come up," he muttered.

"In general conversation?"

He cast her a resentful look. "I don't remember."

"He said he's known you since you were a boy," she persisted, suddenly loath to drop the subject. She decided to bluff her way since Nye was determined to remain a closed book. "Did he say he used to be friends with your father?" she mused as though trying to recall.

His eyelids dropped down, veiling his eyes. "I don't know," he grunted. "You tell me."

It was like trying to draw blood from a stone, she thought ruefully. Perhaps he did let down his guard when with friends and acquaintances, but she was clearly not one of their number, nor like to be. "Do you wish Sir Matthew *had* offered me a post?" she asked with a small wobble in her voice. How funny, just two weeks ago, the prospect of such a post would have filled her with quite a different emotion.

"No," he said, surprising them both. Their eyes met fleetingly, then they both looked away. They drove on a few moments in silence, before Nye cleared his throat. "You haven't asked me what I wanted in return," he said abruptly.

"No, I haven't," Mina admitted. She glanced at him in sudden suspicion. "Is it about my remaining in the parlor at all times?"

He snorted at that. "Much good that would do me."

She turned in her seat to face him. "I'm not used to being idle, you see," she said, deciding to go for open and honest. "And there's so much to be done about the place. It's not as though—"

148

"I understand that," he cut across her.

Mina waited for more, but nothing came. "So...you're agreeable to my helping Edna about the place?" she persisted.

He remained silent a moment. "What I want to know is this," he said at last. "Are you just another pair of hands about the place or do you mean to take up the role in earnest?"

"Role?" Mina repeated.

"Aye."

"What exactly do you mean by that?" Mina asked, sensing there was a deeper significance to his words.

"That of a publican's wife," he said, though his eyes avoided hers.

Whatever she had thought he was going to say, it wasn't that. She paused. "I am a publican's wife, am I not?"

"Are you, though?" His gaze bored into hers. Mina had to struggle not to drop her own. Swallowing, for her throat was suddenly dry, she nodded her head. "That's what you want?" he persisted.

Was it? If she said no, she thought, then she would be doomed forever to this confined life of parlor and attic bedroom. Whereas, if she said yes... A strange and slightly terrifying prospect lay before her. Being a wife to Will Nye in both fact and deed.

A narrow, dull life or the unknown. For some reason, an image flashed into Mina's brain. The cliff edge where she had hovered for one thrilling and horrifying moment, right on the brink.

"Yes," she croaked.

This time, she would plunge right over the edge.

On reaching The Merry Harlot, Nye drove the carriage straight into the courtyard and pulled on the reins. Turning in his seat, he yanked her roughly into his arms. Mina blinked up at him a moment, hot and breathless despite the bite of cold in the air. Nye did not speak, and she was ridiculously aware of the fact they were both breathing hard in each other's faces. Suddenly, his lips were crushed to hers and she was clinging on to his jacket for dear life.

The firm press of his lips suddenly relented and Mina gasped. She would have slid off the bench if he hadn't maintained his ruthless grip of her. She opened her eyes, staring up at him. When had she closed them? How long had she been pressed to his chest like this?

"You've got to breathe through your nose," he murmured, and for a moment she felt indignant, but then she noticed his own breathing was just as uneven as her own and his eyes still fixed on her lips.

"Oh," she said lamely.

"And give me a taste of your tongue."

"How am I supposed to do that?" she asked in bewilderment. "I can hardly talk at the same time."

His eyes gleamed, and for one horrible moment, she thought he would laugh at her. If he had, she wasn't sure what she would have done, but instead he raised one hand to scratch the stubble on the side of his jaw. "I mean let my tongue taste yours," he said gruffly.

Mina gaped at him. "What?" she faltered. She surely had not heard him correctly. One of the horses tossed back its head, and Nye was forced to release her to right his grip on the reins.

"Alright there, Nye?" called a voice, recalling Mina to her surroundings. Her bonnet had come loose and was hanging off her head. She made a grab for it and Nye swore under his breath.

"We'll give it another go," he said. "Later."

"Er…yes," Mina agreed, thankful for her reprieve. "Quite."

She could see other figures milling round in the shadowy courtyard and felt horribly embarrassed they might have witnessed their awkward embrace.

"Reuben, hold her head!" Nye bellowed, and Mina saw the man with the ginger beard spring forward to seize one of the horses as Nye clambered down. She had scarcely retied her bonnet when Nye appeared at her side of the carriage and was holding a hand up to her. Mina took it and precariously started to descend from the perch at the front. She only managed the first step and then found herself swung down with his hands at her waist.

"Get up to bed," he said. "I'll join you later."

Mina's face flamed as she turned away from him to scurry into the inn. He'd join her later? She hung up her cloak and bonnet and took a quick wash in the scullery before hurrying up the staircase. She nearly spilled the wax from her candleholder when Ivy knocked on her door as she was setting it down on the bedside table. "Oh Ivy," she said, looking up with relief. "You did make me jump."

"Just wanted to thank you for my gifts, Mrs. Nye," Ivy said, beaming. "Love a nice bottle of scent, I do, but you didn't have to."

"You're most welcome," Mina said, waving this aside. "And I wanted to. Do you think you'll use the lotion? I wasn't sure which type you favor—"

"Ooh yes, it's ever such a nice one," Ivy interrupted her. "Besides, I always has a different one each time!"

Mina sat on the bed and started efficiently braiding her hair. "Are you not serving behind the bar tonight, Ivy?" she asked.

"Not till after hours tonight," she said with a wink, coming into the room and closing the door softly behind her.

"After hours?" Mina frowned, motioning to a chair. "How can you serve at the bar when it is closed?"

Ivy giggled. "You are a sheltered one and no mistake." She sat in the chair and revealed a bottle she had been carrying under her arm. "Care to take a glass with me, Mrs. Nye?"

Mina changed her mind about her automatic refusal. After all, she was in dire need of some Dutch courage. Instead, she nodded. "Call me Mina," she answered.

Ivy's eyes widened. "I couldn't do that, Mrs. Nye. Wouldn't be right."

"Not even when no one else is around?" Mina asked with a frown. *First Edna and now Ivy.* She sighed, feeling a little forlorn.

"Well, I dunno about that," Ivy replied warily and produced two wineglasses out of her apron. She set them on the side and uncorked the bottle.

"How is it that you can serve an empty bar?" Mina persisted as Ivy poured. "Do you mean you are to do a stock-take?"

Ivy laughed merrily. "Lord bless you, he don't let me do no stock-take," she said, passing a brimming glass of red wine to Mina. "Very jealous Nye is about the state of his cellars. The one time I suggested it, you'd have thought I was a Customs and Excise man." She picked up her own glass and held it aloft. "Here's to a pair of shining eyes," she toasted. Mina hastily held her own glass to chink with Ivy's. She wasn't sure whose eyes they were toasting, or if they were simply expressing a hope for their own. "Chin-chin," Ivy added and took a liberal swig.

Mina took a tentative sip and found the wine to be very sharp yet simultaneously unpleasantly furry on her tongue. She plunked it down. "Very nice," she lied.

"What it means," Ivy said, leaning forward confidentially, "is that there's to be a lock-in tonight."

"A lock-in?" Mina echoed, reaching for her bed socks.

"It's when your regular patrons leave," Ivy explained, "but a privileged few are permitted to remain after the doors is locked. And they're permitted to carry on drinking till the early hours."

"I see," said Mina, drawing on her socks. "And what events determine its occurrence?"

"What?" Ivy asked with a frown, knocking back the last of her wine and reaching for the bottle to pour another.

"I mean, is it a regular thing?" Mina asked, hastily rephrasing her question. She remembered Nye's comment earlier about her being somewhat verbose. "Occurring say, once a month?"

Ivy's expression of confusion lifted. "Oh!" she said. "I take your meaning now." Once she'd refilled her glass, she held the bottle up with a quirk of her eyebrows.

"No thank you," Mina said hastily, taking another minuscule sip of her own drink.

"Well," said Ivy, resting her glass lovingly against her bosom. "It ain't as straightforward as all that. You see, sometimes they'll have ones with the regulars. Now, I don't usually have no part in them ones, I just retires at the usual time and Nye serves at the bar. Then other times it'll be when the prizefighters are here overnight. I'll usually serve at those, cos they likes a pretty face and Nye's usually down to fight."

"The night I arrived was one such night," Mina said aloud. "Though I believe Edna was serving behind the bar."

"I was rushed off my feet that night," Ivy agreed easily enough. "Oftentimes you need two behind bar on such a night."

"How often are prizefights held here?" asked Mina, reaching for her blue woolen shawl and wrapping it around her shoulders. She seemed to remember she'd had the impression Ivy had been with one of the fighters in a bedroom on the second floor, but perhaps she'd had that wrong.

"Oh, fairly regular," said Ivy vaguely. "Usually have at least one bout a month."

Mina wetted her lips with the red wine thoughtfully. "So…tonight's is just a local lock-in?" she said. "Why is Nye not hosting this one?"

"We sort of takes it in turns," Ivy replied easily. "See, sometimes he sits with Gus and Reuben and a few others and they'll be in deep discussion all night."

Mina considered this and could not help but think it rather odd. "Reuben is the one with the ginger beard, is he not?"

"Yes, that's him," agreed Ivy. "He's odd job man and stable hand around here."

From the brief interactions Mina had seen between him and Nye, they did not seem to be on such terms. She wondered what on earth they could find to discuss so intently. Then a thought occurred to her. "So, if you're behind the bar tonight then Nye must be intending to confer with his friends," she said with some relief.

"Friends?" Ivy's eyebrows shot up. "I wouldn't call them that exactly. If he has any, it's that prizefighter crowd. Anyway," she said. "I wanted to hear what happened this afternoon. What's this about some gentleman importuning you in the private parlor?"

Mina choked on her mouthful of wine. "A misunderstanding only."

Ivy cast her a shrewd look. "Only Gus did say as Nye nearly choked the life out of him for his impertinence."

"I think Gus might be prone to telling tall tales," Mina said severely. "By the by, did there used to be a monastery around these parts?"

"Don't know about that." Ivy shrugged. "I'm not from round here though. Not originally," she sighed. "Moved here with my husband, I did."

"Husband? I did not realize you were married, Ivy."

Ivy nodded. "Leastways, I thought he was my husband. Before his actual wife turned up to claim him. Bigamist," she said when Mina's mouth fell open.

"No!"

"Apparently he was always doing it."

"Oh Ivy, I am sorry."

Ivy shrugged. "You lives and learns," she said cheerfully, rising from her chair with her bottle in one hand and her glass in the other. "Anyway, I'll leave you to it," she said. "I'm going for a little nap before I have to go down and take over at ten."

"Good night," Mina called after her. The wine had left an unpleasant taste in her mouth, so setting her still-almost-full glass down on her dresser, she reached for her jar of tooth powder and gave her mouth another scrub. It wasn't that she was concerned that Nye might think her tongue tasted bad, she told herself. Such a consideration had not even crossed her mind. Besides, she did not really expect him to come to her tonight. Not if he was expected to cozily sit with Gus and Reuben in a monthly tête-à-tête.

Retrieving her new jar of Bloom of Roses, she moisturized her face and neck and then heaped her pillows up behind her back to settle with one of her periodicals. So well thumbed was it that it fell open right away at her favorite articles, and she had only run her eyes over the first three paragraphs when her head began to nod and she was forced to put it to one side and extinguish her candle.

11

When next Mina woke, she found herself lying on her side, somehow cocooned and warm as toast. She lay a moment, blinking at the unfamiliar sensation. Had she rolled herself around in her blankets? she wondered as she surfaced from sleep. Then she felt the weight of an arm around her middle and a heaviness pressed against her back and realized she had a bedmate. She caught her breath, spying first the brawny arm slung over her waist. His tanned skin stood out against the pale eiderdown. Then she noticed the rolled-up shirtsleeve and slowly turned her head. Will Nye was lay on top of the bed next to her, fully clothed except for the fact he'd removed his boots and waistcoat.

First light was streaming through the window, but it did not seem to disturb him one whit for his breathing was deep and regular. Despite the fact he'd once boasted he did not sleep, his eyes were closed and he seemed dead to the world. Hastily, Mina turned her head to face front again. When had he climbed the stairs to the attic room? she pondered. She had not heard him, though she had not shoved the chair under the door as was her usual practice either. In truth, she had half expected him after his words to her in the courtyard. *We'll try that again later*, he'd said. But he had not woken her for another half-suffocating embrace. He had let her sleep on. He had not even joined her under the covers.

A sharp rap on the door startled her out of her thoughts and she sat up, dislodging Nye's hold on her. To her surprise, he did not stir, but slept steadily on.

"Mrs. Nye?" It was Edna's voice.

"One moment, Edna." Mina slid from the bed and pattered across the room in her bed socks. Drawing the door open, she found Edna looking harassed. The servant was dressed, but her mobcap sat awry on her head and she had not yet donned her apron to start work. "What is it, Edna?"

"I can't find the master," Edna hissed. "Only there's a pair of Riding Officers downstairs who's asking for his whereabouts most particular." She wrung her hands. "What am I to do?"

Mina cleared her throat. "He's abed. I'll rouse him now and send him down to deal with it."

Edna fell back a step. She could not have looked more astonished if Mina had announced he was sat on the roof. "Oh," she said lamely when she was able to form words again.

"Tell them he will be down directly," Mina said, shutting the door and turning to face Nye. He looked like he had rolled into the spot she had vacated, but still lay fully stretched out and slumbering. "Nye!" she called. No reaction. She walked over to the bed. "Will Nye!" Nothing.

Reaching out, she placed a hand on his shoulder and squeezed. "Nye, you must wake up." When he did not react to that, she felt a sudden alarm. Was he in some kind of drunken stupor? Kneeling on the bed next to him, she took a firm hold of both shoulders and shook him vigorously. Finally, his eyes flew open and he stared up at her. "Nye!" she practically yelled in his face.

"What is it?" he mumbled, his eyes drifting shut again. "Come back to bed."

"There are two Riding Officers downstairs who wish to speak to you," she insisted loudly.

Again, his eyes blinked open and he stared up at her a moment. "Mina," he said distinctly, and why that made her heart beat louder in her breast, she had no notion.

"Yes?" she asked and watched as comprehension stole into his eyes.

He sat up suddenly, causing her to practically fall backward off the bed. "What the hell happened?" he asked belligerently, gazing around the room as though for someone to blame.

"What do you mean?" Mina asked, mystified. "You fell asleep, that's all."

He gave a snort, clambering off the bed. "I don't sleep," he corrected her.

She slipped off the bed and plunked her hands on her hips. "Well you do rather a good impression!" she told him tartly.

He scowled and then cast about the room, looking bewildered. "Where are my boots?"

Mina glanced down at the floor beside the bed. "There they are," she said and pointed helpfully. "And that must be your waistcoat over the chair." She wondered at his confused, helpless manner. He genuinely seemed befuddled and she wondered if he'd spent a night heavily drinking.

After a moment, he sat abruptly in the chair and pulled on his boots.

"Why would there be officers here at The Merry Harlot?" she asked him and was pointedly ignored.

"Put some clothes on," he said, giving her a hard stare, and Mina glanced down at her voluminous white cotton nightgown.

"I will, once you've gone," she answered briskly. He could hardly expect her to start stripping off with him there.

He huffed at that, stood up, crossed the room, and exited it with a slam of the door. Mina pursed her lips and started thoughtfully to dress. She lingered over arranging her hair into a tidy roll which she pinned at her nape. Then she descended the stairs and disappeared into the scullery for her wash. She fancied she heard voices as she crossed the hall, and on entering the kitchen, she found Edna there waiting for her with anxious eyes.

"I've made the tea tray up to bring in to you," she said, turning around. Mina opened her mouth to thank her, though she really did not think it necessary to take her morning beverage in the parlor, when she noticed four cups set out on the tray. "They're in the parlor now," Edna said, seeing the direction of her gaze.

"The Riding Officers?" Mina asked with surprise.

Edna nodded her head. "Will I carry it in before you?" she asked unhappily.

Mina thought a moment. "I'll open the door for you," she said with decision.

She gave the parlor door a swift knock and flung it open for Edna to carry in the large tray which now had toasted muffins and tea cakes as well as butter. Then she paused by the door until Edna had scurried back out again. The servant cast a look of gratitude her way before disappearing back toward the kitchen. Surmising this was an ordeal to get through from Edna's frightened demeanor, Mina drew herself up, then shut the door resolutely behind her.

When she turned around to survey the room, she found two strangers along with Nye. They both stood when she entered

160

though, with some show of reluctance, and she did not appreciate the insolent look one of them gave her, whose stare was very bold. Coolly holding his gaze until he lowered his own, she then glanced toward the other younger uniformed man, whose manner was more respectful.

"These are Excisemen for Her Majesty, Mina," Nye said, clearing his throat. "Mr. Havilland," he said, nodding toward the one Mina had taken an instant dislike to. "And Mr. Guthrie. They're both Riding Officers based nearby at St. Ives. Gentlemen, this is my wife, Mrs. Mina Nye."

"Your servant, madam," drawled the elder very insincerely as the younger executed a punctilious bow. "I had not heard tell that Nye here had taken a wife." He cast a sardonic look in Nye's direction which was ignored.

Mina came into the room. "I am happy to make your acquaintance, gentlemen," she said repressively and headed for a chair before the tea tray. "Can I offer you some refreshment?" she asked in her most colorless tone.

Looking up, she thought she saw a startled look on the one's face and a frown on the other, before they both hurriedly assented. Having ascertained that the elder took lemon and the younger a spoonful of sugar, she poured and, guessing that Nye would take his black, pushed a cup and saucer toward him also. He took it wordlessly and retreated to the window.

"My, how civilized we are today," said Havilland with a sneer. "You will scarcely believe it, Guthrie, but in the five years since I've been posted in Cornwall, I've never been received in this establishment anywhere other than the taproom prior to today."

Guthrie colored faintly, but Mina took a sip of her tea. She glanced at Nye, who was stood feet planted apart by the window, looking supremely unconcerned. She wondered if his attitude was genuine or feigned. Certainly, Edna had seemed badly rattled by this visit.

"One can only suppose," Havilland continued, not having drawn a response, "that a wife must have a civilizing effect even on an establishment such as this." His lip curled. "You are from these parts, ma'am?" he shot suddenly at Mina.

"I am not," she answered mildly. "I was raised all my life in the vicinity of Bath. You are familiar with that part of the country?"

Havilland, seemingly surprised by the conversational turn, did not speak for a moment. While he paused, Guthrie leaned forward in his seat. "I am, ma'am," he answered. "I have spent many a pleasant stay in that city. Both my sisters took their schooling in Bath and I was accustomed to visiting them there."

"Indeed?" Mina asked, turning to him with a smile. "May I enquire as to which school your sisters attended?"

"It was a school situated very near the center," Guthrie responded. "The Alexander Seminary for Young Ladies."

"I know it well. A particularly good school with a solid reputation," she said approvingly.

"You know something of schooling, madam?" Havilland interrupted them skeptically. "Curious. I did not know publicans' wives were so interested in education," he said with a short laugh.

Mina watched Guthrie color at his colleague's rudeness. She placed her cup down carefully. "Perhaps you do not know many publicans' wives who were also schoolteachers for several years," she suggested calmly. His eyebrows snapped together, and she smiled coldly at him. "My father ran a school in Bath for many years." Delighted that she seemed to have taken the wind from his sails, she turned back to Guthrie. "I take it your sisters are no longer employed in lessons."

"No indeed, ma'am," he replied. "To their very great relief. One is lately married and the other employed as a companion to a distant aunt."

Mina's smile grew warmer. "I am sure their schooling will give them an excellent foundation in life to build upon," she said approvingly.

"Your current surroundings," Havilland said, slamming down his cup and saucer with jarring loudness, "must be very different, I'll wager, to the schoolroom." His thin lips twitched. "One cannot help but wonder how the two of you ever met." He raised a supercilious eyebrow at Mina.

"Allow me to assuage your curiosity, good sir," she responded. "We were introduced by a mutual acquaintance. Perhaps you have heard of him? Viscount Faris of Vance Park. He is, I believe, quite well known in these parts." She enjoyed the way Havilland's face froze into an expression of disbelief.

"Lord Faris," Guthrie said, seeming anxious to fill the stunned silence which stretched out. "Indeed, I have heard of him. I believe he keeps a fine stable and often races his thoroughbreds at meets."

This was news to Mina, but she made sure to keep her bright smile intact. "As to that, I could not say," she demurred. "My late father was most opposed to gambling of any sort."

"Such sentiment does him credit, Mrs. Nye," Guthrie responded politely. "I am sure."

She smiled at him agreeably. "Can I refresh your cups, good sirs?" she asked, glancing about. Guthrie passed her his empty cup with alacrity, though Havilland declined with an irritable shake of his head. Glancing across at Nye, Mina was surprised to see him glaring moodily at the younger officer. What was he looking so annoyed about? "Can I persuade anyone to a slice of teacake or a muffin?" she asked, gesturing toward the laden tray.

"I must interrupt these niceties," Havilland said heavily, stirring in his seat, "to ask you a rather delicate question, Mrs. Nye." His tone was deeply sarcastic, and she waited with an impassive expression for him to speak.

"Yes?" she said at last when he continued merely to fix his hawklike gaze upon her without further speech. "Pray ask your question, Mr. Havilland. I will not take offence at any question you ask in pursuit of duty."

His frown deepened. "I must ask you to corroborate your husband's whereabouts," he said, glancing at Nye's blank face. "For last night, between the hours of midnight and four o'clock this morn."

Mina kept her eyes trained on Havilland's face. "Why, as to that," she answered matter-of-factly, "I see nothing sensitive about my answer. His place as a husband was clearly tucked in bed beside his wife. Which I assure you he was, until Edna knocked on the chamber door this morning on your arrival."

"You are a dutiful wife, Mrs. Nye, I perceive," Havilland said dryly. "In this respect at least, you are sadly predictable."

"I would hope I have a healthy respect for the institution of marriage," she replied quietly. "That was the way I was raised after all."

Havilland's mouth worked for a moment as though he was struggling in the grip of some strong emotion. Then he shot out of his seat. "Guthrie," he barked, seizing the hilt of his saber.

"We will take our leave of you, madam. Nye," he said, nodding toward her husband, who nodded in return, but otherwise made no reply.

"Good day to you," Guthrie echoed with another bow. "Good day to you, Mrs. Nye," Guthrie echoed with another bow. Mina nodded and smiled.

"I won't see you out, gentlemen," Nye said, approaching the table. "As I have not yet breakfasted." He pulled out a chair at the dining table as a scowling Havilland wrenched the door open and flung out. Guthrie followed, wincing.

Mina half expected Nye to rise from the table on their exit, but to her surprise, he reached for a muffin and took a bite. When he'd swallowed, he said, "I take two sugars in my tea."

"Oh." She hadn't liked to ask in case it showed a lack of marital knowledge. "Will you take another cup?" Wordlessly, he pushed the cup and saucer across the table at her. Mina poured it out and added the sugar and then handed it back. The whole time she was thinking furiously about that cupboard full of exotic teas and the cellars that Nye apparently guarded so jealously. Was she being fanciful, or did that, in addition with the fact two Excisemen had paid them a visit, seem to indicate one thing?

Could The Merry Harlot truly be a hub for smugglers? She raised a toasted teacake to her mouth before lowering it again. "Are you regularly visited by Excisemen here?" she asked.

Nye shrugged, slathering more butter onto a muffin. "Once in a while, maybe." Seeing her eyes fixed on him, he paused. "This coastline used to be notorious."

"For smuggling?" Mina voiced aloud, and he gave a terse nod. "I see." Wheels were turning in Mina's mind. She could not help but remember the rumbling and dragging noises she heard in the dead of night in a wholly different light. What if it had been shipments of French brandy that were being rolled over the cobbles? Would that not make more sense than a cavalcade of ghostly monks carting bodies toward the cliffs?

She was just pondering how best to broach the subject when a sharp rap was heard on the door. Nye looked up with a heavy frown as it opened, and Jeremy checked on the threshold before sauntering into the room. "Dear me, how very civilized!" he drawled, turning in a slow circle to take in the new features of the parlor room. "Wonders have been wrought here, of which I have ne'er seen the like!" He was looking dapper as ever in a tweed walking suit and was carrying an ebony cane which he twirled lazily before him.

Nye's frown deepened as Jeremy approached the table and threw himself down into a chair. "Good morning, good morning," he caroled, drawing off his gloves. "No, I won't take tea." He shuddered at Mina's murmured enquiry. "Never touch the stuff. Tell me," he said, turning to Nye with interest. "Who were those two gentlemen who passed me in the passage just now? My man Colfax said they resembled nothing so much as a pair of Bow Street Runners."

"Well, he was wrong," said Nye, flinging down his napkin. "Pair of Excisemen come down from St. Ives."

"Tsk, tsk," Jeremy tutted. "Colfax must be losing his touch." He turned to gaze out of the window at a well-built man as blond as himself, though of much heavier build, who was idling outside in the yard. He was dressed as a footman in a blue coat with gold buttons and did not to seem remotely self-conscious in his uniform, even though out of its native setting. Mina watched Colfax saunter over from the carriage toward the ostler with supreme confidence, though Reuben did not look particularly pleased to speak with him.

Nye cleared his throat, and it occurred to Mina that she could more readily believe this Colfax was Jeremy's illegitimate brother than Nye, who was so much darker and heavy-set than he. She wondered also why a footman would consider himself an expert on law enforcement agents, but before she could give this much thought, Jeremy was gently tapping his cane on the table to catch her attention.

"I was wondering, sister dear," he said languidly, "if you might care to join me today for a visit to Vance Park? There is one there who is most anxious to meet with you." She thought Nye looked up rather sharply at this. "My son and heir, Master Edward Vance," he explained with a smile. "He is quite curious to discover the existence of a heretofore undisclosed aunt."

"Indeed?" Mina asked, stirring her fresh cup of tea. "And how old is Master Edward?"

"He is some eight years, or thereabouts," Jeremy answered with a vague wave of his hand.

"I would be happy to make his acquaintance, of course."

"And you could see that portrait of our mother which hangs in the grand salon," he finished, very much in the style of one who reveals a winning hand. "Provided, of course," he added smoothly, "your esteemed husband does not object to letting you out of his sight."

"Why should I?" answered Nye gruffly, getting to his feet. "You could go back with him now," he suggested, looking straight at Mina. "Give you something to occupy yourself with."

She gazed back at him directly. "I could," she agreed. "Though I have plenty of things with which to occupy myself, I assure you." She thought fleetingly of the first-floor bathroom which she had meant to apply herself to today.

"Excellent!" said Jeremy, looking pleased. "In that case, I shall await your leisure."

It did not take Mina long to finish her breakfast, and after collecting her bonnet and cloak, she accompanied Lord Faris out to his carriage. Settling back against its velvety seats brought back some rather unpleasant memories, which she did her best to suppress. How much had changed in just under two weeks! Her time in Bath seemed a lifetime ago.

Jeremy climbed in after her. "Drive on, Colfax," he said, loudly rapping his cane against the roof of the carriage. He turned toward her. "By the by, I feel I should mention I did nip to London to procure that special marriage license I was so remiss as to overlook initially. The archbishop's office was even so obliging as to predate it too, so it matches the registry entry made by Reverend Ryland."

"I see," said Mina, wondering with unease what excuse he must have made for such a favor. On the whole, she did not think she wanted to know. She lapsed into silence for the rest of the ten-minute journey, and Mina watched the approach of Vance Park's neoclassical grandeur with interest. After all, her mother had been mistress here once. It was an astonishing thought, taking in the impressive sweep of the drive with its avenue of trees and its army of white stone nymphs peering out with their blind gazes.

"Well, sister?" Jeremy asked her with a smile playing about his lips. "What do you think of my humble abode?"

Mina's first thought was that it was not exactly subtle, but she swallowed this, instead replying gravely, "I think my mother must have loved my father very much." At his quizzical look, she added, "She never once reproached him with all which had once been hers."

"Ah," he said, enlightenment dawning. "My father always said that running off was the most interesting thing she ever did."

Mina pondered this a moment as the coach drew up. "I'm surprised he granted her a divorce," she said bluntly. "Many husbands would not be so generous. Did he never marry again?"

Jeremy shook his head. "Once was enough, he always said. Besides, by all accounts, he accorded her far more respect once she had left than he ever did during their marriage. He rather liked the story of his once-meek countess, pushed beyond endurance." He pulled a face. "He thought, I fancy, it lent him a gothic air."

Mina frowned as Jeremy sprang down from the carriage then turned back to offer her a hand. She took it. "I already know he did not look like you," she said slowly. "For you look like our mother."

"Quite right." He laughed, drawing her hand through the crook of his arm. "There is a portrait I will show you shortly. You may draw your own conclusions as to who it is resembles my late lamented father."

They were climbing the stone steps now to the main entrance, flanked with Tuscan columns and a pair of large reproduction Medici lions.

"The entrance hall," Jeremy announced, and Mina caught her breath when she looked up to behold the gold ceiling with its pantheon of gods drifting above her on clouds of glory.

"Goodness, how beautiful," she breathed. "Is that the birth of Athene?" she asked, catching sight of a large white marble relief on the far wall.

"It is," he agreed without much interest. "But you must steel yourself to ignore your patron goddess and instead, behold this," he said, coming to a halt in front of a full-length oil portrait of a man in a fancy uniform in front of a vaguely Italianate landscape. "And tell me who he reminds you of."

Mina was obliged to catch her breath on surveying the dark good looks of the subject. For the features were unmistakable from the strong jaw to the bold stare which challenged all viewers unflinchingly.

"William Nye, to the life, is he not?" Jeremy murmured.

Mina colored. "The resemblance is very strong," she admitted.

"You may imagine my father's feelings on the matter. His bastard bearing the stamp of his likeness far more faithfully than his heir ever would," Jeremy mused.

Mina was spared having to answer this by a light step on the stair, followed by a high childish voice.

"Papa?"

Jeremy sighed. "Our respite was brief," he grimaced. "Come, Edward, and greet your aunt Mina."

The steps grew faster, and Mina turned toward the staircase to see a small figure come hurtling down dressed in navy velvet breeches and jacket with a lace collar. Seeing the curls on the child's head, Mina saw Jeremy was spared the indignity his own father had suffered, for Teddy was as blond as could be.

"Good morning, Edward," she greeted him as he came to a breathless halt before her.

"Teddy," he corrected her swiftly. "Are you my aunt Minerva?" He looked her critically up and down. "Why are you dressed like that?"

"I am in mourning," Mina answered firmly. She withdrew her hand from Jeremy's arm and extended it to shake formally with Teddy.

"Have you come to see Grandmama's portrait?" Teddy asked.

"Yes," Mina said. "And meet you too, of course."

"Would you like to see my nursery, Aunt Minerva?" he asked breathlessly. "I've got a toy theater and a sailboat that really floats."

Mina hesitated, turning to Jeremy. "I should love to, if that's agreeable with your father."

"By all means," Jeremy answered affably. "You lead the way, my boy, and I will join you shortly for a game of At the Race Meet."

"That's my newest toy, Aunt Minerva," Teddy enthused, towing her toward the staircase. "We've named all the horses after Papa's."

"Ah yes, I heard this morning that your papa keeps racing horses," Mina remembered.

"Yes, and Son of Bucephalus is my favorite of all, but Jim calls him Pukey Bucey on account of his sensitive stomach."

171

"Is Jim a groom or a jockey?" Mina asked as they reached the second floor.

"Stable boy," Teddy answered with an enchanting smile that revealed his childish dimples. "But he's my favorite 'cause he tells me things."

"I see," answered Mina.

"Father said I'm not allowed to go down to the stables unattended," Teddy said sadly. "And Mama dismissed Nanny as soon as I went off to school, so I have no one to attend me now." A gloom descended on him. "Colfax takes me sometimes, but only when he's got time to spare."

"Will you return to school soon?" Mina enquired as he led her down across a gallery lined with family portraits. "If not, your father must surely hire you a tutor."

"Yes," Teddy agreed without much enthusiasm. "Though I don't want a tutor. Why can I not simply have Nanny back? She used to take me to the stables whenever I asked her."

"Well, because I daresay she has another little boy or girl to take care of now," Mina answered bracingly. "And you are a good deal too big for a nanny and need to take some lessons."

"Another little boy?" Teddy asked indignantly. "But she's *my* nanny!"

"I daresay she had other charges before you," Mina pointed out mildly.

"Them? Oh them," he snorted. "She certainly didn't like them as much as me." His chest swelled out with the boast. "She couldn't possibly like another little boy as much as she liked me." He caught hold of a door handle to his right and swung it open to reveal a large nursery complete with a large rocking

172

horse, a wooden fort, a mechanical carousel, and all manner of picture books, marbles, and quoits strewn about the floor and over the little round table.

"Goodness me, I'm sure Nanny didn't allow your nursery to get in such a mess as all this," Mina said disapprovingly.

Teddy gave her a sidelong look. "Annie should have come along and tidied it," he said evasively. "Only she hasn't."

"I'm sure Annie has other duties than picking up after you, Teddy," Mina said sternly and knew she was right when he reddened. "Let's get these things tidied away now before your papa comes up to play Race Meet with us."

He perked up at this and started dragging a chest into the center of the room. "Let's just throw it all in here," he panted.

"Certainly not," Mina corrected him. "For I can see a bookcase over there for your picture books." She began collecting up the volumes as Teddy sighed and started scrabbling to put the marbles back in their pouch. "There was a battle last night," he confided. "These books were propped up to make the rival fort and these marbles were the cannonballs fired by my soldiers."

"I see," Mina answered, slotting the books back onto their shelves. "I did wonder how the devastation came about."

"The Race Meet game is atop of that shelf," he said, pointing.

"Well, we shan't get that down until we've tidied all this away."

Teddy squinted at her. "You're not like most aunts I've met," he said accusingly.

"How many aunts do you possess?"

"Just one," he admitted grudgingly.

Mina pointed to her own chest in query. He nodded. "Well, it doesn't sound as though your own experience in aunts is extensive," she told him. "And besides, this is what *your* aunt is like."

He gave a snort at that and then started gathering up the hoops from his quoits set. It did not take long before they could once more see the large colorful rug, which must once have graced a far grander room but had been relegated to the nursery once it began to show signs of wear.

"That's better," Mina pronounced, reaching for Teddy's game. "Now, let us set this up on the nursery table as it needs a flat surface."

"I usually just play with it on the floor," Teddy objected as she set it down and lifted the lid off the box to show the six little painted horses and jockeys.

"I daresay," Mina answered. "But you are not hampered by stiffened petticoats."

"You could lie flat on your tummy," he suggested helpfully.

"I most certainly could not!" Mina informed him tartly. "What objection, pray, do you have to this perfectly civilized little table?" In truth, the chairs were a little small for grown-ups, but Mina lowered herself gingerly onto one and watched Teddy extend the six little horses and jockeys away from the box mechanism on their strings.

"What are their names?" Mina asked with interest as Teddy lined the little lead horses up on the starting line.

"Bucephalus, Trojan, Incitatus, Bombast, Braggadocio, and Vainglory," Jeremy recited, entering the room. "They are named after the horses in my own stables," he explained, taking a seat beside them at the table.

174

Mina frowned. "So then, all your steeds are named after historical horses or undesirable characteristics found in man?"

Jeremy looked surprised. "I thought generally the history taught at young ladies' schools was a good deal watered down for a maiden's ears."

"Did you? Perhaps you are unaware of the effect it has on a young woman, to be told certain books are not fit for her consumption."

Jeremy laughed. "So, it was not your good father the schoolmaster who taught you about Caligula, sister?"

Teddy looked up with a frown. "None of the horses are called that," he protested.

"Incitatus," Mina explained to her nephew, "was the name of the emperor Caligula's horse."

"Much like Bucephalus was the name of Alexander the Great's," his father added.

Teddy's frown cleared. "Oh." He cast a look at Mina that seemed to weigh her up anew.

"Now, how do we play this game?" Mina asked. "Is it a winding mechanism that is employed?"

"First you must pick which horse you want to back," Teddy explained. "Mine's Pukey-Bucey," he added quickly.

"Then I pick Incitatus," Mina said decisively. "For I believe it means 'swift' in Latin." She turned to Jeremy for confirmation.

"Or 'at full gallop,'" he agreed.

"Does it?" Teddy looked much impressed. "Rather a good name for a horse. What does Bucephalus mean, Aunt?"

Mina opened her mouth to explain she did not know any Greek, but her brother forestalled her.

"It means ox head," he drawled. "As Alexander's Thessalian stallion was so monstrous in size. He was also said to have had a black coat with a white star at his brow."

"Like our Pukey-Bucey," Teddy crowed.

"Exactly."

"And does your Bucephalus have eyes of midnight blue?" Mina enquired.

"We call it wall-eyed in the racing world," Jeremy corrected her.

"He does have blue eyes!" Teddy said triumphantly. "You named him very well, Papa."

"I'm glad you agree," Jeremy replied gravely. "I choose Vainglory," he said, pointing to the little white horse.

"You *always* pick Vainglory," Teddy said with a roll of his eyes.

"Not true, sometimes I choose Bombast. Besides," his father added, "you always pick Bucephalus."

They spent the next twenty minutes taking it in turns to wind the handle that drew the little lead horses over the finish line. Mina found Incitatus to be a most lucky horse and in all, had the most overall wins from the three of them.

"I believe," Teddy said at the conclusion, "that Incitatus is my second favorite horse," he said, stroking the little brown horse's back with his finger.

"Have you met your papa's Incitatus?"

Teddy nodded. "He's a chestnut, like this one." He carefully started placing the horses back inside the box.

"You must meet my horses sometime, Mina," Jeremy said on impulse, jumping up. "But first, you must come and view our mother's portrait." Mina rose, and to her surprise, Teddy also accompanied them downstairs.

"It's this way," said Teddy, dancing ahead. "In the blue drawing room."

"You go ahead," Jeremy directed her, stopping next to a footman who was not Colfax. "I'll ask for some refreshment to be served to us there."

Mina followed Teddy into a very elegant room with decorated blue silk panels hanging on the walls. "Oh, this is a lovely room," she exclaimed with pleasure as Teddy walked to the opposite end and stood in front of a large portrait of a young woman in a ballgown of foamy pink. "Here!" he said, flinging up an arm.

"Mama," Mina sighed, coming to a halt beside him.

She felt Teddy's gaze on her face as she beheld her mother's pink and white complexion, her gleaming blond ringlets, and the ropes of pearls at her throat. It was quite a feat to look that demure, Mina thought, considering how much of her bare white shoulders were on display. She could of course see it was Mama, but far younger than she remembered her and certainly decked out much more splendidly.

Had she been so very unhappy here? Mina wondered. She remembered Jeremy's words from earlier, about the old viscount only respecting her after she had left him. If he had been anything like Will Nye in temperament as well as looks, she could not imagine her mother would have fared at all well with such a man. Her own Nye would have made a milk jelly of her. Her thoughts made her start. *Her own Nye...* When had she started thinking of him as such?

"Mama wanted it moved," Teddy commented. "And her own portrait hung here, but Papa had hers put on the opposite wall instead."

Mina turned about to look at the opposite wall, where another blond lolled, this time against a Grecian urn full of blooms in a dress of blue satin with an extremely low neckline. Her expression could not have been more different to Mina's mother's if she had tried. Despite her careless pose, her gray eyes were bold and knowing, and the hand that held a blooming white rose to her bosom seemed less to symbolize purity than to deliberately draw attention to her charms.

"Your mama is very beautiful," she said, unable to think of anything more original. Funnily enough, it was the first time that day she had even remembered Vance Park had a current mistress.

"She's lying abed with a sore head this morning," Teddy said impassively. "She never gets up till noon. Last night, she threw a crystal vase at Papa and then spent all evening dancing in the music room with Colfax."

Mina started. *Dancing with Colfax?* For a moment she wondered if she had heard him correctly. "Is your mama fond of music?" she asked with an attempt to steer things into safer waters.

"She likes dancing," Teddy answered with a shrug.

"What do you think?" Jeremy came into the room, and Mina hurriedly turned back around to looking at her late mother.

"I think it's a very beautiful portrait," she said. "And you were quite right, far superior to my own miniature."

Her brother was silent a moment, gazing up at the pretty painted face. Then he, too, looked across at Mina before turning back to it in silent contemplation.

"Are you still sorry I don't resemble her?" she asked lightly, though she did not really know what prompted the question.

"No," Jeremy said after a long pause. "No, I rather think it's for the best all told."

"You don't look a bit like her," Teddy said frankly. "She wouldn't know about Incitatus, would she, Papa? Or Alexander the Great. I can tell," he added darkly. "She'd like dancing and sleeping in bed late."

"Not when I knew her," Mina answered truthfully. "She liked embroidery and sentimental tales about self-sacrifice. Oh, and pictures of kittens and babies in frilly dresses."

Teddy looked, if anything, even more disgusted. Jeremy grimaced. "You almost make me pity my poor father," he said with a laugh. "More and more I appreciate their basic incompatibility."

The way his mouth twisted over these last two words made her wonder if he was thinking of his own marriage. Then a footfall announced their lunchtime refreshments had arrived via the unknown footman. Jeremy dismissed him with a nod and then gestured for Mina to be seated.

The silver tray bore a selection of thinly sliced sandwiches, chicken and cress flavored with celery salt, egg salad with mayonnaise, and roast beef and tomato. This was accompanied by crackers and thinly sliced ham, a plate full of individual glazed fruit tarts, a glistening jelly, and a cream custard. There was a small fine bone china teapot with one cup which Mina guessed was for her and a jug of lemonade for Teddy. Jeremy wandered over to a side table and poured himself something to drink from a decanter.

"You must have a sandwich first, Teddy," Mina chastised when the boy went straight to the fruit tarts.

"You sound like Nanny," Teddy complained, but reached for a sandwich all the same.

"I can see you need a firm hand," she told him reprovingly, but the boy just grinned. "Have you some plan for my nephew's education, now you have withdrawn him from school?" she asked Jeremy forthrightly.

He lowered his glass, blinking. "I haven't really given it much thought," he admitted.

Mina's sharply indrawn breath let him know what she thought of that! "Perhaps a tutor?" she suggested.

Jeremy grimaced, lowering himself into the seat opposite her. "I suppose I shall have to look into it," he answered without much enthusiasm. "Though the last time I engaged a tutor, it did not go well."

"Mama did not like Mr. Jones very much," Teddy confided.

"Is that the impression you gained, my son?" Jeremy said, enigmatically meeting Mina's eye. "Funny, I had almost the opposite conviction."

Mina thought it could only be a good thing that Teddy was too occupied spooning a custard cream into his bowl to pay much attention to his father's words.

"What a pity I did not think to engage you, sister dear, in the capacity of governess," Jeremy continued.

180

She glanced across at him quellingly. It was a little too late for that, she thought, though a couple of weeks ago she would have snatched his hand off at the suggestion.

"I shouldn't want Aunt Minerva for a governess," Teddy interrupted. "She's too strict. Besides, you can't have an aunt for a governess. Even I knew that."

Jeremy laughed. "She would be strict, would she not? But quite apart from that, your aunt is lately married, and I doubt her husband can spare her."

Mina's hand shook slightly as she poured her tea, but she made no reply to this and the probing look he gave her.

"I have an uncle too then?" Teddy said with his mouth full of sandwich.

Mina's startled gaze met Jeremy's. "I suppose you do, my boy," Jeremy answered languidly and crossed one leg over the other. "Your uncle Nye."

"That's a funny name," Teddy said, swallowing the last of his sandwich and reaching for a fruit tart.

A low, husky laugh in the doorway had them all looking up to see Lady Faris, who looked to Mina to still be in a state of dishabille. A frilly white wrapper was drawn over a gown Mina was not entirely sure was meant to be seen by light of day. "Surely you do not expect your son and heir to acknowledge such an acquaintance?" she asked, coming into the room and addressing her husband directly.

"Why not?" Jeremy replied coolly. "Mina allow me to introduce you to my good lady wife. Amanda, this is my sister, Mina."

Seeing that Amanda threw her only the most cursory of glances, Mina did not rise from her seat, but instead poured herself a second cup of tea which she could just squeeze from the dainty pot. "How do you do?" she said perfunctorily and without any expectation of reply.

Amanda rounded the table and helped herself to a couple of grapes from the fruit bowl. She pulled a face. "Everything tastes foul from that hot house," she said. "You should fire that head gardener and get a younger man on the job."

"Hudgins has been here for thirty years, man and boy," Jeremy replied without heat. "Nothing tastes good if you've ruined your palate the night before."

"Ruined my palate—how dramatic," his wife responded, her eyes glittering. "Don't you think your master is ridiculously dramatic sometimes, Colfax?" she asked, looking back over her shoulder, and Mina saw that the blond footman had entered the room in her wake.

"I couldn't possibly comment, my lady," he said without expression, and she laughed.

"My, we are proper this morning," she commented dryly, turning back to her husband. "Is that due to your schoolmistress of a sister's presence?" She shot a mocking look at Mina. "Next you will be inviting orphans and foundlings to dinner."

"My dear," said Jeremy blandly. "You must not squander your precious company on us like this if our little party is not to your liking." Amanda flushed. "I'm sure you have a myriad of things you would rather be doing than entertaining my guest with your antics."

"You—!" His wife bit back her words with effort and Mina saw Jeremy's cold answering smile with something of a shiver.

Clearly there was no love lost between the two of them. She took a deep breath to collect herself. "Oh Teddy," Amanda said, as if she had only just caught sight of her son. "You still here? Isn't it time you went back to school yet?"

"As a matter of fact," Jeremy said before Teddy could answer, "I am not sending him back. There were two cases of consumption last term among the pupils."

"Good God," she scoffed. "He has the constitution of an ox. You're not imagining him some delicate young sprig—"

"Nevertheless," Jeremy interrupted her. "As you did not supply with me a spare along with my heir, I must take all necessary precautions with the one I've got."

Mina darted a look at Teddy, who was now cleaning his plate of jelly.

"Colfax," Jeremy said with a charming smile. "After our meal, would you kindly take my son and Mrs. Nye along to the stables?" Teddy caught an ecstatic breath. "He is most desirous to show Bucephalus to his aunt."

"Of course, my lord."

"You'll see now, Aunt Minerva," Teddy said enthusiastically. "The white star on his brow."

"I look forward to it," she assured him.

Mina spent a pleasant hour being shown around the stables by Teddy and, once Colfax had a word with one of the stable hands, the head groom also. She admired Bucephalus and told Teddy she did not wonder that the handsome steed was his firm favorite. If it had not been for an ill-judged dart into one of the stalls by the boy, it would have been entirely without incident.

Luckily for him, Colfax showed himself to be very quick on his feet indeed, snatching him out of harm's way in an instant.

"And that's why his lordship don't let you come down here on your own, you little bleeder," Colfax told him tightly, setting him back on his feet. Mina looked up quickly, for under the strain, his pronunciation had slipped, betraying a London accent she had not picked up before.

Teddy tugged his velvet jacket back into place and adjusted his lace collar. "I daresay I could have ducked his legs," he said, quite unabashed.

"You would have had your brains dashed out in an instant, Teddy," Mina scolded him. "Now thank Colfax for saving you from a very nasty injury."

Teddy scraped a foot along the ground. "Thank you, Colfax," he mumbled, avoiding the servant's gaze. Colfax grunted and the head groom shot a look of appreciation Mina's way. The rest of the tour went off without any further mishaps, and Teddy bade her a fond farewell on the front steps of the house. "I daresay Colfax will tell Papa I nearly got squashed," he grumbled. "And I won't see Bucephalus for a fortnight!"

"You should be grateful you escaped without any longer lasting repercussions," Mina told him briskly, before bending down to accept his kiss to her cheek. "He may not tell him," she found herself adding, in spite of herself.

"Colfax tells Papa everything," Teddy complained darkly. "Mama says they are hand in glove."

Mina was surprised to hear that, all things considered. "Well, if he does tell, I'm sure it is only out of concern for your well-being," she said reprovingly. "You need to learn to be a good deal less impetuous, Teddy, where your safety is concerned."

He nodded dolefully and cast woebegone eyes up at her. "Will you come and visit me again, Auntie?"

"Should you like that?" Mina asked to mask her surprise and uncertainty how to answer.

"Yes." He nodded. "I don't have any other aunts," he gave by way of explanation. "Perhaps you recall my saying?"

"I do," she admitted. "Well, I, too, should like to further our acquaintance, so we shall have to see what can be arranged, shan't we?"

Teddy flashed her a smile, seemingly satisfied with this. Mina turned and descended back down the steps to the waiting carriage. Colfax extended a white-gloved hand to help her inside and then he swung up on top. Mina leaned out of the carriage and waved to Teddy, who was stood next to one of the large stone lions, waving madly. "Goodbye, Aunt Minerva!" he shouted.

Mina sank back against the cushions with a sigh. She was not sorry to leave Vance Park with its strange tensions and underlying currents, but she had to confess that Teddy had wriggled into her affections already. Dreadful boy that he was!

12

Mina raised a hand in farewell as the coach swept back out of the courtyard of The Merry Harlot. She heard the door of the inn open and shut behind her and had just started to turn toward it when she heard Nye's growl.

"Who brought you back?" he asked abruptly, coming to stand beside her.

Mina did a double take at his surly expression. Had he not urged her to go? Why was he now looking so incensed? "Colfax accompanied the groom, though I hardly needed an attendant to hand me up and down," she commented aloud, remembering how Jeremy had failed to assist her on her previous arrival at the inn.

Nye's eyes narrowed. "Not the likes of him, in any case."

"What do you mean?"

Nye gave her a sidelong look. "There's some that say Colfax has been Lady Faris's lover for years," he said bluntly.

Mina flushed. "Oh," she said lamely, remembering how Teddy had claimed his mother had spent the previous evening. "Surely if that was true, Lord Faris would have discharged him long ago." Nye looked as if he would say more, but then seemed to change his mind. "Teddy told me Colfax and his father are hand in glove," she prodded and, to her surprise, Nye's look of discomfort grew. His eyes shifted away from hers and he cleared his throat.

"None of my business what they get up to at Vance Park," he said dismissively. "If you've any sense, you won't pry."

186

Mina considered this. "Well," she conceded. "I don't know that I shall ever visit again." Nye fell in step beside her as she crossed the courtyard to the inn.

Reaching a hand past her head, he pushed the door open for her and followed her inside. "Why do you say that?" he asked.

Mina removed her bonnet and cloak, hanging them on the peg. "Lady Faris made it quite clear she did not welcome my presence," she explained and patted her hair to make sure it remained in the low chignon bun she had arranged that morning. "Although, I should like to see my nephew again." She eyed Nye thoughtfully.

"What?" he asked, catching her expression.

"He is your nephew as much as mine," she pointed out.

He snorted. "I doubt Faris thinks so."

"Well, that's where you're wrong, for he told the boy quite plainly he had an uncle Nye." She could see he was taken aback at this, though he said nothing as he followed her along the corridor to the kitchen.

"Perhaps Lord Faris would let him visit us here?" she suggested, lifting the lid of the kettle to see if there was water in it. When Nye continued to be silent, she set it on the range and reached for the tea leaves in the cupboard. Glancing back, she saw he had propped his hip against the table and was regarding her broodingly.

"This is an inn, Mina," he said heavily. "And that boy is heir to Vance Park."

"Did not the old earl visit your mother here?" she asked boldly, spooning the leaves into the pot.

"No, he did not," he ground out. "This place was her payoff after he was done with her."

Mina flushed. "Oh." She could not quite bring her gaze to meet with his. "I apologize if I was indelicate." He gave a short laugh as if such considerations were not necessary. Perhaps they weren't. "Jeremy visited us here yesterday," she pointed out. "And Ivy told me he does so frequently."

"Is it Jeremy or Lord Faris?" he asked tersely. "You need to make up your mind."

She reached up to take two cups down from the cupboard. "I know," she admitted. "But I do not yet feel quite comfortable addressing him as Jeremy, so I am trying it out with you."

His eyes glinted. "Maybe there are other things I'd rather you tried out with me."

"Such as what?" The words had left Mina's mouth before she noticed his expression. Then he reached out and gripped her forearm and she was spun around, an arm clamped about her waist and Will Nye's large hand resting against her jaw. Oh, he meant kissing, Mina realized mere moments before his lips descended to hers.

Oh dear, she thought distractedly, what was it he had told her to do last time? Breathe through her nose, she seemed to recall. Then she noticed his lips were much gentler this time, touching tentatively to hers, exerting much less pressure. Not wanting him to accuse her of not pulling her weight, she tilted her head up and leaned into the kiss.

Nye made a noise in his throat that was not a growl, but something very close. Mina's head reeled. Reaching her arms up to wrap about him, she realized she held a cup in each hand, hampering her somewhat, but she flung them around his neck anyway.

Nye's body went taut and he shifted, whirling her around so she was the one now leaning back against the kitchen table. Then his intimidating bulk stepped forward, making her breathless and a little alarmed. If not for the barrier of her skirts, he would be planted between her legs, she realized faintly.

"Nye—" Mina breathed, but his hands were on either side of her face, angling her head up for his kiss. This time when he sealed his lips to hers, she felt his tongue swipe slowly along her bottom lip and jolted with shock. That was it! Last time he had said he wanted a taste of her tongue. Her face flamed hot. No sooner had she let her lips part for him than her mouth was thoroughly taken.

Her eyes closed, Mina gave a muffled gasp before remembering to breathe through her nose. One of the cups fell from her loosened grip and shattered on the kitchen floor. Nye didn't even flinch. One of his hands lowered from her jaw to grip her waist and then skimmed as much of a hip as her stiffened petticoats allowed. He made a noise of frustration. Then his tongue was tangling against hers again and Mina's mind went blank.

What was happening? Every fiber in her being was surging forward to press shamefully close to Will Nye's big, hard body. She could not get close enough to him. His large hand gripping her waist was strangely comforting as it squeezed and relaxed there. She moaned against his mouth, startling herself so badly that she tore her mouth from his and stared up at him in horror.

"Was that me?" she blurted, trying to retreat.

"Stay still," he ground out. "There's broken china at your feet."

189

Mina blinked at him, then lowered her gaze to the jagged pieces lying on the floor. "Oh," she said. It was only then she realized she had dropped *both* cups. And apparently Nye had been fully aware of the fact, unlike her. She bit her lip. "What will I tell Edna?"

He gave a short laugh, releasing her with a show of reluctance. "Tell her I took you by surprise."

Well, that was true enough, she thought, watching him fetch a shovel and brush.

"The kettle's likely boiled," he said, and Mina started, dropping the fingers she had pressed to her lips.

"I'll fetch more cups," she said, hastily stepping around him as he swept up the last of the fragments. *How embarrassing.* She set the cups on the table and then poured the hot water into the teapot with hands that shook. He stepped outside to dump the remains, then came back inside, shutting the door behind him. Mina set the teapot onto the table to brew and hastily sank into a chair. Nye rounded the table and sat opposite her.

"Are you serving behind the bar tonight?" she forced herself to ask. It trembled on her tongue to ask if he intended to sleep in her bed again. He shook his head, watching her intently. "I'm just letting the tea brew," she said, feeling the silence lie heavy on her. Nye didn't comment, just lolled back in his chair, never taking his eyes from her.

Mina doled out the milk and sugar and, after checking the strength, poured the tea. Once she'd pushed a cup across to Nye, she took a deep breath. "So," she said, taking the bit between her teeth. "Should we discuss these additional duties that I'll be picking up now?"

His eyes flared, then he lowered his lids to hide it. "I'll show you tonight," he said, his words dark with promise.

Mina frowned. "Will I ever be expected to work behind the bar?" she asked before taking a sip of hot tea.

"What?" Nye looked thunderstruck at this. "I'm talking about in bed, not in the bar."

Mina bridled. "I am aware of that," she spluttered, setting down her cup on the saucer with a loud rattle. "But we can hardly discuss that now!" She flailed an arm. "I was trying to steer the conversation into safer channels!" A reluctant smile tugged at the corners of his lips, completely astonishing her. "I'm not that obtuse!" she muttered, her face turning red.

"I don't think you're obtuse, Mina," he said. "But you have been sheltered all your life until now."

She picked her teacup up again, wondering why she always grew so flustered when he spoke her name in that rich, deep voice of his. "That may be so," she conceded. "But I'm a fast learner."

"I certainly hope so." She locked up in quick enquiry at his words and he grimaced. "I don't know how patient I'll be," he admitted. "It's not one of my virtues."

"Oh, I don't know," Mina said lightly, remembering how he had carried her home from the cliffs.

Nye frowned and opened his mouth, but before he could form his words, they were interrupted by a hasty step in the doorway.

"Oh! Master Nye," Edna blurted. "I didn't realize as how you was in here."

Mina turned around in her seat. "Is everything alright, Edna?"

191

Edna hesitated. "Oh yes, Mrs. Nye," she answered evasively.

"Would you like a cup of tea?"

Edna's gaze darted once more to Nye before returning to Mina. "I'm still laundering," she said. "I just come down for more washing soda." She darted through to the scullery to collect the soda crystals. "Got them," she said needlessly to illustrate her point and then slipped away.

Seeing Mina's surprised expression, Nye said dryly, "She likely wanted to hear how your morning went at Vance Park and doesn't feel free to gossip in front of me."

"She does seem a bit uncomfortable around you at times," Mina acknowledged. Nye shrugged. "She's very busy about the place," Mina added.

"It's hard to get domestic staff out here," Nye admitted grudgingly. "We're a good quarter of an hour walk uphill from the village."

Mina took another sip of tea to fortify herself. "I daresay the reputation of the place does not help," she braced herself to add. He cut her a look but said nothing. "It being haunted I mean," she added meaningfully.

Nye looked discomforted for a minute. "I wouldn't know," he said brusquely. "I've never seen anything of that sort."

"Gus told me about it, did he tell you?" she prodded, but he just shook his head and refused to be drawn. She sighed. "It's a shame we can't get someone to help Edna," she commented. "As she really does seem to do the lion's share of the work."

"She gets paid more than Ivy, if that's what you're asking," Nye said sharply. Mina set down her cup. It hadn't been and she was surprised by his defensive tone. "Ivy only works the bar in the

192

afternoon and evenings," he pointed out. "And what she does on the side is none of my business. I'm not her pimp."

Mina flushed. "Such a thought didn't even occur to me!" she flung back hotly.

"Like I said. You've been sheltered," Nye responded darkly.

Mina glared at him. "Why do you have to be so disagreeable?" she asked in a grieved tone. "I wasn't trying to pick a fight, just—"

"Just what?"

"Take an interest in the place! A wifely interest," she added painstakingly. "But it seems the only place you expect me to pick up any *additional duties*," she added bitterly, "is the bedroom!" She stood up abruptly. "Excuse me," she said in a brittle voice and stalked into the scullery to don her apron and mobcap. She muttered angrily under her breath as she gathered the cleaning supplies she wanted together in a bucket.

Stalking back out of the scullery, she made to cross the kitchen, but Nye stood in her way, blocking her path.

"What are you doing, Mina?" he asked gruffly.

"I'm going upstairs to clean the bathroom. Those tiles—"

"No," Nye said firmly.

"What do you mean, no?" Mina asked, drawing herself up to her tallest and squaring off with him. For a moment, his eyes gleamed again. Mina narrowed her eyes. If he laughed in her face, she would be furious.

"You're not skivvying anymore," he said loudly. "You've a parlor to sit in. Go sit in it."

"I can't sit in the parlor all day, Nye!" she snapped.

"Why not? You're a lady, aren't you?"

"No, I am not!" she answered shrilly. "I was a schoolteacher and now I am—"

"My wife!" Nye interrupted her, his voice raised to a shout. "And as my wife, I get to dictate what you get up to, madam, and what you do not!"

Mina glared at him, her chest rising and falling. "I understand that you don't want me staring out at the courtyard in the early hours of the morning *and why*!" she added in a low voice that shook with anger. "But if you imagine that you can dictate—"

Suddenly his hand shot out to capture her elbow and spin her about, so her back faced him. Her apron was jerkily untied and then stripped from her shoulders, even as she wriggled to prevent him. "Nye!" she gasped as he snatched the bucket from her grasp and set it on the table.

"Take that thing off your head!" he ordered. Reluctantly, Mina reached up but was apparently too slow as Nye whipped the cap off before her and slung it down on a chair.

"You're abominably rude!" she raged at him as he dragged her out into the hallway. "Sometimes I feel as though I could hate you!"

"Yes, so you've said."

That brought her up short. "When did I—?"

"On the beach," he said tersely.

Mina's face flamed red. "I was very distressed that day—" she began defensively, then noticed he was towing her toward the staircase instead of the parlor. "Wait! Where—?" He did not speak, just propelled her bodily up the first flight of stairs. "Nye!" she panted, trying to free her wrists, but it did no good. He barely even seemed to notice her struggles.

By the time they reached the second flight, he was behind her, his much bigger body shoving her forward. Whenever she tried to turn or even halt their progress, she slammed back against his muscular thighs and was compelled to move again. Her face was red with exertion and anger. "Do you mean to lock me in my bedroom, like a recalcitrant child?" she asked furiously. They had reached the attic rooms now, and Nye flung the door open and jostled her bodily inside.

"No," he said with a short laugh. "That is *not* my intent." He slammed the door shut behind them and Mina fell back a step. She had not expected him to accompany her inside and was aware her expression showed as much. "Well, what now?" she snapped, hiding her uncertainty behind a show of belligerence and plunking her hands on her hips.

Nye leaned back against the door. "Now I show you just what your extra wifely duties involve," he said mockingly. "Take your clothes off, Mina."

She blinked at him a moment, speechless. "It's the middle of the afternoon!" she pointed out, flinging an arm toward the window.

"And?"

"You can't just march me upstairs—"

"I just did, Mina," he pointed out. "And stop stalling. You're no coward." His voice was warm when he said this, bringing her up short. But if his voice was warm, then the gaze that flickered over her was absolutely scorching. It made her catch her breath.

"Though," he added, cocking his head to one side, "you may be the biggest prude in all Penarth."

Her chin came up at this. "I am not a prude!"

"No?" He unbuttoned his waistcoat. "Then prove me wrong." He shrugged it off. "Need some help?"

Mina huffed and reached for the pearl buttons at the back of her neck. By the time she'd unbuttoned down to her waist, her ire was spent, and she was wishing she hadn't let him call her bluff like this. She *was* a prude. What on earth had possessed her to claim she wasn't?

Her insides turned to jelly, and glancing fearfully at Nye, she found him clad only in a pair of clinging white flannel underpants that extended down to his knees. Her eyes bugged out. She had seen his bare chest before, she told herself sternly. There was simply no need for it to draw her eye like this. Had it really had that scattering of dark hair last time though?

Nye tossed the last of his clothing onto a chair and then sauntered over to her. "How does this work?" he muttered.

"You had better leave it to me," she said, batting away his hands.

"You're too slow," he scolded, spinning her around and making quick work of the remaining buttons.

"You'll have to lift the dress over my head," Mina said hurriedly, feeling him give her skirts a tug. "It'll never go over my stiffened petticoats."

"How the hell do you get in and out of this getup every day by yourself?" Nye muttered as he changed direction and dragged her black gown up instead.

"Needs must," Mina answered, lifting her arms obligingly. "Wait," she puffed. "There's buttons at my wrists." Nye's hand shot out to capture her wrist. She saw him roll his eyes at the long row of buttons, however, due to much washing and re-wearing she knew they weren't stiff. Sure enough, he made quick work of one arm, then the other. "I could do it," she muttered, and his eyebrows lifted, though he made no reply.

"Arms up again," he ordered. Mina complied and the black fabric was dragged over her head and discarded. Nye paused a moment, looking over her prim underwear. Suddenly, Mina felt a touch of uncertainty creep in. The dyed black gowns tended to cast an unfortunate shadow over her white undergarments. She hoped they didn't look gray or badly washed. Before she could voice her concerns, he spun her around again and was unfastening the strings of her uppermost stiffened petticoat.

"It'll be easier if you untie all the petticoats first and then I step out of them at the same time," she advised.

"How many are you wearing?" he growled, tugging at a second lot of strings.

Mina thought a moment. "Four."

He made an exasperated noise in his throat.

"Think yourself lucky," she told him tartly, "that you are not similarly hampered on a daily basis."

He yanked her petticoats down over her hips. "Step out," he advised when he had the stiff fabric down so far as her knees. Mina was forced to set a hand on one burly shoulder before she could follow his advice. He was knelt at her feet with his hands at her waist now, as he frowned over her corset fastenings.

"Let me do it," Mina cautioned, her fingers flying to the hook and eyes down the front. "If you mess with those laces, it'll take

197

me an age to get them right again." Demonstrating her own familiarity with her underpinnings, she was soon out of her stays and hanging them on the back of the chair.

Nye rose back up to his feet. "Let me get a good look at you," he said, placing his hands on his hips and planting his feet as his eyes roamed over the picture she made. Mina stilled, glad of the excuse not to have to strip further. All she had left on her now was her cotton chemise, drawers, black stockings and ankle boots.

It seemed an odd request for him to make, then suddenly, she remembered one of her old pupils, Miss Arabella Plimpton, telling the other girls about her brother's French picture postcards. She had listened along with the others in astonished silence to hear that Bella's brother kept a collection of well-thumbed photographs depicting women clad only in their undergarments.

Mina glanced down, doubtful her own appearance would be as alluring. She felt horribly aware that her underclothes were plain and functional without a frill or furbelow in sight. Even her garters were plain white elastic. She could see no reason for him to dwell with pleasure on the picture she made. They weren't even a nice crisp laundered white these days.

"I'm afraid the black dye of my dresses rather rubs off on things," she said lamely. Looking up, she saw Nye wasn't attending her. His eyes were fixed on her legs, she thought with surprise and wondered why. She looked back down, to check if there was a hole in her stocking.

"Take down your hair," he said in a gravelly voice.

A refusal trembled on her lips, but it seemed silly to cavil after she'd stripped off her clothing at his request. Instead, she reached up hesitant fingers and removed her hairpins, unravelling the roll of hair from her nape. She shook her head and ran her fingers through it, until her hair lay loose over her shoulders.

"Turn around."

"Nye—" she started to object, but he interrupted her.

"Indulge me."

She tutted and turned in a slow circle. "I know for a fact I look nothing like a French dancing girl."

"Like a what?"

"You know," Mina retorted, blushing. "Like one of those picture postcards of women in their drawers."

Nye's expression wavered for a moment. "When did you ever see such a thing?" he asked, holding his hand out to her. He looked a little disconcerted.

"I haven't precisely," she admitted, placing her hand in his. "But I know they exist."

He drew her up against him, one hand resting with great familiarity against her bottom. "How do you know you don't look like one, then?" he asked in a low voice. She thought a thread of amusement ran through his words and looked up sharply at him.

"I just know," she said, her gaze sliding away evasively as her chest rose and fell. Ironically, she felt a good deal more breathless since her corset had been removed.

"I don't think you do," he said, placing his other hand at her waist. His fingers flipped up the edge of her chemise, so his hand slid against her bare skin there, making her jump and bite back an exclamation. He stroked a thumb against the indentation of her waist in a leisurely fashion. Mina shivered.

"Let's get these boots off you and lay you on the bed," he said, and she felt unspeakably relieved he didn't expect her to strip naked. At his urging, she sat on the edge of the mattress as he sat on his haunches and untied her laces, casting the ankle boots aside. He hesitated over her stockings, running his palm up and down her calf. "How do you feel about keeping these on?"

Mina stared at him a moment. "My stockings?"

He nodded. "These need to come off, though," he said, tugging at her white cotton drawers.

Mina's face flamed. *Really?* "Can I take them off under the covers?" she asked stiffly. He shook his head. "Why not?"

"Because I want to do something to you here and now."

"Do something to me?" she echoed croakily. He nodded slowly, his eyes glinting up at her wickedly. "Oh." She cleared her throat. "Very well."

He reached up and loosened the strings at her waist. "Lift up," he ordered. Mina lifted her hips off the bed, and he tugged her white drawers down to her ankles, then whisked them off her altogether. Mina forgot to breathe for a moment. She didn't dare look Nye in the face. She was mortified that he was squatting down like that, at eye level with her most private place. She had never even taken a good look down there herself! His hands were on her knees, urging her to part her legs, and heaven help her before she even realized it, she had obeyed his unspoken demand and opened herself to him.

Suddenly, he let out a harsh groan, and Mina's eyes flew to his. He was staring right between her legs. Her mouth went dry. She almost shrank from him when he lurched forward, slid two big hands under her bare bottom, and dragged her to the edge of the mattress. "Nye," she cried. "What on earth are you—?" She forgot to breathe when he went in face-first.

She let out a soundless squawk as she felt his hot mouth there, her brain refusing to believe the evidence of her own eyes as to Nye's depravity. He couldn't possibly be doing that. Not there. His warm breath against her sensitive skin made her shudder. His wicked tongue parting her cleft and sliding through her folds made her gasp. "Nye!" she squeaked. "What do you think you're doing?"

He just groaned in answer, as though incapable of speech. Which he probably was, she thought as her toes curled and she closed frenzied fingers to the thick dark hair at his nape. For his mouth was pressed to her trembling flesh. His tongue seemed to have found a sensitive spot between her legs that made her vision flicker, and he was lavishing it with enough attention to squeeze all the breath out of her lungs.

Her head lolled back on a choked sob. She writhed against his mouth in an abandonment she could never have believed herself capable of, arching her back and craning for the wicked caress of his mouth where she most needed it. Tears started from her eyes and she realized she was being none too gentle, tugging and pulling at his hair, raising her hips to press herself eagerly against his mouth. He didn't seem to mind though, as his hands squeezed her buttocks, urging her to press closer and closer to his questing tongue.

"Oh Nye!" she squealed. "*Nye!*" Then her vision wavered altogether, and she felt herself swoop over the edge of an altogether different cliff, but instead of being dashed against the rocks below, she turned into sea-foam as light as the air and crested on the bobbing waves.

By the time she surfaced from her stupor, Mina found herself lying in the middle of the bed with Nye lying next to her, his hands squeezing and cupping her naked breasts. Mina blinked and raised her head to find her chemise was gone and the only thing she was wearing was her black stockings with their elastic garters. Why had he left just those on? she wondered in confusion. Her eyes sought his, her gaze uncertain, his intense.

"I had no idea what you were hiding under those drab black gowns, Mrs. Nye," he growled. "If I'd had even a suspicion…" His eyes dropped to where his large tan hands were fondling her full white breasts with their rose-pink tips. Mina made a strangled noise in the back of her throat. Her large bosom had always been something of a trial to her. In classical art, the statues and paintings showed women with perky high bosoms. She'd long ago realized hers were not like those idealized depictions.

It was a good thing she still felt drowsy and sated, she realized dimly at the back of her mind, or she would die with mortification at the way he was squeezing and toying with her now.

"You don't need all that whalebone, Mina," he said huskily. "Flattening you out from chest to hip. You must be pinching these beauties half to death." He cocked a quizzical eye at her.

Oh God, he expected her to speak to him while he did these things to her, she realized. With effort, she concentrated on his words. "I…well…" She licked her lips. "Mama always said a decent woman should—" She bit off her words with a smothered squeak as he pinched one of her nipples between finger and thumb.

"I'm guessing your mother wasn't built like you," he said, lowering his head and kissing it better.

202

"N-no," she agreed, remembering Mama's dainty figure. "Not at all."

He sucked her nipple into his hot mouth. Mina gasped. "Wh-what are you doing?"

He ran his tongue around the tip before releasing it. "I'm consoling your poor, abused bosom," he said, moving to the other breast and repeating the process. "After you've been so cruel to it."

She fell back against the pillows. Why did she feel the pull of his mouth between her legs? she wondered with a faint whimper. "What do you mean, cruel?" she forced herself to ask as he shifted over her, inserting one hard thigh between her legs and licking the undersides of her breasts, making her shiver. She knew her wits were scattered right now, but she was sure he wasn't making any sense!

"Smothering them all day long under that constricting corset," he said huskily from the valley between her breasts as he alternated pressing kisses from one to the other. She blinked down at him. "I'm going to be very, very kind to these poor, maltreated breasts," he said with a wink that flustered her. He was teasing her, she thought, but she was unable to muster up even a semblance of resentment about it. With a muffled groan, she arched up, pressing her core shamelessly against his muscled thigh. Oh God, why did that seem to give relief? She shuddered, trying to stop herself from repeating the motion.

Giving a lie to his words, she suddenly felt Nye's teeth close about her sensitive nipple and gave a startled scream. "It's not kind to bite!" she huffed, grabbing the hair at the back of his head and tugging him back.

He ignored her hair pulling and laved her nipple lavishly with his tongue. "Haven't you ever heard of being cruel to be kind?" he groaned. "Ah, Mina."

If he had any respect for her, she thought, he would certainly not be treating her in such a fashion. Unfortunately, she didn't have enough breath to upbraid him about it right now. She was too busy rubbing herself against his hard thigh like a wanton.

"Nye!" she whimpered. He released his grip on one breast and inserted his hand between them, running it down her flat stomach and between her legs. "Nye!" Her head came off the pillow.

"You're nice and wet down here," he said with approval. The slide of his fingers was downright scandalous. His words penetrated the fog that was on her mind right now. *Wet?* Her gaze snapped to his.

"F-from your mouth?" she faltered, realizing she was wet down there. Very wet. She could even hear it. Her ears burned at the lewd sound.

He smiled slowly. "No, this is all you."

She squirmed and felt one big finger slide right inside her. "*Oh!*" He snared her startled gaze as he added a second finger, stretching her and making her wince.

"I can feel it," he grunted with surprise. At Mina's questioning gaze, he added, "Your virginity."

If her cheeks weren't stained scarlet already, they were now. "Nye," she reproached him. "Ow!" She felt his fingers moving ruthlessly inside her. It stung. "Did you just—?" Did he just take her maidenhead with his fingers?

"It would just have been in my way," he replied, and she felt the burn as he added a third finger. Mina winced.

"It's too much," she whined, for the first time not enjoying his ministrations.

"You haven't seen my cock yet," he said wryly.

"Nye!" At her shocked gasp, he shifted again over her. Now it wasn't his thigh between her legs, but his hips. Mina felt the hard bulge pressed against her stomach with trepidation. He still wore the soft worn flannel underpants, but something was spilling over the waistband, bumping against her, demanding attention.

Before she could get too worried, his mouth was back on hers again, hot and wet. Mina's senses reeled. She clutched his shoulders, drove her fingers back into his hair. Her hard nipples rubbed against the dark hair of his chest. It both thrilled and horrified her how much she enjoyed the sensation.

He tore his mouth from hers. "Call me Will when I'm inside you," he said gruffly.

"Will?"

That got his attention. "Yes?"

"I'm just trying it out," she explained breathlessly.

"I'm not inside you yet, Mina," he pointed out.

"Your fingers are," she argued, then felt mortified she'd pointed it out.

"Yes, they are," he growled in wolfish agreement. "I'm going to replace them now with this." He grabbed her hand from his hair and dragged it down to press against the thick tumescent flesh of his manhood. Her eyes flew wide as he dragged her fingers up and down his broad length. *Oh dear*, thought Mina. This was never going to work. She had to stifle an instinctive refusal to even try.

Mina stiffened her resolve. Certainly, she was a fully grown woman and more than a match for the likes of William Nye! 'Twas only fear of the unknown making her quail and quake like this. He released her hand to drag down his underwear, freeing himself from the confines of the flannel. Mina kept her hand curved around him, her breath coming fast. It felt so strange. She had never known anything like it. Almost she wanted to demand a good look at it, but Nye's big body was in the way, crowding her view. She stared at his chest which heaved as though he was running a race. She wondered at it, remembering how he had carried up that cliff without breaking a sweat.

Then he shifted again, withdrew his fingers from her depths, and cupped her mound, stroking his thumb through her curls. "I'm going to enjoy this part more than you, Mina," he admitted roughly. "I've prepared you as much as I can, but you're unused and it's going to be a tight fit."

"Yes," she murmured; she'd heard that much about joinings. "I'm ready."

He shifted over her again, glancing down between them as he adjusted himself to position against her entrance. She squeezed her thighs against his hips as she braced herself. "Relax," he urged her. "Let me in."

She breathed out, nodded her head, and felt him surge forward. Her eyes widened. He hadn't exaggerated. It was going to be a struggle to take him. And oh, it burned.

"Oh God, Mina," he groaned in a strangled voice. "You're so tight."

206

She whimpered, not with pleasure this time. *Ouch*. Her hands flew to his sides and she sank her fingers into his lean hips.

"Just bear with it," he ground out. "I'll go as slow as I can."

She pressed the back of one of her hands to her mouth to suppress a cry trying to force its way out.

"You're doing so well," he praised her and to her surprise, lowered his face to kiss her upraised palm. "*Mina*," he whispered. She was just marveling that he'd never been so gentle with her, when a brutal twist of his hips seated him so deeply within her, they both cried out in unison. Their ragged breaths intermingled a moment as Mina's indignation blazed hot at such rough treatment.

"Say it now," he entreated shakily.

He wanted his name now? Mina seethed. "You nasty brute, Will Nye!" she upbraided him, panting. "That was not slow!"

He gave a breathless laugh. "Does it hurt really bad?"

"I feel like you've buried a sword into my belly!" she flung at him accusingly.

"Oh God, Mina love," he moaned. "You're just going to make things worse for yourself."

"What are you talking about—?" she started, but his hand was at the back of her neck and the next thing she knew his mouth was crushed to hers, his tongue thrusting into her mouth, choking off all words. When he drew back, his eyes were ablaze.

"You're just making me hotter for you," he said thickly, then thrust his hips again, making her gasp.

Mina regarded him speechlessly. Her words were inflaming him? "You're mad!"

"And you're tight," he groaned. "So bloody tight, I'm going to lose my mind." Suddenly, his hand was at her knee, urging her to lift it.

"Wha—?"

"Wrap it around my back." His words were tersely spoken. She had only just rested her heel against the small of his back when he thrust again with a loud, shuddering groan. "Red stockings," he gritted.

Mina was telling herself it did not hurt so much now. She felt alarmingly full and stretched to capacity but not in pain precisely. She frowned. "Red stockings?" she repeated.

"I want you in them."

What? "Why?"

"And lace," he grunted as he settled into a bruising rhythm. "Lots and lots of lace."

Mina's head bumped back against the pillow as he labored above her, grunting and groaning, doing his best to bounce her off the mattress. His hands settled once again, beneath her bare bottom, urging her closer still every time he surged into her.

Broken words and phrases fell from his lips, but she decided not to press him for any meaning. She still hadn't recovered from the prospect of red stockings. The bed swayed and creaked and the brass bedstead smacked against the wall.

Mina was suddenly profoundly grateful it was early. That meant neither Edna nor Ivy would be a-bed to hear the racket they were making. Finally, with a bellow, Nye collapsed on top of her. Without thinking, she closed her arms around him, and the

208

only sound for several minutes was their mutually labored breathing.

Finally, Nye rolled off her with a groan and flung an arm across his face. Mina lay there a moment, her body still trembling in the aftermath. With a sudden curse, he sat up and grabbed her nightgown off the bottom of the bed.

"Don't you dare—" she managed to get out before he leaned over and wiped her with it between her legs.

"It's really all it's good for," he said with a twisted smile and slung her poor, maligned nightgown over the side of the bed. She eyed him with as much annoyance as she could muster, which admittedly was not much.

Even he seemed surprised. "Come on, schoolteacher, is that all you've got?"

"Pass me the bedsheets," she huffed, too tired to even make a grab for them.

To her surprise, he reached down and drew them over them both as he shifted into her. "Reach down and take off your stockings."

In truth, Mina had forgotten all about her stockings. To her surprise, Nye did not relinquish his hold of her while she bent her leg and slipped them off. As he did not let go, she was forced to simply ball them up and throw them similarly over the side of the bed. She wondered if he had been serious about the red stockings and blushed.

Nye yawned on the pillow next to her, and Mina angled her head back to try to look at him. "I thought you didn't sleep," she reminded him.

"I don't. You've worn me out. Demanding woman."

Mina huffed and faced back forward again. *Ridiculous man.* Nye's body was warm against her back and the weight of his arm around her waist was strangely comforting. She would just close her eyes for ten minutes, she told herself as her eyelids dropped down. Just ten minutes and she would get back up and see about those bathroom tiles.

13

When next she woke it was to the sound of raindrops on the windowpane. Persistent raindrops. Raindrops that must surely be hailstones, she thought as one pinged violently off the glass. Then she sat up, dislodging Nye's sleepy embrace. Someone was throwing stones up at the window. Mina hesitated, then turned and shook her husband's shoulder.

"Nye!" she said in a low urgent voice. "William Nye!" Once again, he was out cold. She raised her voice. "Nye, wake up!" She looked around vexedly as a shower of stones struck against the window this time. "For goodness' sake!" Sliding out from under the blankets, she remembered belatedly she was nude. Clicking her tongue, Mina crept over to the chest of drawers where she had a spare nightgown and retrieved it. A loud ping from the window had her drawing in a sharp breath and hurrying over to draw back the curtains and fling the casement open.

"Stop that at once!" she hissed down to the dark courtyard below. "Just stop it!"

A single torch burned in the courtyard below, and she could make out a few shadowy figures huddled round it. They looked to have scarves pulled over the lower parts of their faces.

"We need your man down here now," a rough-sounding voice harangued her. "Send him down, woman."

"I am trying to wake him," Mina answered coldly. "Once I have roused him, I will be sure to send him down. Kindly refrain from throwing stones at my window."

A grunt which she took to be of assent answered her, and Mina slammed the window shut. *Uncouth louts*, she thought, pursing her lips. Bandying words with her at this time of night! Groping for the matches on the side, she soon struck a flame lighting the candle in her holder. Picking up her father's watch, she found it to be half past two in the morning. With a startled exclamation, she turned back to the bed and saw Nye had not moved an inch.

Really, once he was asleep, he slept like the dead. She crossed to the bed once more and commenced shaking him like a dog with a rat. "Nye! Will Nye! Wake up this instant!" She was forced to bawl in his ear when nothing else made an impression.

His eyes flickered open at last. "Mina," he murmured thickly. "Get back into bed."

"I most certainly will not! There's a bunch of ruffians in the courtyard below, demanding your immediate presence!"

His eyes, which had been drifting shut again, reopened. "The yard?" He struggled up onto one elbow. "What?"

Mina darted to the chair to gather up his discarded clothes. "They need you below."

"Time is it?" Nye slurred, rubbing at his eyes. He drew his knees up and moved sluggishly to a seated position.

"An ungodly hour! It's half-past two in the morning," Mina hissed at him. "Your confederates seem to have no consideration for anyone but themselves!"

"Half-past two?" he repeated, seeming dumbstruck for a moment, then he swore under his breath and flung back the covers. She darted forward with his clothes and dumped them on the bed next to him. "Get back under the covers," he told her as he stood up to dress. Mina hesitated, wanting to say something about the nefarious business he was clearly caught

212

up in. As though guessing what was on her mind, he turned and scowled at her. "I won't tell you twice," he warned.

Mina bristled, but decided discretion was the better part of valor. She clambered back into the bed and turned her back to him as he pulled on his clothes, muttering under his breath ill-naturedly the whole while. When he stomped from the room, taking the candle with him, she rolled onto her back and stared up at the ceiling. Well, that was that then. Her suspicions had not been the result of an overactive imagination. Her husband was in league with a smuggler's gang.

She wrestled with the problem for the next hour and a half, waiting for him to return. Finally, she dropped off to sleep, and when she woke again at seven, she was still alone in the bed. For some reason, that fact filled her with annoyance. So, he thought only to share a bed with her when he wanted *that*, did he? She seethed as she pulled on her clothes.

Embarrassingly, almost every item of clothing now made her think of Nye. Her corset made her remember he thought it too confining, her stockings too plain, her garters basic and unadorned. Dragging her hair back to pin at her nape, she stared at herself in the mirror. She was no dancing girl, she thought bitterly. But she was a wife now. The tenderness between her legs reminded her that there could no longer be any question of annulment. Yesterday's romp in the sheets had put paid to that. She was in truth and fact married to an out-and-out scoundrel and a lawbreaker.

She pinned her father's watch chain to her bodice with an ugly cameo brooch that had belonged to her paternal grandmother. Apparently, it depicted her great-grandfather's profile. He had a Roman nose and a jutting chin, and Mina only ever wore it when she was in a bad mood. She slipped the watch into the concealed pocket at her waist and surveyed the result. *There, the very picture of respectability*, she told herself in her dull black gown. For some reason she did not derive from that the satisfaction which she felt she ought.

She found Edna in the kitchen, who took one look at her and pulled out a chair for her at the kitchen table and poured her a cup of tea without once mentioning taking it in the parlor.

"Look like you're in need of a strong cup of tea, Mrs. Nye," she said dourly.

"I am, Edna," Mina agreed. "But I'll just take a quick wash in the scullery first." She slipped through and gave herself a hurried wash. She'd need a bath later too, she thought with a grimace. "Church tomorrow," she observed, raising her voice so Edna could hear her in the kitchen. "And when we get back, I shall help you with the Sunday lunches again." She was surprised when Edna didn't answer, and refastening her cuffs, she walked back through to the kitchen. "Edna?"

To her surprise, Nye was dominating the kitchen with his presence, leaning against the sink, a confrontational gleam in his eye. She started almost guiltily on sight of him, but quickly recovered herself, walking over to the kitchen table to take her seat there.

Edna sent her a pinched look of alarm, but Mina hastened to give her a bright smile of reassurance. "Nye and I have come to a new agreement about my duties," she said in a pointed tone, then raised her cup to her lips and took a sip of slightly stewed tea. Setting it down again, she lifted her eyes to find Nye's narrowed at her.

"This morning," she added firmly in a voice that carried, "I mean to scrub that bathroom upstairs until it's gleaming. Then when I am done, I shall take a bath."

214

Edna gulped the last of her tea, as though she could not get away from the tense atmosphere fast enough. "Yes, Mrs. Nye," she said uncertainly. "Now, if you'll excuse me, I'll get back to stripping them beds."

Mina nodded. "I have some laundry of my own to do this afternoon," she said absently, thinking of her abused nightgown and the bedsheet with its telling smear of blood. She didn't want anyone else's hands scrubbing those clean.

At Edna's hasty withdrawal, Nye walked over to the table. He stopped beside her and waited there until she lifted her eyes to meet his again.

"Seems I've forgotten the terms of our 'agreement,'" he bit out. "Maybe you should remind me of them."

"Very well," she said determinedly. "Now our marriage stands proven both in terms of deed and fact, I shall pick up any household duties I see fit."

He hissed out a breath. "Is that so?"

"It is," she said, raising her teacup to her lips again.

His gaze flickered a moment, then he shrugged. "Seems fair," he said, immediately setting her on her guard.

"It does?" Her eyes darted to his suspiciously.

He nodded again thoughtfully. "You can lord it over household matters," he said generously. "As I mean to be master where it counts most."

"And where's that?" Mina asked doggedly, though she already had a dim suspicion which direction he was heading in his thinking.

"In my bed," he said richly.

"*Your* bed?" Mina huffed. "I don't even know where that is."

He snorted. "You've slept in it since our wedding night."

Her mouth dropped open. "That's your bedroom?"

He looked amused. "Who else's?"

"But…" Her mind spun. "The bed didn't even have any sheets on it!"

He shrugged again. "I told you, I don't sleep."

She gave a derisive snort. "For someone who doesn't sleep, I've never met anyone harder to rouse from slumber than you, Will Nye!"

Annoyingly, as soon as the words had left her mouth, she felt herself blush hotly, remembering the last time she had called him Will. The only time he had bade her call him it. Setting her cup down, she pushed the saucer away and made to stand. His hand on her shoulder prevented her.

"Stay there a minute," he growled. "Unless you want me to drag you into the scullery."

"The scullery?"

"Or maybe bend you over this table," he said huskily.

Mina blinked. *What?* "Bend me over…" Her words trailed off as she noticed the stormy look on his face. Involuntarily, her gaze transferred to the scratched wooden surface. Surely he wasn't serious?

Noticing the direction of her gaze, he growled, and half hauled her out of her chair. "You think I wouldn't?"

"Of course you wouldn't!" she flung at him, but even she could hear an element of doubt had crept into her voice. "It would be vastly uncomfortable for us both, I imagine!" she added, desperately striving for calm.

"No," he disagreed in a low voice, turning her around and shoving her forward against the table. A big hand planted in the center of her back, pushing her down so she was leaning over the surface. "You'd be on your front, like this, and I…" He stepped up neatly behind her, caging her in from the back. "I'd be here, between your legs. Taking you from behind." She felt the hard press of his body on the backs of her legs and felt a surge of panic and something else.

She braced her palms against the tabletop. "Nye!" Her voice rang out, shocked, with the tiniest hint of fear. It pulled him up short. "You'll be master in the bedroom," she said quickly. "But not here, *please* not here."

He stepped back at once, and Mina drew a quick, steadying breath before she turned to face him. She couldn't quite bring herself to meet his eyes. Suddenly, his hand was under chin, forcing her head up. He was silent a moment as he gazed searchingly into her eyes.

"I came on too strong," he said gruffly, releasing her chin and drawing her into his body. His hand shifted up and down her spine in a comforting gesture.

"Perhaps a little," she agreed shakily.

"I sometimes forget," he admitted, exhaling, "how untried you are." He paused. "It's that bold mouth of yours. It leads me astray."

"*I* lead you astray?"

"Yes, you." He moved his head forward to rest his brow against hers for the briefest of moments.

Mina heaved a great sigh of relief when he turned abruptly on his heel and left the kitchen. She could only hope and pray that he never realized the fear she had felt was not of him, but of her own reaction to him.

14

Mina spent a good three hours scrubbing away at the porcelain tiles in the bathroom and was inordinately pleased when the black and white floor tiles shined up as well as the mingled green and patterned tiles on the wall.

She was exhausted by the time she turned her attention to the enormous roll top bath. Along the bottom lay a thick layer of dust, and she could only guess that since the number of maids had so drastically reduced, no one ever bothered to use it anymore as it would take an age to fill. Doubtless everyone simply used the smaller hip bath, as she had done also on that previous occasion.

Gritting her teeth, she finally turned to the pretty matching washstand and forced herself to finish the job. The palms of her hands felt raw from the abrasive suds, and she was just swilling the last of the soapy water from the basin when the door squeaked open and Edna appeared with two buckets of steaming water.

"I've been boiling water for your bath," she said, carrying them in.

"Oh Edna, you're a treasure," said Mina thankfully.

"You've made a lovely job in here, Mrs. Nye," Edna responded, looking around admiringly.

"Thank you. No, not in there," Mina interrupted her when Edna made for the large bath. She pulled a face. "I can't face the thought of how many journeys up and down the stairs that would take."

Edna smiled grimly. "It's a monster of a tub, and no mistake," she agreed. "We all just tends to use this 'un." She emptied the buckets into the smaller hip bath.

"I'm not surprised."

"I'll fetch another two up and that ought to do it."

"Are you sure, Edna? Did you finish stripping the rooms?"

"We only had two overnight guests last night," Edna assured her before scurrying out.

By the time Mina climbed into her tub she wasn't fit to do much more than soak, though she just about mustered the energy to wash her hair before the water turned cold.

She spent a quiet afternoon in the parlor, letting her hair dry before the fire with a bunch of mending at her feet. She had mended the tears in her skirt from her cliff mishap and was just darning the heel of a stocking when she heard the hurried knock on the door.

"Come in," she called.

The door opened and Edna came in bearing a tray with a piece of roast beef. "The master's taking supper with you this evening," she said briskly, setting it down on the dining table before disappearing again to reenter with a bowl of roast parsnips and another of green beans.

"Oh?" Mina glanced at her watch and found it was already six o'clock. "I had not realized it was so late," she said, climbing to her feet. "Is there anything I can do?"

Edna set the vegetables down and shook her head. "He'll be delayed a minute or two," she said. "Only he's just had someone deliver a telegram from the receiving office in St. Ives."

"I see," said Mina, taking a seat at the table. She wondered if she should carve, or if Nye would consider that his province. Edna fetched in a bottle of red wine and a beautiful cut glass carafe to decant it into. Mina exclaimed over this and examined its etchings. "This is lovely."

Edna shot her an enigmatic look. "Seems he's got a few things out of storage since your wedding, Mrs. Nye."

Mina felt herself flush. She didn't care to remember that awful ceremony. Had Edna been there that night in the church to witness her humiliation? She bit her lip, somewhat disconcerted at the idea. Edna bustled back in with a bowl of mashed potatoes and a gravy boat.

"If you don't mind, Mrs. Nye, I'll be going up to my room after this. I've some embroidery I'd like to finish for my aunt's birthday—"

"Of course, Edna," Mina interrupted her. "I can clear away after our meal."

"Oh no, Mrs. Nye!" said Edna, sounding shocked. "You just leave it on the side for me to deal with in the morning."

"We're off to church first thing in the morning," Mina reminded her. "I can certainly wash up afterward."

Edna looked pleased and left the room with a hurried "good night." Mina guessed she was making herself scarce before Nye appeared. She sat a moment twiddling her thumbs, before deciding to go ahead and carve the meat. When she had done that, she uncorked the wine and poured it into the pretty carafe.

She had just laid her napkin down in her lap when Nye strode into the room with a heavy frown on his face and a piece of paper still in his hand. He stared at the table a moment blankly as though he'd forgotten he was even taking a meal. Then with a small start, he sat down opposite Mina and cleared his throat.

"Not bad news, I hope," Mina said, nodding to the telegram he still held.

His brooding expression became more marked. "It's a damnable nuisance," he growled.

Mina's thoughts flew to smuggling, but surely their operation would not be so brazen as to send wires publicly.

With a quick shake of his head, Nye stood up and reached for the roast beef dish, first placing some on Mina's plate and then his own. "It's about a fight to be held next week," he explained grudgingly. "The venue's fallen through and they want to have it here."

Mina spooned some mash onto her plate. "You hold them here fairly regularly, do you not?" she asked with a raised brow.

"No more than once a month," Nye answered tersely. "Usually less. We've never had two in one calendar month!"

"I see." She set the bowl down and reached for the green beans. "Would it inconvenience you greatly?"

Nye gave her a disconcertingly straight look. "It means a house full of strangers," he said bluntly. "Coming from all directions."

"I see."

He gave a short, mirthless laugh. "I doubt you do somehow."

"Doubtless it will mean a good deal of work for Edna," Mina said mildly. "Making up all the bedrooms again for use."

He grimaced. "Aye."

"Well," said Mina cautiously as she reached for the gravy boat. "I could always help—"

"You're to stay out of the way, Mina," he said angrily, slamming his hand down on the table and making her jump.

Color flooded to her cheeks. "I only—"

"I mean it," he interrupted her rudely. "You're to keep out of my business altogether."

Mina froze, then set the gravy boat back down with a thump. She took one breath, then another, then rose shakily from her chair.

"Sit back down!" he ordered her.

Mina glared at him. "There would be little point," she said icily. "As I have completely lost my appetite."

He narrowed his eyes at her, and they both stared a moment in silence. Nye's hand on the table tightened into a fist. "Please sit back down," he ground out. Seeing the effort it cost him, Mina lowered herself back into the chair, though she did not relax her affronted expression one bit. Her own hand trembled as she reached for her water glass.

"Will you take wine?" he asked gruffly.

"No, thank you," Mina answered.

He poured her a glass anyway, which Mina resolutely ignored.

"Eat your dinner," he bit out.

Mina's temper flared, but she picked up her fork and stabbed a green bean with it. She hated him. He was an impossible brute. No wonder Edna fled from him every chance she got.

"I mean it for your own good," he added in a surly voice. Mina gave no reaction. She swallowed a mouthful of potatoes only by sheer force of will. She did not want him to think his actions affected her in the slightest. He was nothing to her, nothing at all. She tasted little of the five mouthfuls she managed to force down, and the atmosphere at table was oppressive to say the least.

Nye ate a hearty meal in heavy silence, then at the end of it he flung down his napkin and gave her an accusatory look. Mina stared stonily at some point on the wall past his right ear. After a moment, he dragged his chair back and exited the room, slamming the door so hard that Mina clapped her hands over her ears. *Mannerless lout*, she seethed as she started stacking the bowls and plates.

It seemed there was only one place she was welcome as far as Nye was concerned, and that was in his bed. Thinking of the return of that prizefighting rabble made her face flame. They would be the same crowd that watched the travesty that had played out the night she had arrived at The Merry Harlot. Only Effie had been kind. As for the rest of them, she was sure they were as bad as Nye himself. She carried the plates and bowls through to the kitchen, her ears craning to catch the murmur of voices in the bar but hearing nothing. She washed and dried and put away before returning to the parlor room and defiantly tossing down the glass of red wine she had shunned earlier. Hopefully, it would help her relax enough to fall asleep. After a hurried wash in the scullery alcove, she climbed the stairs, undressed, and pulled the covers over her head.

When next she woke it was because Nye was climbing into the bed behind her with a whispered curse as he fought to untuck the sheets cocooned around her body. She sucked in a harsh breath when he dragged her against him. He was chilled to the bone. He wrestled with the uncooperative blankets a moment, before dropping onto his back and dragging her over him as if she were the quilt. He gave a loud, satisfied groan when she was fully plastered over him.

She puffed out an irritated breath. "You're cold," she grumbled. He had been out and about, though no decent body had cause to be at this time of night.

"So warm me up."

She gasped when he grabbed her nightgown at the neck and tugged it aside to bury his face in her neck. "You'll tear it!"

"Best thing that could happen to the ugly thing," he said rudely as he rubbed his stubble against her skin.

"It's draughty up here," she pointed out. "And it keeps me warm."

"Take it off."

"It's cold!"

"Take it off," he insisted gruffly. "I want to feel your breasts against me."

She tutted and rubbed her chest against his. "You can," she stated crossly. He was naked, she realized, and not drunk in the slightest. Her body was only covered in a thin layer of cotton.

"Your bare tits," he growled.

"You're such a pig," she huffed. "It's all tangled around my legs, Nye. I'm not—"

"For God's sake!" he growled, bouncing up and dislodging all their covers.

"Nye!"

225

He grabbed at the hem of her nightgown and dragged it up to her waist. "Sit up!"

"It's too cold to be naked!" she complained in a furious undertone as he hauled it over her head and flung it to the end of the bed. "You selfish brute!"

He planted a hand against her breastbone and shoved her back against the pillows, before reaching behind him to grab the covers and drag them back up over them. "Open your legs," he grunted as he dropped down on top of her.

"I hate you!" she grumbled, even as she felt the familiar tingle through her limbs as he pressed all his hard, muscular flesh up against her between her legs. And he was hard. She nearly groaned aloud feeling his manhood bobbing against her thigh. He just grunted an acknowledgment as his hands sought out her breasts, cupping and making out their shape.

"I hate you too," he groaned then leaned down to rub his face over her unbound breasts. "God," he whispered against her nipple, then took it in his mouth and began sucking her.

"Nye!" Mina whimpered. He gave a satisfied moan, then moved to her other nipple, wrapping his tongue around it and drawing it into his hot mouth. With horror, Mina realized she was grinding her hips against him. Her conscious mind told her to stop it at once, but her flushed body wasn't listening. "Nye," she groaned again, arching her back up as she tried to press even closer.

"Thought you didn't like me," he said with a husky laugh as he rocked his hips against hers, increasing the friction. His hardness rubbed against her, making her breath quicken.

"I don't," she panted. "Not at all."

226

"That so?" he asked, sliding one hand down her belly. "You don't want my fingers then?"

Oh God, his fingers... She squeezed her eyes shut. "No?" she lied.

His hand halted their slide through the curls between her legs, making her whine. "No?" he repeated. "You sure about that, sweetheart?"

Mina's eyes snapped open and she glared at him. "No," she said stubbornly, and to her horror, his hand dropped away.

"Fine," he said with a shrug. "You're the one who'll suffer for it."

"What do you mean by that?"

"My cock won't mind, but your little pussy's used to me being more considerate."

Mina's eyes widened with alarm.

He cocked his head to one side. "Maybe you'd like my mouth instead?" he teased.

Mina stared at him. Against her wishes, her eyes dropped to his mouth. Did he mean to kiss her or...?

He gave a low laugh. "You're such an innocent, Mina," he mocked.

"Not anymore," she reminded him bitterly. "Thanks to you!"

"Please, I've barely touched you," he said, shifting down her body. "You liked this last time, so I don't see why this time should be any different?"

"Nye—what are you?" Suddenly she felt his hot breath between her legs and his big hands urging her thighs apart. Mina gave an alarmed squeal as she felt his tongue at her slit. "Nye—don't!" She shuddered and tried to close her legs when he started lapping wetly, but his head was firmly wedged between her thighs. He gave a low rumble of approval in his chest and wrapped his arms around her thighs, holding her firmly in place as his lascivious hot mouth sucked and licked her with every evidence of indecent pleasure. Mina gave a strangled cry and fell back on the pillows. *Oh my God.* She had hoped that her reaction last time had been some kind of aberration. But no, it felt just as good this time. She crammed her fingers into her mouth in an attempt to stifle the broken cries trying to force their way out of her throat. Biting on her bottom lip so hard she tasted blood, she felt the same wetness between her legs as last time and Nye's groan of pleasure that greeted it. "Nye!" she panted. "Oh God, oh God, have mercy!"

Her cheeks burned and the muscles in her thighs strained, but she was no longer sure they were working to escape that wicked mouth, but rather to her shame in collusion with it. "Nye, oh God!" she sobbed brokenly. He gave a growl and released one thigh to bring his fingers to gently spread her cleft. Mina's cheeks flooded with color as she stared down to find his gaze intent on her glistening pink folds. Then he started tonguing her pearl and her body arched up. "Nye!" she gasped. "Nye! Oh! OH!" He groaned again, the vibration shot through her core, and Mina's soul fled with a heartfelt scream right out of her wanton body and flew straight through the ceiling and into the celestial sky above where it floated weightlessly a moment among the stars, serene and blissful. When it drifted back down moments later into her sinful body, it found her collapsed and trembling against the sheets, tears rolling down her cheeks as Nye still lazily lapped at her with his strong, swirling tongue.

Finally, he stopped, his breath heavy and rasping against her tender flesh. "Well, hell," he said, smacking his lips. "I think I enjoyed that almost as much as you did."

Mina whimpered, boneless as he slid back up her body.

"Ah, but you're a hot piece, Mina," he said, spreading her open with his thumbs as he thrust inside her with a grunt. He shut his eyes a moment and drew a ragged breath as Mina gasped in shock to find herself crammed full of his big, throbbing shaft. She was so wet; his cock was sliding home almost without resistance despite his girth. She opened her mouth to protest at such rude treatment, but to her shock, a low moan was all that came out. His eyes flickered open and he gave her a wicked grin that should have been infuriating, but for whatever reason, seeing it made her feel even more heated. "That's it," he said. "Get wet for me, Mina." He licked his lips. "I almost wish I could taste it," he groaned. "But it feels so good wrapped around my cock. Such a tight, wet pussy. And I think it's starting to realize who's master here."

Mina's eyes widened. "You obnoxious—" He flexed his hips to slide the last couple of inches home, making her break off with a groan. "Oh Nye!"

"That's it," he grunted. "I want to see those breasts jiggle when I take you."

Mina closed her eyes. "I wish you wouldn't talk!" she groaned. "You're so offensive!"

He laughed softly against her ear. "Oh really? But your sweet cunt is grasping me so tightly." He thrust against her and Mina bit her lip, resisting the impulse to shout.

"Are you going to stay quiet?" he whispered in her ear. "I don't mind, seeing as how you've already screamed for me tonight."

He thrust again, and she nearly jolted up off the mattress at the sensation of pleasure coiling low in her belly. She shivered and her fingers tightened on the bedsheets as he loomed above her, his eyes half shut with pleasure as his hips pounded into her. "Oh God, Mina," he groaned. "If you knew how good your silky cunt felt on my cock."

But she already knew. Her head tossed against the pillow as she tried to fight the rising tide of sensation. Her knees pressed into his sides as she squeezed her eyes shut against the pleasure. "Nye," she gasped.

"Come on, Mina." His voice throbbed. "I want you mindless again. I need it."

"Oh God, I—Nye—I—" Her hips shifted restlessly as he hammered into her; the slick sounds their bodies made as they moved together were shamefully exciting. She was so wet, her yielding pussy was giving his big cock barely any resistance as he pushed in and out, her suctioning flesh pressing and gripping him as he ruthlessly plunged into her depths.

He gave a low, dirty groan. "If you don't give it to me soon—" His gleaming eyes returned to her full, bouncing breasts, and he adjusted his position so he could take one of her nipples into his mouth again and give it a hard suck. She felt the tug of his hot mouth everywhere and with a startled cry she crashed over the edge.

Five minutes later, when she surfaced groggily from mindlessness, Mina could not really bring herself to feel awkward about the fact she was naked and lying flush against Nye's big, muscular body. He was a nasty beast, she thought as her eyes drifted shut. But he was warm, and after the physical intimacy they had just shared, it was oddly comforting having him there in the bed next to her. Why he would stay afterward when he couldn't even sleep was beyond her, but before she could ponder it for too long, she had slipped into a deep sleep.

15

At church the next morning, Mina was sure she had a lot more nods and cautious good mornings thrown her way. She smiled and nodded in return and enjoyed the walk home in the fresh air with the sun breaking through the clouds and the sky very blue, although the air was still brisk. She and Edna worked side by side once more over the Sunday roast dinners and afterward took their meal together in the kitchen where they conversed easily over a wide range of topics from Edna's aunt's taste in curtains to Mina's experience stitching samplers.

It had been Mina's intention to take a walk along the beach that afternoon, but she had forgotten how long it took to clear away after the meals, and in the end, she and Edna brought their sewing into the kitchen and sat together companionably over their work. Mina did tentatively suggest retiring to the parlor for the afternoon, but Edna looked scandalized, so she quickly gave that idea up. Edna was making herself a new dress for her days out from a flowered calico and Mina had more mending to do.

Many cups of tea were drunk, and Mina's repairs were all mended by the end of their session, and she had even embroidered a handkerchief with her new initials—MN—and a spray of flowers motif that Edna showed her using daisy stitches.

"It's very pretty," Mina said, holding up the square of fabric and admiring the effect. "I believe I shall have to do my other handkerchiefs now to match."

"You could change up the color of the flowers for variety," Edna suggested. "I've some spare colored thread if you have none."

"Thank you, but there's a good quantity in the workbox Nye gave me," Mina remembered. She set her small scissors aside after trimming off a bit of loose thread. "Has he mentioned yet that he is hosting another prizefight here this week?" she asked.

Edna's expression tightened. "Aye, he did." She clicked her tongue. "I'm not saying they don't bring a good deal of business to his door, for they do. But a more disorderly mob you'd be hard-pressed to find." She shook her head. "No better than a pack of heathens."

"As bad as that?" Mina asked in some alarm.

Edna tossed her head so hard she nearly lost her mobcap. "Cutthroats and guttersnipes and scarlet women," she said, lowering her voice over the latter. "Ungodly lot, steeped in wickedness and sin."

Mina blinked, remembering Effie in her scarlet dress. "Some of them must have redeeming qualities," she murmured, remembering she still had the redhead's cream scarf which had been used for a makeshift bridal veil. If Effie was among their number, she could return it to her, she thought, cheering up. "I remember one among them who did me a kindness."

Edna's expression wavered. "Well," she conceded reluctantly, "I suppose even wrongdoers have the occasional good impulse, just as the good flock do sometimes have wicked ones."

"It is not always as cut and dried as we would like," Mina agreed, thinking of her suspicions about Nye and the smuggling trade. She wasn't quite sure where her duty lay in that respect and it troubled her. Of course, she had no proof of her

233

suspicions and a wife couldn't testify against her husband in any case. Still, she felt uneasy whenever she did happen to think of it.

It occurred to Mina that she had not seen Ivy for a couple of days, and she realized that since Nye had started sleeping in the attic, neither of the two maids came to her bedroom anymore. She tapped lightly on Ivy's door before she went to bed. She had just started to turn away, thinking the maid must be behind the bar already, when the door opened, and a flush-faced Ivy answered it.

"Oh Mina—I mean, Mrs. Nye," she corrected herself, looking around in a furtive manner.

"Is everything alright, Ivy?"

"Oh yes, I mean, Master Nye let me come up to my room with a headache. He said he'd tend bar tonight."

"Oh, I see and how are you feeling now, Ivy? You do look a little flushed." To her surprise, Ivy was fully dressed in a warm wool dress with her hair up and a hat pinned atop her blond curls as if to go out.

Ivy's uneasy expression deepened. She hovered a moment, seemingly undecided on some score. Then she stood to one side and let her door fall fully open. "Come inside," she urged Mina, catching her arm and drawing her into her attic bedroom.

Mina looked about and was surprised to see the room looking a lot neater than when she'd seen it previously. On that occasion it had been strewn with Ivy's things, every surface covered with bottles and beads and boxes of powder. Now, the room looked practically bare. Mina noticed two large bags to the side of the door; she caught her breath and turned to Ivy, who was chewing her lip.

"Ivy, are you going somewhere?"

"It's like this, miss," Ivy interrupted her in an agitated voice. She drew Mina to the bed and they both sat on the edge of the mattress. "There's this man as said he'll have me any time these past two years. Sam Rawlings his name is. He knows I'm no better than I ought to be, but he said he don't mind my past, it's my future he's looking to. He's a quiet-spoken fellow and slow to smile, but well, when he do, it's a sight worth seeing."

Ivy looked wistful a moment, before staring down at her hands. "Well, I've always had a fondness for Sam and well…" Ivy took a deep breath. "He's been left some land up Yorkshire way and a cottage and he wants to make a go of it. Says he'll marry me, miss. And what I'm thinking is it's now or never."

"Oh Ivy, that's wonderful, but I don't understand the need for secrecy?"

Ivy stood up and then sat back down again in agitation. "He asked me a month ago, you see, and I gave him a flat no. He's got two kiddies, you see, miss, and I—I never liked my own stepmother. I told you, I think, that I tried married life once before and it didn't turn out so well." She quirked an eyebrow at Mina, who nodded. She recalled that Ivy's husband had turned out to be a bigamist. "Truth to tell it's not an easy life he's offering me." Ivy pulled a face. "I was raised on a smallholding. I've got no illusions. It's hard work." She twisted her hands. "In all honesty, he'd be better off asking the likes of Edna than me." Ivy's expression was rueful.

"I doubt Edna would have accepted him," Mina said truthfully. "For her aunt means to leave her house to her and the true ambition of Edna's heart is to own a Crown Derby tea set and raise three cats."

Ivy gave a startled laugh. "Is it really? Well, she's an odd duck and no mistake."

"You've a kind heart, Ivy. I think you'll make an excellent wife and mother."

Ivy's eyes filled with tears. "Thank you, Mina," she said, taking her hand. "There's no two ways about it, though. I'll be leaving you in the lurch here, doing a moonlight flit. I left it too late to work a decent notice. I daren't tell Nye. Not when he's expecting a regular gaggle of folks for Wednesday."

Mina nodded her head, understanding Ivy's reticence. Nye would be furious. "I comprehend you," she murmured.

Ivy flung her arms about Mina's neck. "Thank you for never standing in judgment over me," she said fiercely as she hugged her. "There's not many who wouldn't have."

"Oh Ivy," said Mina. "You will be missed."

"And you won't tell Nye."

"I won't breathe a word."

Ivy nodded. "You've got the handling of him anyway," she said with a smile. "Any fool can see that."

Mina wasn't so sure about that, but she gave an answering smile of reassurance to Ivy, who was plainly in a nervous state. "Is Sam collecting you tonight or—?"

Ivy nodded violently. "I'm to slip down to the side door." She crossed to her small attic window and looked out. "He's going to park a ways down the road, and I'm to keep a lookout and go to meet him."

Mina looked around the room. "You're all packed? You've got everything you need?"

"Yes, for this past half hour I've been ready and waiting. He said he'd wait till it turned dark and then to watch for him."

"Just give me a moment, I'll be back," Mina said, letting herself out of Ivy's room and crossing the passage to her own. Once inside, she made for her stocking drawer and retrieved the half sovereign she had tucked away. Then she returned to Ivy and pressed it into her palm.

"Oh no, miss, I couldn't!" Ivy gasped, looking down at the shiny gold coin.

"Yes, you can. A good friend gave it to me when I was setting out to the unknown, and now I'm giving it to you. Strictly speaking, I've already spent it once, but it made its way back to me. If you have no immediate need for it, then hide it away for a rainy day." Ivy turned teary again and they embraced. "I will remember you in my prayers, Ivy, and perhaps you will write to me at Christmastime?"

"Oh yes," Ivy agreed. "I will and I'll send you my address so you can write back to me at New Year." She blew her nose as Mina agreed.

"Shall I wait with you now or—?"

"No," Ivy said firmly. "You get you to bed. I need to compose myself for a bit. I'll just sit here in the dark and take my ease while I keep watch for him."

"Very well."

They embraced again, and Mina made for bed.

She wasn't sure how much later it was that she woke, a gust of wind rattling the pane along with a few drops of rain. She lay a moment, listening before she noticed her head was resting on a warm, muscular shoulder. She was tucked against a big, solid body in the bed.

When she went to lift her head, Nye's voice spoke out of the darkness. "Go back to sleep."

Mina blinked. "You're awake," she said in confusion.

"Yes," he agreed. "I've learned my lesson. I can't close my eyes next to you or I'll never get up."

She considered this a moment. "What time is it?" she murmured.

He hesitated. "A little before two," he said briefly.

Clearly, he had to get up before morning for some fell purpose, she thought, but let her own eyes drift shut anyway. It was no business of hers. Her eyes sprang again in the darkness. "Why did you come to bed, if not to sleep?" she heard herself persist.

He didn't answer that, just clamped a big hand to the back of Mina's head and dragged her face back to his neck. Had she been sleeping with her face pressed to him like this? she wondered. "Relax," he said. "I'm not here for anything else."

Mina frowned. "I wasn't worried and I'm not afraid of you," she grumbled, shifting against him. He was wearing his clothes, she realized, feeling the press of his buttons through her cotton nightgown. It was not as comfortable as when he wore his soft flannel.

"You promise?" he said in an odd tone. Mina tried to draw back to get a look at his face, but it was too dark in the room for that.

"I'm not afraid of you, William Nye," she insisted with quiet conviction and felt him exhale. "So don't think you can browbeat me."

He snorted. "If I ever did think that, you soon schooled me different." She felt his hand at her lower back, brushing the backs of his fingers lightly against the base of her spine. It was strangely comforting, and she let her eyes close again.

"Will it be the same people?" she asked suddenly.

"What?"

"The same people as last time," she elaborated. "You know."

"I really don't."

She could hear the frown in his voice. "The same people who bore witness," she said. "That night in the church." She thought she heard his breathing hitch before it levelled out again.

The shoulder under her cheek lurched in what she guessed was a shrug. "Some of them, maybe," he agreed.

"Oh." Even to her own ears, she sounded a little put out.

"Does that bother you?" The words sounded like they were dragged from him.

Mina didn't want to answer. Unbidden, the memories of that awful night flooded into her mind's eye. She felt scalded and raw. "I don't want to see any of them," she admitted, her throat closing on the words. She felt his head turn sharply.

"Why? You have nothing to reproach yourself with."

"I looked a fool," she mumbled against his shoulder.

"No more than I," he said, but that wasn't true, Mina thought despairingly. Every one of his friends had seen the utter contempt he had for her. He had marched right out of the church and left her there and they had all followed him, laughing and carousing. She screwed her eyes shut and to her

239

surprise felt his arms close tight around her, hauling her practically on top of him. "You don't have to see any of them," he said tersely. "You're to stay out of their sight. Understood?" She nodded. It was what she wanted after all. For once their feelings on a subject agreed. "Good," he said throatily. "Now go to sleep."

And funnily enough, she did.

*

Mina woke late and reached for her father's pocket watch on the side table. It told her it was eight o'clock already. She felt the familiar constraint of Nye's arm slung around her waist and looked back over her shoulder to find him fast asleep. Again, she wondered at his insistence that he "never slept" and struggled to extricate herself. His arm tightened, hauling her back against him.

"Nye! We've overslept!" she protested. He slung a leg heavily across hers. "Nye! Really! You're impossible."

He made a grumbling sound against her neck. "It's eight o'clock," she told him loudly and felt his eyelashes flutter against her skin. "Did you hear what I said?" With an exclamation of annoyance, Mina started squirming and wriggling, only to find herself abruptly rolled beneath him. "Nye!" she squealed in alarm.

He reared back at that and blinked down at her, looking confused.

"Let me up!" she huffed. "It's gone eight in the morning."

Nye ran a hand down his face and groaned. "It can't be."

"Well, it is. You fell asleep again!"

Grudgingly, he rolled his weight off her to let her up. Mina scrambled out of bed and started slamming drawers and gathering her outfit together. Nye slowly propped himself up on one elbow to watch her.

"Aren't you going to get up?" she asked pointedly.

"All in good time," he answered, shoving her pillow behind him and lolling back against it. His eyes followed her with lazy appreciation.

Mina lowered her handful of underclothing with a glower. "I'm not putting on a show here," she huffed. "I can hardly dress with an audience!"

"That act would never make it on the music hall," Nye pointed out reasonably. "They'd want to see you take them off, not put them on."

Only by supreme strength of will did Mina stop herself from bristling like an old schoolmarm. "I wouldn't know about that," she said loftily. "I've never been to the music hall."

He gave a slow smile. "You don't say."

This talk of music halls made her think of the covered screens she had used previously, which were decorated with flyers and advertisements for similar acts. "If we're to share this bedroom, I could do with some screens," she mused. "Maybe I should bring those ones up from the scullery."

"That tatty old thing," Nye objected. "It's not fit for anything but the rubbish tip."

"Someone clearly went to a lot of trouble to paste those advertisements all over it," she pointed out. "Who made it?"

He was silent a moment. "My mother," he said finally. She waited, but nothing more was forthcoming.

241

"Oh, well, I expect it could be restored with some work."

He made a rude noise. "It's hardly worth the bother."

Mina pulled her drawers on underneath her billowing nightgown. "Maybe I should strip it down and redecorate it with your news clippings," she said, then wondered why she was provoking him. He clearly hadn't wanted her to see those articles. She shot an uneasy look at him, wondering if she had gone too far.

Nye's eyes glinted at her, despite his relaxed pose. "Well, this is unexpected. Are you teasing me, Mina?"

For some reason, her face filled with hot color. "No," she burst out vehemently.

"It sounded like you were."

Was she? Mina shifted from one foot to another. "I just—spoke without thinking, that's all."

"Maybe you should do that more often."

She bit her lip and tied the drawstring at her waist. "Now you're teasing me," she said flatly. He didn't answer, but when she sat on the edge of the bed to pull on her stockings, she felt his arms close about her from behind.

"I was in earnest," he said gruffly, then nuzzled his face to her neck. Mina gasped, feeling the rasp of his stubble up and down her sensitive skin. "Don't be so starchy." Before she could make any reply to that, he released her with a kiss to her pulse point and gave a ringing slap to her backside that was hard enough for her to feel despite both layers of cotton.

"Nye!" she gasped in reproach as he sauntered across the room to where his clothes lay across a chairback. He just smirked.

"Are those your clothes in the wardrobe?" Mina asked on impulse. "The red silk cravat and the black dress trousers?"

He looked across at her as he drew his collarless shirt down over his bare chest. "Aye, they're my fancy town clothes," he said with a wink. "You should see me rigged out in them, I'm a sight to behold."

"Now you *are* teasing," she answered, but looking at him, found she believed him. Will Nye would be a striking figure in that scarlet striped waistcoat and flashy silk tie. Even when clothes covered his rippling physique, they showed his shape was built of solid muscle over an impressive frame.

He did not possess the polite good looks which graced a ballroom or a tea party, Mina realized. But while he did not have the smooth address of his half brother, Lord Faris, he had something infinitely more disturbing. A sort of earthy, sensual attractiveness. Dressed in his best, he would not cut a respectable figure, but instead the brash kind of figure her father would have crossed the street to avoid.

"I should take you to town," he said suddenly. "One day soon. We could take in the sights. Eat a meal at a fancy hotel, do some shopping, maybe even a show."

Mina was so surprised she nearly dropped her stocking. "Which town?" She wondered if he meant St. Ives.

"Exeter," he answered, pulling on his breeches. "Or maybe London."

"You have business there?"

"No," he said. "It would be for pleasure, not business."

Pleasure? Mina's breathing came faster. He would take her there for pleasure? Or did he mean it would be a pleasure to take her? She hardly dared look at him. It seemed a very intimate thing to be dressing together like this. She slid her plain garters on and reached for one of her petticoats.

"Would you like that, Mina?" His voice was husky and sent a shiver down Mina's spine. She glanced at him to find him knotting a kerchief about his tanned throat.

"Yes, I would," she admitted softly and saw by the gleam in his eye that he was pleased by her words. "But that would mean several days away from the inn," she pointed out. "Is that an easy thing to arrange?" Suddenly, she remembered Ivy's defection and suffered a pang. They would not be going away anytime soon.

"You let me worry about that." He drew on his black waistcoat and reached for his boots.

"Do you have any mending you need doing?" she asked on impulse, feeling herself blush and wishing she could control her reactions to him.

"Very wifely," he said, and Mina lowered her eyes, feeling suddenly rather shy.

"Where do you keep the rest of your things? There's barely any of your effects in here," she pointed out, glad to think of a distraction.

Nye seemed to consider this as he fastened his cuffs. "Here and there. I've a trunk in the stable," he said with a shrug. "There's a bunk in there too. I used to doss down in there for an hour here and there where I could snatch it."

"I see," Mina answered, though she didn't really. Why would he sleep in the stable? It made no sense to her.

As though aware of her thoughts, Nye looked up from tying his bootlace. "I know you've seen precious little evidence, but I really am a bad sleeper," he said. "I can never usually snatch more than a catnap." He frowned. "For some reason, when I'm around you…" He left the rest of the sentence unspoken.

"You get unbroken sleep at my side?" she said with surprise. She wondered if his poor sleep pattern might be because he always had to rise in the early hours to meet unsanctioned ships.

"I don't know why," he said as though he'd heard her unspoken thoughts. "But yes." He straightened up, his gaze flickering over her. Mina suddenly realized she must look a sight still half-dressed and all beneath her nightgown. The petticoat was flaring out, giving it a very strange silhouette. "Soon you won't hide yourself from me, Mina," he said. "There won't be any point."

She made no reply to this, indeed what could she say? He took a deep breath in and then out again. "You can help Edna get the place ready for Wednesday." He said this in the manner of one making a great concession. Mina looked up quickly. "They'll start arriving Tuesday, maybe even as early as tonight. We'll want all the rooms made ready and the bunks in the stable."

She nodded, wide-eyed, pleased to be making progress. "You could bring your own things in, that would free another bunk," she heard herself say rather breathlessly.

He paused a moment before answering. "You want me to do that?" There was a heavier significance to his words that she did not want to examine too closely.

"Of course. A husband's place is by his wife's side," she said primly. "A stable is for horses."

He gave her a crooked smile that said he knew full well she had just told him he was welcome in her bed.

16

Mina had thought it was unlikely Ivy's flight would be discovered before the afternoon, but she was proved wrong in this respect. She was taking a break from stripping the rooms and pouring tea in the kitchen when Edna appeared flushed and distrait.

"Oh, Mrs. Nye!" she said, wringing her hands. "You'll ne'er believe what that wicked girl has gone and done! And us expecting a regular swarm to descend on us any minute!"

"What is it, Edna?" she asked in a steady voice as she poured a second cup for the agitated maid.

"She's up and left! Stripped her room bare of all her worldly possessions and disappeared without a trace." She plunked her hands on her scrawny hips. "Can you believe the like of it?"

"How very odd," Mina murmured. "Perhaps there is some explanation. A sick relative or something of that nature."

"Not her!" Edna answered with spirit. "Too steeped in sin and infamy to have a relative to her name!"

Mina hesitated, wondering what to do for the best. Should she take Edna into her confidence and ask her to delay telling Nye for a few hours or not? Ivy had begged her not to tell Nye, but she had not mentioned Edna.

Overall, she decided regretfully that ignorance was probably the best policy to employ. "Perhaps Nye is already aware of the fact," she said aloud. "And can furnish us with the particulars."

"Not he!" Edna huffed. "For 'twas the master himself sent me up there to roust her as we need all the hands we can get."

"Oh," said Mina lamely. "Then I suppose he cannot know."

A heavy footfall behind them alerted her to Nye's presence. "He cannot know what?" Nye asked, reaching for another cup and placing it before Mina. She hastened to pour him a drink as Edna took over.

"Oh, Master Nye! You'll never believe it! That Ivy's only gone and done a bunk and left us nicely in a stew!" she burst forth, two spots of red in her cheeks.

Mina thought Nye bit back a curse. "You're sure?" he bit out.

Edna nodded, her lips tightly compressed. "All her things are gone, and the bed wasn't even slept in last night."

He swore filthily at that, and Edna clapped her hands over her ears. "The lying jade said she had a headache," he growled.

"Maybe she had her reasons," Mina could not help but put in. Nye threw a scathing look her way, but Edna paid her no heed.

"What are we going to *do*?" Edna wailed.

"Well, we shall simply have to shift for ourselves," Mina said calmly. "Cannot Reuben take a turn behind the bar?"

Nye looked up sharply at that. "What do you know of Reuben?" he demanded.

"He is the stable hand with the ginger beard, is he not?"

He seethed a moment, though Mina could not imagine why he should be so cross she remembered the man's name. "You just said yourself, he's a stable hand," Nye pointed out tersely.

"These events are the only time the stables are full. He'll be needed out there."

"Can you not hire anyone else from the village?" Mina asked reasonably.

Nye rolled his eyes. "I can't find new staff when things are slow, let alone now at such short notice!"

"Well," said Mina, drawing a deep breath. "Then we shall simply have to do the best we can. Edna and I have today and tomorrow to prepare. We can make those meat-filled pastries in advance—"

"Pasties," Edna chimed in.

"Yes, pasties," Mina agreed. "We could cook up the mince and potatoes today in a great batch and then a large quantity of dough."

Edna was tapping her chin thoughtfully. "Aye, that we could," she agreed. "I'll send Reuben down to the village for more flour and potatoes."

"Are you on the roster to box?" she asked, turning to Nye.

"Not officially, but they're bound to have a fighter or two fall through when they realize they have to travel to the wilds of Cornwall," he said dryly.

"I see, so you'll be expected to step into the breach."

He smiled grimly. "Exactly."

"Edna, I'm afraid you will be needed to man the bar in that case, unless…"

"No," said Nye. "You'll not be setting foot in the public bar, Mina." She couldn't say she was disappointed, as in truth she would rather have dreaded it. Still, she had felt obligated to at least show willing. "You're to stay behind the scenes," Nye told her firmly.

Edna made a sound of agreement. "It won't be the first time I've had to serve in the taproom," she said, sounding resigned to her fate. "We've kippers, a ham, and a good quantity of salted pork in the larder for breakfast and supper."

"On the Thursday, perhaps we could offer a roast lunch?" Mina suggested. "I've assisted you twice now on a Sunday and could very likely take over the cooking even if you still have to serve them, Edna."

Edna nodded and, looking a little reassured, wiped her hands on her apron and reached for her teacup. Feeling Nye's gaze on her, Mina turned to him, but he looked away, clearing his throat.

"Well, then," he said grudgingly. "We'll just have to see how we go."

After the two women had stripped the rooms on the second floor and made up the beds on the third, Edna dragged out the largest tub for laundering. Mina was given a sack of potatoes and a sack of onions to get started on the filling for all the pasties they would be serving over the next few days. She set to work with gusto and had filled three bowls with finely chopped onions when the door opened and Gus appeared on the threshold.

"Well now, Minnie," he announced, setting his thumbs into his waistcoat and rocking back on his heels. "This is a very domesticated scene and no mistake!"

"Good morning, Gus." She smiled. "How are you? I have not seen you this past week, I think."

250

"You're keeping much finer company than me, these days I fear," he said, shaking his fluffy white head sadly. At Mina's raised eyebrows, he added, "I hear you've been keeping company with the Farises at Vance Park and now there's a fine gentleman waiting for you in your parlor room."

"A fine gentleman?" Mina asked. "Do you mean Lord Faris?"

"I do not," he said, stroking his moustache. "It's a fine tall gentleman who's waiting on you." He pursed his lips. "And said as his name was Carswell, I believe."

She looked up, startled to see Gus's eyes fixed on her rather hard.

"Sir Matthew?" she asked, standing up from her seat. She clicked her tongue. "I wonder what he could want." The timing could not be worse. "Is his ward with him?"

"His ward?" Gus cocked his head to one side.

It was funny how she had never noticed how shrewd his eyes could look, Mina thought distractedly, for all they were usually so blue and guileless. "A former pupil of mine named Cecily."

"A former pupil, is that the tale?"

She looked around from the sink at his odd tone, but he smiled at her expansively, so she dried her hands and hurried to remove the cap which kept her hair out of the way. "It's unfortunate timing now we're so busy," she muttered. "But I'd better go and see him if he has called out especially. Would you be so kind, Gus?" she said, moving toward him and angling her apron strings his way.

"Of course, dear lady," he obliged. "Nothing could be simpler."

"Thank you." She shrugged off the apron and set it down on a bench. "I won't be long. If you're still here when I return, perhaps we could take a cup of tea together?"

Gus demurred, claiming he would not dream of distracting her when she was so busy, and Mina hurried to the parlor, hoping she did not smell too strongly of onions.

She found Sir Matthew sat with one leg across the other in a seat by the window, his foot wagging irritably. He stood up when she entered the room and bowed. "Miss Walters," he said formally.

Mina crossed the room to shake his hand. "It's Mrs. Nye now," she reminded him and politely gestured for him to be seated. "Will you take some refreshment or—"

"No, thank you." He hastened to reassure her, and she noticed with relief he still wore his caped greatcoat as though he was intending a short visit only. "In truth—" He hesitated. "I was hoping perhaps you might accompany me for a short drive." He gestured to the window where he had a curricle waiting. "Perhaps into St. Ives."

"I'm afraid that is out of the question, Sir Matthew," Mina answered politely. "You find us at sixes and sevens this morning." She sank gracefully into a chair facing him. "We are readying ourselves for the arrival of a large party imminently."

He gave a harsh laugh. "I'm sure I would not like to hazard a guess at what sort of parties would descend on such a lonely spot," he said with a moue of distaste. "Not a respectable one, I'll warrant."

Mina sat straighter in her chair, her gaze very level. "As to that, sir, I am surprised you think it appropriate to say so, considering you must be aware I am married to the proprietor."

Sir Matthew glared at her a moment, slapping his gloves across his shiny top boot. "Yes, I am aware. That is what I—" He broke off distractedly. "That is, after you left the other day, I made enquiry and I might add I have never been so shocked in all my life. To hear you now have ties to an establishment such as this by the bonds of matrimony—" He checked himself again, his icy-blue eyes ablaze. "In short, madam, I cannot think how such a thing came about. I had the utmost respect for your parents. You will have to pardon me, if you find my words unpalatable, but I have made it a habit in this lifetime to speak only the truth."

Mina was silent a moment before answering him. She remembered how her father had held this man in such high esteem and how bitterly he had been disappointed when Sir Matthew had failed to even reply to any of his letters this past year. "I'm afraid I would know nothing of such life choices, Sir Matthew. As a mere woman, I am seldom afforded such luxuries."

He turned rather red at that and stood up from his chair, turning his back to her as he stared out of the window. He was silent a moment before speaking. "I will give you the benefit of the doubt and imagine you are unaware of the evil reputation of this establishment," he said, practically gnashing his teeth. "I cannot fathom how a gently raised woman could find herself in such a predicament. In short, madam, I am appalled that a person I once entrusted my charge's welfare to—that someone who could claim themselves to be a connection—is in any way associated with such a place as The Merry Harlot." His lip curled over the name of the inn, and Mina felt herself inwardly seethe at the pomposity of the man.

"Can you not?" Mina answered, feeling her color rise. "Then allow me to enlighten you, Sir Matthew. My father placed me in my half brother's hands on his death. He had little other option after all our benefactors fell by the wayside and our school failed." She let that barb sink before continuing. "My brother, Lord Faris, arranged this match for me. And if he thought it a fit match, then I cannot see why you should question that."

"Lord Faris?" Sir Matthew wheeled around from the window, an incredulous expression on his face.

"Jeremy Vance, fifth Viscount Faris, is my half brother," Mina confirmed.

Sir Matthew was visibly stunned. "I never heard of any connection between your two families."

"Why should you have?" Mina asked coolly. "My mother was divorced; perhaps you were unaware of the fact."

His expression flickered. Clearly, he had not been aware. "I held your mother in the very highest esteem," he said stiffly.

Mina remembered how her mother had presided so prettily over those gatherings their governors were invited to. "Yes, I expect you would," she said. "Now, if you'll excuse me, Sir Matthew," she said, rising to her feet. "I'm afraid I am terribly busy this morning—"

"Mrs. Nye, it is you who must excuse me," he cut in, striding forward and standing in front of her. "I'm afraid I let my natural feeling run away with me. It was not my intention to insult you and neither is it my place to upbraid you. I was not in full possession of the facts," he said frankly. "In truth, I came to thank you for your intercession the other day." His lean cheeks flushed. "If you had not stepped in, my ward would have been ruined indeed."

Mina inclined her head. "I was glad to do Cecily a good turn, and I'm pleased if you were able to smooth that business over."

"Only by following your advice," he said with a bitter laugh. "My temper would have gotten the better of me on that occasion also if you had not intervened."

"I am happy indeed, if I was able to offer advice that was beneficial for Cecily," Mina answered colorlessly.

"It may be that I can see my way to offer you some respite from your current predicament." He hesitated. "Cecily is at a difficult age, too old for a governess, yet far too naïve to let loose in society as I have recently learned to my cost. I have been thinking and it may be wise—"

"Sir Matthew, allow me to stop you there." Mina cut across his words. "I am not in need of respite. I am a married woman. You mistake my situation."

He fell silent at that. "Do I?" he muttered. "I do not think so, Mrs. Nye. Indeed, I fear there will come a time when you are desperately in need of rescuing from this…place." Mina looked back at him, tight-lipped. When he realized she had no more to say on the subject, he sighed. "I am in your debt, Mrs. Nye," he said tightly. "Something that does not sit easily with me, in light of your current company. But if you will not allow me to make reparation or alleviate your suffering—"

"Again, Sir Matthew, I must remind you that you mistake my situation."

He shook his head. "You are a stubborn woman, Mrs. Nye."

"I thank you for your concern," she said, bobbing him a curtsey. "But I must now humbly beg your leave. Urgent business awaits me."

Sir Matthew held out his hand and Mina shook it. He held it for a beat longer than necessary, and Mina looked up at him in surprise. "I must then remain a debtor to you."

255

Mina pulled her hand from his. "Pray do not give it another thought, Sir Matthew," she said and, turning on her heel, abruptly left the room. As she wrenched the door open, she came face-to-face with Reuben's ginger beard as he straightened up guiltily from the door. "Reuben?" she addressed him in startled accents.

"Yes, ma'am," he stammered.

"Do you have some message for me?"

"No, ma'am," he said, his eyes avoiding hers shiftily. "I'm just going out back now, ma'am." Mina stared after him as he shambled off, and then she made her way thoughtfully back to the kitchen.

She had just opened the sack of potatoes when the door burst open and Nye stood on the threshold, chest heaving. Mina dropped her paring knife and stared up at him. "Now what's happened?" she demanded in exasperation as he slammed the door shut behind him. Really, was she to get no peace this morn!

"Care to tell me what that was all about?" he demanded, gesturing over his shoulder as Sir Matthew's curricle bowled out of the yard.

Tamping down her irritation at having to rake over the whole thing, she forced herself instead to remain calm. "Sir Matthew Carswell called in," she said. "To tell me he did not care for his ward to be associated with me anymore, but that he considered himself in my debt. Something he was most put out about."

Nye continued to watch her narrowly. "So, he didn't ask you to run away with him, then?"

Mina spluttered, retrieving her knife, and sitting in her chair. "Of course not! Where on earth did you get a preposterous idea like that?" He remained tight-lipped, but at the furious look in his eye, she realized something. "Reuben!" she gasped. "He was listening at the keyhole! Well, of all the—"

"So, he did, then?" Nye burst out furiously.

"Of course not!" she seethed. "Reuben could not follow the conversation clearly if that's what he thought. He asked me out for a drive to St. Ives…" She paused at Nye's fresh explosion of wrath. "*Naturally* I declined his invitation as I was far too busy."

"Because your husband would damned well forbid it!" he corrected her hotly.

"Well, as I never entertained the notion for even an instant, I did not think it through that far," she admitted.

"And that was it?" He shook his head. "I don't believe it."

Mina sat up indignantly. "What do you mean, you don't believe me?"

"Reuben said you had to remind him you were a married woman. Even you wouldn't be so outraged at the idea of a mere drive to St. Ives!"

"Even I?" Mina fumed.

"Stop trying to distract me," Nye thundered. "Why did you have to remind him you were married, tell me that!"

"I—because, you were right," she told him helplessly, then saw his gaze ignite. "Not about that!" she said hastily. "But he did want to offer me a position as Cecily's companion. You remember? You asked me if he had before, but at the time, I thought it extremely unlikely and—"

"That bastard," Nye snarled.

"Nye!"

"Next time he comes calling, you do not see him without me being present, am I understood, Mina?"

"I highly doubt that he will ever—"

"Mina!"

"Oh, very well, you unreasonable beast!"

A footfall in the doorway had them both spinning around, and to Mina's embarrassment, she found Jeremy leaning against the doorjamb with an amused look on his face. "Dear me," he drawled. "Marital discord—this place is starting to feel like a real home away from home!"

"What do you want?" Nye growled. "We're busy."

"So I see. I just wanted to see if it was true what I heard in the village."

"What's that?" Nye asked sharply.

Jeremy's eyebrows rose. "That you're hosting another fight here this week."

"Wednesday," Nye replied abruptly.

"Who's appearing?"

Nye looked exasperated. "We're in the middle of a discussion!" he said, gesturing between Mina and himself.

"We're not sure yet," Mina answered, glad to change the subject. "Some of the fighters might be scratched if they're not willing to come to Cornwall."

"Ah, I see." Jeremy was eyeing her curiously.

"Did you bring my nephew with you?" she asked, looking out of the window to where a bored-looking Colfax was stood waiting next to his carriage.

"Not today. Should you like that?"

"I would."

"He talks about you a lot," Jeremy conceded. "You were quite a hit with young Master Teddy."

Nye turned from the window, frowning. "Has Colfax ever boxed?" he asked. "If we lose more than one fixture, I may need a substitute."

Jeremy looked horrified. "I couldn't have one of your louts rearranging his features," he objected.

"He looks about the right build."

"Absolutely not! I refuse."

"Maybe I'll just ask him myself," said Nye, heading for the door.

"He's impossible," Jeremy sighed, sitting on the bench next to Mina. "By the way, there's a most unpleasant stench in here. It's making my eyes water."

"It's onions," Mina told him. "I've still got half a sack to chop."

"My God." Jeremy shuddered. "Did I sell you into indentured labor?"

A smile tugged at Mina's lips. "Don't be ridiculous," she told him sternly. "I'd offer you tea, but I know how you despise it."

He gave her a grin and reached into his jacket, extracting a silver hip flask. "No need." He brandished it aloft and took a swig. "Now we're alone, tell me why did Nye fire up like that when I mentioned news from the village?"

Mina sighed. "He likely thought you had news of Ivy," she admitted.

"Ivy?"

"The pretty blond barmaid."

"I know who Ivy is, but pray tell, why would there be news of her in the village?"

"Oh, because she's run away," Mina admitted. "But I don't think many people know that yet."

Jeremy gave her a long, hard look. "I can see you know more than you're letting on, but I am not concerned about pretty little Ivy. What I want to know is who this fellow is that Nye thinks is trying to run off with you?"

"Oh, you heard that, did you? It was just a misunderstanding, nothing more."

"Don't play coy with me, that's not your style, sister dear."

"Sir Matthew Carswell, JP," she admitted. "But Nye is quite mistaken about what he wanted from me."

"Good idea to keep Nye on his toes though," Jeremy said approvingly. "Clever you."

Mina rolled her eyes. "I told Nye there was nothing in it. I'm not trying to incite him."

"I shouldn't think you had to do much to send him over the edge where you're concerned," Jeremy said with a smirk. "You have surprised me, I will confess. I had not thought you had it in you to bring William Nye to his knees."

"I have done no such thing," Mina said, flushing. Involuntarily, she glanced over to the window to watch Nye making back for the kitchen door.

"Colfax has boxed at country fayres," he announced as he came through the door. "So, he would do at a pinch."

Jeremy threw up his hands in mock horror. "No one listens to me," he complained. Mina sliced into another onion. "Faugh!" Jeremy complained, jumping up from his seat and pressing a hand to his nose. "Foul stench!"

"Well, I'm sorry for your sensitive nose, but I've another twenty to peel and slice before lunchtime," she scolded him.

Jeremy laughed, tipped his hat to her, and sauntered out of the door. She watched as he crossed the courtyard and clapped a hand to Colfax's shoulder.

"Does he usually come to watch the boxing?" she asked.

"Fairly often," Nye admitted, his eyes on her.

"I need to get on with these onions," she said hastily. "It's been one interruption after another this morning."

He grunted, drained his teacup, and strode out of the kitchen, a frown still on his face.

Mina managed to get through the next couple of hours without disturbance, and by the time Edna appeared to make some sandwiches for lunch, she had finished the onions and was halfway through the potatoes.

"There's a sack of swedes needs bringing in for you too," Edna pointed out, somewhat undermining Mina's sense of achievement. She ate her bread and cheese as Edna pinned out the first lot of washing to dry and Nye carried in the sack of swedes on his shoulder from an outhouse.

261

"You may as well bring in your trunk from the stable now," Mina pointed out to him as he set the swedes down next to the table.

He made no answer, but Mina was gratified to see him cross to the stables after leaving the building. She kept an eye on the window as she carried on with the potatoes and, sure enough, five minutes later he reappeared with a battered trunk on his shoulder which he brought in and carried straight past her and out to the hall. When he reappeared, he halted next to the table.

"You'll need to go through it, some stuff needs throwing out, some for mending."

"You're happy for me to do that?" she asked, looking up.

He nodded. "There's nothing interesting, just work clothes, my razor, some spare change. I'm going down to the cellar to sort out some barrels. If anyone comes by, tell them to wait."

"Very well." She watched his back as he left the room and remembered how Ivy had said he jealously guarded over the cellar. She turned back to her diminishing pile of potatoes with pursed lips.

She had just dropped the last peeled potato into a bucket of cold water when Edna appeared carrying a basketful of wet sheets. "This is the last of it," she puffed. "I'll get it out on the line now, weather permitted."

"There's been no spots of rain," Mina said. "Shall I help you? I could do with a stretch of my legs."

Together, they collected in the washing that had dried and hung out the wet sheets. Then Edna joined her efforts parboiling up the cubed potato and swede and frying off the minced beef and onions. Once all the ingredients were prepared, they fetched out the flour, butter, and suet for a mammoth batch of dough making.

They weren't finished with this task until well after six o'clock when they ate a simple supper of leftover fish pie together in the kitchen. Nye joined them to eat a plateful before hurrying back to whatever task he'd left.

Mina allowed herself to be persuaded to take a bath that evening and took a hurried wash in the tin bath in the scullery, listening to Edna banging the cupboards and the pots and pans in the kitchen. By the time she emerged, Edna had formed fifty half-moon-shaped pasties already which she placed under teacloths.

"They're all the better for resting before they're glazed and baked," she explained. "I'll make a second batch first thing in the morning while these are in the oven."

"Maybe I could help, if you could show me how, Edna."

"I'd be glad to. Good night, Mrs. Nye."

Mina made her way hurriedly up the stairs, anxious to avoid all with her wet hair and her petticoats slung over her arm. She was lucky and made it up to the attic undetected. Once there she drew on her nightgown and set about towel-drying her hair.

It was at that point that she noticed Nye's battered trunk set down against the far wall of the bedroom. She stared at it a moment, noticing the straps were unbuckled. He had given her permission to sort through his things, she remembered, and it must only be around seven o'clock. Far too early for her to climb into bed. Pulling on her bed socks, she padded over the floorboards toward it, carrying her hurricane lamp with her. Settling cross-legged before it, she put the lamp down beside her and threw back the lid.

Inside was as Nye had said, a jumble of work clothes in varying condition. Mina soon made a pile for mending and a pile for tidying away into the chest of drawers and the wardrobe. Underneath this was an assortment of penknives, cufflinks, razors, bits of string, handkerchiefs, neckerchiefs, braces, and a collection of old pipes.

Mina was surprised by this as she had never seen Nye with a pipe, but here she found cherrywood, meerschaum, and even clay pipes all looking well-worn and in somewhat sorry repair. Some were carved into curious semblances—a dog's head on one, a naked woman wrapped about the bowl of another. There was even a couple of pipe tamper tools, one in the shape of a mermaid and the other of a lady's stocking-clad leg, but she found no tobacco pouch.

These were assuredly Nye's personal effects, she thought, carrying the items to the drawers on the side of the bed he invariably slept on. Though she found no letters or even postcards among the items, she did find a sheaf of papers pertaining to his ownership of Vance House and the deeds to the inn itself, and the only other paperwork she found was two photographs tucked into a folded piece of cardboard.

The first she took to be of a father and son with their identical flinty glares and stiff studio poses in their Sunday suits. Their expression though was the only likeness between them. The man was of a solid build with a big square jaw, close-cropped hair, and sideburns which Mina judged to be of a sandy light brown color although it was always hard to tell in the black and white of photographs. The boy she knew immediately to be William Nye. He was a tall handsome boy of about eleven years, but much darker than the man whose hand rested on his shoulder, with hair that curled at his nape and brow and straight eyebrows that looked almost black. Was this Nye with the man who raised him and gave him his name? Mina turned over the photograph but found no writing to tell her if she had guessed correctly, only the studio's stamp.

Picking up the second photograph, she saw the features she already knew from the inn's sign The Merry Harlot. This one had two words printed on the reverse. Ellen Nye. The artist who painted it must have used this photograph for reference, she thought, flipping it back over to look at the tumbled curls and the bonny face of the fourth viscount's mistress. Thoughtfully she placed both photographs in the top drawer of the bedside cabinet also.

Mina spent the next twenty minutes hanging up or folding Nye's clothes for the drawers, setting his razor and comb on the washstand and placing his cufflinks on his bedside table until the only thing left was the pile of clothes for mending. These she scooped up and put in a linen bag for later. There, she thought, surveying the room. Now it was truly occupied by a married couple.

Returning to one of her own drawers, Mina took out Effie's lace scarf and contemplated it a moment. She had laundered it, ready to return to its former owner, and she raised it now to examine its rather shabby folds. It looked a good deal better now than on the night she had worn it at St. Werburgh's, she thought ruefully. She could not remember now what she had done with the silver sixpence she had been given in the church. Folding it carefully again, she returned it to the drawer and made for the pile of well-thumbed periodicals she kept under the bed. She settled on one with a juicy tale about a stolen ruby necklace and climbed into bed.

The next thing she knew, she had wakened as a shaft of light fell across her face from an oil lantern coming through the door. She made out Nye's face as he shut the door behind him and came softly to his side of the bed where he was quick to extinguish the lamp and start undressing.

"What time is it?" Mina asked, rolling on her side to face him.

"Late," he answered, climbing into the bed. "Why are you still awake?"

"I wasn't," she assured him and, without conscious thought, found herself shifting closer to him in the dark. He expelled a noisy breath and for a moment she thought he wouldn't take her up on her unspoken invitation, then his hands were at her waist and she was hauled up against him.

"Am I forgiven, then?" he said against her brow.

"What was I angry about?" She had genuinely forgotten by this point.

"My being a damned jealous brute."

"Oh that." It seemed ages ago. "It depends on whether you accept my word or Reuben's on what transpired."

His hands stroked over her buttocks and hips. "Yours," he said raspily. "Mind, I still don't trust that Carswell bastard." She almost *heard* him scowl.

"Do you smoke a pipe?" she asked suddenly and felt his forehead furrow in a frown.

"A pipe? No, do I smell of pipe smoke?"

"No, but I sorted through your trunk and you own so many."

He gave a short laugh. "Already? You don't let the grass grow, do you?"

"I was always urged never to put off till tomorrow what could be done today."

266

She felt him nod and shift back against the pillow. "The pipes aren't mine. They were my father's."

Mina hesitated. "And by that you mean…?"

"The man who raised me," he said quickly with an edge to his voice. "Jacob Nye."

"Was he the one in that photograph with you as a boy?" she asked quietly.

"Yes."

Mina remained quiet a moment, but he did not expand on this. She thought of the portrait of the fourth viscount that she had seen, who looked so like him. "Were you close to your…to Jacob Nye, I mean."

He did not answer at once. "Yes," he said. "He taught me everything I know. Except boxing."

"And who taught you that?" she asked curiously.

"An old groom we had taught me the basics. Samuel Teague his name was." Nye rolled onto his back and propped an arm under his head, the other he kept firmly wrapped about Mina. "When I was nineteen, I went to Exeter to box. I wanted to do it professionally."

"What happened?" She felt his shoulder shrug under her ear.

"I went without Jacob's blessing. He wanted me here."

"What about your mother?"

"She died the summer I was fifteen."

"Oh," she said softly. "And then?"

"I trained, I fought, I won a few cups. I made some money." He was silent a moment. "Then, after a few years my father's health started failing, he wrote to me and I came home."

"So, how long did you end up living in Exeter?"

"Some five years all told."

Mina considered this a moment, staring up at the ceiling. It was somehow easier to ask Nye these things in the dark. "How long is it since Jacob died?"

"Some three years last Christmas."

"Did you know the fourth viscount?" she asked tentatively.

He gave a short laugh. "Know him? No. He had my mother march me out for his inspection a few times until I reached the age when I could refuse."

"How old was that?"

"Ten years or so."

She fell silent at that, imagining him as the boy from the photograph. "And you never saw him again after that?"

"I never said that." He paused. "He used to follow my fights. I saw him in the crowd a fair few times. He even came and shook my hand after one of my more famous bouts. Though we met as strangers, I recognized him alright."

"For him, it must have been like looking at a younger version of himself," Mina mused. "The likeness is extraordinarily strong. Have you never seen his portrait at Vance Park?"

"No," he said without rancor. "There's nothing for me there." He was silent a moment. "He dictated a letter to me from his deathbed, saying he was proud of me and meant Vance House to be mine."

"Vance House?" Surely she remembered that being mentioned before. "Was that not—?"

"Aye," he agreed gruffly, cutting off her words. "The property was never signed over to me at the time. The old lord had never formalized his intent. Landed gentry don't like to break up their estates," he said dryly. "It goes against the grain. Vance House lies on the eastern border of Vance Park on its own ten acres or so."

"That much?" She hesitated. "It must be a sizeable property."

"Aye, it's a handsome house. Queen Anne with access to its own private cove. The Tavistocks, an old bachelor and his spinster sister, are tenants at present. It generates a goodly rent." He was quiet a moment. "Faris finally made it over to me when we wed."

She nodded. "I thought I recognized the name."

He grunted. "I thought you might. I'll show it to you sometime. We might retire there one day."

"It sounds vastly respectable."

He turned his head sharply. "You almost sound disapproving. You'll be telling me next you like being a publican's wife."

"Why should I not?" She imagined living in a beautiful house with a servant and no neighbors that would ever deign to call. Suddenly, it occurred to her that part of her own parents' relative social isolation could have been due to her mother's divorce and their own craving for respectability. "It's interesting living in an inn," she returned evasively. "Something always seems to be happening."

269

"The likes of Sir Matthew Carswell and his wife could call on you at Vance House," he pointed out, his tone rather brooding.

"I should not want them to," Mina retorted. "Even if they did." She wondered again if Nye was right about Sir Matthew's intention to marry his ward. If so, she could now understand why Cecily had run off with the first beau who had shown any interest in her.

"You should be tired, Mina. I've worked you to the bone today."

"Hardly that!" she protested. "I kept long hours as a schoolmistress. When you've boarders to take care of, there are no set working hours."

"Well, go to sleep now," he growled. "No more talking. You're going to be busy over the next few days. I'm *trying* to be a considerate husband."

The next day, which was Tuesday, passed in a whirl of activity at The Merry Harlot. They made batch after batch of the crescent meat pies that Edna called pasties. They dressed and tidied all the bedrooms on the first floor, and Mina polished windows and mirrors until they gleamed. They did not get any arrivals until early evening when Mina looked up from her simple meal of pie and mash to see a smart carriage had pulled into the yard. Nye hurried out from the stable to greet the new arrivals.

"Do you recognize who that gentleman is, Edna?" Mina asked as she rose from the table to take the empty plates to the sink. A dapper-looking gentleman of middling height was climbing out of the carriage to grasp Nye's hand.

"Jones, I think his name is," Edna said, glancing outside without much interest. "He arranges the matches, so I believe. Nasty business," she concluded sourly.

Mina noted his handlebar moustache, bright blue coat, and rather garish yellow waistcoat with interest. "He's certainly a very natty dresser," she observed lightly.

"Not the word I'd use for it," Edna replied.

Mr. Jones turned and reached up to the carriage, helping down a lady dressed in purple silk with a matching fringed parasol, despite the fact it was an evening in early April. Her black curls were piled exceedingly high on her head and topped with a hat covered in purple butterflies. She was not exactly pretty or in the first flush of youth, but she certainly drew the eye. On her left rouged cheek was a large beauty spot which somehow seemed to add to her attraction, rather than detract. "Is that his wife with him?" she asked.

Edna sniffed. "Calls her his 'business partner,' he does." She lowered her voice. "But they share the same bedroom and that's a fact. You go on and take your wash, Mrs. Nye," Edna urged her. "I can finish up in here. There's water just boiling on the range for you to use. You don't want to be running into any of these folks if you can help it."

Mina tarried a moment, to see how Nye would greet the purple-clad lady, but other than a nod, he barely seemed to acknowledge her. Feeling too tired for an excess of curiosity, she had a wash and took herself off to bed. Nye did not come upstairs until midnight, but when he did, he curled around her and fell into a deep sleep almost immediately and Mina joined him.

Wednesday dawned with a very blue sky and bright sunshine despite the bite in the air. Mina hurried down to breakfast

271

informally in the kitchen and immediately noticed unfamiliar faces milling about the yard outside the window.

"Folks have started arriving," Edna confirmed, following the direction of Mina's gaze. "We've had two coaches already before eight."

"Good gracious," Mina observed, raising her teacup to her lips.

"Soon as it's noon they'll start swilling ale," Edna said bitterly. "You just see if they don't."

"I'll get started on the vegetables for the roast dinner as soon as I've finished my toast," Mina reassured her.

Edna nodded. "The mutton's already in the oven, roasting with rosemary and garlic for the evening meals. If you do the veg, then we're as prepped as can be expected."

Mina moved to take charge of the piles of carrots, beets, and turnips and commenced duties there.

Once they were peeled and chopped and set into pans of cold water, she moved them to the side where they could be placed on the range when needed.

New arrivals kept sweeping into the yard and making their way through to the public bar and even sitting in the sunshine outside on a low wall with their tankards.

Edna was forced to run in and out of the kitchen, trying to cover her many duties. She had only just started bearing the stacked platters of hot pasties into the barroom when she was called away again to show another couple up to the bedchamber they had paid for.

"Mrs. Nye," she said with an agonized glance at the piping-hot pastries. "I knows as how you're supposed to stay out of sight, but I don't suppose—"

272

"Never fear, Edna. I am sure I can carry the last of these through without catching anyone's attention."

The harried maid smiled at her and darted out into the hallway. Mina's prediction proved true for the first two platters which she carried through without comment. For the third and final platter however, she was not so lucky.

Mina set the laden dish down on the nearest table to the door and turned to make her escape. She almost collided with a solid figure standing there. It was one of the prizefighters who had stepped into her path.

"Careful, miss." He laughed, throwing his hands up. "No need to flee before us. We're not as scary as all that I hope!" He looked her up and down. "You'll be Ivy's replacement, then?"

"No, I—"

A second boxer stepped forward. "I remember you," he hailed her cheerfully. "You were here last time. You came into my room, then ran away before we could get acquainted." He grinned at her.

Mina's eyes widened with surprise. "I'm sure I did no such thing!" she denied promptly. Then she frowned, for now she looked at him, it did seem to stir some hazy memory. All at once, she recalled him sprawled out on a mattress on the floor, waiting for Ivy to finish with the occupant of the next room. "Oh," she said uncomfortably, raising a hand to her lips.

"You remembered me now?" he asked. "Few people could forget this face," he boasted with a wink, displaying his profile obligingly for her. He was good-looking, she acknowledged with his tanned face and nut-brown hair. "You should have stuck around. I never object to passing the time of day with a pretty woman."

273

Mina looked frowning from one to the other. They looked remarkably similar with their long, lean builds and twinkling hazel eyes. "Are you brothers?" she asked.

"That's us, I'm Jack Toomes and this here's my brother, Frank."

"We've another brother who fights too, but he couldn't make it here tonight," said Frank, stroking his sideburns. "He's—er— indisposed." From the gleam in his eye, Mina guessed the third brother was up to something even more reprehensible than fighting.

"'Ere, you boys," interrupted a villainous-looking old woman from a few tables away. "You blind? That ain't no doxy." She gave a toothless cackle that seemed to echo in her memory. "You're wastin' your time trying to sweet-talk this one, she's took," she said, knocking back a large glass of gin.

Frank's and Jack's heads whipped around. "What you talkin' about, Ma?" Jack demanded.

"We'll see who's wasting their time," said Frank. "You workin' the bar tonight?" he asked, turning back to Mina. "What time do you finish your shift?"

"I don't actually serve behind the bar," Mina started to explain. "You see—"

"What the bloody hell's going on here?" roared Nye from the other end of the bar. He had just come through the other door with a large barrel over his shoulder. "You pair of bastards step away from her and Mina—get back in the kitchen this minute!" he bellowed.

Mina's face flamed scarlet. Thanks to Nye's yelling and bawling everyone had turned to look at her with interest. "Don't you speak to me like that, William Nye!" she replied, her spine stiffening with outrage.

"Mina!" cried Effie, standing up from her table. "How are you, my darlin'?"

"Bloody hell, I didn't expect her to last more'n a week at most!" someone else observed loudly nearby.

"I'm very well, thank you, Effie," Mina replied with as much dignity as she could muster. "How are you?"

"Never mind that!" Nye boomed. "You have no business being in here—get out!"

Mina gasped, turned on her heel, and rushed out of the room, blinking back tears. Before she even knew it, she had rushed out of the front door and was hurrying across the courtyard as fast as her legs could carry her. Dimly, she heard the door burst open and someone in boots striding across the cobbles behind her. She had just reached the gatepost when strong arms closed about her from behind.

"Oh no, you don't, my girl," Nye said lividly as he lifted her off her feet. "What the hell is it with you and taking off running?" When she started struggling, he swung her around so she faced back toward the inn, then did a double take when he saw the tears streaking down her face. "Mina!"

"Leave me alone!" she flung at him, dragging her forearm across her face, and trying to barge her way past him back toward the inn.

He seized her about the waist again, hauling her against him. "Why are you crying?" he demanded roughly.

"I'm not speaking to you!" she told him shakily as he placed two large hands on either side of her face.

He lowered his face to hers. "You know I didn't mean it like that!" he said in a low, compelling voice. "I just meant the taproom, not—"

"I don't care what you meant!" Mina flung at him, her voice raw and throbbing. She shoved at his chest hard, but he didn't move back an inch. "I don't even want to look at you!"

"Mina!" He sounded frustrated. "Don't make this into something it isn't."

"Our marriage you mean?" she demanded. "No, you're quite right. Trying to make the best of it is an utter waste of my time!"

His expression hardened. "That is not what I meant, and you damned well know it!"

"If you would be so kind as to release me," she said icily. "Then I will get back to my rightful place in the kitchen." The effect, she thought, was probably ruined by her tearstained face, but she couldn't do anything about that right now.

He gave a low growl. "If you take off again, I'll put you over my knee." He seized her chin and tipped it up to meet his gaze. "Don't test me."

"Just leave me alone, Nye," she said, suddenly exhausted from all the emotion. "I've had enough."

"What does that mean?" he asked angrily, grabbing her arm. "Mina?"

"I'm tired of all of this," she said wearily.

"No, you're not!" he growled at her, tightening his grip on her upper arms, and shaking her roughly. "You're in your bloody element, so don't lie to me!" Mina caught her breath and stared at him. In her element? What did he mean by that? "Don't tell

276

me you've had enough of this because I don't accept that. I won't accept it."

"Wha—?" Mina tensed, but it made no difference as he dragged her against him and crushed his mouth to hers in a cruel, possessive kiss that masked her lips against her teeth. His fingers drove into the hair at her nape, almost painfully, holding her fast so she could not escape his embrace. Instinctively she knew that to struggle would be a mistake, so she remained rigidly still until he released her, his breathing ragged and the light of battle in his eye. Mina's gaze shifted over his shoulder to the faces all pressed against the inn windows.

"We have an audience," she pointed out.

"Let them look," he hurled back at her, his fingers closing about her wrist and dragging her in his wake. "If it means I'll be spared the sight of you being accosted by all and sundry, then so be it."

"Accosted?" she spluttered. Once he'd hauled her over the threshold, to her surprise he towed her toward the public bar and not the kitchen. "Nye?" she asked, trying to come to a halt and starting to panic. His strength made her dragging feet pointless.

He flung back the door and hauled her up against his side, his hand at her waist. "Everyone!" he announced. "This is my wife and I'll thank you all to remember it!" He glared about the room aggressively and Mina winced. "Anyone got anything to say about that?" he challenged.

"What's her name, Nye?" someone called out jocularly.

"Mrs. Nye, to you," he replied, lip curling. "Anyone else?" His narrowed gaze seemed to wither any remaining questions on their tongues. "You'll see her about the place this weekend, but

277

I'll ask you to keep a civil tongue in your heads or you'll answer to me. Am I understood?"

There were some cleared throats and shuffling of feet at that. "Aye, you're understood," another voice responded to a chorus of ayes. Mina tried not to meet any gazes, she felt so mortified.

Nye lowered his mouth to her ear. "You can invite Effie and any of the womenfolk you want to sit with you in the parlor," he said, surprising the life out of her. "But if you allow anyone to be overfamiliar, I won't be answerable for my actions, Mina," he warned direly.

When he released her, Mina stumbled forward before recovering her step. She lifted her chin and picked her way through the tables and chairs toward Effie's bright puce dress. When she reached the table, she realized Effie was sat with the raven-tressed partner of Mr. Jones. Today she was wearing a striking dress of striped black and white and a matching hat with a black feather.

"Here, darlin'," said Effie, drawing a seat back for her. "Park yourself here wiv us girls. Can't think when I've been so entertained! Allow me to introduce Miss Dottie Jones," she said, gesturing toward her companion. Then casting a shrewd look over Mina, she nudged her own glass toward her. "Take a swig of this, you'll feel more the thing then."

Mina nodded toward Dottie, who was surveying her with amused incredulity, and accepted Effie's kind gesture by taking a tiny sip of the gin. She managed it without pulling a face or shuddering. "Thank you," she said, returning the glass to Effie with a forced smile. "I'm afraid Nye won't permit me to sit in the public bar," she admitted. "But if either of you ladies would like to join me in my private parlor, then I would be glad to receive you at any time. I can generally be found in there or the kitchen."

278

"My, my," drawled Dottie Jones. "A private parlor, we are privileged."

"I'll join you and gladly," Effie announced. "Jeb plain ignores me when he gets wiv all his boxing cronies and that's a fact." She laughed. "But probably not till tomorrow though, Mina. We've got the bouts to watch and you'll likely be done in by then and all. You're run off your feet."

"Yes," Mina agreed. "Perhaps you'll join me there for breakfast tomorrow morning, say at nine o'clock?" With a slightly unfocussed smile, Mina turned and made her way out of the bar with her head held high. She fancied she did not imagine the swell of conversation as the door swung to behind her, but if there was any justice in the world then Nye's name was being just as bandied about as her own, if not more.

She was glad to escape to the kitchen after her ordeal but even there was not quite the refuge she would have liked. She heard Edna's voice upraised in the kitchen, and when she pushed the door open, she saw she was talking heatedly to Reuben. On her appearance, they both shut up like clams.

"If those is ready, I'll take 'em out now," Reuben said in a surly voice, clearing his throat.

Edna tutted. "Ten minutes ago would have been preferable," she snapped. He picked up the platter of hot pasties with ill grace and stomped out of the kitchen with them.

"Right sorry I am, Mrs. Nye," Edna said, turning to her without preamble. "It's my fault the master took on so—"

"No, no, Edna, I knew how he would be, it's not your fault," Mina interrupted her hastily. She could not bear to hear Edna speak of what had happened. "We are so short of hands that it really ought to be every man, woman, and child on deck."

Edna bit her lip. "Yes, Mrs. Nye," she said repressively. "Least now with the lunchtime rush, things will quiet down for a few hours till evening."

"I suppose so," Mina agreed. "What time will you be required in the taproom?"

"Not till six," Edna said, pressing her lips into a thin line.

"It's a great pity Reuben cannot take a turn at serving behind the bar," Mina observed, rolling up her sleeves and crossing to the sink to wash the large quantity of glasses and tankards that had appeared from the bar dirty.

"That stupid fellow!" Edna spat bitterly. "Could not be trusted as far as he could be thrown."

Mina filled five trays with clean drinking vessels before the sink was cleared enough for the next lot. "These will all need taking through to the bar, Edna, and I confess I am not equal to the task."

Edna nodded grimly, setting down the potato she was peeling ready for the suppers. "It's not to be wondered at, Mrs. Nye," she said, rounding the table and picking up the first lot. "If I find Reuben, I'll send him through for the rest," was her departing shot over her shoulder.

Mina, who had spotted Reuben through the window setting down hay bales in the yard, did not have the heart to disillusion the crosspatch maid. She wondered a moment what the bales could be for before she realized he was marking out a crude ring for the opponents to spar within.

When Edna returned, the trays now stacked with dirty glasses once again, she piled them next to the sink.

"Can I leave you to take charge of the pots, Mrs. Nye?" she asked, making for an overhead cupboard. "Only I need to make the dough now for the loaves for morning."

"Of course, Edna. And once I've done these, I'll wash up. I cannot bake bread, so you need to concentrate on that."

"Yes, Mrs. Nye," Edna agreed, looking gratified. They worked silently for the next hour and a half, moving purposely around the kitchen. Once Mina had fetched and boiled clean water for the sink and cleared the dirty dishes, she made a pot of tea which they shared as she washed and dried all the glasses and mugs.

At one point, a grumbling Reuben appeared bearing the empty platters which now only held crumbs from the devoured pasties.

"Not there!" Edna scolded him when he tried to set them down on the clean table. "Over by the sink for washing, you lummox!"

He changed direction and slammed them down, but Mina cut off his hasty retreat by pointing out the clean glasses for the bar. "You'll need to take those back through now, Reuben," she pointed out coolly. Reuben muttered under his breath but followed her directives all the same.

"After this week, Nye really needs to take a good look at the staffing of this place," Mina said darkly.

"He'll never sack Reuben," Edna said bitterly.

"Why not?" Mina frowned, looking up in surprise. "Is his stable work really so indispensable? He seems a surly, disobliging fellow to me."

"It's not his work in the stables the master cannot do without," Edna muttered and would not meet Mina's steady gaze.

Mina pulled the plug on the sink and let the dirty water drain away as she considered this. Was it possible that Reuben was in on the smuggling business? she wondered. She collected the bucket from the corner of the kitchen and carried it outside to the pump to refill with water for boiling. Feeling eyes on her, she looked up to see Effie's man and another muscled prizefighter both smoking cigars as they sat on the low stone wall in the sunshine.

"Mrs. Nye," they said both said, removing their cigars from their mouths politely before they spoke. Neither of them wore a jacket but were sat in their shirts and waistcoats as if relaxing in their own gardens.

She nodded. "How do you do."

"I'm Jeb Morris," said the first, who had very pale blue eyes. He nodded to his companion. "This here's Clem Dabney."

"How do," said Clem, eyeing her curiously. His waistcoat was pink and black with gold stitching and he wore no cravat, his collar slung negligently open as if he were still shaving. Mina wondered if it was due to his thick, muscular neck. Perhaps neckcloths were uncomfortable for him to wear?

Jeb hesitated. "You probably don't remember us," he said. "But we were at your wedding." She wasn't sure, but she thought she saw a twinkle in those almost colorless eyes as he replaced his cigar between his lips.

Mina seized the arm of the pump and worked it, glad for a distraction. "Yes," she said after half filling the bucket and pausing to rest her arm. "I do remember both of you as it happens. You were with Effie, who was very kind to me, and as for you, Mr. Dabney, your companion broke a mirror in your room and threatened to see you hanged if I remember correctly."

Clem Dabney let out a surprised guffaw. "Aw, Goldie didn't mean anything by it, Mrs. Nye," he told her with an easy grin. "She's just got the temper of a fiend."

"Is she not here with you this weekend?" Mina asked.

He smirked. "She's otherwise engaged."

"Don't listen to him, love," Jeb recommended. "He's already moved on to pastures new."

"Not all of us are ready for a leg shackle like Nye was," Clem protested.

"*Not* a very flattering way to describe Mrs. Nye, Clem. You're ungallant, so you are," Jeb chafed him.

"Nay, that wasn't my meaning, Mrs. Nye," Clem said hastily. "I make a point always to be gallant to the ladies."

"Such gallantry I believe I can live without," Mina said dryly, and Jeb laughed uproariously as Mina worked the pump until the bucket was filled and then stooped to pick it up.

"Nay, let me," Clem said, sliding off the wall and taking the bucket from her. "I'll prove I'm a gentleman and all!"

Mina nodded to Jeb, who was still wiping tears from his eyes, and led the way back to the kitchen with Clem following docilely behind her. "Thank you kindly, sir," she said as he set it down on the kitchen table.

He turned to where another two empty pails stood next to the door. "Let me get these for you, Mrs. Nye," he said, pointing his thumb toward them with a lopsided grin. "It's the least I can do."

"It would be a kindness," Mina said, inclining her head. "And I thank you."

He strode off with the remaining buckets, and Edna gave her a wide-eyed look from where she was kneading the dough.

"We can use all the help we can get," Mina reminded her.

17

The clock struck six and Edna finally disappeared into the bar after the last of the plated roast dinners had been carried through to the bar by her and Reuben. Mina was scrubbing the pots in soapy water when she heard a footfall in the doorway.

"Mina!" Jeremy greeted her exuberantly. "Here you are, like Cinderella confined to the kitchen."

"Auntie!" chorused Teddy, who was being carried in his arms.

Mina pushed a lock of escaped hair out of her face and beheld them speechlessly. "You have surely not brought my nephew to watch this barbarous sport?" she blurted out in shocked accents as they sauntered into the kitchen.

"We rode over on Papa's chestnut hack," said Teddy. "Papa says I'm old enough to watch the lightweights fight," he boasted, rushing up to her as soon as he was set down on his own two feet.

Mina bent down to kiss his proffered cheek. "You did not bring the carriage?" she said in surprise. Although now she came to think of it, the yard was rather full with coaches and likely could not squeeze another in.

"Not us," answered Jeremy lightly, then changed the subject. "Lightweights generally spar earliest in the evening," he informed her, looking about the kitchen with great interest. "Not to mention, boxing is a good deal less barbarous than taking him to watch some other country sporting event on offer locally, such as cockfighting."

Mina shuddered and snatched up a tea towel to dry her hands. "I don't understand how grown men can watch such nasty things," she said with disapproval. "I suppose at least men are rewarded for their participation and freely choose their fate, unlike dumb animals."

"Quite so," Jeremy agreed absently.

"I thought it was the sport of kings that interested you, Teddy," she said, moving away from the sink.

"Horse racing," Jeremy explained, seeing his son's blank face.

"Oh! It is," Teddy agreed readily enough. "But I do want to see them fight. Do you know any of the boxers, Aunt Minerva?"

"As a matter of fact," Mina said, arching a brow, "I was conversing with two just now outside."

Teddy rushed to the window and pressed his nose against it. "What are their names, Auntie?"

She walked over to stand next to him. "That one in the extraordinary waistcoat is called Clem Dabney," she said. "And the one next to him is called Jeb Morris."

"What funny names!"

"I once won a golden guinea on Clem Dabney," Jeremy said. "Who's he fighting?"

"I haven't the faintest notion," Mina retorted.

Jeremy laughed. "Your uncle Nye is also a boxer," he told his enraptured son.

"Will I see him fight, Papa?"

Jeremy shook his head. "He's a heavyweight, m'boy. He'll be midroster, I suspect, and we're only staying for the first fight."

Teddy's face fell. "Oh, *please*, Papa," he wheedled.

"It would not be at all nice for you to be here after it grows dark," Mina told him sternly. "It would not be respectable."

Teddy huffed out a sigh and thrust out his bottom lip.

"I had hoped to secure a private parlor," Jeremy sighed. "But they're all taken. Everyone got here devilish early it seems."

"Well, you can use mine," Mina said as the thought struck her. "It has a window out onto the courtyard."

From the gleam in Jeremy's eye as he thanked her, she realized he had expected her to offer this for his use. She did not mind though, as she would have been appalled at the idea of him taking a child of such tender years into a common taproom.

"Let me show you through."

She took them through to her private parlor, and Jeremy went to the bar to secure lemonade for Teddy and something stronger for himself. Mina demurred, but he brought her back a bottle of wine in any case which he set on the side.

"Is this room for your use alone, Auntie?" Teddy asked, opening the lid of the music box and setting off its pretty chimes.

"Yes, your uncle Nye had it set up for me."

He looked frowningly at the walls. "Where is your portrait of Grandmama?"

Mina smiled. "My portrait of her is only little and I wear it here, around my neck." She reached up and unfastened her locket. "Come sit beside me and you shall see."

287

Teddy came and sat on the sofa next to her, and she passed the open necklace to him which he gazed at for a moment. "Yes," he agreed solemnly. "That's her." He looked at the other miniature. "Is that my uncle Nye?" he asked.

Mina shook her head. "That is my own dear papa. He was a schoolmaster."

Jeremy poured him a tumbler of lemonade from a jug and passed it to him.

"What are the dogs' names?" he asked, restlessly getting up to wander the room.

"Dogs?" Mina looked up to see him gazing at the china Staffordshire dogs on the mantel. "Fiddly and Dee," she improvised.

Two dimples appeared in Teddy's cheeks. "You made that up!" he accused.

"Of course," she agreed with raised brows. "That is my prerogative. I have another china dog upstairs that an ex-pupil of mine named, and you would not believe the preposterous name she gave it."

"Bill Barnicoat," Teddy guessed promptly.

Mina gave a startled laugh. "Now that is a funny name."

Jeremy smiled, sitting in a seat by the window. "It's a local Cornish name," he said. "And don't go poking and prying into all your aunt's personal things," he admonished the boy.

"I don't mind," Mina assured Teddy, who was peering in her workbox. He extracted two silver thimbles and set them on his thumbs.

"They're taking their coats off for the first bout, my son," Jeremy said, taking a sip of brandy.

Teddy rushed over to the window. "Colfax is out there!" he said, pointing. "Can we not go outside, Papa?"

"You'll cramp his style. Besides, your aunt's feelings will be hurt if we abandon her."

"You may carry a chair over to the window if you like, Teddy," she offered. He made haste to take up her suggestion.

No sooner had he clambered into his seat, his face next to the glass, than he gave a startled exclamation. "Grandpapa from the picture!" he gasped, pointing a finger to the pane. "There!"

Jeremy looked amused. "That is not my father, but your uncle Nye," he explained. "He does look very like that portrait of the fourth Viscount Faris, does he not?"

Teddy frowned. "But why does my uncle Nye look like Grandpapa?" he asked.

Mina's gaze darted to Jeremy, but he looked perfectly composed. "Because Vance blood flows in his veins too, my boy. Why else?"

"But my aunt…?"

"Your aunt has no Vance blood like us," Jeremy reminded him gently. "You know she shares my mama's but not my papa's lineage."

Teddy's frown cleared. "Oh." He glanced sidelong at Mina. "So, if my aunt and my uncle had a little boy, he would be more like a brother than a cousin to me."

"He would still be your first cousin." Jeremy laughed. "But a very close one indeed." Teddy seemed satisfied with this and pressed his nose to the glass. "Mind you do not fog that windowpane," Jeremy admonished him. "Your aunt is forced to clean those with her own fair hands."

"Have you no servant, Auntie?" asked Teddy in surprise.

"Only one," Mina admitted. "It is too bad, but no one wants to work for us here at such a lonely spot."

"You have not yet replaced Ivy?" Jeremy asked with a yawn.

Mina shook her head. "Nor like to, apparently."

He nodded. "Let me ask my housekeeper if they can find you someone," he suggested. "We often turn people off if they displease my wife," he observed with a grimace. "What was the name of that unfortunate girl your mother flew at last week?" he asked, turning to Teddy.

"Corin," Teddy supplied sadly. "Mama pulled her hair and slapped her cheek so hard, it turned quite red."

"She'll be a local girl and looking for work, no doubt," Jeremy hazarded.

Mina lowered her voice. "If she's respectable, I have been reliably informed she will not want a position here."

"Ah," said Jeremy, holding up a finger. "But that was before. All Penarth now knows there's a mistress now in residence and a highly respectable one at that. She attends church every Sunday and has swept through with a new broom. Is that not so?"

Mina regarded him in surprise. "All of Penarth?"

"Assuredly," he agreed. "I promise you."

"Well, if you can find us another pair of hands, we would indeed be grateful, but we are badly in need of bar staff and I'm sure a former maidservant from Vance Park would not fall so far in grace as that."

"No, but a footman might," Jeremy suggested wryly. "Only Colfax stays the course, we get through them at a rate of knots as well."

"What about Herney?" suggested Teddy without taking his eyes from the window. "He said he will work his notice and not another day. I heard him tell Harbottle so only yesterday."

"I did not realize he was working his notice." Jeremy looked startled. "Ah well, our loss may be your gain, sister."

"Well, that would be wonderful indeed if you may work such a miracle," Mina said doubtfully.

"Leave it with me," Jeremy said confidently. "And now, silence while we enjoy the bout."

Mina watched for a couple of minutes but found the prospect of two bare-chested men repeatedly thumping each other in the face, while the crowd shouted and jostled excitedly around them, to be one she did not savor. She slipped back to the kitchen as Jeremy explained the precise science of the counterpunch to his son and heir.

Soon she had stacked the washed pans against the draining board and started on the gravy-smeared plates which started to appear via a sulky Reuben. He did not speak as he plunked them down beside her, so Mina did not trouble herself to either.

She had soaked through two drying cloths already and was fetching a third freshly laundered tea towel from the drawer when her brother reappeared, once more carrying Teddy.

291

"We're off now, Mina. Night is falling and I'd better take this one home."

She nodded and came forward to kiss Teddy's cheek. "Will you need to collect Colfax from outside?" she asked.

Jeremy shook his head. "I shall not spoil his fun."

"Teddy will not slip from the saddle while he's asleep?" she fretted.

Her nephew's eyes flickered open. "I'm not so tired as all that!" he objected.

"He's an excellent seat." Jeremy laughed. "Besides, I should not let him fall." He looked at her critically a moment. "You're overworked here, Mina. I shall speak to my housekeeper without delay."

"I would appreciate it," she admitted. "It has been a long day, but I shall take myself off to bed directly."

He nodded.

"Will you not kiss Papa good night?" Teddy asked from his father's shoulder.

Mina started. "Of course, we are brother and sister after all," she said bracingly and stepped forward to lightly peck Jeremy's cheek. "Good night, Jeremy," she said and saw a flicker of surprise in his expression before he smiled back at her, looking pleased.

"Good night, Mina."

She did not watch them depart through the window, but instead finished up in the kitchen and then went through to the scullery to wash before bed. She was just fastening the buttons at her neck as she walked into the connecting passageway to the hallway when she paused, hearing a burst of husky laughter. She could see the shadow against the wall of two figures, just out of view, who were intertwined at the foot of the stairs.

"Finally noticed me, have you?" the voice asked flirtatiously. "I been waiting for you to cast your eyes in my direction for an eternity, Clem Dabney. I thought that Goldie had sunk her talons in you good and proper."

"You're a local then, are you, my beauty?" he responded gamely. "Now that does surprise me, for you've not the regional way of speech at all."

"Good God, no!" the woman replied, sounding annoyed. "I'm no Cornish maid!"

"I'm glad to hear that," Dabney replied, lowering his voice. "For I've no use for maidens, none at all. I prefer a more seasoned hand at the plough."

"Prefer to ride below the crupper, do you?" she asked huskily. "I must confess I've no use for novices when it comes to ploughing my furrow."

Mina flushed. She ought not to be listening to this, she thought. The terms might be agricultural, but she knew from their tone they were not discussing anything as wholesome as farming. She was just sliding her foot back for a stealthy retreat when she heard the front door open and close and a third voice raised to join the throng.

"Ah, there you are, Clara," said a booming voice. "I've secured a prime position in the courtyard and mean to sit atop our carriage to watch the next bout."

"I was just telling Mr. Dabney here, my dear, how you'd laid your bets on him at the last three fights," his lady answered, bold as brass.

"That you, Dabney?" asked the voice in surprise. "Good gad, sir, I'd have scarcely recognized you rigged up like a gent."

"Oh yes, it's me alright," Clem Dabney answered good-naturedly. "By habit, I don't tend to walk about stripped to the waist."

"No," mused the gentleman, sounding surprised, as though he'd never considered that prizefighters might have lives outside the ring. "I suppose you wouldn't, by God."

"I'll be out shortly, Cyril dear," his companion dismissed him. "Mr. Dabney was going to introduce me to his lady friend, Miss Gold."

"Oh," the unfortunate Cyril responded without interest before another aspect occurred to him. "Now don't you get distracting Dabney before his fight, Clara," he reproved her. "Needs all his concentration on defeating that bruiser Nye. Devilish ugly customer he can be. I lost my shirt when he defeated that Frenchie last June."

"Nay, sir, she won't distract me," Clem said easily. "Besides, there's some of us that benefits from a last-minute distraction. I get too wound up if I've nothing else to focus on."

"Oh?" Cyril sounded interested in this technique. "Well, in that case, proceed, my dear fellow! You'll join me when you're ready, Clara," he said, his voice drifting away.

Clara giggled. "I didn't realize you were fighting William Nye." Her voice was breathy with excitement. "Maybe I should wait and offer the spoils to the victor," she purred.

"Nay, one so beautiful could not be so cruel," Clem murmured. "You'll not abandon me so fast? Not when I'm so anxious to play the swain."

She laughed at that. "You'll not escape so easily, my big, strong ox," she told him. "For I mean to put a yoke on you before this night is ended, my fine, lusty ploughboy." Mina hearing a rustling sound, and guessed they were kissing.

"Oh, very well," Clara conceded with a sigh. "In that case lead me to your rustic hayrick forthwith."

"Aye, and gladly," he responded. "We've got half an hour, for I fight at eight."

Hurried footsteps mounted the staircase. Slowly, Mina advanced into the hall. She was trembling, she noticed as she reached for the banister, with anger. So, the lady considered she might offer herself as a winner's trophy to her husband, did she? Mina inwardly seethed as she climbed the steps to the attic. She did not know if Clem had been allotted a bed on the second or third floor, but she went slowly to ensure she had provided them with plenty of time to have ensconced themselves in his room.

She reached her bedroom without further occurrence and once there, made haste to don her nightgown and bed socks and an unflattering nightcap besides. She drew the covers over her head and thought about the people currently spilling from every door in the inn. Disreputable types, she thought them. A mix of sportsmen and villains.

Her mother would have been shocked to the core at such goings-on under her roof, she thought. But then, Mama's own experience of life at Penarth had set her on the ruinous path to divorce. She was not sure how Mama subsequently wound up marrying a respectable schoolmaster, for her parents had never spoken to her of such things. She supposed they must have drawn a discreet veil over Mama's previous life. On reflection, perhaps it was not so strange that she had not known Jeremy even existed.

She turned over on the bed, furiously dragging the sheets with her. It took only a few moments with her eyes squeezed shut before she realized she was not going to get a wink of sleep. With an exclamation, she sat up and reached for the matches, lighting her candle. She would read the highwayman story, she told herself. She had only managed the first few pages before dropping off the previous night.

Still, try as she might, she found it hard to immerse herself in the story tonight. Other thoughts kept intruding, then, too, there was the background noise from the yard below. Though she could not make out any precise words being shouted she could hear the hoots and jeers drifting up to her window though it was shut fast against the cold night air. She pulled her nightcap down about her ears and to that added her shawl which she draped over her head also, to muffle out the sound. Then she rested her elbows against her raised knees and glued her eyes to the well-worn pages of her periodical.

By sheer dogged determination, she managed to wade her way through the words on the page, though she took in truly little of the story. She wasn't sure how much later it was that the bedroom door was flung open and Nye came in, stripped to the waist, a candle in one hand and a cloth in the other which he held to his eye.

She sat up straight in astonishment. Surely it wasn't as late as all that? She lowered her shawl from her head. She fancied she could still catch snatches of conversation in the courtyard below.

He limped across the room. "Need to sleep," he said, lowering himself down onto the bed with a stifled groan. Watching him, Mina almost winced herself. He was a mass of cut and sore flesh. His left eye looked to be the worst; there was a deep welt above it which looked only freshly healed.

"What are you doing up here at this hour, Nye? They're surely still drinking the bar dry?"

"Dottie's taken over the bar," he said briefly, collapsing back onto the pillows.

"Dottie?"

"The brunette who came with Jones, the promoter. She's run several bars in her time. She knows what she's doing, and she won't stick her fingers in the strong box."

"Well, you look terrible," she said, remembering she was still cross with him from earlier. She shifted over to make room for him as he was already crowding her with his much larger body.

He gave a crack of laughter. "And you're all heart," he said, reaching over and snatching the book from her hand.

"Nye—!"

He threw it across the room. "Get over here," he said, seizing her under the arms and dragging her body across his. Mina froze a moment and then started to struggle.

"Ow!" he objected. "Keep still or I'll give you something to squirm about."

"Get off me, you brute!" she huffed, even though she stilled her limbs out of consideration for his injuries.

He gave a grunt and relaxed back against the pillows again, dragging the cap from her head and tossing it over the side of the bed so her hair spilled down over his shoulder.

Mina squeezed her eyes shut. It was extremely undignified lying spread-eagled in this fashion! She felt her face warm at the feel of all his hard muscle. All he was wearing was a pair of long underwear. "This can't possibly be comfortable for you—" she started reasonably.

"It is, so shut your yapping and go to sleep."

"You rude beast!" She braced her arms on either side of him to lever herself off, but his hands seized her immediately, keeping her in place. One at the top of her thigh and one at her waist.

"All I want to do is sleep," he growled. "But if you want to make it into something more, then I'll happily oblige."

To her alarm she felt something stirring against her thigh. "No," she burst out, for the inn was full to the rafters.

"Then give me what I want."

She pondered this a moment and forced herself to relax back against his hard body.

He gave another groan and shifted against her.

"Nye, you said—"

"Everything hurts," he explained curtly.

Which didn't explain his erection, she thought with annoyance, but she was too much of a lady to point that out. Which the brute was probably counting on, she thought, gritting her teeth. Fine! If he could ignore it, so could she. She moved her head, resting her cheek against his shoulder, and tried not to jump when his hand came to rest familiarly on her rump.

"Nye..." She frowned.

"Don't suppose I could persuade you to take this damnable nightgown off?"

"Certainly not!" she huffed indignantly.

He sighed, cursing under his breath. Then his hand moved, she heard a rustle, and when it slid back it was against her bare skin.

"Nye!"

"Just give me this," he muttered. "I'm in agony."

"It's your own fault, if you will partake in such brutal sports," she tutted. "I have no sympathy for you."

"You're a hard woman," he said, and she jumped when his thumb stroked over her backside in an idle caress. "But you do have a nice arse," he added thickly.

"You are the most aggravating man, Will Nye!"

"And extremely nice breasts," he added appreciatively.

"Stop it!"

"If you had any Christian charity, you'd take this bloody thing off and let me feel them bare against my chest."

She gasped. "You're an utter disgrace!" she said angrily, raising her head from his shoulder. She couldn't really make out his face in the dark, but she could have sworn she could see his eyes gleaming beneath her. And he was definitely hard against her thigh now. "You said all you wanted to do was sleep!" she pointed out.

"I do," he groaned. "But now I need a quick tumble to take the edge off."

"Well, there are plenty of whores around, so I suggest you go and find one!" she retorted angrily with a directness that shocked even her. Of course, if he had done any such thing, she was uncomfortably aware she would have hit the roof. What was going on with her these days? She struggled to rise up off him, but it was futile.

"I don't want one of them," he said huskily, and suddenly his hands were at her neckline, roughly yanking the thin cotton until a loud rent was heard.

"Nye!" she gasped, feeling the cool night air against her bare breasts. Then his mouth was there, wet and lascivious. He sucked the tip of one breast until he had taken as much of it into his mouth as possible and moaned around it loudly.

Mina gasped, her hands clutching at the pillows behind him as he pinched and plucked her other nipple, his hands roaming over the big, soft globes of her breasts, rubbing and stroking them, as his tongue licked over and underneath and between the valley as he switched from one to the other in indecent worship. "Nye!" she whimpered as he sucked the other nipple into his mouth and laved it with his tongue, making her whole body jolt in reaction. "Oh God!"

"Mmmm, that's it, comfort me," he groaned against her wet flesh.

To her horror, she realized she was now fully astride him, writhing against his muscular stomach as he suckled and nursed at her full breasts in turn. It was so wrong, she thought distractedly as she shifted over his hot mouth, pushing her other breast forward for his attention. Sucking in a shuddering breath, she was glad it was dark, so he couldn't see her wantonness!

"Take the rail," he growled, releasing her breast before fastening greedily on the other.

"What?"

He seized one of her hands and pushed it toward the iron headboard.

"Grab a hold of it," he growled. "With both hands."

300

Mina groped blindly for the metal headboard as he reached down and roughly tugged the remains of her poor mauled nightgown out of his way. Then she felt his thumb stroke over the most private hair between her legs, making her shiver. His cock was standing firm against her buttocks now, rubbing against her for attention.

"Are you wet, Mina?" he asked hoarsely.

She watched him run his tongue over his full bottom lip as his fingers slid into the warm folds of her quivering cleft. Mina's fingers gripped hard around the brass rail of the headboard.

"Nye!" she gasped again, and he gave a satisfied growl.

"Drenched," he said, tracing her slit as he coated his fingers in her moisture. "I want you to ride me."

"What?" Even as her shocked words burst forth, he slid two fingers deep inside her, making her eyes water as she clamped down on him. "Oh Nye!"

"Hmmm," he hummed, throwing back his head to look up at her face. "I always forget what a sweet little pussy you have. Far too sweet for such an obstinate woman."

He moved his fingers, and she squirmed at the sensation coiling in her loins. "Ohhh!"

"I bet I could make you come from this alone," he mused, pumping his fingers, but even as she undulated against the firm stroke, his hand halted. "No," he said as she suppressed a groan of disappointment. "I want you wild and wanton for it."

"What? I don't…"

He shifted again underneath her until she felt his rampant shaft between her legs, hard and urgent. "That's it," he grunted as he aligned the tip against her slit.

"But…I don't—"

"You do the work this way, as I'm too banged up." The fingers of one hand spread her open as the other grabbed her thigh, guiding her down over his staff. Mina bit her lip and groaned as the thick head pushed into her where she ached and throbbed.

"Nye," she groaned as he eased into her inch by inch. "It's—it's too much."

He gave a husky laugh. "You can take me," he said, tugging on her thigh and pushing his hips forward. He spoke the truth, for she felt him lodged there firmly before his hands came to grab her buttocks and urge her forward onto his cock. She tried to stifle the satisfied moan that rose to her lips as he slid deeper. She could not manage to suppress it when he slid the last couple of inches home. Luckily, he drowned it out with his own loud grunt. "Yesss!"

He dropped back against the pillows with a sharp exclamation. "Woman, you're going to kill me," he groaned. "You're so tight."

Mina's hands dropped from the rail to either side of his head on the pillows. The bed shuddered as she felt him reach up instead to seize the metal frame with his hands. "Ride me," he groaned. "Now."

"I don't—"

"Yes, you do. Move your hips," he ground out, sounding in pain. "Use me."

Mina blinked down at him. She felt so full at this angle, she was a little concerned she might do herself a mischief. She bounced forward experimentally, and he groaned. Resettling her knees against the mattress, she rose up and then sank back down on him. She couldn't help crying out at the thrilling sensation of propelling herself like this on him.

"Harder," he grunted.

Mina repeated the action with more vigor this time. "Are you sure this isn't hurting you?" she panted when she heard his ragged breathing as she rose and fell, rose and fell against him. She could feel her own bliss approaching, climbing up her spine as she arched her back and ground down against him in a steady rhythm.

"You're not sat on my face," he pointed out. "That's where I'm cut up."

She muffled an objection that would have been a waste of breath in any case. "Then," she panted, "you'll tell me, won't you?"

"What?"

"When you want me to stop. So, we can change back to the normal position," she said, face flaming hot.

"By normal, you mean missionary?" he asked with a raised brow. "Besides, you won't make me come like this," he said with supreme confidence. "And I told you, call me Will when I'm inside you."

"Oh." She fell forward, bracing her hands against his chest. "Will," she sobbed, twisting her fingers in his dark smattering of chest hair, and tugging sharply. She couldn't hold off much longer, a few more strokes and she'd ignite. Holding off her pleasure, she stopped bouncing and just undulated against him, tightening her inner muscles around him, taking him deep. "Will," she whispered brokenly. "You feel so good."

She felt him throb within her as she came apart, and suddenly his knees rose up behind her. The bed jerked as he released the headboard and sat up, his hands hard on her hips.

"Minerva!" he choked, and she blinked in the dark as she felt his breath on her face, his shocked voice in her ear. For a second, she thought she'd hurt one of his injuries, but then she felt him spilling within her. "W-Will!" she gasped, but his hands held her rigidly in place and suddenly, his mouth was on hers, hot and devouring. He wound a hand in her hair as he stroked his tongue in her mouth, the other grabbed at her backside, holding her firmly in place on his spurting shaft.

He moaned into her mouth as his hips surged hard against her until he was spent. Then he just held her there a moment as they panted in each other's arms. He released his grip on her hair and ran his hand from her neck to her middle back. Nipping at her bottom lip, he lifted his mouth from hers, still breathing hard. "Witch," he whispered and fell back onto the pillows, taking her with him. Too tired to protest, she let her eyes drift shut and fell fast asleep in his arms.

18

Predictably, if distressingly, it was a hammering on the door that awakened her the next morning.

"Mrs. Nye!" shouted Edna's voice. "They're asking for the master below!"

"Alright, Edna!" she yelled back and glanced down at Nye's sleeping face. His eye was not so swollen this morning, she was relieved to see, though he still looked rather battered with a purpleness coming out below it. Both his arms were outstretched and, as per usual, he was out cold. She shook his large shoulders and saw him wince. He must be sore, she realized, quickly releasing him.

When she started to peel herself off him, he grumbled in his sleep, "Leave off your squirming, wench. I'm not done with you yet."

"Wench? I'm your wife, you heathen! And you most certainly have done!" she scolded him. "It's morning and I'll thank you to remember I'm a decent woman."

He sighed at that, though his eyes remained closed. "So long as you don't remind me of it at night, I'm content," he said in a gravelly voice.

Mina turned her head sharply to look at him, but he hadn't moved, so she crossed to the dresser and helped herself to clean stockings and drawers. She had managed to clamber into her chemise and corset before his eyes finally opened, and he watched her stepping into her petticoats.

"I'll cure you of that respectability yet, Mina Nye," he rumbled ominously.

She stuck her nose in the air. "Seems to me you need some semblance of it around here. You're utterly shameless."

"Is that so?" He sounded more amused than anything.

"Brazen," she added. "And so are your clientele…" She hesitated.

"What is it?" he asked, swinging his legs around so his feet hit the floor. "It's not like you to hold back," he observed before continuing. "I told you, you shouldn't mix with them. They're a rough crowd. If you heard something that offended you, then I did warn you—"

"I'm not talking about the prizefighters," she burst out. "At least, not directly."

He eyed her warily. "What then?"

"Do you know who—" She flailed a moment for the right term. "*Accompanied* Clem Dabney upstairs yesterday?" she asked.

His eyes narrowed. "Clem?" he said with rising ire. "What of him? If he said anything to you—"

"No, no. He did not even know I was there." She hastened to stem the flow. "It was some married lady, I think. Her husband was a spectator in the crowd and yet still she went upstairs with Mr. Dabney." Nye blinked. "You do not look shocked," she said, feeling like the wind had been taken out of her sails.

He said nothing for a minute, just pulled on his long underwear. "This will be hard for you to fathom, Mina," he said dryly. "But very few would bring their wives to watch a boxing match. She was likely his mistress, and if she went upstairs with Clem, then he would not have forced her."

"I know that!" Mina flushed. "I may be sheltered but even I knew that much." She took a deep breath, lowering her gaze. "Have married women ever—" She broke off a moment. "To you, I mean," she said stiltedly. When she mustered the courage to look at Nye, he had his hands on his hips and was watching her under lowered brows.

"Offered to toss their skirts up for me?" he asked dryly. "If they did, those days are behind me now. And I was never particularly interested in respectably married ladies. They expect you to do all the work and then be grateful for it, in my experience. They're not worth the bother." Mina gasped at this and pressed her hands to her hot cheeks. "I'm doing you the favor of being frank with you," he pointed out. "If you ask me a direct question, then I'll give you a direct answer, whether you like it or not."

"What makes you think I was not satisfied with your answer?" she asked boldly, lowering her hands from her face. "If you *had* enjoyed making sport of other men's wives, I would have been seriously displeased!"

"Oh, would you now?" he asked, going from tense to amused. "For your information, I am only interested in one married woman and that's my own." He surprised her by crossing the room to haul her into his arms and soundly kiss her. "Now put on your dress," he growled. "Before I'm tempted to drag you back to that bed. More tempted, that is."

At the gleam in his eye, Mina hurried to free herself and fetch a clean black dress from the wardrobe. She would not put anything past him when he looked at her like that.

"I've invited Effie and Dot to take breakfast with me this morning in the parlor," she said over her shoulder as Nye pulled on his breeches. "At nine o'clock."

307

He looked skeptical. "I doubt they'll be up before noon," he predicted. "It would have been a late one last night. People will likely stick around until this afternoon before they start leaving with sore heads."

"Well," Mina reflected, moving to the mirror and taking up the hairbrush, "I shan't be offended if they do not show up. But I shall have to prepare in any case."

When she made her way downstairs ten minutes later however, she found Effie drifting out of the kitchen in a sea-green dress and cradling a cup of tea in her lace-mittened hands. "There you are, Mina," she greeted her with a yawn and a kiss to her cheek. "I've left Jeb abed, but I wouldn't have missed our cozy catch-up, not for the world!"

Mina showed her to the parlor and bade her take a comfortable seat while she saw what was for breakfast. She found Edna stacking smoked kippers onto a plate.

"Morning, Mrs. Nye," she greeted her. "Sorry about having to wake you like that, only that Mr. Jones would insist he needed to speak to the master first thing."

Mina waved the apology aside. "Not at all, Edna. What can I do?"

"Nothing, Mrs. Nye, these kippers are for your breakfast guests. I've buttered some bread slices there for you and I'm about to make a fresh pot of tea, so if you'll just take those through with you presently, then all is sorted."

"Wonderful," said Mina approvingly. "What should we do without you, Edna?"

The maid snorted but looked gratified.

Mina disappeared into the scullery to wash and when she reappeared some minutes later, Edna informed her, "There's hardly anyone up yet, except for that Mr. Jones smoking a nasty cigar outside the back door. Everyone else is still snoring."

"I'm sure it's not to be wondered at," Mina observed, buttoning her cuffs. "I could hear the merrymaking out of my window into the small hours."

Edna pursed her lips, then lowered her voice. "I'm lucky that bold-faced one with the mole on her cheek, what calls herself Mrs. Jones, took over the bar at midnight so I could go up to bed. I'm grateful to her for that if nothing else."

"Indeed, that was good of her," agreed Mina. "For it meant Nye could retire at a decent hour to repair his wounds." She colored faintly as she picked up the dish of kippers in one hand and the bread and butter in the other, for that was not all he had done.

"Only fancy, she's had me light the fire in her room this morning, so she set her curling iron to the flames," Edna said with obvious disapproval. "The vanity!"

"You must have been very busy already," Mina said, conscience-stricken. "Really, taking breakfast in the parlor this morning was most thoughtless of me."

"Nonsense! You're mistress here, and other folks needs to know it! You go on ahead," Edna told her bracingly. "I'll bring in the tea as soon as it's ready."

Mina thanked her and made for the parlor where she found Effie admiring the blue and gold tea set.

"Lovely bit of china, this," she said, looking up at Mina's entrance. "What a fine room! Do you know, I had no notion this was even here?"

"Oh, it wasn't," Mina told her, setting down the dishes and pulling back a seat at the table for Effie. "Nye had it set up for my use."

"Fancy that!" Effie's eyes were very wide. "That's handsome of him, and no mistake."

"Yes, I'm very fortunate," she said, setting the silver cruet set down on the table. "Do you think Mrs. Jones will join us this morning?"

"Who?" asked Effie blankly. "Oh, you mean Dot!" She sank into her seat and leaned forward confidingly. "She ain't really married to Nat you know, love. She just goes by that when she accompanies him out and about."

"Nat?"

"Nat Jones, the fight promoter. You must have seen him yesterday."

"Oh, of course. In the yellow waistcoat."

"That'll be him."

Effie helped herself to a kipper and a slice of bread and butter. "Well, this is grand," she said, looking around the room. "I declare I feels as if I'm havin' breakfast wiv a duchess."

Mina smiled wanly, but Edna sailed through the door with the silver teapot and milk jug before she could reply. "There you are, Mrs. Nye," she said, setting them down. "Can I fetch you anything else?"

"I think we're very amply provided for, thank you, Edna."

"Don't you talk nice," Effie said admiringly as Edna retreated. "A proper lady. Everyone says so."

"Nye thinks it's down to too much book-learning."

Effie shook her head. "Now that's where he's wrong. You can never have too much of that," she said. "That's what my old dad used to say, and he should know, 'cause he couldn't read nor write, poor old sod." Mina was too startled to know how to reply to that, but luckily Effie did not seem to notice. "Besides," she said bracingly. "My Jeb said you've a pert tongue in your 'ead and not too prim to give someone a taste of the sharp side of it." She giggled.

"Oh! Well, that was—kind—of him," Mina choked out as she selected two cups and saucers for them. "Do you take sugar?"

"Three when I can get it," Effie admitted. "Yes, he said you soon had Clem with his tail between 'is legs and bashful as a schoolboy!"

Mina had a sudden uncomfortable recollection of Clem's rather racy dialogue with the female in the hall the night before. "*Bashful* is not the word I think I would use for Mr. Dabney," she observed dryly.

"Never tell me he was saucy with you!" gasped Effie. "I wouldn't have thought it of him!"

"Oh no!" Mina interrupted her quickly. "Not at all. To me, he was politeness itself."

Effie collapsed back into her chair in exaggerated relief. "Well, thank gawd for that!" she said. "Or Nye would have torn him limb from limb! Anyone can see how jealously he guards you." Mina paused before lifting the teapot but could find no words for a response. "I don't mind tellin' you," Effie continued. "All the fellas was talking of it yesterday after that exhibition he put on in the bar. Not in his hearing, mind. None of them had a death wish." Effie winked and Mina poured the tea.

311

"He is not so bad as all that," she protested weakly.

"Oh, isn't he?" Effie snorted. "You didn't see how he ripped at Frank when he reminded him of how he'd left you standing at the altar all forlorn. Proper fuming, he was. It's my belief if my Jeb hadn't got between them, Nye would have planted him a facer there and then and he wasn't even down to fight Frank Toomes!"

"He fought Mr. Dabney, did he not?"

"S'right," Effie agreed, taking a large swig of tea. "Shame he wouldn't let you watch, but I daresay it's not a very genteel thing for a lady to do." She sounded sympathetic.

"I hope Nye does not think of me as a perfect lady," Mina murmured absently, remembering what he'd said about fine ladies not being worth the bother.

"Maybe you'll bring him round given time," said Effie, who was clearly one of life's optimists.

"Perhaps," agreed Mina, who was not sure she'd ever be a boxing enthusiast.

The door opened, and Mina was surprised to see Dot sail around it dressed in a lilac spotted gown with a profusion of pleats. Mina noticed that the mole on her cheek was a good deal less prominent this morning and realized with surprise that she must enhance it with charcoal to make it darker as some people did with their eyelashes. Her hair, however, just as Edna had predicted, was tightly ringleted in a profusion of jet-black curls showing evidence of her curling iron.

"Good morning," she greeted her, getting to her feet. "Please take a seat, Mrs. Jones, and I'll fetch you a cup."

The newcomer gave her a level look. "That's not my name, Mina," she said, pulling out a seat at the table. "Though Jones is my name, funny enough, it was because my father bestowed it on me, not Nat. It's Miss Jones, but you can call me Dot," she said handsomely.

Mina fetched her a plate, cup, and saucer and made haste to pour her a cup from the silver teapot.

"You are an early riser, Miss Jones. I had thought you might sleep in after my husband told me you had manned the bar last night."

"I couldn't loll abed like the Quality," said Dot agreeably. "Not for a hundred pound. My old ma would have had a good deal to say about lying in for all hours. Never taken breakfast in bed in my life, though I keep a parlor maid now and a kitchen one too."

Mina passed her a brimming cup which she took with murmured thanks. "Do you live in Exeter?" she asked politely, nudging the dish of kippers her way.

Dot shook her head. "London," she said succinctly. "I don't like to be away from the capital for more than a few days at a time. Can't abide the backwaters, I can't."

Mina was unsure if she was referring to Penarth or Exeter in these disparaging terms, but Effie extended her cup hastily for a refill, so Mina was spared having to answer by her hostess duties.

"Well, well," drawled a voice from the doorway, making the three of them turn their heads. "What a dainty gathering."

Mina drew in a breath of surprise for it was none other than Lady Faris resplendent in a royal blue riding habit complete

313

with whip and mannish-looking hat which did nothing to detract from her blond beauty.

"Lady Faris," she exclaimed. "Is my brother with you?"

Jeremy's wife had sauntered into her room as if she had every right, and Mina was tempted to point out this was a private room. However, she felt somewhat hampered from doing this as she had so recently visited Vance Park.

"Can I help you to a cup of tea, Lady Faris?" she asked instead with cool politeness.

Amanda Vance gave a dismissive wave of her hand. "I wouldn't dream of interrupting your little tête-à-tête," she said with a curl of her lip. Effie sucked in her cheeks and directed a wide-eyed look Mina's way. Dottie remained unperturbed by the interloper, tucking into her breakfast with relish.

"I understand my husband attended your sordid festivities last night," Lady Faris continued, sounding nettled. "And saw fit to bring my son with him."

"I'm afraid you will need to take it up with him, if you disapprove of prizefighting," Mina pointed out.

Lady Faris shrugged. "Quite the contrary, I assure you. 'Tis only that I fail entirely to see why I should be excluded from such a party. It is doubtless hard for a daughter of the middle classes such as yourself to appreciate," she said condescendingly. "But one who has had the benefits of a truly enlightened upbringing can have an appreciation that you would be wholly lacking."

Lady Faris's eyes grew round and avid as she watched Clem and Jeb walk across the courtyard from the stables. She walked toward the window and stared out at them quite unabashed. "Magnificent specimens," she murmured, then turned with a

314

smug smile toward Mina. "Of course, a sheltered little schoolmistress like yourself couldn't possibly understand the exhilaration of watching something as primal as two rough men going at it like animals." She gave a dramatic shiver.

Mina rolled her eyes; she could feel not only Effie's but also Dot's eyes on her, waiting for her to react. "I'm so glad you're enjoying the view," she said with the blandest politeness, hoping Effie would not fly out of her seat at any minute.

The blond looked annoyed by her mild response, as though she had been hoping to shock her. "Of course," she persisted. "The fighters would be very riled up after such a set-to. They require certain inducements to calm back down of which you would be entirely ignorant, you poor little thing." She tapped her chin with one finger. "I remember when I traveled to Spain with my father, how the bullfighters would send in a cow to calm the most savage bull."

"I'm sorry," said Mina sweetly. "Are you actually comparing yourself to a cow in this metaphorical scenario?"

Effie giggled, and Dot let out a surprised gurgle of laughter.

Lady Faris gave a high, unconvincing laugh. "I must say, your attitude toward extramarital encounters is quite refreshingly cosmopolitan for one of your ilk," she said snidely. "Nye must be eternally grateful of the fact. I doubt very much you know in whose bed he spent the night celebrating or drowning his sorrows."

Mina set down the milk jug she had just picked up with a thud, but even as she opened her mouth to speak Dottie forestalled her, lowering her knife.

"Every man in that bar heard Nye resolve to take himself off to bed to his wife at ten o'clock," she said loudly. "So, there's no mystery as to whose bed he slept in last night."

"No one knows as well as I where my husband spent the night," Mina said calmly, but with a hint of steel in her voice. "You have missed the mark, Lady Faris. I beg you will not embarrass yourself further in front of my guests."

Amanda Vance's color was exceedingly high in her cheeks. She gave an irritable shrug of her shoulder. "Oh, well, if you are resolved to be a dead bore over it, there is nothing more to be said."

"I am not broad-minded and have never claimed to be," Mina said as if she had not spoken. "My marriage is not a *fashionable* one," she said scathingly, "such as the ones I understand the nobility frequently partake in, and neither would I want it to be." She let that sink in a moment, pausing to see if Lady Faris would make some response, but when she only tossed her head, Mina turned back to her guests. "Is there anything I can get for anyone else? Dot—more kippers?"

"I don't suppose you've any coffee?" Dot asked apologetically. "Only I've got in the habit of taking that of a morning rather than tea."

"Of course!" said Mina, getting out of her chair. "Would anyone like anything?" Lady Faris only turned a cold shoulder and stared out of the window. Dot and Effie both demurred so Mina made her way through to the kitchen where she could hear someone talking in a loud jocular fashion to the accompaniment of boisterous laughter.

She had hoped to escape the tense atmosphere in the parlor for a moment to cool her heated cheeks. She had never felt so tempted to forget she was a lady and could only be grateful that

316

she and Nye had discussed the question of remaining faithful to their marriage vows only that morning so she could answer Lady Faris with perfect composure.

As soon as she stepped over the threshold, the conversation fell quickly away, and she felt several alarmed gazes follow her as she walked to the kitchen range. She wondered what caused their expressions and could only hazard their conversation had not been fit for her ears. "Good morning, gentlemen," she said in passing to Jeb and the Toomes brothers, who were stood about in various attitudes of relaxation, their shirts unbuttoned and their necks bare. Through the open door she could see Clem and Nat Jones smoking cigars.

"Morning, Mrs. Nye," several voices chimed discordantly.

She nodded. "I trust you all slept well."

"Aye, tolerable well," said a Toomes, she wasn't sure which.

"Well enough," concurred the other. "Though my head was fair ringing from the clout I received in the third. Fair cruel it were," he said sadly and shot a meaning glance at Jeb, who grinned.

"You'll live," he told him callously, but Mina could see they were all friends in here.

To her relief, she realized the overwhelming aroma in the room was coffee which meant they did have it. She never drank the stuff, but her father had used to be partial to a cup in the morning. She made for the range and poured a large cup for Dot.

Nye cleared his throat. "The boys have clubbed together to pay for us to spend a weekend at a fancy hotel," he told her. "To celebrate our nuptials." He scratched the back of his neck and Mina thought he reddened slightly.

"That is very kind of you all," Mina marveled and meant it. "Only the other day, Nye said he would take me away for just such a weekend."

"Seems the least we can do," said Frank cheerfully. At least, Mina thought it was Frank.

"It was Nat's idea," admitted Jeb. "But we didn't mark the occasion last time we were all here, so…"

Nat Jones came in from outside, and Mina noticed he was the only one dressed correctly in a cravat and waistcoat. "Dear lady," he cried. "Allow me to felicitate you. It is too bad of Nye not to have introduced us till now."

Nye glowered. "This is my wife. Mina, this is Nat Jones, who organizes the matches."

Nat bowed gracefully over Mina's hand.

"Quite the gent, ain't he?" said a Toomes brother, nudging Mina. "To look at 'im, you'd never guess he was raised in a circus, would you?"

She didn't say so, but to Mina, his manner did hold something of the theatricality of a ringmaster in a big top. His tailcoat this morning was of delicate lavender and his waistcoat of emerald green.

"I'm very happy to make your acquaintance, Mr. Jones," she said aloud.

"I dare swear I have never seen such a change in a man," he said, sweeping his glance over Nye. "Only look at him this morning. Well rested, shaven, dressed. I doubt more than a drop of liquor even touched his lips last night. Usually the next morning his eyes are bloodshot and his vocabulary mere monosyllables!" Nye's frown deepened. "You have wrought a miracle, Mrs. Nye! A modern-day miracle!"

"Aye, well that's enough said of that!" Nye grouched, folding his arms. "Let's not get too carried away."

"I must get back with Dot's coffee," Mina excused herself, leaving them to their ribald conversation to rejoin the others in the parlor.

They were deep in conversation when she entered the room, and Mina looked around in surprise to find no sign of Amanda Vance.

"Did Lady Faris depart already?"

Dot gave a short laugh. "She only waited for you to disappear and made good her escape," she said contemptuously.

"Feel sorry for the poor bugger what's joined his lot wiv 'ers in life," said Effie.

Mina colored faintly as she set the coffee down in front of Dot. "She is married to my half brother," she confided, returning to her seat.

"She never is!" Effie gasped. "And her making sheep's eyes at my Jeb out the window, bold as you like!"

"I don't think their union is a happy one," Mina admitted.

"Fancy your brother being some posh nob, in these parts," Dottie marveled, taking an appreciative sip of the dark fluid. Mina nodded, interested to see she took it black and bitter. Dot sighed when she set the cup down. "That's better," she said. "Well, wonders will never cease. 'Course, I could tell you had something about you. We were just discussing it. I wish me and Nat had been here that weekend of your marriage now."

Mina grimaced. "In truth, you did not miss much," she assured her. "But that reminds me, I have your lace scarf," she said, turning to Effie. "Which you were kind enough to lend me for a veil."

"Oh no!" said Effie, looking shocked. "You're not to return that. That's to be kept in your top drawer along with your lucky silver sixpence and your dried blue bouquet."

Mina started, remembering how she had pitched the delphiniums over a stone wall on her lonely march back to the inn. "That's very kind of you," she said, "but you see—"

"Wouldn't hear of taking it back," Effie said staunchly. "You can lend me something borrowed if I ever get Jeb up that aisle."

"Very well, I will treasure it," Mina said awkwardly. "I don't precisely know what I did with the silver sixpence in truth, and I'm afraid I threw away the flowers in a fit of temper. I wanted to strangle Nye at the time," she admitted as Dot gave a gust of delighted laughter.

"You're a dark horse and no mistake," she said appreciatively. "When you asked that snooty piece of goods if she was comparing herself to a cow! I hardly knew where to look!"

Effie joined with a peal of mirth. "She didn't know where to put herself!" Effie gasped, wiping her eyes. "I wouldn't have missed that, not for a month of Sundays! Told you she was a rare 'un," she said to Dot.

"She's certainly not in the usual style," Dot agreed, though Mina was not sure this was precisely a compliment.

"I think the lads were disappointed to find that pretty Ivy up and gone," Dot commented when their laughter subsided. "Whatever happened to her? Nye seemed to have no clue." She shot a keen look at Mina. "If I'm not mistaken, you'll know more about the matter than he." She tapped her nose. "Women always do."

"A man, like as not," Effie chimed in. "I hope the poor little devil found a better one than the last she hitched her cart to."

Mina set her knife and fork down. "She did," she said. "A widower with two small children who wanted to marry her and set up house."

"Well, I never!" Effie whistled.

"Good for her," said Dot. "I only hope it may work out for her."

"She seemed realistic about the life he offered," Mina said, pouring another cup of tea. "And was entering into it with her eyes open."

"Can't ask for much more than that," Dot opined, pulling a face. Effie agreed with a sad sigh. They passed the rest of their meal amicably, and from the rumbling of wheels and the clip-clop of hooves in the courtyard outside, Mina observed that people were already starting to drift away after last night's excitement.

By lunchtime, most of the overnight guests had cleared out. They served what was left of the pasties cold to any who were desirous of lunchtime refreshment, and to her surprise, Nye summoned her to the door to wave goodbye when Nat, Dot, Clem, Jeb, and Effie departed in two coachloads. She hurried to his side and he wrapped an arm about her waist. A cart drew out behind them carrying the Toomes brothers and their disreputable toothless old grandmother, Ma Toomes.

"Where *is* their third brother at present?" Mina asked as they waved them off.

"Exeter jail," Nye answered absently. "Why?"

"'Tis of no matter," she hastened to assure him.

19

The rest of the day passed in a blur of bed stripping and laundry. She and Edna pegged three lots out to dry on the line in the sunshine. Mina walked to the edge of the drive and shielded her eyes against the sun to gaze into the distance. It was a clear day and she could see the sea which looked a sparkling turquoise next to the gray granite and green headland. It was so beautiful she could almost believe it an illustrated plate from a storybook.

"You'd best not be thinking about flight again," a voice rumbled behind her, and Mina swung around to shoot a reproachful look at Nye, who was stood watching her, hands on his hips.

"I keep thinking I should incorporate a walk along the beach to my day," she admitted. "Perhaps before breakfast. I imagine it would be a wonderful start to the day."

"Depends what the weather's up to," he retorted. "On a day like this when all's calm it would be well enough. But the Atlantic Ocean in a storm is none too pretty."

"I expect it's still a sight to behold," she argued. "And if it was too choppy then I should not venture down from the cliffs."

He frowned. "I wouldn't want you walking those cliffs on your own. It's a lonely spot and you're not familiar with the terrain. Then there's the tides," he added. "You can easily get trapped when it comes in fast."

"Well, you could always come with me," she pointed out, turning on her heel and walking back up the path. "If you're that worried."

When she drew level to him, he reached out and caught her wrist, drawing her toward him.

"Evening is better," he said. "Come, take off your apron and we'll go now."

"Now?" She felt a spurt of excitement.

He nodded. "It's after six."

"You're free now?"

"For an hour," he confirmed. "Before the drinkers start pitching up."

She struggled with her apron strings before he could change his mind. Something about her haste seemed to amuse him, for he laughed and spun her round to help.

"I can take it in—" she objected, but it was too late, for he had balled it up and cast it over the wall.

"We'll collect it on the way back," he said, taking a firm hold of her hand.

"I do not have my bonnet," Mina murmured, though she did not think she would miss it so very much.

The wind whipped Mina's hair about her face as they approached the cliffs. In the yard, the sun had felt warm, but the breeze was stiffer the closer they came to the sea, and Mina almost wished for her cloak. Once they started down the cliff path however, the rocks sheltered them, and she soon started to warm up again. Nye went before her and she was glad to put a steadying hand to his shoulder for parts of the path were very steep and not easy to negotiate.

They paused at the halfway point and Mina caught her breath when she beheld the blue waters, dazzling against the pale sands in the cove beach.

"I think this must be the most beautiful place I have ever been," she murmured. Nye stood silent beside her gazing out, but she felt it was a companionable silence and groped for his hand again. He took hers in his own and squeezed it.

"The private beach with Vance House has a prettier view than this," he said.

"I can't imagine one prettier."

He shook his head. "You'll see."

"We should have brought a picnic," Mina mused.

"Next time," said Nye, and Mina felt herself warm again, from the inside out this time. It took them a further ten minutes to reach the bottom, and she was glad to walk along the flat beach, for the balls of her feet ached from their climb down. Heeled ankle boots were not the most suitable for cliff walking, and privately she acknowledged that navigating the path by herself would not have been sensible.

Glancing back at the crescent shape of the cliffs behind her, she could readily imagine that you could easily get caught out by the tide and would face a desperate climb to escape it coming in. She shuddered and Nye passed his arm about her waist.

"Cold?"

"No, just thinking," she said, her answer almost drowned out by the screech of the gulls.

"We can walk right the way around to the village at low tide," Nye told her, pointing into the distance.

"It is low tide now?"

He nodded. "We could walk back up through the village, though it's a steady climb."

"I'm familiar with it," Mina reminded him. "I walk it every Sunday for church."

He nodded. "So you do."

The decision made to walk along the shore into the village, they picked up their pace. Mina gazed out to sea at the boats she could see bobbing in the water.

"What would they be fishing for?" she asked.

"Pilchards likely as not." She pulled a face. "You have no liking for the humble pilchard?"

"It is not my favorite," she admitted. "I do not think I've had them above twice in my life."

"You've had it more than that since you've lived here," he said. "In Edna's fish stew. We keep a barrelful in salt in the pantry."

Mina shrugged. "Edna's fish stew is tolerable but not a dish I'd choose to eat."

He grinned. "Maybe I should tell her to bake you a Stargazy pie."

"What's that?"

"You've not heard of a Cornish Stargazy pie?"

"You're teasing me," she said, narrowing her eyes at him.

He shook his head. "I cannot believe you've not heard tell of it. It's baked pilchards with egg and potato in a pastry pie."

"It sounds foul," Mina said frankly.

"It's a local delicacy," he corrected her.

"Why is it called Stargazy?"

"Ah, because the pilchard heads are arranged to peer up through the pie crust toward the stars."

Mina halted and stared at him. "How macabre!"

"It's a sight to behold."

"I believe I'll pass up the Stargazy pie."

He laughed, tugging her hand to get her to moving again. "Don't let any locals hear you say so."

"By the by," Mina said as they neared the walkway up to the village, "Jeremy said he might be able to help us to some staff for the inn," she said, pushing the hair away from her brow. She did not think her low bun was fully intact by this point as most of her brown hair seemed to be streaming along in the sea breeze.

"How's that?" asked Nye skeptically.

"By all accounts, they have a high turnaround of staff at Vance Park. Jeremy said just recently a local girl was given her marching orders and they have an ex-footman who might be induced to work behind the bar."

"Is that right?"

"You sound doubtful."

"Let's just say, I'll believe it when I see it."

She shook her head but did not argue as they made their way up the beach. She had expected him to drop her hand as soon as they stepped off the beach and onto the track that led to the road, but he pulled her arm through his instead. Several fishermen were sat on barrels with lobster pots, and Nye nodded as they gazed at them with open curiosity, their pipes bobbing in their mouths as they wished them a good evening.

"Do any of the fishermen frequent The Merry Harlot?" Mina asked. Nye shook his head. "I seem to remember Edna told me they frequent The Ship instead."

Nye nodded in the direction of a black and white inn on the seafront. "That's it there."

Mina looked at the rather shabby little whitewashed inn. "It's not as grand as The Harlot," she said critically. "It's a shame we cannot poach some of their staff."

He smiled at that and Mina eyed him curiously, thinking she had never seen him so agreeable. "Your knuckles look split and sore," she observed. "Do they still hurt?"

He gave a small shake of his head. "Nothing to signify." They were climbing the bank now up away from the village.

"You cannot have had long to recover between your fights this time," she observed. "When we get back, I will bathe your cut eye in salt water."

He grunted. "Don't fuss. I'm used to taking care of such things." Then he shook his head.

"What?"

He looked rueful. "You did not even ask me who won my match."

With surprise, Mina realized this was true. "I suppose I took it for granted that you did," she admitted with some embarrassment.

Nye laughed at that. "Touching you have that much faith in me." Catching her suddenly troubled expression, he asked, "What is it?"

"Oh, it's nothing," she replied evasively. "Just something Lady Faris said."

Nye eyed her warily. "Oh yes?" he prompted. "And what was that?"

Mina hesitated, for the confidence she had felt only that morning when repudiating Lady Faris's claims had faded, since she had noticed a loophole. "She seemed to think I must have very lax views about marriage," she answered.

"Why?" he asked pointedly.

"Because she could not believe that you would tolerate anything else in a wife."

He came to an abrupt halt in the road, pulling Mina to a stop also. "I thought we had already cleared this up this morning."

"You said you were not interested in any married women save for your own," Mina reiterated.

"So where does the confusion lie?"

She gazed over his shoulder. "You did not mention *unmarried* women."

He gave a startled laugh. "Are you serious, Mina?" he asked, pulling her into his arms. He rested his chin on the top of her head. "You need have no worries on that score."

"Are you sure?" she blurted, staring at the tanned skin that showed between his collarless shirt and necktie. "I saw how those women clamored around the fighters these past two days."

"Aye, but did you see me paying any heed to them?" he answered lightly.

"I did not see much of you at all," she mumbled.

One hand moved from her waist to tilt up her chin. "You do not need to trouble yourself about any women, wed or unwed," he reiterated, his gaze capturing hers. "And my own marital views are far from lax. You might have noticed when I bawled everyone out in the bar, staking my claim? If you did not, then everyone else was sure to mark it, I promise you."

Mina's face reddened. "Well, yes," she agreed evasively. "But sometimes gentlemen expect fidelity from their wives without the expectation of reciprocating."

"Not me," he retorted promptly.

Her eyes sought his and whatever she saw in his dark gaze reassured her. She gave a short nod. "Very well then," she said. "Thank you for the clarification." She went to pull away, but his grip on her did not slacken. "Nye?" she said consciously. "We are standing in a common highway."

"Aye, so we are, wife, and not one more step will we stir until you give me the kiss I want."

"Nye!" She felt herself become flustered in an instant. "We are not some…courting couple!"

He looked amused. "Nay, for we skipped that stage," he agreed. "So, let us make amends for that now." He cocked his head to one side, looking suddenly thoughtful. "We'll walk out together like we did tonight and keep company of an evening at least twice a week."

"Keep company?" she echoed, trying to imagine Nye sat in the parlor with her in his fancy suit of an evening. Even twice a week that was some feat of imagination. What was she supposed to do with him? She could not imagine having him sitting with a book of poetry like her father had used to do or helping her to wind her yarn. "You'd need someone else to cover the taproom," she pointed out uncertainly.

"Well, according to you, Faris has that matter well in hand," he reminded her glibly.

She spluttered. "You, however, seemed to place little confidence in his abilities!"

"The longer you stall giving me those pretty lips, the longer we'll be stood in the middle of the road, at the mercy of passing carts," Nye pointed out.

Realizing he was not going to let her off the hook with this, Mina took a deep breath and squeezed her eyes shut, tipping her face up to receive his kiss. He did not immediately take her up on her invitation, and for a moment indeed, she thought he would not.

She was just starting to feel foolish when his lips descended on hers, in a kiss such as Will Nye had never bestowed on her before. His lips were soft yet firm, and infinitely sweet as he molded them to her own. After a moment, she felt his hands cup her face almost tenderly and run his thumbs along her cheekbones in what she could only consider to be a caress.

Never in her wildest dreams would she have imagined that Will Nye would ever touch her thus. When he lifted his face away from hers, he looked almost as surprised by it as she. He stared

331

at her a moment before taking her hand again. "That was the kiss I should have given you atop the carriage that time," he rasped.

"The carriage?" Mina faltered, feeling her wits had gone a-begging.

"The first time," he replied abruptly.

Mina remembered the suffocating embrace that had been her first and almost agreed. But if he had kissed her like this back then, she was not sure how she might have reacted. It would have been far too intimate. This kiss, she realized dazedly, was a courting kiss. It was a kiss given to sweethearts.

She traced her lips with her finger and reddened. When Nye turned a heated look her way, she could not quite meet his eye. "Have you ever been courting before?" she heard herself ask and wished she had not.

"Courting?" He shook his head.

"You seem rather good at it," she said, casting him a sidelong look. "As though you might have had some practice."

"You're not so bad yourself, love," he answered with a wink.

"You've never had a sweetheart?" she persisted recklessly, her color heightened.

Again, he shook his head. "Don't forget, I went to Exeter at nineteen. I had no time for walks on the beach or making up to the local lasses."

Mina narrowed her eyes. "Maybe not, but I expect there were lots of women in Exeter," she said darkly.

"None that would have expected me to court them," he answered frankly. Mina pursed her lips, then decided it was better to focus on the future and not the past. "What of you?" he asked in a low voice. "Did your father never hire a young schoolmaster that caught your fancy?"

Mina turned her head sharply at the odd tone in his voice. Now it was his turn to color slightly and avoid her gaze. "Nay," he said roughly. "Don't tell me, for I've changed my mind. It would be better not to know."

"There was no one," she admitted. "Not a single suitor. My parents did not mingle in society, and we saw no one that was not connected with the school. I did not consider it before, but I fancy the fact my mother was divorced might have been a reason for that."

He was silent a moment. "Were they happy?" he asked with a rasp, sounding, as though unaccustomed to such conversation.

"My parents?" He nodded. "They were devoted to one another," she said simply. "Weren't yours?"

Nye frowned. "I think they were, in their own way. My father, old Jacob Nye, was not much of a talker."

"He did not wear his heart on his sleeve?" Mina ventured.

Nye hesitated. "Some would say he was a hard man to know, but he raised me as if I was his own. My mother was…" He paused as though searching for the right word. "Very uneven in her moods. She would be happy one minute, laughing and joking with the best of them. Then the next she would be cast down in the sullens, saying her life was ruined and all chance of happiness gone. You never knew which way she would go."

Mina thought about this. "That must have been difficult for a child to understand." She remembered the decoration on the screens and wondered if Ellen Nye blamed her son for the fact she had ended up a publican's wife and not taking up a life treading the boards. Or did she blame the fourth viscount for casting her off as a mistress with a handsome payoff? Had her pregnancy been the reason their liaison had ended when it did?

He shrugged. "I soon learned not to seek her out, but to leave it to her whether she wanted me or no."

The inn was in sight now, and Mina made out two figures in the yard stood watching them approach. As they drew closer, she realized it was Gus and Reuben.

"Good evening!" Gus hailed them cheerily with a wave. His pipe smoke puffed over his head in a thick trail of clouds while Reuben, looking surly as ever, moved abruptly away as they turned into the courtyard.

"What's amiss with Reuben?" Nye asked as they drew level to Gus. He kept a firm hold of Mina's hand in his, and she thought Gus's eyes dwelt there a moment before he answered.

"Amiss? Why nothing," he said heartily. "What should there be amiss on a fine day such as this?" He nodded at Mina. "Mrs. Nye," he added affably. She noticed he did not call her Minnie today.

"Mr. Hopkirk, good evening," she responded as Nye towed her in the direction of the kitchen door.

It opened before they reached it, and Edna hurried out, drying her hands on a tea towel. "Oh Mrs. Nye," she said. "Lord Faris is here with two others. I hardly knew where to direct them, though I showed them into your parlor in the end. I hope I did right."

"I'm sure you did, Edna," Mina told her soothingly, though she could not imagine why Edna had been reluctant to show them into her private room.

Nye released her, and Mina hurried through the hallway, pausing only next to the mirror to tidy her windswept hair. She twisted the loose tresses back around what was left of her bun and reinserted two pins and hoped for the best. Nye had followed her out of the kitchen at a slower pace, but he caught up with her outside the door and entered the room directly after her.

"Ah, here you are!" Jeremy exclaimed, getting up from a chair with his ready smile.

"I'm sorry I kept you waiting," Mina responded as her eyes traveled over the two neat figures who had been sat on wooden chairs against the wall but now stood to attention. Her heart leaped. Could these be the two domestics he had mentioned? She turned her gaze back on Jeremy and he beamed.

"I see you have anticipated my mission." He extended an arm in a sweeping gesture to incorporate the room's other two inhabitants. "I have brought Miss Corin Goode and Mr. Edward Herney for your consideration, as promised."

"I am very pleased to make your acquaintance," Mina said as they bobbed a bow and a curtsey in her direction.

"May I present my sister, Mrs. Mina Nye, and Nye, the owner of this establishment."

From the corner of her eye, Mina saw Nye was a good deal surprised to see Jeremy had proved good on his word. He nodded to Corin and turned a considering eye on Edward Herney, who was tall and slim and aged no more than twenty-two or -three years.

"Ever served as a tapster before?" he asked.

Mr. Herney stepped forward. "I confess, sir, I have not, though I have received some training in the butler's pantry. I know how to tap a keg and have taken instruction on the care and serving of wine and spirits."

Nye nodded. "That should stand you in good stead," he said, and Herney's expression brightened.

Mina turned back to Corin, who had large anxious eyes, hair so blond it was white, and resembled nothing so much as a frightened rabbit. "How old are you, Corin? Have you much domestic experience?"

"I'm nineteen, ma'am." Corin bobbed again. "Please, Mrs. Nye, I have worked as both scullery and kitchen maid before now."

"Well, that sounds very satisfactory," she said, smiling at the girl. "You will have your own attic bedchamber next door to our other maid, Edna, who will help with your instruction."

Corin's eyes grew even wider. "Yes, ma'am," she whispered, then looked at her feet.

"Edna takes Monday as her day off. Should you have any objection to taking either Wednesday or Thursday for your own?"

"None, thank you kindly, ma'am," Corin squeaked.

"You'll have a bed above the stables," Nye told Herney. "There's several bunks in there and you can take your pick. Reuben, the stable hand, sleeps in there and no one else at present." Ed Herney nodded. "You can take a midweek day off for your own, I little care so long as you give me a few days' notice. Weekends are our busiest time."

"Understood, sir," said Herney keenly.

Nye looked a little pained. "Call me Nye," he said. "When can you start?"

Herney turned to Jeremy. "Lord Faris has my trunk on his carriage. If you're agreeable—?"

"I am," Nye said curtly. "If you come now, I'll give you a tour of the place." He nodded at Jeremy, and he and Herney both left the room.

"Did you bring Corin's trunk also?" Mina asked, turning to her brother.

"I did. Prepared fellow, aren't I?"

"Excellent. I'm sure Nye will get Reuben to carry it upstairs for us. Will you stay to take some refreshment, Jeremy?"

He shook his head regretfully. "Alas, I must see my steward on my return and cannot tarry. Perhaps I will return in a couple of days' time to see how you're all faring."

"That would be most agreeable and thank you, for I did not expect you to act so promptly, in truth."

"Catching people unawares is one of my chief delights in life," he mused with a small bow and left.

20

Over the next couple of days, Herney and Corin proved themselves to be adept at learning the ropes at the inn. A rocky start with Edna was soon smoothed over when she realized Corin knelt every night beside her bed to say her prayers and was a regular churchgoer.

As for Herney, he seemed wholly unaffected by Reuben's grumpiness and did not seem to mind turning his hand to whatever his master or mistress asked of him. He was clean-shaven, had a sister who lived in Penarth, and was teetotal, which was the only thing that made Nye look at him askance. In truth, as Mina pointed out to Nye, they had much to be grateful for.

On Sunday, both new members of the household accompanied Mina and Edna to church in their Sunday best, and Mina started to daydream that she could look forward to that weekend away with Nye sometime soon.

That evening to her surprise, her husband joined her in the parlor. She lowered the letter she had been reading which was from her old maid, Hannah, back in Bath. "I did not realize you would be able to join me this evening," she marveled. "Is Herney serving behind the bar?"

"He is," Nye agreed, adding another couple of logs to the fire before sinking into the chair opposite her. "I've told him I can be fetched if I'm needed."

Mina nodded, a faint pucker between her brows. Had Ivy not said something about conferring with Gus and Reuben on a Sunday evening in the taproom? Or had she got that wrong?

"What's that?" he said, nodding at her letter.

She gave a start. "Oh, a letter from Hannah, who used to work for us in Bath. She took a position with a young widow when the school closed. She writes assuring me that she finds her new situation very agreeable." She did not tell him the content of the rest of the letter.

Hannah had been astonished to hear that Mina was lately married and had quoted Mr. Samuel Johnson's maxim on marrying in haste, repenting at leisure. It did not seem right to Hannah that Mina should be wed whilst in deepest mourning, though she acknowledged it was only right she be led by her remaining family member, Lord Faris.

She finished by sincerely wishing that Mina would entreaty her husband to change the wicked name of their hostelry, for she had felt quite mortified having to write the direction for her letter and wondered that Mina could bear to live under the roof of such a loose, immoral sign, be it ever so old. *For antiquated things*, she urged and underlined twice, *were not always respectable.*

Mina cast her letter aside and picked up her bag of mending. She had two shirts of Nye's that needed repair, though she felt a little self-conscious working on them in his presence. "How is Herney working out in the bar? Are the customers taking to him?"

Nye shrugged. "He's likable enough, though…a tad respectable maybe for their tastes."

"He's a pleasant, clean-living young man," Mina said severely.

His eyes gleamed. "Exactly. I see you take my meaning perfectly."

Mina suppressed the answering smile that rose to her lips. "I'm sure he will win them over eventually."

"How's the girl?" he asked abruptly.

"Corin? A very willing and helpful young woman," she said with approval. "I think with pointers from Edna, we will soon have another treasure on our hands," said Mina, warming to the theme.

"Come and sit on my lap, Mina," Nye interrupted her.

She lowered her sewing and blinked at him. "Nye!"

"What? I want my treasure in my hands," he said warmly.

Mina gaped at him. "Are you calling me your treasure?" she asked, her voice oddly constricted.

"What else? Now stop staring and bring your sweet arse over here."

To her own astonishment, Mina found herself setting her sewing down beside her and rising from the sofa. "This was not precisely what I had in mind when you said you were going to keep company with me of an evening," she said uncertainly as she crossed the room toward him.

He reached up and drew her down onto his lap. "Wasn't it? But it was what *I* had in mind, I assure you."

"I can well believe it," Mina retorted as he wound an arm around her waist. "But I thought we were discussing household matters."

"We can still do that with you on my lap."

Mina looked down at him suspiciously. "Really?"

"What else needs to be said?"

Naturally, her brain chose this moment to turn blank. With Hannah's words in mind, she asked, "Was this inn always known by its current name?"

Nye's eyebrows rose. "Nay," he admitted. "I have the old sign in one of the outhouses, but I doubt you'd like it."

"What was its original name?" she asked, though she had a dim memory someone else had told her it once.

"I warn you, it's no more appropriate than the one it bears now." She could see he was deriving some amusement from this subject by the smile lurking in his eyes.

"Tell me," she said, tightening her arms around his neck.

"Very well then, it was called The Quiet Woman."

Mina looked down at him. "Wretch," she said, and he laughed. "Why would I not like the sign?"

"I'll show it you sometime."

"What does it depict?"

He sighed. "A headless woman carrying a tray of cheese and wine."

"Headless?"

"Only a woman without a tongue in her head is quiet."

"Is that a quote?"

"It's inscribed on the sign."

Mina pulled a face. "I think I prefer The Merry Harlot," she said dryly.

Again, Nye's smile flashed out, but he soon turned serious again. "Do you want to change the name?" he asked lightly, but to her surprise, Mina saw he looked in earnest. "I've been thinking of late of some changes that need to be made around the place." His thumb rubbed against her waist in the gesture she was starting to find familiar.

"What sort of changes?" she asked curiously.

"Certain associations," he answered evasively, and Mina wondered with a surge of optimism if he meant his ties with the smuggling trade.

"You mean," she said carefully, "that we should try and entice more locals away from The Ship?"

He shrugged. "As to that, I doubt we'll ever lure the villagers away from a more convenient watering hole. But we could think about become a coaching inn again with teams of horses running along the Exeter road. There's probably only about ten years or so left before rail connects this whole country," he mused. "But ten years is still a considerable amount of time."

Mina considered this. "The whole country connected by steam train?" she said in surprise.

"Twenty years at the outside."

Mina turned thoughtful. "A small place like Penarth would never get a station though."

"It's unlikely," he conceded. "But nearby St. Ives likely would. An inn might survive, but there would be no need for posting stations for the mail coach."

It was a sobering thought. "Well then," Mina agreed. "We ought to concentrate on amassing our fortune now while we may." Nye looked amused. "What would we call our new and improved coaching inn?"

He shrugged. "I've not yet given it much thought." He was silent a moment. "The Good Wife?" he suggested and cleared his throat.

"Why William Nye," she said in surprised accents. "You flatter me." He growled and she dropped a swift kiss on his brow, for he was clearly not used to paying compliments of the respectable kind. "I have a better idea." She gazed down at him. "What say you to The Prizefighter?"

Now it was his turn to look surprised. His gaze flickered. "You would not think that as disreputable as its current name?"

"Certainly not!" She turned thoughtful. "I think it's a vastly good idea. The fights bring us a good deal of business and we could still hold them once a month."

His brow crinkled. "I like it," he admitted. "I like it a lot."

She smiled down at him and met him halfway for the slow, exploratory kiss they shared. For all it was tender, when they drew back, both of them were breathing hard.

"Let's go up to bed," Nye said abruptly, sweeping her up from the sofa.

"It's not yet eight o'clock!" Mina pointed out but found this objection ignored completely as he carried out of the room. "I see now our courtship would have been quite scandalous," she muttered as they mounted the stairs and Nye grinned.

"That's your fault," he rumbled. "For it's my understanding the woman is supposed to set the moral tone of the courtship at the outset."

Mina gasped at this, quite outraged, and Nye burst out laughing before they had even reached the attic.

*

This new state of harmony between them lasted all of two days before Mina received a postcard from Harrogate. She turned it over curiously to read Ivy's careful writing which stated her marriage to Sam had taken place that morning and all was well.

"Well, that's a relief in any event," Mina said briskly, passing the postcard to Edna.

Nye folded his arms across his chest, regarding her narrowly. "Are you going to claim you had no knowledge of this?" he asked. Mina colored slightly.

"Sam who?" puzzled Edna, lowering the card.

"Rawlings," Mina answered absently.

"So you did know!" Nye thundered, looking disgusted.

"What difference does it make?" Mina asked, plunking a hand on her hip and regarding Nye in a martial light.

Edna speedily excused herself to go and finish the tub of laundry she had left to soak in the bathroom upstairs.

Reuben hovered a moment in the doorway, before slouching off again.

"Your loyalty should be to me, Mina," Nye said tightly.

Impulsively, she reached out and put her hand on his chest and he went very still. "Nye, don't." She paused a moment. "I know that, and it is. Please don't make more of this than is necessary."

He stared down at her hand, and both jumped when the unlatched window slammed shut with a bang. When she went to move her hand away, he caught it and carried it to his lips, pressing a quick kiss to her knuckles.

"Very well, we'll say no more about it," he said gruffly. "I'm headed back to the cellar if you need me." He flung abruptly out of the room, slashes of warm color along his cheekbones.

Mina stood staring after him abstractedly, when she became gradually aware that Reuben had appeared once again in the doorway he had only vacated moments ago.

"There's a carter outside," he said abruptly. "Says he's brought something for you?"

Mina turned away from the sink in surprise. "For me?" He nodded. "I have not ordered anything, Reuben, and neither am I expecting anything."

"Mebbe someone ordered it for you, then?" He shrugged. "Will you come outside and take a look? He's waiting for it to be unloaded so I need your instructions."

Mina glanced at him in surprise. Usually, Reuben resented every order she gave him. Crossing to the window, she looked out. Surely enough there was a cart stood in the courtyard with a hunched figure in a smock sat at the front with the brim of his hat pulled low on his head. Suppressing a sigh, she flung open the door and strode over to the waiting cart, Reuben hot on her heels.

He reached past her shoulder to fling back the tarpaulin and show her the cart was empty save for two hay bales. Mina frowned and half turned to look back at Reuben.

"I fail to see—"

There was a blur of movement behind her and a sharp sudden pain before everything turned black.

21

The first thing Mina became conscious of was the low murmur of voices. At first, she tried to drown them out to spare her poor pounding head. Then, as her senses returned and she felt the cold stone of the floor beneath her cheek, she realized she needed to regain consciousness and fast. The chill of her unfamiliar surroundings told her she was in trouble. She shouldn't be here. Even the sounds were echoing and strange. It was almost like she had been thrown into a cellar.

Had she been thrown into a cellar? Someone had spoken recently of cellars. She thought it was Nye. He would never have thrown her into any cellar though. She was sure of that. Mina's eyes cautiously opened. Wherever she was, it was dark, dank, and chilly. She concentrated on the voices. Surely she knew them? They were familiar, but danced on the edge of her memory, elusive as dreams on waking.

She was lying on the ground, and her first thought was that she was injured. If she had fallen down the cellar steps, maybe she had hurt herself? Gingerly, she tried to move her feet and felt them scrape against the stone floor. Then her hands. *Ouch.* Her head was aching fit to bust and her side felt bruised and tender. She wondered if she might have broken a rib.

Mina struggled into an upright position, sucking in her breath against the dizzying pain. Her movements had alerted the other occupants she was conscious, and she heard their feet approach.

"Where am I?" Mina asked, raising fingertips to her temples.

"Don't you tell her!" said an angry voice, which she recognized at once as Reuben, the stable hand from The Harlot. A memory surfaced of turning to see Reuben with a rock in his hand. With incredulity, she realized he must have struck her head with it.

"Now, lad," Gus said with reproach. "There's no need to take on so. Mrs. Nye won't be informing on us, will she?"

"Gus?" Mina blinked up at his fluffy white-head feeling befuddled.

"Aye, it's me," he told her encouragingly. "Right glad I am your brains weren't dashed out, girl. Our Reuben was a touch overzealous, I'm afraid. I only told him to stun you, not to try and stave your skull in."

"You told Reuben to stun me?" she repeated through lips that felt numb.

"I'm afraid so," he said with a gusty sigh. "Needs must, you see. You've had a most unfortunate effect on Nye." He tutted. "Never would have believed it, if I hadn't seen it with me own eyes."

Mina gazed up at him uncertainly. "I'm not sure I follow," she faltered, drawing her knees up to her chest.

"Pass that blanket here, Reuben. For she's trembling, either from the shock or the cold, one or the other."

"Damned if I will!" retorted Reuben angrily. "Where's the sense, when the plan is to throw her off the headland in any case?"

Mina's heart contracted as Gus sent the younger man a reproachful look. "There's no need to be churlish, Reuben! And nightfall's not for a few hours yet." He reached across for a green plaid blanket and draped it about Mina's shoulders. "How's that, my dear?"

"Yes, much better, thank you." She squinted at the dim light thrown out by a single hurricane lamp on the floor. It looked like they were in a subterraneous cavern of some sort. "I don't understand. Where are we?" she repeated. Her mouth felt dry and dusty, and when she reached a tentative hand to the back of her head, she could feel a matted patch of hair that was likely dried blood and a throbbing bump from where she had been struck.

Noticing her discomfort, Gus looked about. "Where's that flask?" he asked Reuben, who glared back at him. "Not the whisky, you needn't worry. I mean the water."

"I still say we shouldn't waste it on her," Reuben muttered.

Gus gave an exclamation and stooped to pick something up. "Here, take a drop of this, Mina. It'll clear your head for certain."

She took it from him but was unable to unscrew it, so weak did she feel.

Gus took it back from her. "Stupid fellow that I am!" he reproached himself. "Here now, I've removed the cap for you."

She took a sip of the water, then another, before easing back against a packing case and taking a third. It refreshed her, and she clutched it to her chest as Gus removed a hip flask from his coat and took a pull of spirits. He held it out for Reuben, who scowled and shook his head.

"Why am I here?" she asked in a raspy voice. "How long have I been here?"

"Only a couple of hours," Gus said soothingly. "Reuben bundled you in the back of a passing cart and he brought you here." He winked at her. "'Course, the carter was an associate of ours, if you know what I mean." He tapped his nose and laughed uproariously.

Reuben twitched with annoyance. "Keep your voice down, you fool! Do you want the Tavistocks to hear you?" he asked in a furious undertone.

For a second, Mina thought she saw a spurt of annoyance pass over Gus's features, then almost immediately it was gone, and his face settled back into its habitually amiable expression.

"Nay, lad, don't be daft. I never could resist a pretty woman, they've been my downfall all my life," said Gus wistfully. "I misdoubt I'll be cured of that in my advanced years."

"Old fool," Reuben muttered. "A pretty pass if the guvnor hears you've been spilling your guts to the likes of her!"

Mina watched a sudden expression of cunning steal over Gus's face and it horrified her. It contorted his round cherubic countenance into something quite different and full of malice. For some reason, Reuben's words filled him with an unholy sort of amusement. It seemed to be some sort of private joke, for when Reuben glanced back at him again, Gus's face relaxed back into his usual semblance of geniality.

It didn't make sense to Mina, but it frightened her all the same. Reuben was half Gus's age and of a stout, strong build. But Gus was far from scared of him. Her head hurt too much for her to fathom what was going on, but she felt all the same that Gus was the real threat for all Reuben's apparent menace.

"Have I been kidnapped?" she asked hollowly.

"In a manner of speaking, yes," Gus agreed cautiously. He stroked his fluffy sideburns. "Though, we're not holding you to ransom. Not but what I expect that man of yours would pay any price for your safe return!" He chuckled. "He's that smitten with you. It would be funny how hard Nye's fallen, if it weren't so damned inconvenient."

Mina winced, trying to piece his meaning together through the fog of her head. "Inconvenient?"

Gus sighed, and plunked himself down on a nearby barrel. "We're land smugglers, you see, Mina. When the boats deliver the goods, we collect and distribute the booty all around hereabouts. We're a tidy, organized bunch, a goodly number, and none of us know above one or two other members by name."

"Except the guvnor," Reuben growled.

"Oh-ho yes!" said Gus richly. "Save for the guvnor, who is the mastermind of our little group, so to speak."

"And Nye? He's one of your number?" Mina asked with a gulp.

"Oh yes. A most valuable member."

"Leastways, he *was*," Reuben interjected, an ugly expression spreading over his face.

Gus sighed. "Until you got your clutches into him, my dear Minerva, and gave him a yearning for respectability."

Mina stared up at Gus. "Nye?" she could not help but clarify. "Nye hankers after respectability? It's the first I've heard of it," she managed with a burst of her usual spirit.

He nodded back at her ruefully. "For your sake, he has determined to throw off all ties with our disreputable company. It is the most lamentable business. Really, most lamentable."

"Which is why you're going to have an accident," Reuben told her harshly. His mouth tightened into a thin line. "Tonight."

"Without you, he will have no incentive to clean up his act, do you see?" Gus pointed out gently with a regretful sigh. He walked over to one side and beckoned Reuben. They exchanged a few low spoken words, and Gus retreated out of sight. Mina listened to his footsteps echo over the cold stone floor and was surprised to count a good dozen steps before she had to crane her ears. Wherever they were concealed was not a small space but extended at least a few feet.

Cold crept over Mina as it sunk in that they weren't holding her to ransom or the promise of her return over Nye's head. They genuinely thought to find her husband more manageable with her out of the way. Up until a certain point, she'd had the vague idea of throwing herself on Gus's mercy, but after she saw that wicked expression on his face, she had banished that notion completely. For all his bluff, Gus was clearly senior to Reuben in the smugglers' chain of command.

She pulled the woolen blanket closer about her as her mind groped for some way out of her predicament. Now why was it that Gus had looked so irritated with Reuben for a moment? she tried to recall. Reuben had appealed for him to quieten his voice in case the Tavistocks heard, she thought slowly. *The Tavistocks*. Now where had she heard that name before?

She racked her brain and took another gulp of the water Gus had left with her. Suddenly it came to her. Nye telling her about Vance House, the reason he had married her in the first place. A fine Queen Anne residence he'd said, with ten acres and its own private beach. His father, the fourth viscount, had left it to him on his deathbed but had not included it in his will. Jeremy had only made the deeds over to him when he had married her. The Tavistocks, he had mentioned, were the elderly current tenants.

Keep your voice down, you fool! Do you want the Tavistocks to hear you? What else could Reuben have meant other than they were somehow concealed somewhere at Vance House? She frowned. Could this be the cellar? But no, it looked far too roughhewn for that. Perhaps a cave on the private beach, she conjectured. But if that were so, why would the Tavistocks overhear them, unless they happened to be on the beach itself?

She stole a sidelong look at Reuben, knowing he was in fact the weaker link than cunning old Gus.

"How interesting," she said aloud. "I've always been curious about Vance House."

He wheeled around and regarded her with narrow eyes. "No doubt you're thinking that Vance House is the ideal place for a fine lady such as yourself," he said with a pronounced sneer. "But let me assure you, woman, you'll never get your hands on it. Over Nye's dead body. So, don't even think it!"

Meaning to rile him, she cast a look of disdain his way. "I assure you, that as his lawful wedded wife, that would be the one condition whereby I *would* get my hands on it," she pointed out. "Any property of his would then come to me by law. But in any case, Nye has told me we shall retire here to Vance House, so I shall certainly be mistress here someday, whatever you say, Reuben."

He balled his fists and took a hasty step toward her as Mina heard Gus's approaching footfalls draw closer. "Let her alone, lad," he said with a chuckle. "You're not her equal for verbal sparring. She'll run rings around ye, so she will."

"I'll give her a split lip if she keeps testing me," Reuben said sullenly.

"Ah no," Gus scolded him. "That's no way to talk about a lady."

Reuben spat on the ground. "For two pins I'd cut her throat now," he snarled.

"Nay, lad," Gus said, shaking his head. "When we dispose of her, she'll go over the cliff with not a mark on her. "She's threatened to jump before and that'll be what folks think happened this time."

"I have never threatened to jump from a cliff!" Mina said indignantly.

"Have you not?" Gus stroked his chin. "But to be sure, that's what they're all muttering in the village for weeks now. You told Nye you would sooner go over the cliff than mind his shameful ways and that's how you brought him in line."

"I did no such thing!"

"Well, Minnie girl." He shrugged and spread his palms wide. "You can appreciate how these rumors get started. Now you can't deny, you did run up to those cliffs very dramatical that time."

"I wanted to get away from the inn, not fling myself off!" Mina disputed hotly.

"Aye, well, there's always a grain of truth to such rumors but often not much more than that," Gus admitted with a grin. "Reuben said you and Nye had just had a dustup about that Ivy's disappearance. He'll blame himself no doubt for being too sharp with you."

"Nonsense!" Mina huffed. "Reuben quite mistook the matter. We did not quarrel and Nye will know I was not remotely distressed."

"Shut the bitch's mouth, or I'll do it for her!" Reuben interrupted them in a low growl.

Mina glanced curiously at Gus's face. It was clear that he gave the orders, for he had instructed Reuben to abduct her. Yet for some reason, Reuben seemed to forget this in the face of Gus's affability. It was almost like he was taken in by the "salt of the earth" act and forgot that was just a mask the older man wore. Having seen it slip, Mina knew she would not forget Gus's real face in a hurry.

Gus seemed to notice her scrutiny, for he gave her a sly wink before sauntering over to Reuben and dealing him a vicious blow across his face. Reuben reeled and was forced to clutch at the rockface of the wall to keep standing upright. "Now Reuben, my lad," said Gus in his kindly tone, rocking back on his heels. "I'll not say it again. You'll keep a civil tongue in your head around Mrs. Nye. I'm the one gives you your orders and not t'other way about."

Reuben's face turned a dull, ugly red. He choked back the angry words that sprang to his tongue and turned away to retreat skulking into the shadowy distance.

"Don't you mind him," said Gus jovially. "He'll toe the line alright," Mina said nothing, for in truth she was far more frightened of Gus than she would ever be of Reuben. "Just think, Minnie my girl," Gus sighed, pulling out his tobacco pouch. "You'll very likely end up another ghost story, like the one I told you about those dastardly monks." His eyes twinkled at her like a kindly uncle. There was something truly horrible about it.

"I'll probably be a good deal more romantic and tragic in the retelling," she managed to joke feebly.

He chuckled. "Ah yes. You'll be beautiful as the day, with a crude brute for a husband. The quintessential wronged wife, no less." He transferred some tobacco to the bowl of his pipe with his thumb.

"No doubt a gray lady," Mina forced herself to expand on the theme. "The ladies are usually gray, I find, when forced to roam the earth weeping and wringing their hands."

Gus nodded, removing his pipe from his mouth to consider this. "Very true," he rumbled. "'Tis a pity you've not a spectral hound to keep you company, so it is."

"I will not haunt the cliff, though," she assured him. "Instead, I would haunt you."

He paused a moment in the act of striking a match. "Would you now?" He chuckled again. "I believe if it were in your power you would."

"Naturally my afterlife would be in my power," she told him coolly.

"Well," Gus said, holding the flame to his pipe. "I've had a few wives, you know, and most of them swore vengeance on me at the last." His eyes glazed over as if in fond memory. "The one I prized best of all, ah, she spat in my face that she'd be revenged with her last breath. Such a spitfire she was, my Jenny! But she never troubled me, after I'd put her in the ground. Never heard so much as a peep from her." He shrugged.

Mina stared at him. "How many wives have you had?" she croaked.

Gus cocked his head as if considering. "Well, five, give or take. A couple of them was only common-law so to speak," he said cagily.

"You *killed* them?" Mina heard herself ask faintly.

He shook his head. "My Lucinda she died in childbirth and the babe with her. And Connie, she was always nesh. Fever fetched her off. But as for the other three…" He let the words dangle and shot her a sly look.

"I don't believe you," Mina said obstinately, and Gus laughed. "It's no different to your other fairy tales. I knew you lied about the monks," she said obstinately.

"Lied? Not a bit," he rumbled, but Mina only shook her head.

"Spectral monks? I think not. And I know who Grayking was, even if you do not." He lifted his bushy eyebrows at her in query. "He was a goose, not a saint."

Gus removed his pipe again and stared at it a moment. "Well now," he said ponderously. "Stranger things have happened. I have heard tell that there were dogs sainted at one time and even a woman once made pope."

"Fancy that," Mina said sarcastically, and he chuckled again. Somehow hearing him continue genially was far more frightening than Reuben's ugly threats. "Nye will know I didn't fling myself over a cliff," she persisted. "I'm afraid your confederate's understanding is far from strong. One time, Sir Matthew Carswell offered me a carriage ride and Reuben reported he had asked me to run away with him."

Gus frowned and puffed furiously on his pipe. "And?" he prompted.

"This is just such another misunderstanding. We are on perfectly affable terms. The last thing Nye did was kiss my hand."

Gus pondered this a moment, before breaking into a smile. "I won't deny, you've got Nye panting on a chain for you, but you'll have to admit, Minnie dear, that you fight as much as you reconcile. That's just the sort of couple you are." He beamed at her. "It won't be hard for folks to believe he drove you to it. Not a gently reared, respectable soul such as yourself."

"Edna won't believe it either," Mina said, raising her chin.

"Edna Lumm's thought an odd body in these parts," he said mildly. "There's not many will set much store by her ramblings." He spread a piece of sacking over the barrel and sat back down on it again. "You've got to resign yourself to it, lass. There's none will be the wiser for your untimely end. It's a pity, but there it is. You're a fine spirited lass after my own heart, but business is business, and none can get in its way. Started out as a wrecker I did when I was naught but a boy. You have to be utterly pitiless to succeed in that profession. You mustn't think I'll let my fondness for you stay my hand."

Mina felt her blood run cold. *Gus, a wrecker?* The wicked men who deliberately lured ships with false lights so they were dashed on perilous coastlines and their cargo plundered. She had read accounts that had made her shudder of poor victims washing up on the beach and being clubbed to death by the wreckers waiting there for any survivors who might tell the tale.

No, she could not depend on Gus showing her any mercy when the moment came to push her off the headland. As for Reuben, he heartily despised her. She would have to rely on her own wits to escape. If the time she had spent since leaving The Hill School had taught her anything, it was that she had a strong survival instinct and deep inner reserves of strength.

For some reason, Nye sprang uppermost to her mind. What would he do without her? Probably go to the devil completely, she thought, without her to keep him on the straight and narrow! She shot a considering glance at Gus. He was garrulous and liked to while away the time with conversation. She would have to work with what she had.

357

"We are, I collect, under the cellars at Vance House?" she mused. "Did you know this place was the reason Nye accepted our marriage?"

Gus looked amused. "Why bless your soul, Minnie, of course I did! This place is vital to our operations. This here passage," he said, taking his pipe out of his mouth and pointing with it into the distance, "extends all the way from the cellars of Vance House to the beach."

"A secret passage?" Mina asked with a glimmer of interest despite herself.

"Oh aye," Gus agreed. "None other."

"I wonder that Nye did not throw out the tenants as soon as he had the deeds to the place. Surely it must have put you in danger of discovery?"

Gus shook his head. "The Tavistocks are an elderly pair who mostly only use the second floor of the house these days. Rheumaticky he is, and she's deaf as a post. They retires early of an evening without fail and keeps no dogs. Precious little trouble we've had of 'em these past five years."

"I see," Mina murmured. "Gus, will you tell me truthfully? How deep is Nye in this business?"

Gus shifted on his barrel into a more comfortable position. "Well, about as deep as he can be," he admitted, shaking his head. "Now, I don't say as it was his fault entirely. Old Jacob Nye as acted as his pa, was up to his ears in the trade. In the end, there weren't a drop he served that had paid any custom." Gus chuckled as Mina took in the fact Nye had not chosen to become embroiled with smugglers.

"When Nye come back from Exeter, fair flummoxed he was to find his old man hand in glove with a pack of smugglers. In the five years he'd been gone. The Merry Harlot had been run into the ground, so it had. It weren't used by any of the posting coaches to stop at no more. The stables were in disrepair, the teams of horses all sold. The old man had lost interest since his wife had died and his boy up and gone. He never showed it, but he had a heart under that stony exterior."

Gus shook his head. "A mistake, I'd urge him against time and again, but he'd never listen. 'You never raised any young 'uns,' he'd say to me and I'd say, 'No, I made sure to clear out long afore I got saddled with any brats!'" Mina watched his face and the subtle change it underwent again in the shadows when he showed his truly callous nature. It chilled her.

"So," she said softly. "Nye returned and found he could not disentangle himself or The Merry Harlot?"

"Now, Mina," Gus said reproachfully. "Don't go deceiving yourself that man of yours is a saint. He objected at first, it's true, but when he saw what a loss The Harlot was running at, and how locals shunned the place, he knew he had little choice but to throw his lot in with ours." Mina pursed her lips. "Promised old Jacob, he did, that he'd get the place back up on its feet."

"They were reconciled?"

Gus sucked in his cheeks. "Well, they were never really what you'd call estranged," he pointed out. "Nye had dreams of being a boxer, not a landlord. Jacob never objected, but he said it wasn't a sport for any man past his prime of life. You need something to fall back on, after you made your fame so to speak."

"How about smuggling?" asked Mina with a touch of acerbity. "Is that a job suitable for a man past his prime?"

Gus chortled. "Well, you has to leave the brunt of the more physical side of proceedings to the younger men, it's true," he reflected. "But when it comes to cunning, Mina…" He touched his nose. "Old dogs and foxes know best. Those young cubs and puppies don't have nothing on us." He gave a quick gesture for her to be quiet now, hearing Reuben's footsteps approaching.

"Ah, here you are, my lad," he announced cheerfully, though Mina thought it was plain to see the younger man was still in a sulk. His cheek looked swollen from the blow Gus had struck him, and he would barely look him in the eye. Mina wondered if there was some way she could use their rift to her advantage, though nothing sprung immediately to mind.

"It's growing darker out," he muttered resentfully. "There's a squall rising."

Mina wondered how long she had really been missing from The Harlot. If it was growing dark, then it must be about six o'clock at least, and it had not been long past lunch when she'd been struck on the head. She wondered how soon someone would raise the alarm that she was missing. She did not think the household would be complacent. After all, she had ventured little from the inn and had no friends or acquaintances in the village.

Then again, she *had* told Nye she wanted to start walking on the beach, but maybe that could work to her advantage? If they meant to drag her to a clifftop to throw her off, surely the one closest to the inn would be the most logical. She had escaped once to clamber down that cliff and the fact was well known. She had walked that cliff path with Nye only recently too. Perhaps they would be searching for her there, even now?

The next period of time crawled interminably. Gus and Reuben moved out of her range of hearing, and though she could hear snatches of their murmured discussions, none of it was intelligible. They spent some time shifting cases or barrels from one area to another. She could only suppose they were expecting a new shipment of goods at some point.

Mina closed her eyes and tried to relax to ease her throbbing head, but it was hard. Her ribs hurt, though she no longer believed they were broken, and she could not get comfortable on the hard floor. She had just managed to achieve a light doze when her side was nudged with a boot.

"Sit up," said Reuben harshly, though she little knew why he bothered, for the next moment, he was jerking her shoulder forward and cramming a rag into her mouth. Mina turned her head away and began to struggle almost as a reflex.

"Less of that!" He cuffed the side of her head and jerked her upright. "Come and hold her!" he bawled at Gus. "I'll knock you out again if you keep this up!" he warned. He was trying to pass a cord about her wrists now, Mina realized, and she redoubled her efforts. All was in vain though, and now her head was dizzy as well as aching.

Gus tutted when he joined them. "That's too tight," he said, feeling her bound wrists. "You'll leave marks on her flesh and then the cat will be properly out of the bag. Haven't you got the sense you were born with, lad?"

"You do it then," Reuben fired up angrily. "For I've no patience with her."

Gus adjusted the cord and then the strip of cloth about her mouth. "Right sorry I am, Minnie my girl," he muttered. "But we can't have you crying out when we're scaling the cliffs. Reuben," he said as the thought struck him. "Whatever you do, don't go pitching her over the side until we've taken this gag from her mouth, d'ye hear me? Never knew such a hotheaded young fellow."

"I'm not a total fool!" Reuben griped, then froze. "What was that?" he hissed and turned to look over his shoulder. Mina's heart lurched as she knelt on the floor of the passageway, for she had heard it too. A scraping noise above them. "Someone's in the cellars, moving stuff about!" Reuben said hoarsely.

"Nonsense!" Gus scoffed heartily. "You think Nye would bring anyone here? And give away his knowledge of the operation? He's not such a fool, I tell you!"

"He's a fool for her!" Reuben seethed. "And my ears are better'n yours, old man. I tell you, someone's up there!"

Something seemed to catch Gus's ear now, for he turned sharply and stared toward the left. His expression turned grim, and he darted to fetch something. Mina was dismayed to see it was a pistol.

"Let's get out of here," Reuben said, also drawing out a pistol. He looked at Mina with open loathing. "I've half a mind to put a bullet through her now."

"Don't be an idiot," Gus urged. "We may have need of a hostage yet. Help me get her to her feet."

Mina braced herself as the two of them grabbed none too gently under her arms and dragged her upright. Mina was sure the scuffle they made had caught someone else's ears, for she heard a muffled voice and cursed the fact she was now securely bound and gagged.

"Let's go," Reuben said, viciously yanking her arm.

Mina gave a stifled sound of pain and Gus seized her about the waist. "You'll have her over, you're so rough," he upbraided Reuben, who only growled back at him like a cur.

She wasn't sure how far along the passage she was forced to stumble and trip, but after a few minutes, the passage took a steep incline and seemed to have grown very narrow.

Reuben was forced to lift and push her through a tight opening, and she felt the sea air on her face and heard the crash of the waves. She saw nothing though, as her eyes had not yet adjusted from the gloom of the passage. They paused for a moment as they all three of them caught their breath.

"Take her arm, Reuben," Gus puffed. "For she's no balance with her arms tied behind her."

Reuben swore and seized her arm none too gently as she stumbled over uneven ground. She wished she had a better idea of where Vance House was situated, but all she could remember Nye saying was that it was on the outskirts of Jeremy's estate.

Her eyes were finally accustoming themselves, but little good it did her, for night had indeed fallen. She caught once again the gleam of a pistol barrel and remembered both men were armed. Her blood ran cold. Try as she might, she could figure out no happy outcome from her predicament. Her feet dragged as she wondered how far she was expected to walk in her bound and weakened state.

As she tripped again, Gus caught her and whispered to Reuben, "You'll have to put her over your shoulder, lad."

"Damned if I'll carry her," Reuben argued back.

"She'll be going off in a swoon if you don't," Gus pointed out.

It suddenly struck Mina this was an excellent suggestion. She could not slow them down any more than if she made them carry her dead weight. And why should she aid them when every step drew her ever closer to her demise? Taking her cue from Gus, she swayed and then dropped like a stone onto the rough track they were following.

"I told ye, ye young jackanapes!" Gus said roughly. "Now look what ye've done!"

"Me?" Reuben carped back at him. "How's this my doing, I'd like to know?"

"Because ye bloody near caved her head in this morning, that's why! Bloody idiot!"

At this a loud, clear voice rang out. "Halt in the name of the law!" and all hell broke loose.

Mina rolled into a ball at the sound of a gunshot, and only the fact she was gagged prevented her from screaming. She fancied it was Reuben who had fired, and now another gun made reply from elsewhere.

"Hold hard, you fool. You'll give them our location!" Gus swore as Mina scrabbled about on the floor, trying to roll to her knees. She would not put it past Reuben to turn his pistol on her, so strong was his dislike, and her first instinct was to try to get as far from him as possible. Luckily, he was darting this way and that, peering wildly into the darkness as though to pierce the shadows for their attackers. Very likely, he still thought her unconscious.

Feeling deafened, Mina managed to find her feet and stagger back until she hit a convenient boulder, which she made haste to scramble around while her abductors were distracted. She had just taken another step backward when two arms closed about her and a hand clamped across her mouth.

She rolled her eyes, trying to see who this newcomer was, when she heard him swear to find her already gagged. At the sound of his voice, she sagged with relief, for it was Nye. She could have cried if she hadn't been so paralyzed with fear. Before she knew it, she was scooped up and borne a few feet away behind some gorse bushes. Even as Nye set her down, she heard Reuben's bellow of fury at finding she had gone.

"Where is she? I'll kill her! I'll kill her!" he roared.

"Untie her—check her wounds," Nye said in a furious undertone, and Mina perceived he had handed her into the care of Edward Herney.

She made a muffled attempt to warn Nye and would have grabbed at him to stay him if it were not for her bonds. She made a sound of distress in her throat as Herney fumbled to open his penknife to free her.

"Be calm now, Mrs. Nye," he tried to soothe her, but Mina paid him no heed for she could hear shouting and scuffling down on the beach. Her ears craned for another gunshot, and when she heard two more shots in quick succession she flinched and turned so fast she almost fell.

"Nay, I'll cut you if you can't keep still," Herney reproached her in the ominous silence.

"Herney?" called a voice. "Herney? Do you have her?"

To her surprise, Mina found she recognized that voice. It was Guthrie, the younger Riding Officer from St. Ives.

"Aye, sir," Herney responded. "Though I have not managed to free her yet, poor lady."

"Step forward, I say! Bring forth the woman!" called another voice arrogantly. That would be Havilland, Mina realized, recognizing the voice of the older and far less agreeable officer.

"Yes, sir," Herney called out, and apologizing to Mina, he took her about the waist and lifted her out to where a semicircle of uniformed men who seemed to belong to the local militia were stood brandishing lamps and swords. There must be eight of them, Mina thought blankly, staring about her. Then she noticed the dark heap on the ground. It was Reuben.

Gus was kneeling nearby, very pale, his eyes squeezed shut and blood pouring from his shoulder. Her eyes scanned the company with painful anxiety for her husband. At last she hit on him, stood with his hands behind him and a rifle pointed to his middle back. He stared stoically into the distance and did not meet her eye. He was under arrest, she realized despairingly.

"Look out!" shouted Officer Guthrie, hurrying forward, then Mina's whole world slipped sideways, and everything turned black.

22

"There now, poor thing," crooned a voice near Mina's ear, and she caught a whiff of sal volatile under her nose. Twisting away from it, she opened her eyes to find a plump, elderly matron bent over her with a look of extreme concern.

"Wha—?" Mina scanned the dark room to find herself in a comfortable lady's sitting room, lying on a sofa. "Where am I?"

"Why, you're safe here at Vance House, Mrs. Nye. I'm Nellie Tavistock and the officers bade me to keep you quiet and get you rested—"

"I must see my husband at once!" she said, sitting up and dislodging a good deal of cushions. Her head swam and she nearly sank back down again. That was what she got for crying wolf, she thought contritely.

"There now! You mustn't go upsetting of yourself, Mrs. Nye!" the plump old lady said as Mina moved a hand to the back of her head which was now dressed with a bandage. "I bathed your poor head myself and your wound is nicely cleaned and covered."

"Thank you." Mina flushed. "I do not mean to sound ungrateful, Miss Tavistock, but—"

A knock on the door interrupted them. A look of exasperation passed over Nellie Tavistock's amiable countenance. "There now if it isn't them again! You stay there," she ordered and hurried over to the door.

Mina listened to the low murmur of voices, steadily rising, until poor Miss Tavistock was thrust aside and Officer Havilland brushed past her.

"She's conscious now at least," he said, looking Mina up and down as his colleague stayed by the door apologizing to Miss Tavistock, who was a good deal ruffled.

"I certainly am," said Mina, swinging her legs onto the floor with a wince and shooting out a hand to the arm of the sofa to steady herself.

"She'll be fetched off again in another swoon, like as not!" cautioned Miss Tavistock, who was becoming less amiable by the minute. She scurried to Mina's side and turned a ferocious expression on the officers.

"That can't be helped, my good woman," said Officer Havilland briskly. "I must needs have an account from Mrs. Nye immediately."

"The good doctor," Miss Tavistock bridled, "said as she was not to be bothered—"

"Where is my husband?" Mina cut across this interchange. "Not another word will I speak until I have had some speech with him!"

"He has been taken to the holding cells at St. Ives," said Guthrie apologetically.

Mina gasped as an irritated expression passed over Havilland's face.

"That need not be your utmost concern, I assure you," Officer Havilland said with a sneer. "The onus is now on you to clear your own name from our investigations."

Mina turned to Miss Tavistock. "Would it be possible to send word to Viscount Faris? I believe he was your landlord until very recently?"

Miss Tavistock looked flustered. "Lord Faris? Of course, but—"

"Please tell him his sister is in dire need of his support and his legal counsel."

"His sister?" Miss Tavistock quavered, looking from Mina to the outraged Riding Officer. "Of course, my dear," she faltered. "But I could not in all conscience leave you alone with these two..." Words failed her. "Gentlemen," she finished with barbed disapproval.

"I assure you, not another word will pass my lips until you return to me, my good ma'am."

A martial light entered Miss Tavistock's faded blue eyes. "You can count on me, my lady!" she said, whisking past the two officers and leaving the salon in a whirl of sensible skirts.

"I apologize if we seem unduly hasty in our questioning," Guthrie started appealingly. "But you see—"

Mina turned her pale face away from them and stared sightlessly through the window at the dark night. Nye had been taken to St. Ives. They had taken him at gunpoint. She had not even had the chance to assure him she was still in one piece. Tears filled her eyes and spilled over her cheeks, and Officer Guthrie bit off his words in dismay.

"Mrs. Nye—!" Officer Havilland started hotly, but a rheumy old gentleman stumped into the room at that point in a brocade dressing gown.

"M'sister sent me," he said awkwardly. "Now what's this to-do?" He caught sight of Mina and gave an outraged yell. "Nellie said you was brow-beatin' her and I thought she must be exaggeratin'! Now, m'dear, there, there," he said, scuttling into the room, stabbing the carpet with his walking stick. "Doc Hadley said you wasn't to be harried!" He flung a look of acute dislike at the Riding Officers. "Pulling about me cellars and now distressin' of this lady! Demned outrage I call it!"

"I didn't even get to see him!" Mina sobbed as he extracted a handkerchief from one of his pockets.

"Now, don't go upsettin' yourself, my dear." He turned back to the officers. "Pass me that glass!" he barked. "Can't you fellows do something useful for once? Cursed nuisances!"

Mina took the handkerchief with thanks and gave way to an excess of emotion. She had been knocked unconscious, threatened, prodded, poked, and manhandled. She had been in fear of her life for hours and had also been tied so barbarously her wrists were cut, and gagged with a rag she could only hope had been halfway clean.

"There's a poorly dear," Mr. Tavistock murmured. "You cry it out. Good for you."

Mina, who had always despised herself for showing any weakness, found this was all the encouragement she needed. She gave vent to her utter misery and despair for a good couple of minutes. During this time Miss Tavistock reentered the room and joined the battle. Her sweet, kind face had transformed into that of a raging virago, and she had swept the room of officers and banged the door in their faces, informing them she had re-sent for Doctor Hadley, who would likely bring an action against them.

Mina allowed the Tavistocks' kindness to wash over her as she drank a glass of water and took a slice of bread and butter. Miss Tavistock bathed her wrists and dressed them as well in bandages, and by the time a tea tray had been brought in for her, they heard horses in the drive outside and a little maid ushered in a concerned-looking Jeremy in a many caped driving coat.

Jeremy took one look at Mina's swollen face and bandages and hurried to kneel at her side. "But what is this, my dear Mina?" he asked in a voice of such concern that she went off again in a storm of tears. "This is not like you," he said, a good deal shaken, clasping one of her hands. "What has occurred?"

"They've taken Nye away!" she managed to wail between sobs. "And put him in prison!"

"Some nasty smugglers abducted poor Mrs. Nye this morning and put her in a concealed passageway beneath our cellars, my lord," Nellie Tavistock hastened to inform him. "Her good husband, Mr. Nye, is our landlord now. He brought them Riding Officers here and bade us cooperate fully. And now she's been restored, what do you suppose those villains have done, but taken Mr. Nye up in chains!"

"Concealed passageway? Good God," echoed Jeremy. He hesitated. "And the smugglers?"

"Reuben's dead," Mina sniffed. "At least he looked dead. And Gus Hopkirk was shot, but only in the shoulder."

"Hopkirk, you say? Good Lord! He wasn't a smuggler, was he?"

Mina nodded, her eyes filling with fresh tears. She turned to the Tavistocks again. "But where is Edward Herney, our tapster?"

"God bless you, miss, he's sat in our kitchen getting the grilling of his life. They're a-trying to pin the charge of smuggling on

371

him too!" Miss Tavistock said with kindling anger. "And anyone with eyes in their heads can see he's a good Christian lad with never a stain on his conscience!"

"Herney is no smuggler!" Jeremy said in shocked accents. "He was my second footman until last week!"

"Runnin' amok, that's what they're doin'," broke in Mr. Tavistock wrathfully. "Marching round me house and tryin' to clap everyone in irons! Why they'll be after us next, my dear," he said, turning to his sister. "Saying we were aiding and abetting criminals in our cellars!"

"I'd like to see them try, Amos!" his sister said indignantly.

"Jeremy." Mina leaned forward impulsively and took his hand in a firm grip. "You must help me."

He glanced down at her bandaged wrist. "Of course, sister," he said comfortingly. "You must not excite yourself, for you've clearly had an uncomfortable time of it."

"Uncomfortable?" burst forth Miss Tavistock. "Someone beat her about the head so hard, it's a mercy her skull wasn't cracked!"

Jeremy straightened, a martial light gleaming in his blue eyes. He shrugged his cape onto the floor and flicked an invisible piece of lint from an impeccably cut sleeve. "I believe I will now see who's in authority here," he drawled, every inch the fifth viscount, and Mina relaxed limply back onto the sofa.

*

Mina was taken up to bed shortly after by Miss Tavistock herself and shown into a handsome guest bedroom. She was swathed in one of that good lady's tentlike nightgowns, and a stone hot water bottle was placed at her feet. Her head ached and her eyes were heavy from something a grim-faced Doctor Hadley added to a glass of water. He gave several sharp exhortations that his patient was not to be bothered for a good twenty-four hours and left after promising to visit with her on the morrow.

Jeremy looked in before he left, but Mina could not properly focus on what he was saying, save that he promised he would return first thing in the morning. Mina's eyelids drooped down, and she gave way to a deep, dreamless sleep.

When next she woke, sun was streaming through the window and she stared at the ceiling for a good few moments before recalling her precise whereabouts. Indeed, when first she had woken, she had thought herself a schoolteacher still, in Bath.

Sitting up, Mina was surprised to see an assortment of her own items laid out on the chair by her bedside. One of her black dresses and some clean underclothing and her own bottle of lotion. Someone had been to The Harlot to fetch her things, she realized, flinging the bedclothes aside and sliding gingerly from the bed. She felt bruised and a little shaken, but her head no longer pained her except when she touched a hand to the bandage. Doubtless she had a bump there, but it could have been a good deal worse, she reflected as she padded over to the porcelain washstand where a jug of tepid water stood waiting for her. It was still warm enough for her to wash, so she set about her ablutions hurriedly and did her best with the hairbrush around her bandaged head.

She was dragging her black dress over her head when a knock on the door heralded the arrival of the maid Annie who was a good deal dismayed to see that Mrs. Nye had already mostly dressed herself. She helped with the buttons and hooks and laces until Mina was presentable and then ushered her downstairs to a small parlor room where she was brought tea and toast.

Jeremy joined her as she was midway through her second cup and shut the door quietly behind himself, raising his finger to his lips. "The officers have been told you are under strict doctor's orders to see no one," he said in a low murmur, joining her at the table. "We can count on the Tavistocks to help us avoid them."

"Have you been to The Harlot this morning?" she asked.

"I have. Edna packed your things. I trust you had everything you needed."

She nodded. "How were they?"

"Subdued," he said. "They send their love. Edna's eyes were very red, and she seems to be throwing herself into her work to occupy her mind."

"She always throws herself into her work," Mina said with a small smile.

"She says Corin is a tower of strength in her time of need."

Mina was a little startled by this. She thought of timid little Corin and marveled that Edna should describe her so. "Well, I'm glad of that in all events. Was Herney allowed to return there last night? Without him, there is no man present to—"

"Do not fret." Jeremy gave a wry smile. "He was permitted to return in the small hours of this morning. Even Officer Havilland was forced to admit he could not bring any charges against so blameless a character. I have sent Colfax along to help at the inn. He can turn his hand to most things."

Mina thanked him and pushed her toast away half-eaten. "Now we have skirted the subject long enough," she said, taking a deep breath. "How stand things with Nye?"

Jeremy was silent a moment before subjecting her to a hard look. "Tell me, sister, just how attached are you to things as they stand?"

Mina's heart thudded almost painfully. "What do you mean?"

"Mina." He reached across and took her hand. "When I married you to Nye, I did so in the throes of a—" He cast about for words. "Distempered freak." His lips twisted. "I had been on a week-long binge at that point and was never more than halfway sober for the duration. I was feeling bitter and disillusioned about my own personal circumstances, and you were forced to suffer for my poor judgment. I can make no defense for the role I played in—"

She stiffened. "What are you saying, Jeremy? This is all water under the bridge now and hardly helpful!"

"In marrying you to a man of poor moral character," he continued as if she had not spoken.

Mina wrenched her fingers from his. "You dare to speak to me of moral character?" she asked in a shaken voice. "Yes, I could tell you were half-cut the entire journey from Bath. Let me tell you I felt far more endangered in *your* company than I ever did in William Nye's."

He flushed. "Mina, please." He waved his hand helplessly. "I regret my role in what has happened, most heartily. If you will only allow me to make some reparation." He broke off, taking a deep breath. "Amanda and I are separating. Our marriage has brought us nothing but misery."

"And Teddy," Mina pointed out through gritted teeth.

"One good thing," he acknowledged. "She talks of moving to the Continent almost immediately." He leveled a look at her. "How should you like to be mistress of Vance Park? You could take up the reins as my sister. Help me raise Teddy right." Mina shook her head. "I'm persuaded your parents would have approved of such an outcome," he urged.

"But I would not, my lord. I am married to William Nye and I do not hanker for any other role," she assured him vehemently.

"Even our mother was divorced, Mina," he pointed out seriously. "If she could muster the bravery to take such a step, then I am sure that you could."

"Divorced?" Mina burst forth. "Good God, sir! It is *you* who needs to procure a divorce, not I!" She gazed at him with exasperation. "Really, Jeremy! You will allow that brazen wife of yours to skip off to the Continent without legally severing your ties?"

He looked suddenly tired. "Mina—"

"No, Jeremy! It is not solely I who needs to face up to harsh truths. I know that I am married to a smuggler," she said in an urgent undertone. "But you are a fool if you let that woman flounce off to Europe with a claim still on your name and title. What if she shows up years from now, quite dissipated, steeped in infamy, demanding you give her the dower house for her old age? Only think of the vicious company she could expose Teddy to! The rumors and conjecture, the demands on your purse! Even if you never see her again, no respectable woman will ever ally herself with you when there is no possibility of marriage. Do you really mean to deprive Teddy of a decent female influence in his life?"

"He has you for that," he said mutinously. "I am done with women."

She gave a short laugh. "A pretty face like yours won't repine for long. I daresay our mother thought she would never remarry, but it must have been mere months before she took the plunge again!"

It took a moment, but she saw the glimmer spark in his eye. "Think me pretty, do you?"

"You're vastly pretty," she said briskly. "Just like she was."

"And Nye's an ugly customer like m'father." He sighed. "But you're devoted to him, aren't you?" Mina nodded, unable to speak the words. "Lord, what a mess I've made of everything!" Jeremy groaned.

"Don't you dare think of sinking into despair, or another bottle!" Mina upbraided him. "If you truly want to make amends, then help me now, my lord."

He nodded. "If that's truly what you want, then gladly."

Mina huffed out a sigh of relief. "In that case, I need you to bring your carriage around, for I need an escort to Upton Gadsby."

"Upton Gadsby?" Jeremy echoed, clearly mystified. "Why, what's there?"

"Sir Matthew Carswell, Justice of the Peace," she replied promptly.

23

On the ride over there, Jeremy explained that it had been Edna who had raised the alarm. Happening to glance out of the bathroom window, quite by chance, she had seen Mina struck down and bundled into the cart. By the time she had run downstairs and into the yard, the cart had already trundled away. She had thought it was a local man, Tom Rowley at the reins, but as she had only caught sight of his back, she could not be certain of that fact.

By the time Nye had been summoned from the cellars and the story told to him and the bloodied rock discovered in the yard, so much time had lapsed that there was no sign of the cart and a frantic search had found no Reuben either. Nye had saddled one of the horses and ridden first in one direction and then the next, for Edna had not waited to see which way the cart had gone.

A grim-faced Nye had returned an hour later empty-handed and announced his intention of riding to St. Ives to enlist the Riding Officers aid in recovering Mina. Everyone had been a good deal shocked, for such a step meant exposing his own involvement in the smuggling business, but Nye had remained unswayed in his determination to set forth immediately.

At this point in the retelling, Mina wondered if Nye had known how close to death she had come. Had he had an inkling of just how ruthless Gus Hopkirk could be? She wondered if Nye, too, believed that Gus was the true brains behind proceedings. He could surely have not realized how deeply Reuben resented her or he would not have kept him on at the inn.

"So, Nye confessed to knowledge of the secret passage beneath Vance House?" Mina said aloud.

"As to that"—Jeremy shrugged—"he had only very recently taken ownership of the place. I suppose my father must have told him it existed, for I did not know." He hesitated. "What if I said that I had been the one to tell Nye of it, on handing over the deeds?" He darted a glance at Mina. "I could say I was concerned that the passage had been disturbed of late and had asked Nye to check this. What do you think?"

Mina nodded. "That might be a good thought," she agreed. "Nye is far from talkative. I should think it unlikely that he told the Riding Officers much information other than that he believed I was being held a prisoner down there."

"If he could have," he pondered, "very likely he would have gone after you alone. It must have gone against the grain to get the law involved. I daresay he thought the risk too high to do anything else."

"Apparently he had cut his involvement with them," Mina admitted. "They thought by getting rid of me, they would draw him back in their circle again."

"Getting rid of you?" Jeremy queried.

"They were going to fling me off a cliff and hope it passed for suicide of an unhappy wife."

Jeremy looked shocked. "I had thought they meant to control him in some way by ransoming your return." She shook her head.

"How are we to approach this business with Sir Matthew?" he asked with a frown. "Have you considered?"

"I have," Mina admitted. "Are you content to be guided by me in this matter, brother?" He inclined his head, gesturing for her to continue. "I would like you to take a high tone with him," she admitted. "'It is absurd that my brother-in-law should be embroiled in this matter,' that sort of thing. Sir Matthew is something of a snob and will set much store by your title."

Jeremy's lips twitched appreciatively. "You also mentioned something about his being in your debt, I think?"

"Ah yes, although in truth, that fact irks him and it would not put him in the best humor to remind him of it outright," she admitted. "I have not precisely considered how that angle can best be used as yet."

On reaching Sir Matthew's residence, however, they were told by the butler that Sir Matthew had ridden over to St. Ives on business. Mina and Jeremy exchanged glances, for they both fancied they knew what business that would be.

Jeremy handed over his card and the butler's eyes widened. He took a step back from the door, opening it for their admittance. "If your lordship and your companion would be so good as to come inside to wait in the drawing room, I am sure that Sir Matthew will be back within the hour."

"Thank you, you are most kind," Mina answered, leading the way. Jeremy fell in behind her, and they were led into a handsomely appointed drawing room of blue and white.

"I will fetch you some refreshment, my lord," the butler said, backing out of the room, but Mina forestalled him.

"Could you be so kind as to convey a message to Miss Carswell for me?" she enquired cordially. "And let her know that Miss Walters awaits below and would very much like to see her."

The butler hesitated. "Miss Cecily is still abed, I fear."

Mina's eyebrows rose. She had not expected that Sir Matthew would allow such indulgences in his house as lying abed until eleven in the morn. "I believe she will very likely receive me in her room," she said with a confiding smile. "We are very old friends, you see, from Cecily's schooldays in Bath."

The butler's brow cleared. "I see, miss. I will certainly let Miss Cecily know." He disappeared, only to reappear five minutes later, beckoning to Mina from the doorway. She excused herself to Jeremy, who looked resigned to kicking his heels, and followed him upstairs to a very charming bedchamber done out in rose pink. Cecily was wearing a frothy lace wrapper with her golden hair still loose over her shoulders. She squeaked at Mina's appearance and hurried forward to embrace her warmly.

"My dear Miss Walters," she gushed, drawing her into the room. "I am so happy to see you delivered from the jaws of certain death!" she gabbled before noticing that they were not alone. That will be all, Fimble," she said grandly to the butler in dismissal.

Mina cleared her throat. "A cup of tea would be most welcome, Cecily dear," she prompted.

"Oh! Of course!" Cecily turned back to the butler. "My usual tea and toast," she said vaguely. "With an extra cup for my guest." She shut the door after Fimble and begged Mina to take one of the pink and gold boudoir chairs. "Forgive me for being so thoughtless," she said with a charming smile. "Only I had thought—with everything that has happened—that you would not be able to eat or drink a drop! I vow I could scarcely eat any supper yesterday after I had been apprised of the awful goings-on!" She gave an eloquent shudder before crossing to her dressing table and seating herself there.

So, thought Mina, Sir Matthew had been kept fully apprised of the business. Very likely the Riding Officers were hoping to go for a conviction.

"I do hope you won't mind my seeing to my toilette," Cecily ran on apologetically. "But I simply must be presentable by the time dear Sir Matthew returns." Mina saw with surprise that Cecily colored slightly as she said this and anxiously scanned her pink and white complexion in the mirror for any flaws.

"Of course not," Mina said, folding her hands in her lap. "In truth I am very relieved that you have been apprised of what has occurred. I was not sure if Sir Matthew would think such matters fit for your ears."

Cecily took a pretty pink bottle up and lifted the stopper to apply rose water to her face. "Oh, as to that," she said, not quite meeting Mina's eyes in the looking glass. "Things have undergone a slight *change* between Sir Matthew and myself." She simpered as she opened a box of pearl powders. "Since that unfortunate contretemps that you so kindly extricated me from." She dabbed a large powder puff to her nose and chin. Swiveling on her seat, she looked earnestly at Mina. "I will not scruple to tell you, my dear Miss Walters—"

"Mrs. Nye," Mina interjected smoothly, but Cecily took no notice of such a trifling detail.

"—that you must wish me happy in the very near future." She fidgeted with the ribbon at her breast. "Only fancy! Quite unbeknownst to me, Sir Matthew has been madly in love with me all this while! He finally declared himself in a fit of passion when he railed at me for being taken in by that unworthy scoundrel, Mr. Brinson. It seems poor Sir Matthew wished for me to make up my own mind, but when he saw I could be so easily taken in, he said he will no longer permit my being out in society until we are safely married. We are only waiting for my twenty-first birthday next year and then we shall tie the knot."

Mina frowned. "And what do you think about that, Cecily?" she asked, feeling somewhat taken aback.

"Oh, well I am fully sensible to the honor that he does me," Cecily answered, preening herself. "I daresay none of my schoolmates will marry so well as I." Mina remembered that Eliza Hinch had married a baronet but thought it would not be fortuitous to bring that up at this precise moment. "It does still take me aback that I should have captured his heart," Cecily admitted in a burst of confidence. "For he always seemed so stern and forbidding, that I never once thought of him in the role of lover, but now that I do…" She blushed. "Well, I have to own he is the very finest man I know. And not so very old at six and thirty. We are only related by marriage, and besides, Sir Matthew has promised that he will take me to Rome for our honeymoon and that I may have one of my cousin's litter of Maltese dogs for my very own companion. They are such dear little things, like little balls of white fluff! Oh, I shall be so happy to have both a husband and a little doggy of my own," said Cecily, clasping her hands together and gazing at her reflection in the mirror raptly.

"I see," said Mina, though in truth she found it extremely hard to imagine Cecily as the wife of dry Sir Matthew. She wondered, for instance, what on earth they could have in common to talk about of an evening. For Sir Matthew was cool and sardonic where Cecily rattled on like a pea goose. While it was true that Cecily still seemed to feel some vestiges of her former awe around her guardian at present, Mina did not doubt this would soon dissipate and then she would regale Sir Matthew with her every empty-headed thought. Still, she reflected, it was highly likely that people thought she and Nye made a strange couple. Perhaps Sir Matthew would simply sit

Cecily on his lap as Nye did with her. "I am happy things are going on well for you, my dear," she said aloud.

"Oh yes," Cecily agreed dreamily as she threaded a riband through the front of her locks. A discreet knock on the door heralded the arrival of a tea tray which was set down on a gilded occasional table.

"Would you be so kind as to pour, Miss Walters?" Cecily asked, her eyes not leaving the mirror.

"Of course." Mina nodded and thanked the parlor maid. "I do wish you would call me Mina, Cecily. For our own ages are not so very disparate, and we have been acquaintances now of many years. And with you so very soon to be entering matrimony, it seems foolish that you should address me so formally."

Cecily wheeled around at this, her expression rapt. "I would be delighted, my dear Mina!" she exclaimed. Mina wondered at it, but it seemed Cecily was in deadly earnest. The only reason Mina could think of was that Cecily could write to her former schoolfellows, now proclaiming them to be bosom friends. For her to think of this as a social triumph was so patently absurd that Mina could not help hiding a smile, despite her own mood at present.

Cecily applied perfume and then rang the bell for her maid to help her into a dress of lavender with a profusion of ruffles and lace. Mina had poured their tea and eaten half of the toast before Cecily dismissed her maid and sank into a chair beside her.

"Now tell me *everything*!" she urged. "Dearest Mina, spare no detail, for I want to hear it as though it were one of those wonderful stories you used to tell us at school."

Mina regaled her with an extremely expunged version of all that had befallen her since their perfidious stable hand abducted her and secluded her in an underground passage. Of Gus Hopkirk's involvement she mentioned precious little, save that he had implored the villainous Reuben not to let her freeze to death, or offer her unnecessary violence.

"What a terrible man that ostler was—so cruel and brutish!" Cecily shuddered. "For you to be at the mercy of such a ruffian turns one's blood quite cold!"

Mina agreed. When she came to the part of the story where Reuben had gagged and bound her for her journey to the cliff edge, Cecily shrieked and clapped her hands to her cheeks. She did not utter a word until she reached the Riding Officers taking Nye into custody along with Gus Hopkirk.

"No!" cried Cecily, sitting up indignantly. "But why should they do such a stupid thing?"

Mina spread her hands wide. "I think because Nye owns Vance House and was Reuben's employer they think—"

"But how foolish! As if that were his fault!" she expostulated. "I vow and declare I never heard of such stupidity! After they abducted his own wife!" She stood up and then sat down again in great agitation. "But where is your husband now?" she asked.

"He sits in the holding cells at St. Ives, awaiting transfer to Bodmin jail."

Cecily gasped. "But we must tell Sir Matthew at once!"

Mina looked down demurely at her gloved hands. "I must own that was my mission in coming here this morning. To throw myself on Sir Matthew's mercy…"

"Of course!" breathed Cecily approvingly. "It is the only thing to be done!"

"Alas, he was from home when I arrived—"

"Oh, but I am sure I heard his carriage come up the drive some twenty minutes ago," said Cecily blithely.

"Really?" Mina said, turning toward the window. "I did not notice it."

When they made their way downstairs moments later, they found the drawing room empty and the murmur of male voices from Sir Matthew's study.

"Who was it who accompanied you this morning?" Cecily asked in a whisper as they hovered on the threshold.

"My half brother, Lord Faris," Mina responded and saw Cecily's jaw drop.

"Lord Faris?" she gasped. "Lord Faris is your brother? Dearest Mina!"

"Yes," Mina confirmed, craning to make out any of the words through the door. "I did not find out until recently, however. Should we knock?"

Cecily looked horrified. "Oh no! On no account. We must sit and wait for them to join us after they have talked business. Sir Matthew does not approve of women who put themselves forward in an odiously pushing manner," she stressed.

Mina gritted her teeth but sat beside her ex-pupil on a sofa all the same. They had not been sat there for more than a couple of minutes when Jeremy emerged, his usual urbane self, though there was a pucker between his brows Mina did not care for. His gaze sought hers for a reassuring smile before Sir Matthew checked on the threshold to the room.

"Mrs. Nye, I had not realized you accompanied Lord Faris."

"Dearest Mina was visiting with myself when you arrived home, Sir Matthew," Cecily told him, fluttering prettily.

He stiffened and Mina thought a little color entered his hollow cheeks. "Indeed," he said, his gaze darting between them. Whatever he saw did not seem to make him any easier in his mind. "Er—Cecily has ordered you some refreshment?" he asked.

"Oh yes," Mina agreed. "She has been a most considerate hostess. Jeremy," she said, rising to introduce her brother to Cecily. "This is my good friend, Miss Carswell. Cecily, this is my brother, Lord Faris."

"Enchanted," Jeremy said, bowing over Cecily's hand. She blushed prettily and became quite flustered. Mina noticed Sir Matthew's brows snap together as he watched her brother at his most charming.

"You have seen my husband this morning, Sir Matthew?" she asked pointedly.

"What? Oh—er, as to that, I'm afraid I only managed to look in on him very briefly, ma'am." He dragged his eyes from Cecily to address her. "I spoke with Officers Havilland and Guthrie and only had the time to really speak to that hardened charlatan, Augustus Hopkirk, if that even is his name," he added cynically.

Mina remembered that Gus was not from around these parts and reflected with surprise that it may well be an alias. "I see."

"Surely, Sir Matthew, there is something you can do for my friend?" Cecily appealed, moved to tears. "It is too cruel that her husband should now be held prisoner! And most unjust."

Sir Matthew looked uncomfortable. "I will own that I was not fully apprised of the facts," he said after a slight pause. "But there are certain matters we need clarification upon," he added pompously. "And we cannot act in haste on these matters, my dear Cecily."

"Well, Carswell," said Jeremy, taking up his hat and cane, "I have made my next actions plain. My solicitor will be engaged to act on behalf of my brother-in-law, and we will lodge an action against any move to transfer him to Bodmin immediately."

Sir Matthew's expression tightened. "As you say, my lord," he said with a stiff bow.

"Come, Mina," said Jeremy, offering her his arm. With heightened civility, they took their leave.

"What did he say?" Mina asked in a low voice as they pulled away from the house.

"He offered Nye a custodial sentence this morning, if he turned Queen's evidence against Hopkirk."

Mina gasped. "What did Nye say to that?" she asked in dismay.

Jeremy cast her a speaking glance. "Nothing. He is not easily coerced or intimidated, as you may imagine."

"At least then he would not hang," Mina said, biting her lip.

"You would still be married to a convicted felon, however."

"But not a widow," she pointed out.

"There is that," he conceded.

"I think you put him out a good deal talking of legal representation. They had not expected Nye to have such backing."

"It was not mere bluff," Jeremy assured her. "I will ride to see Havering this afternoon."

"Did he tell you nothing else?" Mina persisted.

"Carswell said Hopkirk is playing the lovable rogue card to the hilt. Just a bluff old sailor out of his depth and manipulated by more unscrupulous types."

Mina cast a quick glance at Jeremy. "Does Gus try to throw the blame on Nye?"

"Quite the contrary. He claims Reuben issued all the orders and says he knows of no other members of the gang. He acts bewildered by the fact Nye is in custody. Hopkirk says he was horrified to find Reuben had kidnapped you. Asserts he did everything in his power to make you more comfortable and protect you from the fellow."

Mina pursed her lips. "Like all convincing lies, it has some truth to it, though precious little." She looked Jeremy straight in the eye. "I believe Hopkirk was 'the guvnor,'" she admitted. "And very likely the mastermind behind the whole smuggling operation. But I doubt it could ever be proved."

Jeremy gave a low whistle. "Hopkirk?" He gave her an uncertain look. "Carswell is determined to bring someone before a jury for punishment."

Mina stared straight ahead of her. "If I was willing to testify against Gus—"

Jeremy shook his head. "If he truly were the head of the gang, that could be dangerous, Mina. We do not know how many make up his company of men. There could be dozens in the locality waiting to wreak their revenge."

"True," she admitted. "And I have no proof. Only suspicions and some stories he told me." She hesitated, remembering the truly horrible things Gus had said about him being a wrecker and the fates of his former wives. "The trouble is, he has told me a good many tales and all of them are tall ones. He could have been just trying to frighten me, but—" She broke off, remembering Gus's expression of malignant glee in the lamplight. "I do not think it."

They were quiet for the rest of the homeward journey, and when Jeremy set her down in the courtyard of The Harlot, Mina was met by Colfax, who seemed to be seeing to outside duties. He informed her that a Riding Officer was awaiting her in the parlor, and Jeremy immediately said he would accompany her inside.

"No, please," Mina said, turning back to stop him from leaving the carriage. "I would be much more comfortable if you went to see your legal man on Nye's behalf. I am much recovered now and will be more than equal to their questions."

Jeremy relented, though Mina could see he was not happy about it. Corin was waiting in the hallway to take her cloak and bonnet, and she impulsively hugged Mina and then hung up her things. Edna, upon hearing her voice, came hurrying out of the kitchen with a suppressed sob to fling her skinny arms about her.

"That wicked oaf, Reuben!" Edna said in a low voice that shook with anger. "Oh, your poor head," she exclaimed, seeing the bandage beneath her bonnet.

"It is nothing really, a clean wound that the doctor is assured will heal nicely. Forgive me, Edna, I must go into the parlor now to deal with this officer."

"I have a tea tray ready to bring in with you," Edna responded, making haste to fetch it.

Mina had been girding her loins to confront the unpleasant Havilland, so she was considerably taken aback to find it was the younger and more personable Riding Officer that awaited her. Leaping to his feet, Guthrie bowed punctiliously and greeted his hostess. Edna set down the tea tray and retreated, and Mina bade Guthrie to take his seat.

"I trust you are feeling better today, Mrs. Nye?" he asked as she sat opposite him.

"My bumps and scrapes are healing, thank you, Mr. Guthrie, though it is not pleasant coming home after my ordeal without my husband by my side."

He winced. "I understand."

"Can I ask about the night he has spent in custody?"

"He is tolerably comfortable, I believe, ma'am."

She supposed she would have to make do with that, she thought, setting out two cups and saucers and pouring the tea.

"My brother, Lord Faris, intends to engage his own legal man for Nye's defense," Mina told him steadily and watched him blink over this as she passed him his cup.

"Indeed?"

"Can I ask the intent of the Crown in his arrest? Do you mean to posit that he is implicated in my kidnapping?"

Guthrie swallowed. "We do not believe that your husband was involved in your kidnapping," he admitted. "Otherwise, he would scarcely have requested us to accompany him to ambush Hopkirk and Prouse last night. My superior, Officer Havilland, believes it to have been a 'falling out among thieves' situation. He thinks the most likely scenario is that your husband was trying to disentangle himself from the association and your abduction was a bargaining tool on their behalf to ensure his continued cooperation."

Mina took a sip of her tea and then replaced it on her saucer before speaking. "And what of Gus Hopkirk? Can he shed no light on the matter?"

Guthrie looked pained. She noticed he was rather pale today and suspected he had not been allowed much sleep the previous evening. "Mr. Hopkirk maintains he knows precious little about the matter," Guthrie admitted. "He claims he has been a foolish old man, slipped the odd bottle of rum to impart his local knowledge. According to him he was shocked and dismayed to find Reuben Prouse had abducted you and expected him to stand guard over you in that passage below Vance House."

Mina looked up quickly and Guthrie nodded. "He knows he faces a hangman for his part, so he is striving to appear fully cooperative. They dug that bullet out of his shoulder yesterday and he looks fair to mend. Hopkirk claims Reuben showed him the passage a month or so ago and swore him to silence. When asked to meet him there yesterday, he apparently had no notion of the kidnapping plot. Indeed, he claims he only knew Reuben Prouse as the face of the smugglers and none other."

"He does not implicate my husband, then," Mina pointed out.

"No, he does not," agreed Guthrie slowly. "Hopkirk begs for me to carry word to you that he is most anxious you are recovered from your ordeal and restored to your husband. He acted quite bewildered that Nye should be in custody at all."

Mina could only feel herself greatly relieved that Gus did not mean to try to pin the role of mastermind to Nye. It seemed absurd to her that anyone could think Reuben a commanding figure, but she supposed he had little else to fall back on.

"He says you will bear him out that he was most careful of your health and well-being and acted as champion against Prouse's repeated threats of violence."

Mina nodded. "That is true enough."

Guthrie, she noticed, looked visibly frustrated by her words, though he did not press her. "As for Tom Rowley, he insists he is a 'peaceable man' with a large family and says he never saw hide nor hair of him anywhere near the place." He hesitated. "We want to know if you will testify against Tom Rowley, Mrs. Nye."

"I'm afraid I cannot," Mina answered with perfect truth. "I was quite insensible after Reuben struck me, and I did not catch sight of the carter's face at any point."

"Your maid, Edna Lumm, now says she cannot be sure the man was Tom Rowley who drove the cart out of here yesterday afternoon. She only says she took him for Tom Rowley at the time."

"Edna is one of the most truthful people I know, Mr. Guthrie. If she says she cannot swear to it, then I must believe her."

Guthrie's look was rather hard before he dropped it. "Rowley was taken into custody but released again this morning," he admitted. "Indeed, I start to fear, ma'am, that we will not get a successful conviction against any of the ring at this rate."

"You have no expectation of identifying who the mysterious 'guvnor' they spoke of might be?"

Guthrie shook his head. "Hopkirk talks ceaselessly, but it's all sound and no substance. To hear him talk, Prouse was the villain of the piece and he a poor duped old man." A look of disgust passed over his face. "I believe, ma'am, that he would vastly enjoy appearing before a jury."

"They would be eating out of his hand before the trial was over," Mina predicted softly.

Guthrie shook his head. "You have no other detail to impart that might help us with our investigation? No new angle that might aid us in our enquiry?"

"I'm afraid not," Mina said quietly. Helping their enquiry build a case was not exactly her priority, but she could hardly admit as much.

He looked disappointed, but not surprised, and took his leave of her shortly after. Edna and Corin rallied around with Edna exclaiming she had never liked Gus and always thought him a smooth-tongued villain. It was Corin's half day that afternoon and the girl said she would not take it, but Mina insisted.

"You must go into the village, Corin, and visit with your granny as usual. And you must make sure to tell her anyone else you meet there that Edna and I have both told the Riding Officers most unequivocally that we cannot identify Thomas Rowley, and neither would Gus. Only Reuben's involvement with my abduction is confirmed with witnesses."

Edna shot her a sharp look at this but lowered her gaze as Corin agreed wide-eyed that she would do so.

"The Rowleys are a local family," Edna said after Corin had set out with her bonnet and her basket for the village. "And there's powerful many of them living hereabouts." She hesitated. "I told true when I said I couldn't positively identify him, but—" She broke off frustratedly. "I did take it for him at the time, Mrs. Nye, and that's the God's own truth."

"I understand perfectly, Edna," Mina assured her. "We cannot send a man who may be innocent to the gibbet."

Edna paled. "What of the master?" she asked hoarsely. "Has he queered his pitch sending for those officers? You could have knocked me down with a feather when he said that was what he was doing. For he must have known—"

"My brother, Lord Faris, is speaking to his solicitor on Nye's behalf, and I have spoken to the local Justice of the Peace. I hope between them they may negotiate Nye's release. He had already broken with them, Edna," she added quietly. "That was why—why they took me," she said simply.

Edna reached across the table to clasp hands with her. "I knew you would bring him around," she said staunchly.

Mina could only hope she had not inadvertently sent him to the hangman.

24

The next three days were a sore trial to Mina. The only news she received was a scribbled note from Jeremy assuring her he had met with his legal man, Havering, and he was taking the matter under his consideration. They received no more visits from Riding Officers, but they did receive all manner of other visitors to The Harlot.

The first were the Tavistocks, who came in a very antiquated carriage and stayed for a roast mutton dinner in one of the private parlors. Mina tried in vain to get them to take their meal in her own private room as her guests, but they would not be convinced. It dawned on her that the elderly brother and sister were showing support for their business and she could only be grateful, though she did not know how much sway they held locally.

They were firm in their opinion that the elder and more objectionable of the two Riding Officers was in gross dereliction of his duty and so they told anyone who would listen. "For it stands to reason, my dear. If Nye was implicated in this business, he would hardly have brought them to his own door!" Mr. Tavistock said with a decided nod of his gray head. "Pack of nonsense, depend upon it!"

The second night, a straggling bunch of working men came up the hill from the village and trooped into the empty taproom at The Merry Harlot. Corin had to run to the stable to fetch Herney, who had been polishing the carriage. He hurried inside to serve their customers and Corin made haste to inform Mina that at least three of the group were cousins to Tom Rowley.

The third night even more drifted up the bank from the village in two and threes. Some only stayed for one drink, but others hung around for longer, making the taproom buzz with conversation. Reuben Prouse had not been a popular figure and people were happy enough to allot him the lion's share of the blame. Of Gus, they seemed less censorious and seemed to think he had been led astray, more sinned against than a sinner.

Mina sat in the kitchen with Edna and Corin, who were sewing new dresses for church. She had her handkerchiefs to embroider, but in truth managed precious few stitches. She simply did not want to be alone with her thoughts these days, which often turned bleak.

She wondered how long it would be before she had news from Jeremy. He had thought that Sir Matthew Carswell would communicate far easier with him, and Mina was forced to agree. She did not know what Mr. Havering's opinion had been of their chances of Nye escaping conviction, for Jeremy had been uncommunicative on that score. She drew his note from her waist pocket again and stared at the well-read words.

"Your cup of tea will be getting cold, Mrs. Nye," Corin ventured timorously.

Mina flashed her an absent smile and drank the beverage down. "I think I'm for bed," she sighed. "I'm good for nothing else. I've sewn this same petal three times already and unpicked it again just as many times."

She had washed and was walking back through to the kitchen when she heard the horse hooves in the yard outside. She was surprised, for it was nigh on ten o'clock. Glancing out of the window, she saw the rider dismount and was startled to see it was none other than Jeremy.

Hurrying through to the hallway, she flung open the door and waited for him to hand his horse over to Colfax, who was still helping out where needed. Jeremy did not tarry to speak to his employee but strode immediately to where Mina waited. "Let's go to your private room," he said in a low voice, and Mina led the way with her heart in her mouth.

As soon as he had shut the door behind them both, she turned to him, almost trembling with apprehension. "You have news? Please tell me."

He reached into his jacket and withdrew a folded paper which he held fast a moment before passing it to her.

Mina's hands shook so badly she could scarcely open it. "What is it?"

"Release papers."

Mina cried out, almost dropping the papers to the floor. "For Nye?" She fixed her eyes on him with an intensity that was almost painful.

Jeremy smiled. "They are signed and ready for presentation to the officers at St. Ives."

"Then, why do you not present them immediately?" She glanced at the clock and cursed the lateness of the hour.

He cocked his head to one side. "It's my belief that you should perform that office, sister. First thing on the morrow."

"Me?"

Jeremy's expression turned grave. "It's my opinion you will need to exercise the full force of your charm on him, I warn you."

Mina felt a spurt of alarm. "What do you mean?"

"When I saw him yesterday, his frame of mind was grim. He—er—was not contemplating the future with relish."

"Well, no. He would hardly do so with the gallows looming on the horizon," she reminded her brother somewhat tartly.

His lips quirked. "When I spoke of any possibility of cheating the hangman, he talked of disappearing to Exeter and leaving you in staid respectability at Vance Park."

Mina turned quite cold. "What?" she cried.

"Either that or having you divorce him before he perished on the scaffold."

"Divorce!"

"I'm sure it was only his depression of spirits that prompted such talk," Jeremy hurried to assure her. "But I could not rouse him from it, try as I might. I think if I were to take these papers to him, he would disappear for at least a month or so."

"Disappear? For a *month*!" Mina's ire rose.

"No more than that, I'm persuaded, but even so I do not think you should be made to do without him at present."

"No indeed!" Mina fumed, plunking her hands on her hips. "Why, the very idea!"

Jeremy gave a sudden laugh. "You'll bring him about; I have no doubt."

"Certainly, I shall," Mina responded in high dudgeon. "You may depend upon it." When he turned toward the door, she reached out to stay him, her mood changing abruptly. "Jeremy, wait. I have not thanked you for everything you have done for us—"

"No, and I beg you will not do so," he interrupted her. "You are my family, and I have more need of that now than ever." He hesitated. "It will be your turn to return the favor in coming months. Comparatively, 'tis of little import, but I have started divorce proceedings as you advised. Amanda is not taking it well." He grimaced. "I have no doubt that things will get a good deal worse before they get better."

"Oh, Jeremy." She squeezed his arm with a rush of sympathy. "It must be very hard, but I am convinced you are doing the right thing. We will be here for you, of course."

He nodded, smiled at her, and left Mina still clutching the piece of paper to her heart.

*

It was not even six o'clock when Mina rose the next morning. She dressed hurriedly, but when she went to place her father's watch in the inner pocket of her skirts, she was surprised to find something hard concealed in there already. Drawing it out between two fingers, she found it was her missing bridal sixpence.

She stared at it a moment, lost in thought, then, taking it for a good omen, she went downstairs with a lightness in her step that had not been there before, in search of Ed Herney. He was already up and dressed, and on confiding the errand was to fetch the master home, he showed every pleasure at the prospect of driving the coach and went to put the horses to. Colfax assured her he would hold the fort while they were gone.

Mina had finished a piece of bread and butter and a cup of tea by the time Edna appeared in the kitchen.

"You're early this morning, Mrs. Nye," she said with surprise, then added anxiously, "Not bad news, I hope?"

400

"On the contrary, Edna," Mina told her with a smile and produced the paper. Edna screeched and rounded the table to embrace her over the news.

There was just time for a second hurried cup of tea before she climbed into the carriage and then she was on her way to the holding cells at St. Ives. She clutched the papers in one gloved hand and drew her cloak close about her. Rain was steadily falling, and she peered out of the carriage window wondering if the April showers were going to turn into a downpour before the morning was over.

The rain slackened off by the time they reached St. Ives, and they had to stop while Herney took directions, having never had occasion to visit the cells before. They were soon proceeding down a side street, and seeing a uniformed individual alighting from a nearby doorway, Mina called up to Herney to halt the carriage.

"I will get down here. You must circle around and return in a half hour or so."

"You're sure you won't wait for me to stable them and accompany you, ma'am?" he yelled down as she alighted.

"No, no. That won't be necessary, thank you, Herney." She was already making determinedly for the steps.

Once inside, a forbidding-looking gentleman approached her. Before he had even opened his mouth, Mina informed him crisply that she wanted to speak to whoever was in charge. Ten minutes later, after her papers had been duly inspected, she was ushered into an antechamber to await the prisoner's release.

Mina took her pocket watch out no fewer than three times as she waited for them to bring Nye to her. Would things have gone smoother if she had brought her brother along with her or even Colfax? she wondered. The officials had seemed affronted that so important a document had been delivered into their hands by a mere female.

No, she thought on reflection, for Jeremy had warned her that Nye had a mind to be difficult. She would be better able to handle him on her own. The door opened and Mina sprang to her feet as Nye was ushered inside by an attendant.

"You're to wait here," the attendant said heavily. "And we'll bring out your belongings."

Nye turned toward her, his chin dark with stubble and his clothes rumpled. It was his expression, however, that gave her pause for thought, for it was closed and far from inviting.

Mina took a deep, fortifying breath and walked forward, but he made no answering move toward her. Coming to a halt in front of him, she reached out to take his arm, but he stepped away from her, preventing her.

"What did you do, Mina?" he asked in an ominously quiet voice. She frowned a moment, unsure what he meant. "To ensure my release," he added through gritted teeth.

"I did only what needed to be done, nothing more, nothing less."

"Wait!" he said, his hand shooting out to grab her arm where she stood. His grip was hard, and Mina only just managed not to wince. His nostrils flared and he dragged her close until his face was inches from hers. "Did you let him touch you?" he asked harshly.

Mina's jaw dropped. "What? Who are you—?"

His eyes narrowed. "Carswell. Answer me."

"William Nye—!"

402

"Because if you did, it was a one-time-only deal. I'm not sharing you."

"Sir Matthew is a respectable man!" she hissed.

"I don't give a fuck if he's the lord mayor of London, he's not sleeping with my wife."

"Of course not!" she spluttered. God, she'd forgotten what an unreasonable swine he could be! She let a crack show in her veneer and took a shaky breath, leaning into him. "Nye, can we please just leave this wretched place? I promise I'll explain everything to your satisfaction as soon as we're out of here!"

His hands tightened on her upper arms a moment before he gave a nod and released her. Someone coughed behind them, and they realized the attendant had returned holding Nye's watch and penknife. He took them from him and stuffed them in his waistcoat pockets. When Mina moved instinctively to his side to slip her arm through his, he shook her off. Mina swallowed down the hurt she felt at his rejection.

"I'm a state," he said, avoiding her eyes and running a hand down his jaw distractedly. "I haven't shaved in two days. Walk ahead of me."

For a moment she considered arguing, but he planted a hand squarely in her middle back and pushed her toward the door. Gathering her shredded dignity around her, Mina headed out into the fresh air. To her horror, she felt her eyes prickling with tears. No doubt it was the fallout of the strain of last two days, but it was hard to shrug off her husband's accusing words. Well. At least now she knew what he thought of her!

Catching sight of the carriage at the end of the street, she made for it with her head held high. She could hear Nye's boots against the pavement behind her but did not turn her head to

403

look at him. Seizing the handle to the door of the carriage, she flung it open, but even as she lifted her skirts to place her foot on the step, big arms closed around her from behind and Nye boosted her up into the carriage before him.

She was surprised when he climbed in after her. She thought he'd have taken a seat up top with Herney rather than ride passenger inside. She had only just arranged herself onto the seat, stony-faced, when the carriage lurched forward.

"I'm waiting," he said harshly.

It was funny to think the large angry man sat opposite as a sight for sore eyes, but that was how it seemed to Mina, even though she currently wanted to throw something at him. She let her gaze roam over his dark hair and smoldering eyes. Then she caught the expression in those eyes and thought she'd better make haste to explain her role in his release.

"Jeremy engaged his legal man to take up your cause, a Mr. Havering. I believe the Vances have employed his firm for many generations," she answered in freezing accents.

His eyes flickered, but he made no comment on this. "And?" he prompted. "I saw whose name countersigned those papers, Mina," he added dangerously. "So don't even think about lying to me."

"Very well, I did approach Sir Matthew," she admitted. "But never alone. Jeremy accompanied me to Upton Gadsby. He spoke to Sir Matthew as well as I. In fact"—her voice rose with indignation—"I barely spoke to the man. I concentrated my efforts on Cecily, so she would bring her influence to bear on him." He gave her a withering look. "They are engaged to be married," she added pointedly. "At least, unofficially they are." He made no comment on that, and Mina started to feel a little desperate. "In any case, if anyone owes an explanation, it's you!" she flung at him accusingly. "What on earth were you thinking telling Jeremy that you wanted to divorce me or go running off to Exeter?"

"I'll tell you what I was thinking, Mina," he retorted angrily. "I was thinking that when I was swinging from the gibbet, you'd be set up in a fine house, befitting of a lady like yourself!" His eyes avoided hers, staring unseeingly out of the carriage window.

"Well, that's not what I would want," said Mina firmly.

He swung around, an incredulous look on his face. "Well, if that isn't just bloody typical of you, woman, then I don't know what is!"

"I'm not a fine lady," she carried on, calmly ignoring his outburst. "I'm a publican's wife, and I'm more than happy with my lot."

He snorted. "How about a convict's wife?" he asked bitterly. "I don't think you'd have suited that fate, Minerva."

"Certainly, I would not," she agreed. "But as you had renounced your former way of life, I had no intention of allowing that to happen."

He stared at her incredulously. "You had no intention?" he echoed, then shook his head. "You've got no idea, woman."

"On the contrary, I knew full well what *I* was about. But as for you, how dare you make plans to leave me? Do you have any notion—?"

"Do you have any notion how *I* felt?" he broke in heatedly. "When I found that rock covered in your blood? That rock Edna told me Reuben had smashed against the back of your head—" His voice was thick with emotion, and for a moment, his throat

405

seemed to close on him. "I knew full well whose fault it would have been if you were found somewhere cold and dead with all that spark and fire of yours extinguished," he carried on unevenly after a moment's pause. "Mine! All mine. Mine was the blame for carrying on with that pack of—" Words failed him again. "The blame was mine, and so should the punishment have been."

"Nye—"

He waved her words aside. "I'm not a fit husband for you, Mina. I never was. Do you think I'm unaware of the fact? Faris was insane to have even thought of such a scheme, and I'm a villain to have taken the bargain. Do you understand? I married you to get my hands on Vance House because the smugglers had been using that passage and the cove there for years."

"Yes, I had realized that," she admitted coolly. "But why then, on gaining it, did you not immediately evict the tenants? More importantly, why did you tell the smugglers that you were quitting the business altogether?"

Nye brooded a moment, then took a deep breath. "I was not bothered about a pair of old, stone-deaf sitting tenants," he said dismissively. "And as for quitting…" He gave a short, harsh laugh. "I was crazy to think they would even consider letting me get out of it."

"Likely because Gus was always so personable," Mina mused. "He's very good at hiding his ruthless nature."

He shot her a troubled look. "I don't even like to think about how you must have felt when you came around in that passage."

"I won't lie, I was badly frightened when I caught a glimpse of Gus's true self. I think personally he was the real leader of operations, do not you?"

Nye looked startled. "I don't—" He frowned and directed her a look beneath his brows. "Gus?"

"Every time Reuben spoke of 'the guvnor,' Gus was practically laughing up his sleeve. He did not trouble to hide it from me."

"He always spoke of receiving orders from another," he said slowly, but his expression was thoughtful.

"Is it true that no member knew more than one or two others of the company?" He looked evasive. "I remember that night they called up to the window for you they had scarves over their faces." She could see he was still reluctant to speak on the matter and sighed. "Edna has told the Riding Officers she could not identify the man who drove the cart that carried me away, for she only caught sight of his back view."

Nye's gaze met hers. "Did you see him?" he asked.

She shook her head. "His hat was pulled low and I only glimpsed him for an instant before Reuben struck me."

He tensed at her words, then exhaled noisily. "Probably just as well," he muttered.

"The Rowleys have taken to frequenting The Harlot of an evening," she told him.

He sat up in his seat with a quick frown. "What? Have they said anything to you? To Edna?"

She shook her head. "It's not so much an intimidation tactic as a show of support," she assured him. "Corin and Herney spread it in the village that we are not identifying anyone apart from Gus and Reuben."

"Reuben's dead, I saw to that myself," he said abruptly.

Now it was Mina's turn to sit up. "What do you mean?" she faltered. "I thought he got shot in the struggle?"

Nye shook his head. "I broke his neck," he said briefly. "He should not have touched you."

"Broke his—?" Mina stared at him a moment, then gave herself a quick shake. "Well, it's of no matter now."

Nye shielded his eyes from her with his hand. "Gus may still turn Queen's evidence, you know," he said gruffly. "To save his skin. If he were to implicate my own involvement over the years…"

A horrid thought occurred to her. "Was that one of the reasons you wanted to disappear to Exeter?" she asked, suddenly stricken.

"No." He looked impatient.

"In any case," said Mina, "I don't believe for one minute that Gus would do such a thing." She hesitated. "You see, his whole defense angle is that he was an ignorant old man who was taken advantage of by the wily smugglers. A bit of flattery, a few bottles of rum, and he was putty in their hands. That sort of thing. He won't blow that apart now by admitting to knowing much more about the business. Officer Guthrie told me Gus acted quite bewildered that you had been taken into custody. He told them that Reuben gave him his orders and you were nothing to do with it."

Nye looked a good deal taken aback by that. "Reuben giving orders?" he repeated skeptically. "No one would believe that."

"They would if they wanted to. It turns out Reuben was not well-liked in the village. The officers did not even know him. I

408

bet you the guards are already warming to Gus and allowing him extra portions of tobacco and gin," Mina said with a snort. "He's a cozening old rogue. Or at least, that is the face he presents to the world." She thought fleetingly of the more sinister things he had told her but pushed that resolutely out of her mind. It could have been lies, she told herself. Gus Hopkirk was first and foremost a spinner of yarns.

Nye looked conflicted. "Still," he hesitated. "If he truly was the one in charge…"

"Put it out of your head," Mina begged. "It's my belief such a thing would never be proven. It is just a notion of mine after all, and one I will not so much as mention to anyone else save yourself." When he continued to be silent, she added, "Besides, he bore you no ill will. He told me himself that you were drawn into smuggling by old Jacob Nye and that you had little choice about it."

Nye did not look appeased. "If he gave the orders to have you kidnapped, Mina," he started wrathfully, "then—"

"But don't you see? That was nothing personal. It was just business. Indeed, he scolded Reuben for treating me poorly. He did not dislike me." It occurred to Mina that Nye did not realize Gus had intended for her to be flung off a cliff edge. She decided not to enlighten him. Likely it would just put rash ideas into his head about getting Gus convicted at all costs. "Now that the smuggling ring is broken quite apart, I daresay he will bear no malice, but will instead focus on swaying the jury in his favor."

"Aye, and he'll probably escape with a custodial sentence," said Nye darkly. "I wouldn't put it past him."

"And what's that to us?" Mina shrugged. "I doubt he'd come back to Penarth. He's not from round these parts and likely he's left many such skirmishes with the law in his wake. He'll probably go whistling out of prison and take himself another name and pitch up at some other seaside spot. A salty seadog with a wealth of tales and a winning manner."

"And that's it, is it?" Nye asked. "We just forget about the ordeal he put you through?"

"Yes," she said firmly. "We put all that behind us. At least—" A sudden thought struck her. "I may write him a letter to be given in prison."

"What?" Nye thundered.

"Just to let him know that I will never breathe a word of what I learned in that passageway and that you refused to turn Queen's evidence so he knows he has nothing to be revenged against on that score."

"They read and censor every letter a prisoner receives—" Nye began, but she fluttered a hand at this.

"I know that of course! I would couch everything in exceedingly careful terms. For instance, I would thank him prettily for preserving me against Reuben. He would be vastly pleased by that, I think, and read it aloud to his jailors at every opportunity, for you see it backs the line he means to take. Then I could tell him that you had been released and how vexed I was that anyone could be so foolish as to suppose you had been involved." She tapped her chin distractedly. "Perhaps I could finish by assuring him I bear him no ill will and wish him well in his trial."

Nye looked irritated. "And if he should call on you to testify in his defense?" he pointed out testily. "Could you swear in a court of law that he intended you no harm?"

410

This floored her for a moment, before she rallied. "I could truthfully say that he upbraided Reuben for repeatedly threatening me. And besides, I don't think he would want me on the witness stand for he would know I would not actually lie on his behalf."

"No, except by omission," he said caustically.

Mina directed a swift look at him. She had almost run out of steam now and had precious little left in her arsenal to distract him from his current mood. "Well," she ventured, going for broke, "I have discovered some new friends in any event. The Tavistocks are an exceedingly nice pair, and I beg you will not dispossess them of Vance House, for they seem very settled and have been there some twenty years all told." When he did not immediately respond, she rattled on. "There is not the smallest need to evict them on my account, Nye, for I have no intention of being set up as a fine lady while you go haring off to Exeter!" She folded her arms and firmed her mouth. "So, you need not think it!"

All of a sudden, she found herself pushed back against the cushioned seat and her mouth taken in a bruising kiss. "Mmmffff!" Mina made an annoyed sound around his tongue as he covered her body with his own, dominating her with his far bigger size and frame. "Nye!" she protested when he finally dragged his mouth from hers.

"You'll not be satisfied with any outcome that does not include me by your side, is that what you're saying, Mina?" he asked in a gravelly tone, his hands roaming over her back and down her hips as he maneuvered her where he wanted her. She felt him reach for the hem of her skirts.

"Nye!" she squeaked in outrage. "Not here in the carriage!"

411

"Aye, here in the carriage. I'm having you, on your back." His eyes were dark with desire, and Mina blinked up at him in alarm.

"'Tis only a half hour's journey before we're home—" she reminded him reasonably.

"Now!" he growled, unfastening his crotch. "I cannot wait."

She huffed "Oh, very well!" as the uncouth lout tossed up her skirts and started dragging her drawers down her legs. "But I think it very unmannerly of you!"

Suddenly, to her surprise, he froze. "Your head," he said, his eyes flying to hers.

"Oh, it's fine now," she assured him. "Just a little cut, entirely cleaned and mending."

"Let me see," he said, reaching for her bonnet strings and untying them.

"You can't, it's mostly covered with hair."

He ignored her, casting off her bonnet and turning her head this way and that.

"Satisfied?" Mina felt a little flustered, sat like this with her drawers around her ankles and Nye practically on top of her.

"There was so much blood," he said uncertainly. "I saw it."

"I imagine you know more about head wounds than I," Mina pointed out. "They bleed a lot. After all your own eye has barely recovered from your recent boxing match."

"It doesn't pain you?" he asked gruffly.

"Barely at all." She gazed at him, touched that his ardor had been so quickly doused by concern for her well-being. "And

412

you were quite right," she told him, taking the bull by the horns. "In what you said before." When he looked blank, she added quietly, "Unless you're by my side, then I won't be happy, Nye. I happen to be in love with you, you see."

He went completely still at that, his eyes growing dark with emotion. "Then I'd better make sure to keep you happy," he said, his voice rough with desire as he sank to the floor of the coach between her legs, shoving her petticoats out of the way.

"Nye!" she squealed, realizing his intent with dismay. "I'll fall off the seat!"

He lowered his face to the juncture between her thighs and growled against her, making Mina feel quite weak. She reached up to brace her hands against the seat back as he opened his mouth directly over her and started placing open-mouthed kisses there. "Oh Nye!" she groaned. "Don't let me fall!" He must have heard her as his grip on her thighs tightened and he pinned her harder into the seat as he feasted on her like a man half-starved. Mina closed her eyes and shivered. "Nye!" she whimpered. "Have mercy." She thought he gave a stifled laugh, as she uttered a hoarse cry and came apart completely, with embarrassing haste.

She was only vaguely aware when he ripped open the bodice of her dress, scattering the buttons.

"This bloody corset," he complained as he unhooked the front to free her breasts. She should protest at such treatment, she thought dreamily. She would look a state by the time they reached the inn. Then again, she could just draw her cloak about her, and no one would be any the wiser. He was palming her breasts now. "Ah God, Mina," he groaned. "You're so beautiful."

413

She blinked at this epithet. *Beautiful?* He must be the only person who thought her so. For a moment, she almost wished she were dressed in frilly undergarments to please him. Red stockings, she seemed to remember, were to his particular liking. Maybe she would work up the nerve someday to purchase a pair?

"What did I ever do to deserve all this bounty?" he said huskily, lowering his face to nuzzle against her breasts.

She clasped a hand to the back of his head, stroking his dark hair as he worshipped at her bared bosom. She sent up a fervent hope that no other carriage would pass them on this country road, for if they chanced to glance through the window, they would surely get an eyeful. Then he opened his lips against the tender swell of her flesh, and she forgot such considerations in the delight of his tongue and the scrape of his teeth and the sucking depths of his hot, devouring mouth.

Pinning her to the edge of the seat, he reached down to free himself from his breeches and she felt the bold thrust of him against her belly. "Hurry, Nye," she implored.

He cast a wild glance out of the carriage window. "We've plenty of time."

"That's not what I meant!" she sobbed, crowding against him. "I can't wait any longer. Please, Nye."

He was still for a heartbeat. "Ah, Mina, love," he said thickly. "It needed only that…" He caught her behind her knee and hooked it over his hip. "Tell me again."

"I can't wait, I want you—oh! Oh, Nye!" she keened as he thrust and her eyes watered as she felt him lodged within her, sinking into her slowly but surely. His hands were not gentle as he jostled her, forcing his thick inches deeper, dragging her hips

414

down as he bumped her against the seat, until she had taken his entire length and their bodies were tight and flush against each other.

He gave a harsh groan, his brow beaded with sweat, and she realized he had been exerting some will after all, to temper his actions and not grow frantic. "Ah, Mina," he breathed. "God, I couldn't ever give you up. I was lying to Faris, to myself even."

She wrapped her arms around his shoulders, looking deep into his eyes. "Good," she said simply, and he surged into her, making them both moan aloud. "Will," she whispered, rubbing her hands across his shoulder blades. "I—I don't want you to go slow."

He gave a suppressed laugh again. "So, then tell me to go *fast*," he recommended, illustrating with a hard buck of his hips. Mina uttered a yell, which startled her greatly and made Nye's eyes flash. She tightened the grip of her leg about his hip, wishing she could wrap the other around him, but the tangle of her petticoats prevented her.

"Tell me, Mina. I'll do anything you say," he vowed throatily.

"Yes, yes, faster," she implored, tightening her arms over his shoulders. "Faster please! *Oh yes!*"

At this point, he illustrated so thoroughly an understanding of what she needed that Mina lost her wits completely. She shivered and moaned and wailed her way through an orgasm that saw her lose control of her limbs and her inhibitions so completely that they ended up sliding from the seat into a tangle of limbs on the floor of the carriage.

She managed to pull herself together just in time to watch Nye's own expression go from agonized, to ecstatic, to spent. With a loud groan, he fell forward, his face burying into her neck

415

where his ragged breathing tickled her sensitive skin there, as his shaft still pulsed inside her, flooding her with his seed.

She reached up and ran her fingers into his hair, her heart swelling when he closed his eyes, pressing his head closer as he not only allowed but showed every evidence of enjoying her caress. They lay a moment in each other's arms on the floor of the carriage as it bumped and jolted along its way home. She didn't want to speak. Didn't want him to speak. Just wanted to lie there limp and happy and satiated.

Finally, he lifted his head to look down at her, one hand coming up to brush the hair from her face. "I love you," he said. "Mina Nye." A slight pucker appeared between his brows. "Did you know that already?"

"Not for certain. Not until you mentioned my blood on that rock," she admitted. "And were so upset about it."

"Don't," he said, closing his eyes a moment. "Don't spoil this moment with that. I thought you were likely dead. That was why I didn't care anymore."

"About implicating yourself?" she asked softly. "I can't believe you rode to fetch the Riding Officers. It was practically an admission of guilt."

He murmured an agreement. "It didn't matter what happened to me," he admitted. "Not at that point. I wanted them all to swing for it. For daring to raise a hand against you. No one will ever do so again," he vowed. "I'll kill anyone who ever tries."

"I know." She thought briefly of Reuben's crumpled body before shutting that memory away. If she could have cuddled into Nye closer, she would have, but there was not an inch to spare between them.

He met her untroubled gaze frankly, then shook his head. "Now tell me about every minute you've spent away from me."

She reached up and pressed the pad of her forefinger to his frowning brow as she told him the whole unvarnished story as swiftly and in as economical words as possible.

He didn't interrupt, even if he did breathe in sharply and narrow his eyes at a couple of points. At the parts about Sir Matthew she slid her hands up his shirt and stroked his muscular back by way of comfort, marveling that he could be so jealous. It seemed ridiculous to her, but she trod carefully all the same. "So, you see," she said teasingly, "my virtue is firmly intact."

His eyebrows rose at this. "You're lying on the floor of a coach with your tits out and my cock still in you," he pointed out.

She slapped a hand against his back. "Nye!"

"It's the truth, love." He smirked. "Your ideas of virtue have taken quite a battering since we got wed."

"There's no need to be crude," she said, pressing her lips together.

He gave a soft laugh. "That prim look doesn't work when I'm buried between your thighs, Minerva." He dropped his words, low and intimate, and flexed his hips, eliciting a soft moan from her lips. "God knows, it's my favorite spot in all the world."

"Nye," she whispered, feeling him grow hard again.

He dropped his mouth to hers for a tender kiss. "Get up on your knees, love. We've still got a good ten minutes of even road."

She gaped. "Nye, we need to set ourselves to rights! They'll be waiting for us at the inn, wanting to shake your hand and wish you well—"

"Well, I only care about what I want, right now," he growled, pulling out of her and dragging her up from the floor. "Because I've been in abject misery for three days thinking I'd lost my future with you." He bent her forward, so her chest was pressed into the cushioned seat, and then settled behind her, bunching her skirts to her waist.

"But that's ridiculous—" She broke off with a groan as he thrust back into her, the front of his powerful thighs pressing into the backs of hers. "Oh, Will!"

"Mmm," he grunted, one hand sliding around her hip and diving between her thighs to rub against her most sensitive spot. "I think you like being ravished in a coach, wife."

Mina turned her face, so her cheek was pressed against the cushioned seat. "Oh!" she panted. "Oh, Will." Her eyes drifted shut.

"Tell me," he insisted.

"Yes," she sobbed. "Anywhere with you."

He started a vigorous pace, driving into her so briskly, she struggled to catch her breath. "Anywhere?" he echoed, sounding intrigued. "What if I'd wanted you in my cell? With your back against the bars?"

She gave a choked laugh. "As if you'd ever ask such a thing of me," she couldn't resist pointing out.

"Don't be so sure…" he answered darkly.

"You wouldn't even look me in the eye in that holding room!"

His hands slid up over her waist, urging her to straighten up from the seat. When she did, he cupped her generous breasts, pulling her back firmly against him, even as he kept thrusting. "Don't imagine for one minute that I didn't think about it," he

418

panted. "Because the thought of never spending inside your hot little cunt again nearly made me weep."

Mina reached down and grasped the seat hard. "Nye!" she gasped.

"You're mine, Minerva," he said richly. "Say it."

"I'm yours."

His mouth nuzzled at the back of her neck. "Don't you ever forget it, wife."

"Or you," she panted, making him give a broken laugh.

"I'm not likely to," he groaned, his hips picking up the pace further. "Everyone knows you keep me on a short fucking leash, woman."

Minerva made a sound of explosive disagreement as he ran his thumbs hard over her nipples.

"Oh yes, you do," he whispered huskily against her temple. "And I don't give a fuck who knows it." He planted a hand on her upper back and propelled her forward again until her upper half lay against the seat again. "You want to know something really messed up, Mina?" he asked in a raspy voice.

His hips were really hammering against her backside now, and Mina knew she was lost. She gave a low scream as he pushed in deep and pinned her hard against the seat. She clamped down on his shaft as her shuddering orgasm ripped through her. Only when the tremors had subsided did he buck his hips forward in another hard thrust which tore a grunt from his own throat. "I. Fucking. Like. You. Owning. Me." Each word was punctuated with a thrust.

Then she felt him stiffen and swell inside her for a moment before his seed gushed inside of her in a long spurt which drew a satisfied moan from him. He carried on rocking his hips as he gave her it all, and she reached back to clasp his hip, holding him close. He dragged her chemise out of the way, in search of the spot where her neck met her shoulder. When he found it, he kissed it lingeringly, before letting her feel the scrape of his teeth. "And now you know," he said with a ragged breath, wrapping his arms around her tight.

Epilogue

One Month Later

Hotel de Maris, Exeter

Mina sighed as Nye leaned over and topped up her champagne glass. "Nye, I fear I may be a little tipsy already," she confided, noticing the lace wrapper she wore was hanging open, the sky-blue ribbons negligently untied and affording him a view of her cleavage. "I drank at least three glasses at the restaurant."

"Good," he responded promptly. "I like it when you're tipsy." His voice lowered intimately. "You afford me so many more liberties." He dropped a kiss onto her lips, then sauntered through to the adjoining room, replacing the bottle in the ice bucket and unfastening his cuff links.

Mina glanced down at the vast array of boxes that littered the floor of the dressing room in their hotel suite. "How on earth are we going to fit all of this into a coach on the way home?"

"We'll have to hire our own," he answered promptly, sounding wholly unconcerned at the prospect.

She twisted around on her seat to show him a disapproving expression. "Nye, the extravagance!"

He smirked. "You'll be wearing some of it, I hope," he said.

Mina gazed down at her new wedding ring and sipped the delicious bubbles as she surveyed the bewildering array of new things she had amassed over the last three days. Silk, satin, and lace undergarments spilled out of a variety of pretty colored boxes, and her new black silk dress hung up in all its glory over the back of the wardrobe door. Not only that but she had accumulated a dozen pairs of thigh-high silken hose, so far removed from her old black stockings as to be virtually unrecognizable as the same garment.

Nye had wanted to buy her a whole new wardrobe of pretty gowns, but she had only to explain to him in a quiet aside that she wanted to keep on her blacks for Papa for at least a twelvemonth, and he had acquiesced at once without a single objection.

After that, he had concentrated solely on her underclothing. She was now the owner of pink, lilac, pale lemon, and ice blue drawers and chemises, trimmed with profusions of lace and pearl buttons. So pretty were these garments and so delicate that she could scarcely believe their purpose was to be hidden away from view. She had satin nightgowns with ribbons and wrappers to match, every bit as fancy as those Cecily or Amanda Vance had worn.

He had insisted, too, on new corsets, or "French stays" as the lady in the store had called them. They started much lower, concentrating on her waist area alone, not going anywhere near her bust or hips at all. "Madam is quite right," the assistant had told her. "With such an admirable figure, you do not need to be so laced in like a fat old dowager from shoulder to thigh." Nye certainly appreciated the scantier corsets and the pretty underwear, but to her surprise Mina found she delighted in them as well.

She had been spoiled rotten these last three days. He had not only replenished her wardrobe, but also bought her a number of trinkets and toiletries, enough to cover the dressing table back home. Something had only to catch her eye and he would summon immediately for it to be wrapped up in tissue and ribbon for her.

She had a cut-glass bottle of new French perfume, pearl powders, lip salves, and a traveling case lined with sea-green silk, decked out with an array of silver-backed brushes, a matching manicure set, and a vanity mirror all engraved with her initials. She had new delicate gray gloves trimmed in black, a fashionable new bonnet with a puffed and gathered crown, and the smartest pair of new ankle boots of the softest leather.

Not only that, but Nye had wined and dined her, taken her to the theater, to the Italian opera, though he had yawned throughout the performance, and to the museum and the art gallery. That very evening they had been out for what Nathaniel Jones had called a "slap-up" celebration meal at one of the finest hotels.

It had been attended by several of Nye's fellow boxers, who were in Exeter for some sporting event. Nat Jones had treated all of them as his guests, and Mina dreaded to think of the size of the bill he must have picked up afterward, for there had been six courses and a procession of bottles of the finest champagne.

Mina had been quite agog to see what everyone wore for their night on the town. Clem had been resplendent in a lilac cravat with a diamond-studded tiepin in the shape of a lucky horseshoe that she had been quite dazzled by. He had escorted no one on his arm, though he eyed many passing beauties with his lazy smile of appreciation and seemed to draw just as much covert attention back from them.

Jeb had brought Effie, who had been decked out in a low-cut gown of purple satin trimmed with gold lace that Mina had quite blinked to behold. Dot had not been there, for Nat had been unable to tear her away from her beloved London, but there was a young buck called Barty Ewell, with pomaded locks, who Effie told her in a whisper was expected to be the next big thing in lightweight boxing.

Barty escorted a very giggly blond called Ruby who Effie said was a dancing girl "with airs above her station." Mina, who caught Ruby eyeing Nye speculatively on not one, but two occasions during the meal, was inclined to agree and kept a beady eye on her, until the girl got the message that Nye's "missus" was proprietary.

Deep down, Mina could not really blame her, for it seemed to her that Nye in his black dress trousers and scarlet striped waistcoat was quite the handsomest man in the room, despite the strong competition from their own table. She could barely keep her eyes from him and found herself reaching for his hand on several occasions in a public show of her affection quite unlike her previous self. She couldn't seem to stop herself from touching him these days. Luckily, he appeared to like these bursts of spontaneous affection and actively encouraged them.

When the main course was served, a toast was raised to "Nye's pretty bride," and Mina blushed as though she were indeed a newlywed and not a wife of nearly two months standing. When she'd raised the first spoonful of lemon trifle to her lips, she had paused as everyone had let out a wild cheer. Looking down in astonishment, she'd found a gold band set with three diamonds glinting up at her from the swirl of cream and sponge.

"Don't swallow it," Nye had advised, leaning forward. "It's your wedding ring."

"Oh, Nye!"

He had wiped it clean with a napkin. "Not sure that was such a good idea," he'd murmured ruefully as he slipped it on her finger.

"We must be bankrupt after this weekend," she said. "But I cannot regret it!"

"Not bankrupt." He laughed. "Though I have spent all my ill-gotten gains. Just as well." He winked. "In case those Riding Officers ever come poking and prying into our affairs again. Let them," he said recklessly after he'd kissed her soundly to the accompanying whoops and cheers of his companions. "For they won't find any skeletons now."

Mina had bit her lip and drank down her glass of champagne, for she knew she was sadly straitlaced compared to their current company and did not want everyone to think Nye's wife uptight or prim. If they thought it, they did not voice it, and after her second glass of champagne, Mina no longer felt conscious of the stares of everyone else in the restaurant. Indeed, she was quite sure half of them were looks of envy, for theirs was quite the liveliest party in the whole venue and certainly with the most striking-looking men.

Mina sighed now as she removed the mother-of-pearl clips from her hair that Nye had bought, and ran a brush through her locks. "Effie was in fine looks tonight, I thought. I wonder Jeb does not marry her," she mused aloud. "She'd make him a fine wife, I'm sure. She's so exceedingly kind-hearted."

Nye snorted. "She was a pickpocket from an east end slum when Jeb took up with her. Don't go running away with the notion she's some sweet thing from the wrong side of the tracks. She'd cut your purse strings soon as look at you."

Mina set her brush down, her breath coming fast. "You're wrong, Nye, and in any case, I don't care if she was a thief or where she's from. She was the only person who was kind to me on my wedding day, and I will never forget that!" Her voice broke with emotion over the last few words, and flushing to the roots of her hair, a mortified Mina bounced up from her seat and ran into the adjoining bathroom, bolting the door shut.

"Mina!" Nye hammered on the door, close behind her. Indeed, she'd only just managed to slam the door in his face. "Open this door!"

"No, I'm getting undressed, give me a minute," she lied in a wobbly voice. Why, oh why were tears coursing down her cheeks? She was acting like a complete fool! She made a grab for a face cloth.

"I'll break this door down," he threatened, rattling at the catch.

"Nye, please just give me a moment!" she begged, furiously wiping her eyes. *"Please!"*

There was a loud bang and a splintering of wood, and Mina screamed, wheeling around as the door swung violently back and lurched off its hinges. "Nye!" she gasped in dismay. He was already striding through, yanking her roughly into his arms. "Nye—the door!" she wailed, looking at where it hung drunkenly off its hinges.

"Fuck the door," he said succinctly and scooped her up into his arms. An urgent hammering started at the door leading from the corridor. Nye strode straight over to it, with Mina still in his arms, and threw it open.

"Sir!" started an outraged hotel employee.

"My wife fainted in the bathroom," he said coolly. "Put the damages on my bill." Then he pushed the door shut with one booted foot. Mina, her eyes very wide, saw the tight disapproving faces of a few other guests focused on them. *"Riff-raff"* she heard one old woman whisper loudly to her companion.

Mina gave a hysterical giggle. "Oh dear. I seem to have turned into one of those women that causes scenes," she murmured. "This reminds me of that first night I arrived at The Harlot," she said as Nye carried her over to the bed and laid her carefully down.

"How?" he murmured, sliding onto the bed beside her. "Tell me, I want to know." He rolled into her, capturing one of her hands in his in the pillows above and twining their fingers.

"Well, because I was so shocked as I went from room to room, trying to find somewhere to sleep." She wiped her eyes with her other hand. "I had led such a sheltered life till that point," she mused wryly. "You wouldn't believe what an eye-opener it was. That night, you'd had a boxing match in the yard." Her eyes rose to meet his, and she was disconcerted a moment by the expression his held.

"I remember," he said gruffly. "Keep going."

"Well, the place was full," she said uncomfortably. "I'm sure you recall. I met you on the second landing." Her eyes slid away, but his long fingers caught her chin and drew her back to face him.

"How is this like that night?" he persisted.

Mina gave an awkward laugh. "Well, there were prizefighters all over the place and—and their company," she said.

"Mmm," he agreed, his hand sliding down to cup her between her legs, over the pale pink silk. Mina gasped. "Like you're my *company* now?" he suggested huskily.

"Yes," Mina agreed breathlessly. "Someone—I'm not sure who, for I did not know everyone's names at the time—well, he was fighting with a woman in the front bedroom. At least…" She frowned. "Now that I think about it, it must have been Clem, for the female shouted 'I'll see you hanged, Clem Dabney,' or something of that sort." Nye's thumb had started to lightly stroke over the silk covering her mound and Mina's breath caught.

"So, Clem was fighting with his doxy?" he put in smoothly.

"Yes, they broke a mirror. I think she threw something at him. Possibly a shoe."

"Mmm, then what?"

"Then—" Mina had to make a concerted effort to concentrate. "Um—oh yes. I heard Ivy in with someone…" She broke off distractedly. "Oh wait, I think it must have been Frank Toomes, for when I went into the room next door, his brother, Jack, was lying on a mattress on the floor and he said 'Are you finished with Frank now?' Because, you see, just for a minute he believed I was Ivy."

Nye's thumb immediately stilled. "He spoke to you?" he asked sharply.

"Yes, you see, he thought—"

"He thought you were Ivy, yes," Nye said tensely. "What reply did you make?"

Mina gazed up at him. "I don't really remember, in all honestly," she added at his heavy frown.

His eyes narrowed. "Mina—"

"I think I just uttered some kind of apology and ducked out of the room," she said truthfully.

"That was it? The full exchange?" Mina nodded, wondering at the intensity of gaze. Why was he so wound up about it? She watched his shoulders relax. "Then what?"

Mina cast her mind back and flushed. "I don't remember!" she prevaricated.

A smile curved his lips. "Little liar," he contradicted her. "That's when I happened upon you. Outside Jeb and Effie's room."

"Oh yes," she admitted weakly.

"Listening to them rolling in the sheets."

"Nye! I was not!"

"Your face was red as fire," he teased. "And when I spoke to you, you jumped two feet in the air and shook like a leaf." The playful look left his face and he looked regretful. "You were scared of me."

"No," she contradicted him uncertainly. "It wasn't as straightforward as that. I felt really, really *angry* with you." She heaved a great breath. "On the walk back from the church, I had wound myself up into a huge temper with you. Even at the time," she mused, "I knew it was strange that I blamed you more than Jeremy."

"Did you?"

She nodded and bit her lip. "Because, I felt—" She broke off her words. "It's silly really."

"Tell me," he insisted.

"I felt that we'd been forced into it together and—" She heaved a breath. "But you didn't feel that way at all, and I was so *humiliated* in the church." She squeezed her eyes shut and felt him shift closer into her, crowding her with his bigger body. His hand stroked over her hip encouragingly, until she spoke again. "I couldn't really make head nor tail of anything that night," she recalled wonderingly. "And I didn't know anyone save you and Jeremy. Everyone else were complete strangers to me. And I knew there was *something* between you and he, but I didn't understand then what it was at all. I just knew I was completely in the dark." She paused and his fingers squeezed her waist. "And when you grabbed my elbow, I just felt myself *relax*, because for some reason, I trusted you in the dark to steer

429

me right." She swallowed. "But then you—you left me behind. You walked out of the church and everyone followed you. And when I tried to catch up, I fell over my shoe—" She broke off as a tear rolled down her face. "So stupid."

"Yes, I was," he said gruffly. "Because you were right. We were in it together, and I had no right to blame you like that. I was a fucking idiot to leave you in that church. I showed myself up, not you."

She looked up quickly at that. "Well, but—"

"Do you know why I was angry with you, Mina?" he asked softly.

"Yes. Because you didn't want to marry me."

"No," he contradicted her. "It was because I thought you were Jeremy's cast-off mistress."

Mina gasped. "Oh yes, I had forgotten about that," she admitted. "Ivy explained it to me later."

He looked grim, but she knew his anger was directed toward himself. "I thought he was giving me his leavings, like his father did to mine." She regarded him speechlessly a moment. "And I was furious about it, really furious. I wanted to break his neck. Not yours," he added. "Never yours. But I didn't want you. Not then."

"Well, I'm not surprised." She gulped. "Not if you thought that!"

"I wanted you at the top of the stairs though," he said gruffly.

"What?"

"When you stood there, looking so fucking embarrassed." He reached up and scratched the side of his jaw. "It really threw me off."

"You had to put your mouth by my ear to make me hear," she recalled. "Because Effie was making so much noise." She cleared her throat.

He smiled. "And you shivered and dropped that ugly bag of yours as if I'd touched you. And I thought, why the hell does he want to be rid of someone as sweetly responsive as that?"

"Is that really what you thought?" Mina marveled. "I thought you despised me at that point."

He snorted. "No. If I had, I never would have sent you up to my bed."

"Your bed you didn't sleep in!" she pointed out.

"Till now."

"Nye?" she whispered. He turned his head to look at her. "Did you really want me then? That first night, I mean?" He nodded. "Oh." She smiled at him.

"Nothing like as much as I do now though," he admitted, reaching down and dragging her leg over his hip. He twisted his body so he lay on his back, bringing her over him. "When I think about how I left you to walk back to The Harlot like that in the dark and on your own—" He broke off angrily. "I hate that I did that. Can you forgive me, sweetheart?"

Mina relaxed her body into his with a sigh. "Yes."

"Really?" She nodded and the expression in his eyes grew warm. "You're so good to me, sweet Mina."

Mina hid her hot face against his shoulder. *Sweet Mina?* "You wouldn't say that if you knew what I fantasized about doing to you all the way up that hill," she mumbled.

He let out a laugh, then dropped his voice. "I hope it was filthy."

She swatted his shoulder. "Of course it wasn't! I was a virgin bride at that point and hopelessly clueless."

"What was it?" She squirmed, and he grabbed her backside and ran his thumbs under the lace covering her buttocks. "Tell me."

"Pulling off my shoe and flinging it at your stupid, handsome head," she admitted.

He chuckled, then looked instantly contrite. "And instead you dripped candle wax all down your poor little wrist." He sounded so regretful, Mina looked up in surprise.

"I didn't realize you'd noticed me do that."

"Of course I noticed it. I wanted to pull up your sleeve and check your skin, but I thought you'd likely piss yourself with fright if I touched you at that point."

She made a rude noise. "I probably would have snapped and boxed your ears," she said.

He laughed. "It's just as well you didn't do that."

"Why?"

"Because then *I* would have snapped," he said. "I don't think my little virgin bride was ready for me at that point." He grew suddenly serious. "When I said that about Effie tonight, I only meant that none of those women have your sweetness, Mina."

"You're the only person who ever found me sweet," she answered honestly. "Even my father said I had a sadly sharp tongue at times."

He laughed again. "I like your tongue. But I still don't know why you think tonight reminds you of that first night at The Harlot."

"Oh." Mina's frown cleared. "I meant those people out in the corridor looking at us with such disapproval and shock. That was like me on that first night. My face must have worn the same expression." She giggled, then covered her mouth. "I'm definitely tipsy," she said. "I never giggle."

"I think you *are* a little tipsy," he agreed with a slow smile. "You may have a sore head in the morning."

"Really?"

"I won't mind," he said agreeably.

"Because you won't mind missing our planned trip to the botanical gardens?" she asked archly.

"We can just go later in the day," he said with a shrug.

"I'm sorry I caused a scene," she whispered, lowering her face to touch her brow to his. "I don't know why our wedding day keeps springing so forcibly into my mind today. It makes me overemotional."

"I do," he said. "It's because this is what it should have been like. A celebration. An occasion. I wish it had been," he said regretfully. "I regret so much—"

"But not marrying me," she interrupted anxiously.

433

"God no!" He carried her hand to his lips and kissed her palm before setting it down over his heart. "That's one thing I will never regret."

"Then the rest doesn't matter," she said softly. "For we have the rest of our lives to do things the right way." She bit her lip. "Though, I do think we might be one of those couples that fight as much as we reconcile."

"So, we'll never grow bored." Nye shrugged. "Besides." His eyes gleamed. "The fighting's just part of the making up. And I *really* like making up with you, Mina."

"Yes," she murmured in agreement, smiling as she tried to remember who it was that said that about them first. Then she realized it was Gus and hastily changed the subject. "We must stop referring to it as The Harlot now," she reminded him. "For it is not The Harlot anymore."

A new sign now swung over the courtyard, one that bore the likeness of a man hunched in a fighting stance, stripped to his waist with his fists clenched. It looked rather like Nye, and Mina admired it excessively.

He nodded. "I will probably slip up every now and again. It was The Harlot for a long time."

"Well, now it is The Prizefighter, named in your honor." She dropped a kiss on his jaw. He angled his head for her to kiss the other side, and she obliged with a spurt of laughter. "Edna is thrilled about the change of name, and so is Corin's granny. And you must own, we seem to be gaining a good deal of new customers."

"Mmm," he agreed, his gaze locked to hers. She ignored the blatant message in the dark depths of his eyes and leaned an elbow onto the pillow behind his head. It thrust her lace-clad bosom practically into his face, but she pretended not to notice this or the way his gaze was riveted to it.

"The new name means I can now invite my old maid, Hannah, to stay with us as our guest next summer, for you must admit it sounds a good deal more respectable. Even Teddy is now permitted to ride over and visit with us, so long as he brings a groom. By the way, we must remember to pick him up a present before we return to Penarth. Preferably something pugilism themed, for he is becoming almost as enthusiastic about boxing as he is horse racing." Nye's hands settled firmly on her hips. "Perhaps we should take the opportunity to buy an engagement gift for Corin and Herney now they are walking out together? For I'm sure it will not be long before—" Her words ended in a shriek as he rolled her under him. "Nye!"

"Tease," he breathed. "You do know I adore you, Mina, and that I always will?"

She caught her breath and nodded. "I know it, William Nye," she confessed. "And I wholly reciprocate the sentiment. As for teasing you, I bought you a present this morning." She colored faintly. "It's in your bedside drawer."

He frowned but reached across to open the drawer, withdrawing a slim cream cardboard box. He lifted his eyebrows and flipped up the lid. What he saw there made his gaze catch fire. "Red stockings?"

She nodded. "The store assistant seemed a good deal shocked. She could barely look me in the eye as she wrapped them."

Nye laughed, rolling off her at once and propping himself up against the pillows. "Put them on now and do it slow."

"Like a showgirl?" she asked, sitting up and slipping her wrapper off her shoulders. "You know, you'll have to take me

435

to the music hall if I'm to learn how to do this properly." She shook out a red stocking.

He shook his head. "None of them are the equal to you, Mina. Not in my eyes. No one is."

She smiled at him as she drew the red silk stocking over her toes and up her calf. "I feel the same about you, Will Nye," she assured him warmly. Then she did her best to prove it.

THE END

If you enjoyed this book, please consider leaving me a rating on Goodreads, Amazon, Bookbub or wherever else you leave your reviews. I would be very grateful.

You can find my website at: www.alicecoldbreath.com where you can sign up for my monthly newsletter and find out what I am up to.

Also, please do check out some of my other stories!

Many thanks, Alice.

If you want to read more about prizefighters, then the next book in the series is Benedict's story:

A Substitute Wife for the Prizefighter: *Victorian Prizefighters Book 2*

Plain, respectable Lizzie Anderson is in a devil of a fix. After catching sight of something she was not supposed to, her whole family is torn apart by the ensuing scandal. Lizzie's steadfast principles means she cannot deny the evidence of her own eyes, and as a consequence finds herself thrown out onto the street! Her only ally in her time of need comes from a very unexpected quarter indeed…

Benedict Toomes has long thought Lizzie a thorn in his side, but after seeing her staunchness in the face of adversity, he finds himself picturing her in a totally different role in his life: a stand-in for the betrothed he no longer wants to marry…

Find out how this unlikeliest of couples navigates life together after a rocky start and finds their preconceived notions about the other could not have been further from the truth!

If you want to read more stories about Penarth, then Jeremy's story can be found in:

A Foolish Flirtation: *The Reversal of Fortune Series Book 1*

At eighteen, Emmeline Ballentine's father splashed out on one London season to introduce his daughter to polite society. Sadly, for Emmeline, polite society was not terribly receptive to a city trader's daughter.

She only ever caught one gentleman's fancy, the dishonorable Jeremy Vance who made her head spin as he singled her out for attention at the balls and assemblies. Her worldly chaperone warned her he was making a May game of her, but Emmeline had not heeded her warning. Consequently, her dreams were dashed, when at the close of the season, Jeremy announced his engagement to another.

Ten years later, their paths cross again in Bath. Emmeline is older and wiser, and a good deal poorer, and Jeremy is divorced. There is absolutely no chance of him making a fool of her again with his shocking offer of marriage. Is there?

OTHER STORIES FROM ALICE COLDBREATH YOU
MAY ENJOY:

The Vawdrey Brothers Series

*Book 1 – **Her Baseborn Bridegroom***

Lady Linnet Cadwallader has been raised a helpless invalid in
her own castle. Brought up to believe she will "never make old
bones," she lives a quiet and lonely existence, hiding away her
excessive freckles and red hair from a world that believes her to
be hideously misshapen and ugly.

Until one day her uncle arranges a marriage of convenience for
her, a marriage in name only with a young puppet groom…but
Sir Roland does not show up. In his place turns up his baseborn brother Mason Vawdrey. And dark, forceful Mason is no
one's puppet.

Things are about to get interesting at Cadwallader Castle. And
Linnet is about to discover that maybe a golden leopardess does
not need to change her glorious spots.

The Brides of Karadok Series

Book 1 – Wed by Proxy

Thrice wedded, but never bedded, Mathilde Martindale has long
lived in the shadow of her indomitable mother, and meekly
done as she was told. Until one day she decides to become
mistress of her own destiny and leave the royal court to find her
own path.

Married by proxy, Lord Martindale has never even met his
bride of three years. Wed as part of a peace treaty, he bitterly

resents the mercenary wife who cares only for wealth and prestige. And then he meets her...